I0817870

PANGOTHA

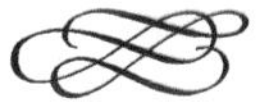

SAMMY JONES

WHIMSICAL GNOME PRESS

This is a work of fiction. Names, characters, places, and incidents either are the product of the author's imagination or are used fictitiously. Any resemblance to actual persons, living or dead, events, or locales is entirely coincidental.

First Edition: July 2024

ISBN 978-1-7357385-3-6 (ebook)
ISBN 978-1-7357385-4-3 (paperback)
ISBN 978-1-7357385-5-0 (hardcover)

Published by Whimsical Gnome Press
www.authorsammyjones.com

DEDICATION

This book is dedicated to my wonderful husband, children, and readers. Thank you so much for your time, patience, and support!

CHAPTER 1

"The advisors are calling for your head as justice. They want to prevent an uprising," said Carter. "I don't know what to do."

With glazed and bloodshot eyes, Linx focused on the dungeon's damp stone wall behind Carter. Every word that left his mouth violently speared her heart.

Once reality set in, Linx shouted, "They want me dead? They want to kill me? Carter, you can't let them! Please help me!"

Prickles blanketed her back, quickly traveling up her neck. How was she going to convince Carter she didn't kill his mother?

"I'm going to do what I can. I have to go speak with them now. I'll be back, Linx. If you think of anything, let me know," he said, turning to exit the dungeon.

"Carter! Carter! Please don't let them kill me! I'm innocent!" Linx shrieked as the guard slammed the door after Carter left.

"Shut up!" yelled the guard.

Broken and betrayed, Linx lowered her head. Her blonde hair draped around her soft face as burning tears singed her cheeks, dripping to the ground. She thought to herself, *Why didn't he believe me? Would he really kill me? He couldn't kill me. I've sacrificed everything for him. He wouldn't kill me, would he?*

Fear consumed Linx while thoughts flooded her mind. She remembered Carter's lack of trust in her when they arrived in Crystal Woods. If he was willing to kill her then, he wouldn't think twice about avenging his mother now. Raising her head, she shook her hair away from her face. Squeezing her eyes to drain the remaining tears, Linx took a deep breath.

With the magic-suppressing straps still wrapped around her arms, Linx hoped Carter had loosened them enough earlier so she could escape. She attempted to pull one arm out and then swiftly wriggled herself free before anyone entered the room. Standing to her feet, she stumbled as she moved toward the wooden dungeon door.

As Linx was about to transport herself outside the castle, she thought about Poba's cape inside the queen's chamber. She had to retrieve the cape and return it to the trolls. They needed closure for their dear friend. Instantly, an unsettling vision appeared in her mind. Linx despised having no control over when the visions came.

She saw figures march over grasslands, swinging swords and clubs by their sides. As she focused, Linx held her breath, realizing the trolls were marching toward the castle in Crystal Woods. Images of trolls chanting war cries while holding torches ran through her mind like a film. She thought, *What are they doing?* It was then she saw the torch's light flash off of crystals and gems—*Poba's cape. They wanted to seek revenge for Poba!*

As quickly as the vision came, it ended, leaving Linx to sort out the details.

"What do I do?" Linx whispered to herself. If she reclaimed the cape, it would still cause a massive war between Violet Woods and Crystal Woods. On the other hand, how could Crystal Woods be trusted with the cape and the powers it holds? When Linx had gone to confront the queen about hoarding the cape, she was framed as a murderer. Who knew how they would twist any relationship in the future? With Crystal Woods holding a troll's cape, others could be in danger. As Linx contemplated what to do, voices could be heard approaching. Rushing back to where they left her, she waited patiently. *Maybe Carter had a change of heart!*

"Carter?" Linx screamed. "Carter, is that you?"

"Didn't I tell you to shut up?" the guard shouted, peering through the rusty bars on the door.

Jingling through his keys, the guard looked down, breaking eye contact with Linx. Now, it was all or nothing.

I am my only friend. I don't need anyone else, she thought to herself. *Now gather yourself, and let's get out of here.*

Without another thought, she transported herself out of the dungeon and near the queen's chamber. Darting for the shadows, Linx waited to see if anyone was near before moving toward the chamber door. Around the corner, a scuffle in the hallway spooked Linx, so she threw up a force field to hide against the wall. She waited while some low mumbling passed through the hallway. Once she could no longer hear anything, Linx slowly dissolved the force field. Stepping out of the shadows of the hall, she noticed a familiar girl walking toward the queen's chamber. It was the servant—Crystal! Although Carter had no qualm with her, Linx didn't trust her one bit.

Crystal had a dark aura around her, and Linx could not pinpoint why.

Linx quietly followed Crystal from a distance, wondering what her plans were near the queen's chamber. Although Linx needed to leave the castle as soon as possible, something inside her head told her to refrain from teleporting into the room. Goosebumps climbed up her arms as she stalked Crystal from a distance. Hoping no one would see her, she silently sprinted closer to Crystal. When Linx got close, she let out a faint sigh to calm her nerves. As the air left her nostrils, Crystal paused in her tracks and turned her head to listen for anyone approaching. Linx's face dropped in horror while tiny beads of sweat lined the top of her neck and forehead. *Oh, no! Oh, no! What should I do?* she thought to herself.

Crystal swiftly continued down the hall, and Linx thankfully rubbed the side of her face. She couldn't believe her luck. Her hands felt clammy as she squeezed them into fists. She could feel the thumping of her heartbeat vibrate in her throat as they got closer to the queen's room. Once Crystal reached the doorway, she paused, placing her hand on the wall. *What was she waiting for?* Linx froze as she watched Crystal's smooth fingers transform into a wrinkly, aged hand. Within a matter of moments, Crystal's plain dress turned into a dark, hooded robe that Linx recognized immediately—the elder. *But how? How could this be possible? I thought the elders had died with the queen!* Linx shouted in her mind. Nervously observing the elder's next move, Linx felt her stomach turn into knots.

"My dear, what are you doing here?" the grumbling voice taunted.

No! No! Linx screamed in her mind. She waited with wide eyes, hoping they were talking to someone in the room.

"Ah. It's not polite to ignore your elder, Linx." The creepy figure spun around to face her.

Linx swallowed what felt like a prickly ball, leaving her throat dry. "I don't know what to say."

"Never mind. There's no time to chat. I need to get the cape and bring it back to Violet Woods!"

Linx ran over to block the elder from entering the queen's chamber. "I can't let you take the cape!"

"Move out of the way, you fool! There's not enough time to be playing games," the elder said, blasting Linx out of the way.

With a stinging burst of energy, she flew against the wall and fell to the ground. Enraged, Linx floated to her feet. Swirling her hands, she shot a bright burst back at the elder, sending them tumbling down the hallway.

In the distance, a commotion could be heard approaching them. Linx noticed the sound of guards running through the halls.

"Linx, you fool! What are you doing? Why do you think I killed the queen? She stole Poba's cape. It belongs to Violet Woods," the faint voice said.

"You—you were the one who killed the queen? You killed the queen and framed me?" Linx shouted as her rage ignited a fireball in her hands.

The elder stumbled toward her. "L-Linx, what are you doing? Look, there are times when sacrifices must be made for the good of our people. It had to be done."

"No, the curse was true. You wanted to be set free! You are a danger to our people, and I won't let you leave with Poba's cape," Linx said, red streaks visibly filling her eyes.

A guard shouted from a distance, "You there! Stop in the name of the king!"

The elder begged as they tried standing up, "Help me, Linx! You don't know what you are talking about!"

A spark of magic behind the elder caught Linx's eyes. The elder swung their arm around to whip a ball of energy at Linx, but she anticipated the betrayal. Linx slammed the elder with the fireball and darted for the queen's closet.

"Woah! What was that?" shouted one guard.

"In there! There's someone in the queen's chamber!" shouted another guard.

Breathing heavily, Linx swung open the closet door. Her anger ceased as her eyes absorbed the magnificent secret—Poba's cape. Numerous gems and crystals sparkled from top to bottom, tempting anyone to grab it. However, slightly repulsed by the thought of a dead troll's cape hanging in front of her, Linx hesitated to touch it.

Voices shouted as others realized the body in the hallway belonged to an elder. "Men, this creature is the same as the one that was on the lawn."

"How many are there?" asked another guard.

"I don't know. Hurry! Go check the queen's chamber!"

Linx ran out of time. She needed to grab the cape—or she risked losing it. Reaching out, her fingers barely grazed the bumpy surface when a vision surged through her mind. The trolls chanted as they invaded the castle. They battled Carter's guards as they pushed through the hallway. One troll shouted, "Kill them all!"

She shook her head as the vision left her mind. Knowing what she had to do, guilt ate away at Linx as she secured the cape in her arms. She didn't know why, but she was compelled to give Carter a fair warning of what was to come. Unsure if she would regret it, Linx cultivated a note that rested in the closet and read—Prepare for war.

"You! Stop!" a guard yelled to Linx.

With flaming eyes, Linx glared. "You'll never keep me within these prison walls. I'm taking this with me, too. Your queen stole it from our allies. I'm bringing it back to where it belongs. Tell *your* king that I expected more from him. I gave him everything, and I would never kill his mother. That evil creature in the hall was her murderer. I will never forgive him for what he did."

As two guards charged Linx, their hands reached to grip her arms. Before their fingertips could clamp down, Linx disappeared into thin air. Baffled by what had happened, one guard noticed the note sitting on the floor of the closet. "Get this to the king right away!"

CHAPTER 2

Appearing on the castle's front lawn, Linx scanned the surrounding tree line, debating on what to do. As she held Poba's cape, she knew she had to return it to the trolls. They deserved to know the truth, and they should be the ones to decide what happens with the cape. The trolls had waited so long to learn who invaded Violet Woods and killed their beloved family members. Nevertheless, Linx feared that potentially other elders may be lingering. Danger lurked on her journey, and now she traveled alone.

Letting out a long exhale, Linx acknowledged she needed to leave quickly, despite feeling exhausted. Many creatures wanted her, so she couldn't afford to get caught. Linx transported herself behind the castle to flee toward the forest. She hoped no one would think to look for her in this section of the woods. Linx anticipated Carter would search through the areas where they had traveled before.

Once she reached the tree line, Linx sprinted into the woods without looking behind her. As she darted down a hill, it became steeper and harder to maneuver. She attempted to slow down by grabbing a tree, but it was too late. Linx's foot snagged a root bulging from the soil, causing her to trip and tumble down the hill. Throughout the fall, Linx tried to save herself, but she couldn't teleport to a safe location. Her shoulder slammed against a rock, and her knee cracked off of a rotting log. As she continued to roll, Linx's face narrowly missed a violent kiss from a thorny bush. After a few seconds, she finally came to an abrupt halt, wrapping around a tree trunk.

Slowly standing up, Linx hunched forward due to the impact of her lower back hitting the tree. While pain crawled throughout her spine, she felt disoriented from twirling down the hill. Linx couldn't understand how she had fallen like that. She knew she had to be quiet since there was a possibility of running into the wrong group of creatures. Once she had a moment to gather herself, she couldn't believe the intense irritation that radiated from the base of her neck. *I must have pulled or scratched something from the fall,* she thought to herself.

Within seconds, Linx heard yelling in the distance. She was unable to hear what was being said, but she knew that it must've had something to do with her escape and the cape.

"The cape! Where's the cape?" Linx shouted. Looking around on the ground and up the hill, she couldn't locate where the cape had gone. "Oh no! Where could it be?"

The itching intensified on her lower neck as time went on, and an uncomfortable pressure pressed on her wings. Reaching up to touch her skin, Linx's heart sank when her hand rubbed against a rough surface. Each finger slowly rolled over foreign bumps and sharp edges until her fingertips came across her own skin. She panicked in her mind.

Poba's cape? No! No, no, no, no! How could this be? I must've rolled on it when I fell down the hill! As the thought flashed in her mind of a dead troll's cape fused to her back, a hot, nauseating wave of sweat washed over her.

Sprinting through the trees, the cape swayed from side to side. It whipped against a tree before getting caught in a low-hanging branch. Frustrated, Linx yanked it off and continued to snake through the woods. As she ran, Linx quickly became winded. A layer of pins and needles coated her throat as the sensation of her esophagus closing overcame her. Dodging her pursuers' line of sight, Linx took a moment to gather herself. A nearby dense bush perfectly concealed her body. Depleted of energy, she had no direction, no plan, and no ally to protect her. Linx desperately hoped she could lose them soon.

A symphony of music danced down from the vocal birds above, taunting Linx. Their happiness, carelessness, and freedom resonated within the beautiful notes of their song as she fled for her life. Knowing she couldn't teleport to the Violet Woods, she pressed on. Linx wondered if she'd ever be able to go back, but what would they say if someone found out about the elder's death? Actually, both of the elders. Maybe her fate would be worse there.

Echoing from the top of the hill, a voice said, "Spread out! She can't be far from here."

"What do you mean? She's a fairy! Who knows where she could've gone," a deep voice argued. She sensed hatred in his voice—the overly involved or too invested type.

A soft, familiar voice mumbled with a touch of sorrow, "Linx is here. I can feel her presence."

Her heart fluttered. *Carter! How did he get here so fast? What am I going to do?*

"She's not from around here, so she can't make it too far. She'll probably run into the ecknids if she went this way." The first voice laughed.

Linx whispered, "Ecknids? I thought ecknids roamed Pangotha. There is no way—oh no! Crystal Woods neighbors a small edge of Pangotha. I can't believe this is happening."

Dread seeped deep into her arms and legs as she recalled the stories of the ecknids. Monstrous, tree-like creatures that walked the mountainous lands of Pangotha. When an uninvited guest arrived, they could never escape because the ecknids informed each other of the trespasser. The winds that blew through their peeling bark would quietly carry their secrets to every neighboring tree. No one knew what happened once a trespasser was spotted.

Linx shook her head at the ridiculousness of her thoughts. *How could anyone know about them if no one ever escaped?*

A guard shouted, "Down there! I think I see her! There she is!"

Oh, no!

Sprinting through the brush, Linx steadied her breath as she slid around a large tree. She immediately spotted a dark cave disappearing into the side of the mountain. Hopeful she could escape, she pushed every ounce of energy into her feet. With every breath, she felt a soreness in her lungs that trickled into her heart. *Almost there!*

"Down that way!" a guard yelled to others.

Linx couldn't tell how many were following her as the sun started to set. The crunches on the forest floor and yells of others faded into oblivion as she focused on the dark hole. Although she didn't know what waited inside, she knew it was safer than any other place in her world now. Every person, creature, and place always seemed to fail her. Linx understood that once she let her guard down, reality would crush her hopes. This was all her fault. She let her guard down with Carter, even after he killed her. Why? Why couldn't she learn? She wanted to help Carter, her people, and find closure for the trolls. Well, this was now her consequence. She was destined to be alone.

With tears pooling in her dim green eyes, she dove into the dark cave and held out the palm of her hand. Lighting a flame above her middle fingertip, she glanced around to see what accompanied her. Moss and splotches of water covered the walls. As she started to walk deeper, she heard a whisper.

"Linx?"

Turning around, Linx's eyes grew bright and her heart sank when her gaze locked with Carter's. Speechless, she inhaled a heavy breath.

As his dark hair gently flowed in the weak breeze, he panicked. "What are you doing?"

"What? Are you going to turn me in?" Linx's eyes raged with fire.

"No, I wanted to get to you first. I didn't want them to find you." Carter rubbed his neck.

"But you are their leader! You can tell them to stop!"

"Maybe before. I don't know if I can now," he said, quietly.

"What do you mean? You said before that you didn't know what would happen to me." Linx furrowed her brows and tightened her lips.

"Before, yes. They found the elder's body. I know that you didn't murder my mother, but you stole the cape. Not to mention, you left a note insinuating war. They believe you are a danger to Crystal Woods."

"You know I'm not! I helped you get here!"

Looking behind him, he said, "I—I don't know, Linx. Once I found out the cape was missing too, it put me in a hard spot to defend you. Where is it? Maybe if you give it back . . ."

"Give it back? Crystal Woods feels so entitled they think I should give it back? Someone murdered an innocent soul and stole his cape right off of his body. And you want me to give back their sick trophy? They ripped a cherished part from him, and you want it back?" Linx laughed. "How pathetic are you?"

"At this point, Crystal Woods wants you dead. I'm not saying they're right. Maybe I can convince them to spare you if you hand over the cape. This will show your loyalty," Carter said.

"My loyalty is with no one now."

Carter sighed. "Linx, I—"

"Plus, I can't." She looked away.

"What do you mean that you can't?"

It was then that Carter caught a glimpse of fading light, bouncing off of the cape that rested on her back. "Linx! Is that —why would you do that?"

"Well, I couldn't trust you with it."

Perplexed, he stood silent for a moment before asking, "So you put it on?"

Linx scoffed. "No! It wasn't intentional."

"No one around here knows how to remove them! What are you going to do? You can't go back to Violet Woods like that! How will they believe any of this?"

"My well-being is no longer your concern," she coldly said.

As Carter stood dumbfounded, Linx swirled her hand in the air and slid a dark energy wall between them. Before he reached her, the force field sealed shut. Dropping her chin to her chest, she squeezed her eyelids shut as a burning droplet fell from the corner of her eye, singeing her cheek. Wiping away the disappointment and regret, she knew he was right. Where would she go? If she went back to Violet Woods, she would be exiled or killed for everything. Lighting a flame once more, she pushed forward to venture alone into the darkness of the cavern tunnel. As an inviting and secluded area appeared along the path, Linx set up a protective shield so she could finally rest for the night.

CHAPTER 3

As the magnificent ships sailed over rough seas, Carter found himself mesmerized by the painting that blanketed his room. Focusing on every stroke from the paintbrush, he sensed his mother's passion and sadness as she artistically journaled her thoughts so long ago.

"Your Highness." A guard swiftly knocked on the door, pulling Carter from his daydream and back into his lonely world.

"Y-yes, come in." Carter rubbed his eyes, pulling his thick covers up to his shoulders.

His door gracefully opened as the guard swiftly entered. "Your Highness, it's your coronation today. You must get ready at once! Guests are pouring in, waiting to see you!" The guard attempted to veil his disgust with Carter's lack of motivation.

Carter stumbled out of bed with half of his hair reaching for the ceiling. "That's today? I thought Hyde said the coronation was in four days?"

Sticking his nose in the air, the guard whispered while shaking his head, "Yes, he did . . . four days ago."

Sliding his robe over one arm and then another, Carter darted toward the vanity mirror. Scrambling to flatten his chaotic hair, he frantically patted down the brown flyaways. As he blankly stared into the mirror, he noticed what were once speckles of beard hairs were now layers beginning to cover his face. His eyes were sunken in, lightly cupped by dark bags.

Hanging his head over the dusty vanity, Carter curled inside of himself. "I don't know how I'm going to do this."

"Your mother would be ashamed if she saw you like this," the guard mumbled.

Like a switch, Carter grabbed a decorative, spiked metal ball, clutching it tightly in his palm. "What did you say to me?"

"Your Highness, how do you think she would feel if she saw you like this? You haven't bathed in . . . I don't know how long. You've been holed up in your chambers, and you forgot about one of the most important days in your monarchy," the guard said, scanning the room while holding his breath.

Carter whispered, "Get out."

Stepping back, the guard asked, "I beg your pardon?"

"Get out!" Carter spun around and launched the spiked ball mere inches from the guard's head, shattering a mirror behind him into hundreds of pieces.

Ducking down, almost falling on the floor, the guard yanked the door open and dove into the hallway. Sweat poured over his forehead as an advisor met him outside Carter's chambers. He stood tall, wearing a brown outfit with thick gray hair pulled into a short ponytail.

"I assume it went well?" the advisor asked.

"Lowe, he's a monster in there," the guard whispered.

"Well, I wouldn't expect any less, but I'm sure it's not that bad." Lowe chuckled, pulling his jacket down firmly.

"You're mad if you think it's not that bad in that dungeon. My eyes were screaming from the putrid odor that was flourishing in there. Maybe you can talk some sense into him because he nearly took off my head."

Lowe laughed, waving his hand in the air. "You were never gifted with the skill of communication. You may go."

As he fixed his attire once more, Lowe walked up to the door and sharply knocked twice. Carter hurled an object straight at the door before yelling, "Go away!"

Letting out an amused sigh, Lowe turned the knob while keeping his head protected behind the door. A vase exploded near the door opening as Lowe waited before saying anything.

"Don't you listen?" Carter shouted. "Go away! Leave me alone!"

Popping his head in quickly, Lowe said, "I wouldn't do that if I were you."

Midway through grabbing another object off his table, Carter paused to hear out Lowe's threat. "And why is that?"

Sidestepping into Carter's chambers, Lowe quietly closed the door behind him. Unfazed by Carter's tantrum, he walked up to him, staring with bright blue eyes. "Look around, Carter."

"Lord Lowe, you should be speaking to me as your ruler," Carter said with fiery eyes.

"Mind your temper. When you act like one, I will."

Raising his eyebrows, Carter lifted his arm, preparing to whip the next object toward the advisor. "Excuse me?"

"I'm not joking," Lowe said. "If you want to be respected, you need to set standards for yourself. If this kingdom thinks their ruler is ill—be it physically or mentally—it leaves room for a usurper, like your mother, to snake their way into power."

"How dare you?" Carter shouted.

Holding his open hands in the air, Lowe continued, "You can be upset as much as you like, but I'm not wrong."

Firmly clenching his jaw, Carter crushed his lips between his teeth as he fell back onto his bed. "What do I do, Lowe? I have no motivation to move forward."

"The first thing is to knock off the hysterics. The other advisors and your people will not take kindly to child-like behavior on the throne. There is so much uncertainty since your mother has passed. Don't fail them, and don't fail yourself."

Grabbing a nearby pillow, Carter covered his face while he let out a scream that sent shivers up Lowe's back. The pain within his esophagus could be heard with every crack in his voice.

"Your Highness, let it out, but only let it out in here. Don't let others see your weakness."

Throwing the pillow to the edge of his bed, Carter faced Lowe. "I have everything, but I have nothing. My heart hurts because anyone I have ever loved is gone, and it's all my fault. All of this is my fault. My mother would've still been alive if I didn't seek her out. Linx would still be with me if I hadn't pushed her away so many times. And now, I have no idea where she is, what she will do—possibly for revenge, and if she will ever face me again."

"So you are concerned that someone, who you call a friend, might seek revenge? Doesn't seem like a friend to me," Lowe said, laughing from shock.

"Not out of anger." Carter walked back to the antique vanity. "If she wanted revenge, it would be to set things right."

"Your Highness, we thought she killed your mother."

Slamming his fist on the table, he shouted, "I know! And I should've believed her. Instead, I went along with everyone else out of fear of what they would think of me. I betrayed her—again. This time, I'm not sure I can fix it."

Shaking his head, Lowe rolled his eyes with a sneering smile. "Your Highness, enough is enough. You beat yourself up over a girl—a thief. She is not worth your time or energy. If she cared, even the slightest bit, she would've returned the cape."

"She can't."

"Yes, she can."

"Lowe, you don't understand."

"I understand plenty, Your Highness. You are trying to defend a thief of the kingdom. If she came back and returned what is rightfully the kingdom's property, then there would be no more issues. She can just play dumb. You know, what they're good at." Lowe squinted his eyes suspiciously.

"What's that supposed to mean?"

Snickering lightly, Lowe explained, "Oh, fairies. They're mischievous creatures. I'm sorry, but it's hard to trust them. Look at what the elder did to your mother."

"But that was the elder, an evil creature. I don't understand what you are trying to get at, Lowe. Who cares about the cape? Why can't we move on?"

"Who cares about the cape?" Lowe puffed up his chest, sending his flared nostrils toward the ceiling. "We do! As should you!"

"I thought no one even knew about it."

"That's the point! No one did except those who needed to. They harnessed the defensive power to keep our kingdom safe, and now that it's gone, we better start to beef up our borders."

Carter furrowed his brows as he shook his head. "Wait, what? All of the security surrounding Crystal Woods relied on Poba's cape?"

"Your Highness, it's a matter of time before you discover how unstable and disliked Crystal Woods really is. I would recommend getting yourself dressed as quickly as you can. You have a coronation to attend." Walking toward the door, dread swept Lowe's face as he envisioned all enemies joining forces to storm the kingdom. "I will send your servants in at once."

Carter's gaze dropped to the ground. What has he been unknowingly sucked into?

A middle-aged servant quickly entered his room and began brushing his hair. Carter discreetly studied her face, looking up only when he thought she wouldn't notice. She had a warm presence and smile, but permanent worry lines etched her olive skin, dividing her forehead into several sections.

As she assisted with his hair, another servant rushed into his room to attend to his attire. Everything felt like a whirlwind while people tugged at his hair, arms, and clothes—making sure his appearance reflected a proper ruler instead of an insecure and immature child.

Once Lowe returned to check on Carter, his eyes looked him up and down before he released an annoyed sigh. The clicking of his shoes pierced Carter's ears as he gracefully rushed over to fix Carter's collar.

"You need to be feared, and no one will fear a poorly put-together young man," Lowe whispered, patting Carter's white tunic.

Raising an eyebrow, Carter stared at the ground, trying to pay attention to Lowe's advice. "Feared?"

"How else can you hold a kingdom together?"

"You just told me to tone it down, but now you're saying I need to be feared. That guard feared me. What's the difference?"

"That guard? That guard!" Lowe shouted, slamming the palm of his hand against the dresser.

The servants fled the room with various items and clothes overflowing in their arms. Leaning back in a chair, Carter didn't know how to respond to Lowe's increasing volume.

Walking up to Carter's chair, Lowe's face shifted to a red tint. "*That guard* is Brent Fille. His grandmother was caught stealing from the queen prior to your mother ruling the land. She was beheaded, and his family has been working off the incurring debt ever since. After turning in other family members and pledging his life to the kingdom, along with a very heroic act on the battlefield, he earned the position of a kingdom guard."

Running his hand along the side of his head, Carter looked in the other direction. "Oh, um, I didn't realize."

"If you want to be a king they remember *and fear,* remind him that you know every detail of his life, along with everyone else he loves, and what will happen if he ever crosses you again. Take notes." Lowe walked over and pulled open the door. "Send for Brent immediately!"

Slamming the door, Lowe walked over to a tiny marble table standing in the corner of the room. He picked up a delicate teapot and poured hot water into one of the two teacups. As he lifted the cup to his lips, Brent came rushing into the room and bowed toward Carter before turning toward Lowe.

"My Lord, you requested my presence?" Brent stood tall, awaiting a response.

"Yes. Yes, I did." Lowe set the teacup down gently on a thin saucer. “I was just explaining to our new king about how you worked very hard to get where you are today. Not many disgraced families had the same outcome as you.”

Humbly nodding his head, Brent said, “Um, yes, My Lord. I am very grateful for the chance to redeem my family’s name.”

“Right.” Lowe smirked, clasping his hands softly together. “Well, I just wanted to address your tone with our king earlier.”

Rubbing his neck, he quietly said, “I am so sorry, My Lord.”

“Don’t apologize to me.” Lowe rested his hand against his chest as he chuckled.

Sweat formed across Brent’s pale forehead as he turned toward Carter. “Your Grace, please accept my deepest apologies. My comment was disrespectful earlier. I’ll do anything to regain your trust. Please forgive me.”

Carter looked him up and down before dipping his head to accept his apology. Immediately, Brent’s eyes darted toward Lowe, unsure of what would come next. Uncomfortable silence held the room hostage, with all eyes waiting on Lowe’s next thought. Carter witnessed how powerful fear was . . . how powerful silence was. Brent, nearly in tears, hadn’t moved a muscle, awaiting his fate. But it also caused Carter, as a ruler, to wait patiently and see what would happen to one of his subjects. Although he was aware of the power he held to stop it all, he understood whatever advancement Lowe took was an intentional move to help educate Carter—or so he hoped.

After a few moments, neither of the men knew what would happen if Brent spoke before Lowe, so Carter decided to break the tense mood. “I think that is all, Brent.”

Slowly holding up his hand, Lowe cynically smiled. “Your Grace, if I may add one more thing.”

“Oh, of course.”

Lowe lifted his nose in the air, gliding toward the guard. "Brent, my good man, if you ever disrespect *any* nobility again—"

"My Lord, I will never again," Brent said, shaking his head from side to side.

Lowe grabbed his face and brought it close to his own. "You'll find yourself buried alive, right next to your grandmother's filthy, rotten corpse."

Carter's mouth nearly fell to the ground as he witnessed Brent drop to his knees, begging Lowe for forgiveness.

"Leave this room now, you disrespectful swine, before I send the hangman knocking on your family's door."

With tears streaming down his face, he turned once again to Carter. "Your Grace, I'm so sorry!"

Without another word, he sprinted out the door, and his footsteps echoed down the hallway.

"Was that really necessary?" Carter shook his head in embarrassment and sympathy.

"Your Majesty, some rulers are surrounded by men they know nothing about. They simply view them as mice doing their dirty work. Yes, some are nothing to think twice about. But others are—infected."

"Infected?"

"They harbor a disease that, once spread to others, can destroy your reign." Lowe gracefully lifted his teacup to his lips.

"And what's this disease you speak of?"

"The thirst for power."

CHAPTER 4

Making his way into the Great Hall, Carter looked around, examining the guards and the people of Crystal Woods. Surrounded by strange and unusual faces, a cold ache of loneliness spidered over his back and wrapped around his stomach. He trusted his advisors to guide him into making the most effective decisions for the kingdom, but that spark of hope, comfort, and genuine friendship was missing.

A handful of adults elbowed some children to stand up straight while a motherly woman adjusted a boy's shirt. Sauntering down the aisle, Carter lowered his eyes and nodded in the woman's direction. Some individuals smiled as he walked past them, and others just stared. Whether it was amazement, disapproval, or envy, Carter couldn't tell.

Countless people packed themselves together, hoping to get a good view of the new king. Joyous laughter faded into a hush once he reached the end of the aisle. Briefly turning to find any familiar face, his attention ultimately rested on Lowe. Despite Carter's face turning pale, Lowe's expression remained solemn and detached. Carter locked his fingers in front of him, squeezed his biceps into the side of his body, and released a heavy exhale from his nostrils. Spinning back around, the massive crown captured his attention while sitting peacefully on a pillow of red silk. The points came up to razor blades, threatening anyone unworthy who dared to touch it.

Although the ceremony was relatively quick, Carter's nerves transformed the experience into a painstakingly long event. Within the crowd, he wondered who was there to support his success and who wanted to watch him burn. There was no way to tell who the nobility or his mother had wronged, yet he would be the one to pay for it. Thoughts flooded his mind of the journey that led him to this very moment—the death, the unknown. Gracefully turning around to face *his* new kingdom, Carter smirked as a strange sense of calm rested over his shoulders and mind.

With Carter now the newly crowned king, countless heads bowed as he walked back through the aisle that divided the crowd. Lowe patiently waited at the end to accompany Carter. Four other well-dressed men silently stood beside him, gripping their hands in front of their bodies.

Softly clapping his hands, Lowe held a slight smirk. "Bravo!"

Carter was astounded by the lack of emotion in their collective demeanor. Unsure of how to read them, Carter's face remained firm. Was he just being self-conscious? Dismissing the awkward body language, Carter confidently approached them as he pulled his shoulders back and raised his head.

"Your mother would be so proud," a noble said with a straight face.

Nodding, another noble asked, "King Carter? You are so lucky to have reconnected with your mother. Quite lucky, indeed. Can I ask something?"

Shrugging with nothing to hide, Carter sighed. "Of course."

"There was a rumor that your father . . . wasn't the most pleasant fellow."

Impatiently interrupting, Carter demanded, "And what's your question?"

Amused, the noble pulled back in an exaggerated manner. "Oh, I didn't mean to ruffle any feathers. I was simply curious to see if you felt maybe there'd be another reunion in the future. You know, a family gathering of sorts with daddy and son."

Scowling, Carter said, "I don't follow."

"I just didn't know if there was a family *secret* that we could get in on. I had a wife and kids, ya know. I miss them." The look of suspicion faded to sadness in the man's eyes.

As the noblemen's eyes burned into Carter's skin, he found it to be the perfect platform. "Look, I don't have any idea what occurred prior to my presence in this world. I came in confused and, frankly, terrified. Unfortunately, my time with her here was limited—but much appreciated. However, it gave us very little time to talk."

"I see," the nobleman replied in a condescending tone.

Taken aback by the tension, Carter opted to walk toward the courtyard for fresh air. From the corner of his eye, he could see the men gossiping amongst each other. Lowe didn't appear to contribute to the conversation, but he certainly didn't try to stop it either. It was imperative that Carter managed his emotions. He couldn't afford a complete breakdown or worse—releasing chaos within the castle.

Stepping outside, he graciously accepted the offerings of the crisp breeze that gently caressed his face. As the warm sun beamed down, Carter strolled toward a line of fruit trees to make distance between him and the fake party that celebrated his ascension to the throne. His heavy heart lightened when he heard children giggling nearby.

Looking up, three children sat underneath a tree while a nobleman and servant solemnly accompanied them. A rush of guilt overcame him as Carter realized he had never noticed them before. Caught up in his own dramas, he neglected his main duty of caring about the people. Although he didn't completely agree with Lowe's tyrannical approach, he was right about one thing—he needed to know who his subjects were and their stories.

"King Carter!" the nobleman shouted, briefly waving his hand. "What are you doing out here? You have a party to attend!"

"Lord Grant, don't get me wrong," Carter began while approaching the tree, "I appreciate the notoriety, but all of the hubbub can be a tad overwhelming. I just wanted to relish the little things for a moment."

"I can't blame you there." Lord Grant smiled while glaring at an antsy child.

Inhaling deeply, Carter turned to the children. "It's nice that you are enjoying this beautiful day."

The small boy was speechless as he stared at Carter. His innocent blue eyes tugged at Carter's heart while the girl beside him looked into the sky, twirling her strawberry-blonde hair. The third child, a little girl with deep brown skin and piercing green eyes, raised the corners of her lips ever so slightly before tousling her curly black hair and turning her attention to the other children.

All three appeared to be skin and bones, so Carter asked, "Are you hungry? There's a giant feast in there. You're more than welcome to join everyone inside."

The children's eyes immediately lit up with excitement before reality hit. Once they looked over toward Lord Grant, mentally begging to go, their smiles soon faded.

"Oh, no. Thank you though. They'll be fine," Lord Grant quickly declined.

"Well, I don't want to keep you." Carter smiled. "I hope you get to do many fun things today. Maybe I shall see you all soon."

Lord Grant rested his arm on his bent knee, nodding his head toward Carter. "Enjoy the rest of your celebrations."

Walking away, Carter peered in the direction where Linx had escaped. Every feeling came rushing back—regret, embarrassment, and shame. *I failed you again, Linx. I am so sorry,* he thought to himself. Why did he care about any of this? Why did he care that she had the cape?

Deep in his heart, he knew that his mother was in the wrong for taking part in stealing the cape. It didn't matter whether she was the individual who killed Poba or ripped his cape off, she still knew that something awful had happened and benefited from it. Instead of doing what was right, she put on a stolen body part from a dead troll. That cape didn't belong in Crystal Woods. It was better off with Linx anyway, but how could Carter help the noblemen see that?

CHAPTER 5

With clicking and grinding of the pebbles beneath her feet, Linx found herself sinking into the earth with each footstep. As echoes of her sniffles sharply bounced through the tunnel, Linx solemnly walked into the unknown. Her tiny flame's flicker barely reached the ragged tunnel walls when she noticed a green shimmer coating the inside of the cavern. Forcefully concentrating on her hand, the flame grew to the size of her head. Although surprised by her growing power, self-doubt consumed Linx's soul. Where did this tunnel lead? Did she have the power to save herself if she encountered a dangerous foe? After all, she succeeded in previous battles with the help of others, but now—she faced them alone.

"Who cares?" she mumbled aloud. "Really, I've always been alone. What's so different now?"

Trying to console her aching heart, Linx found her mind

wandering—to a very distant time when her well-being and life should've been protected by another. Hidden by magic, time, or something else, forgotten images flooded her mind. A young voice shouted in her mind, *Papa!*

A familiar yet obscure image appeared in Linx's mind. The picture was of her father calmly standing by a lush fruiting tree. His light blue eyes sparkled as he gazed at Linx. The days were always sunny, warm, and filled with laughter. She started to recall chasing each other through the field while picking juicy wallo fruit to bake into a scrumptious pie once they got home. Her little sister, Lyla, soon bopped around behind them on their fruit-picking trips too. What was this life she was remembering? What was going on? Oh, how visiting the past hurt! Such detailed and warm memories became beautiful spears, piercing a once-happy heart.

Linx continued through the cavern tunnel, smiling at the affectionate moments that filled her early childhood. Boy, she never realized she would miss something as simple as biting into a sweet red wallo, picked fresh from a tree. Nothing in this world ever compared.

Her thoughts quickly drifted to the tragic day that changed everything. As if that day was like any other, her father wore his signature smile—one that could befriend the hardest soul.

"We'll play when I get back! I love you!" He smiled, closing the front door and cutting off the sunshine that poured in.

Later that day, Linx's mother called outside for her father. Fresh soup simmered on the stovetop, emitting a savory smell throughout the house. Her mother, Gaela, spent the early afternoon prepping a hearty meal the whole family loved.

"Rydan! Are you almost finished?" Gaela's voice echoed throughout the field and dissipated into the woods.

Linx's father, Rydan, loved to embrace nature and found a sense of accomplishment in manual labor. When the garden needed tending, he picked the weeds by hand. If their house had fallen into disrepair, Rydan gathered his tools to renovate or fix the issue. It took no one by surprise when he opted to cut down trees or split logs by himself. And that's what he did. He chopped down a giant tree, and the next day, he would split the logs. Once he finished for the day, his heavy boots would crunch through the woods, and long strands of wheat whipped his legs as he traveled through the field toward their home. Rydan neatly stacked pieces of wood alongside the off-white cottage for whenever they needed them.

However, on this day, when the sun hid behind the distant mountain, he couldn't be found. With skies turning from a soft pink to deep violet, Gaela became curious about his whereabouts.

She yelled to the girls, "Linx! Lyla! I'll be right back. Your father is late for dinner. Keep the doors locked."

"Okay, Mama!" they replied in unison.

Linx could picture the flowing yellow dress her mother loved, fluttering in the wind. The pleasant smell of the soup still lingered in Linx's nostrils. She remembered how that delicious smell taunted her senses for hours as she awaited her parents' arrival.

"Linny, my belly hurts!" Lyla whined, holding her stomach.

"I know. Mine too. I wonder where Mama and Papa are," Linx replied.

"What are we going to do? It's so dark out. I'm scared!" Lyla shuttered with the sides of her lips pulling down toward her chin.

Linx took a deep breath. "Lyla, I'm going to find them."

"You can't leave me here alone!" Lyla tossed her dark, tightly-curled hair away from her green eyes that matched Linx's.

"I don't know where they are, and we have no way to know if they need help."

Lyla scoffed. "How can we help them?"

"I'm going to find them, but you have to stay here. What if they come back? They won't know where we went. You need to stay here and make sure you lock the doors. I'll go check down behind the waters. If I'm not back in twenty minutes, go to the Nelsons' farmhouse."

"Fine."

"Thank you! I'll be back soon. And don't open the door for anyone!"

"No one else lives near us." Lyla pouted, rolling her eyes.

Linx sighed. "I'm saying . . . just in case."

"In case of what?" Lyla pestered.

"I need to go!" Linx shouted, quickly slamming the door.

Lyla had a good point—how could she help them? Linx slid her hand over her forearm, brushing her fingertips over her chilled skin.

The thick weeds felt taller than normal, scratching against her soft, fragile skin. As Linx turned her head to peer down the side of her home, she noticed the sun had set so quickly she couldn't see beyond the first window. An eerie cloud blanketed Linx's mind, and bumps prickled down the skin covering her spine. She felt the burning glare of eyes watching her every move. Peering over her shoulder, she didn't see anyone, but the feeling of a ghostly presence lingered. Who was out there? Was anyone out there?

The crickets softly chirped in the distance, calling out to anyone who would listen. Linx took comfort in their song as nature's staccato music whirled around her body. Oh, how Linx wished she was home, sitting at their old, creaky table while Mama generously heaped each bowl full of soup. She could picture Papa gushing about his luck of having such a wonderful family and a delicious meal.

Instead, she walked alone into the thick darkness—into the unknown. Isn't it strange that places once welcoming and warm become terrifying once the sun disappears? The trees hypnotically sway, distracting helpless souls as their intuition screams to turn around. Sounds that normally go unheard cause hearts to race and cower with fear.

Linx repetitively scanned her surroundings, fiercely begging the universe to protect her. Where could her parents be? Suddenly, her power and confidence melted, dripping into the ground below. Mountainous goosebumps smeared over her skin as curiosity pushed her tiny body forward into the foggy woods.

Carefully walking alongside the rushing creek, Linx's breath quickened and her chest stung as the heavy air expanded within her lungs. Her feet squished into the saturated ground, almost suctioning her in place. Right when she contemplated turning around to run home, a burst of wind pushed a metallic odor in her direction. The light, rusted metal smell infiltrated her nostrils, causing her brain to panic. The intense sting of dread snaked across her body, slithering to her feet.

Inhaling through her bone-dry mouth, she cautiously reached for the support of a nearby thin, smooth tree. Holding herself up, she glanced around the woods, hoping to see or hear her parents. Sounds felt as though they were amplified nearly one hundred times their normal level. *Where are Mama and Papa?*

Linx shuffled forward through dead leaves and sticks, grasping onto a few more thin trees. The distinctive smell grew as she continued until she stumbled upon something that would never leave her mind again. Dark splatters violently painted four surrounding trees, dribbling down and around each groove within the bark. Temporary denial comforted Linx's mind as she analyzed an incomprehensible sight, cushioning any doubt. Sensing disturbances on the forest floor, Linx held her breath as she dropped her gaze. Her eyes fell upon a devastating sight that left her excruciatingly heartbroken.

Blood-soaked clothes and chunks of limbs were savagely scattered in a chaotic frenzy as red coated the trees, bushes, and dirt floor. She brought her hand up to her mouth, muting her agonizing screams. An uncontrollable tremble surged through her legs, driving her knees to the ground. Reaching out in front of her, Linx stroked a familiar yellow fabric, loosely draped over a bush branch. Her life, happiness, and safety all disintegrated within a split second, fluttering away in the wind like her mother's shredded dress.

The moonlight peered through the dense woods, exposing the struggle from hours before. Unable to stomach anymore, Linx's internal organs tightened and twisted, wringing out any substance that rested inside. Turning her head as she pushed herself up, tears streamed down her face, thinning the blood beneath her as they fell.

At that moment, Linx fought the urge to scream for help. *Who would come running?* Everyone who could help or protect her lifelessly rested in front of her eyes. Everyone except—Lyla!

Oh, Lyla! She desperately needed to find Lyla! She had to reach her before anyone or anything else did. When Linx spun around to race home, her weight shifted to her toes as a shadow twice her height blocked her path. Inhaling enough force to scream for anything to hear her, she barely muttered a word before the shadow gripped her throat, lifting her body off of the soft ground.

Squeezing her eyes closed, Linx dug her nails into the hands of the unknown monster. Her breaths turned into wheezing as her esophagus started collapsing beneath the evil fingers wrapped around her neck.

As pressure built in her head, she opened her eyes to witness her killer.

Confused, her grip dropped from the firm hands to his wrists as she muttered, "Papa?"

The familiar deep voice whispered, "Linny, I'm so sorry. I wish you stayed home."

"Wh-why?" Linx's eyes filled with tears while she slowly began losing consciousness.

"Linny, you're too young to be pulled into this. She was cheatin'. I found out she was in love with someone else. Linny, why did you have to come out here? All you had to do was stay home with Lyla a little longer, and nothing would've ever happened. We would've moved on, happy as could be. Now, I guess it's just going to be me and Lyla from here on. I'm sorry, Linny. I gotta do this. I really loved ya a lot. You brought so much light into our family. I know Lyla's gonna miss ya. I will too." His eyes were blank and empty, glaring at the mess he created.

Linx hadn't thought the clothes mixed with her mother's were someone else's. She assumed, due to the darkness and dismemberment, she had stumbled upon the grizzly remains of her parents. Little did she know, her father was the cause of this devastation.

"Pl—" Linx tried to plead.

"I wish you would've stayed home, Linny," he repeated, squeezing her neck as her eyes began to slowly close.

CHAPTER 6

While mentally reliving her forgotten past life, Linx's mind had disassociated from her body as she followed the path in the cavern tunnel. She walked until the tunnel formed into a narrow walkway that split into two paths. With her flame barely flickering, she found herself gasping for air. Despite the close quarters, she pushed forward down the path to the right.

"This tunnel has to lead somewhere," she mumbled. "Plus, where would I go anyway? Who knows what Crystal Woods would do with me."

As she trudged forward, jagged rocks protruded from the walls, almost forming horizontal spears. Water lightly streamed down the walls and dripped from the pointed rocks. She quietly snaked by, attempting to minimize the volume of each step. Darkness soon engulfed Linx's path. She focused on brightening her flame to help guide the way. Once the flame grew to a healthy size, she realized she was standing at a dead end.

Disoriented, she spun around while intense trepidation trickled down her back. A crunch echoed throughout the tunnel, triggering her mind back to the horrendous moment with her father. Her breathing quickened as her heartbeat became painfully rapid. The dark walls appeared as though they were closing in, and she felt vulnerable and trapped inside.

Attempting to calm herself, Linx welcomed the cold air to fill her lungs. With a slow exhale, she almost caught herself—until pebbles rattled in the distance. Sweat melted down her back as her throat forcefully tightened. She stood—trapped—in unfamiliar territory . . . alone. What was coming her way? With no friend and many a foe, she could see no positive outcomes.

Her fear poured from her tense biceps down to her trembling hands as the sound grew closer. Referencing all her previous battles with Carter, she didn't know if she could take on an enemy alone. As adrenaline released into her body, assisting by quickly pumping her muscles with fresh blood, she could no longer contain herself. The power within Linx surged through her fingertips—blowing a hole into the dead-end wall, disintegrating the stone into rubble while revealing a glimpse of open bright green land surrounded by peculiar trees.

Linx quickly darted toward the opening in the cavern wall to view the landscape. Glancing around, her eyes illuminated with vivid colors and intriguing vegetation. Bright lime green grass danced with the wind while a clear blue creek gently bubbled in the distance. Linx carefully stepped down a mountain of debris from the explosion, slightly sliding on the rolling pebbles. Where was she? Linx couldn't see anything or anyone moving at all.

Once her feet reached the wispy grass, a sweet and fruity smell tickled her nostrils, elating her senses. Linx's heart felt oddly calm and at peace. Her body and mind transcended to a level she had never experienced before. A jolt of joyous energy surged from the soles of her feet up to her heart, shooting intense energy through her fingertips. As she soaked in the warm sun, tiny bumps rolled across her body while a euphoric breath filled her nostrils.

"Wha-what is this place?" she whispered aloud, hopping over the refreshing water from one stone to the next.

As she delicately bounced onto the last two protruding rocks, pearlescent fish wiggled beside one another downstream, lightly skimming the water's surface. A powerful wind gracefully brushed Linx's hair over her shoulders, spiraling each blonde strand in the air. This beautiful land rejuvenated her spirit.

Twirling in a circle, Linx noticed the ground vibrating under her feet. Looking up, she gasped as countless bare trees in the distance eerily bent to their sides, creaking as their sharp branches pierced into the soil. Linx held her breath, watching the dark trees grip the ground and propel themselves forward in a circular motion. The eerie noise picked up speed as they began crawling in her direction. What was happening?

Turning around, Linx sprinted toward the cave opening. She could hear cracking and creaking following close behind. The vibration of the noise rumbled over her skin. As she glanced behind her back, the pointed trees dug their razor-sharp branches into the ground to thrust themselves forward.

I'm not going to make it! I'm not going to make it!

Linx did the only thing she could think of. She quickly swirled a protective bubble around herself before the crawling trees could reach her. Sealing the top, she fell to the ground as the trees swarmed her. They jumped on top of her force field, attempting to stab their razors into the bubble. One after another, creatures attacked her protective bubble, burying her beneath them.

What am I going to do? Too many keep coming! Maybe I can teleport to the cave, but I don't know what else is in there.

The pounding of her heart became uncontrollable as she began breathing rapidly. Another idea came to mind, but she didn't know if it would work. Mindfully gathering and compressing her strength and power, Linx released a destructive explosion, sending the creatures in several directions. Grabbing a broken branch with a sharp, blade-like end, she swung the powerful weapon in the direction of one of the oncoming creatures. As the branch came into contact with the being, Linx's branch sliced through the creature. When the bark fell to the ground, the chaotic madness abruptly froze.

"Enough!" a high, raspy voice yelled from the distance. "You must stop now! The Gemenii's prophecy is coming to fruition before our eyes. Has our guardian finally found us?"

Gripping the branch with a sweaty palm, she held it steady, ready to fight. Something inside of her told her to stay—not to run or teleport. Holding her ground, she scanned over her enemies, threatening the same fate the other creature endured.

She studied the strange beings that stood still, mere feet away from her. The eerie tree-like creatures had two openings that appeared to be eye sockets with a giant hole beneath them. Linx neither saw nor heard of such a creature before. *What are these things?*

"We are ecknids," whispered a faint, winded voice.

Dread seeped down her spine as Linx realized she was face-to-face with a creature believed to be a legend—a myth. Instantly, all of the terrifying stories she had been told flooded her mind. The stories mainly included missing men who never got the chance to leave once they encountered one.

I need to go—now.

One of the creatures crawled forward before standing upright. With deep brown and gray bark, it moaned as the tree stretched tall. The pointed branches bent to form hooks, seemingly ready to attack. Nevertheless, Linx did not move a muscle.

Bowing itself toward her, it whispered, "My lady, please accept our apologies. We didn't know the prophecy would come true. We thought the arrival of the guardian was . . ."

"The arrival of who?" Linx shook her head, attempting to understand what was being discussed. "What are you talking about?"

"The guardian of Pangotha."

Unable to comprehend the situation, Linx stood in shock as she confronted the being. "I have no idea what you're talking about. I . . . am no one's guardian."

She adjusted her weight evenly onto both feet, preparing in case this was a trick to distract her. What could they possibly be talking about? Linx couldn't believe her eyes as these creatures shifted from their arachnid stances and transformed tall alongside one another, forming a forest before her eyes. A wave of heat traveled through her body as her eyes scanned from one side to the other. She sensed the hollowed stares piercing into her soul. In a matter of moments, a deadly and dark wall encircled Linx in the vibrant grass.

Linx firmly grasped the unorthodox sword in her right hand, igniting a flame in her left.

"My lady, you don't have to worry. We didn't realize that you were the guardian. We're under attack by many men."

"I'm not falling for your trap!" she screamed, lashing down a strike toward an ecknid and quickly blasting another with a rolling ball of fire. "I don't know what kind of game you are trying to play with me!"

As her wooden blade sliced into a branch of the first ecknid, the tree stood still, exhaling a wind of pain. The ecknid's arm cracked and fell to the ground. The second ecknid swiftly swayed, dodging Linx's deadly flame.

An exhilarating gust of wind pushed through the field. But this time, a wall of words soaked through her brain as the breeze lifted her hair into the sky.

"We won't fight you, my lady. We are your guards—your protectors. We fight for you, we die for you, and we die for Pangotha."

Taken aback, Linx tossed the sharp branch on the ground and pulled her arms toward her chest, clenching her fingers in regret. With tears forming in her eyes, she shuddered while chills coated her back. Her bottom lip parted from her top, searching for words that were not there.

A high, raspy voice startled Linx. "Well, well! So, you've finally come. It's true! The prophecy is true!"

Peering over her right shoulder, Linx examined a fuchsia puffball hopping over. The petite creature appeared so vulnerable and gentle—until it lifted its head to look into her eyes. Linx jumped back, staring into its giant, solid black orbs. Long, pointed teeth poked out from a mouth that almost split the creature in half.

Bouncing closer to her, the creature said, "You act like you haven't got a friend in the world."

Shaking her head, Linx frowned. "Why is my life any of your concern?"

"Well, it ain't. But you don't need to be rude about it. I

thought a guardian would've had some grace or manners. Guess we all gotta be wrong sometimes." The creature snorted, puffing out its fur.

"Who are you anyway?"

"The name's Pygo, my lady. It's a pleasure to meet you. We've been waiting for the guardian's arrival for quite some time!"

"I'm not a guardian! Why is no one listening to me? My name is Linx, and I belong to Violet Woods—or at least I used to." She lowered her eyes to the side, thinking about her cape predicament.

"Exactly."

Scrunching her face, Linx asked, "What do you mean?"

"Linx, you used to belong to Violet Woods, but your new home is here—Pangotha. This kingdom has been waiting for you."

"How can this be my kingdom if I've never been here before? I've only heard stories, and I have no knowledge of this land."

"The destiny of Pangotha was to be saved by the jewel-caped fairy, guiding us to a state of safety, prosperity, and peace."

Running her hand through her hair, a rush of anxiety spread across her chest. She whispered, "I . . . I need to sit down."

Pygo bounced over to Linx. "Do you need some time alone?"

"Um, I don't know." She raised her eyebrows as she made her way to the bubbling creek.

The ecknids parted a path for Linx as she made her way out of their company. They sensed a change—a bump of power that sparked hope and the possibility of transformation.

Linx walked toward the bubbling water. Her body felt very heavy from the weight of this strange news, and this nonsense felt like it would push her over the edge. Gracefully sitting on a rock that dipped into the water, Linx let out an audible sigh.

"My lady, are you not happy to see us?" Pygo screeched as he bounced over.

Linx turned her head to face this new creature. She felt slight chills swirl over her arm and back as she looked into his eerily dark eyes. The more she stared, the deeper her vision traveled into this creature. The same feeling came over her when she stared into the sky, and she could continue to see a new level into the space beyond. What was this creature?

Taking a deep breath, she explained, "I don't know who you are. How can I be anyone's guardian?"

"Let her leave," a new deep voice mumbled. "She doesn't want to be here. She's not our guardian."

Linx furrowed her brows as her eyes searched for the irritated voice. Her gaze locked onto a tall, built male figure standing behind an ecknid. Pygo glared in his direction.

As the figure made his way toward them, he continued, "If she is your guardian, then she can win in a duel against me."

The lean man stepped in front of the ecknids, dawning a dark, form-fitting suit of armor that reflected a deep green tinge in the sunlight. The material appeared to be lightweight, yet durable. Strapped across his chest and shoulder was a thick leather harness that held a sword firmly against his back. His black, wavy hair framed his deep brown face and dark eyes, falling softly on his shoulders.

Flustered with his attitude, Pygo yelled, "You're talking nonsense!"

"No! The Gemenii, the same creature that described *your* guardian from their premonition, stated she can beat anyone—especially on her soil. I'm tired of listening to that superstitious garbage. If it's true, she can easily win against me. You're willing to believe anything that devil tells you."

"You best watch your tongue, Jaut!" Pygo's fur tinted to a flaming red.

Jaut smirked. "Aww, do you really think that you've found your precious gem?"

"Even the ecknids sense her presence!" Pygo sneered.

Spinning around to face the wall of ecknids, Jaut laughed. "Is this true?"

A whisper pushed through the spiny trees and blew through Jaut's hair. "Yes."

"Lies! She's an enemy!"

Shrugging, Pygo replied, "Jaut . . ."

Clenching his jaw, a rage cooked inside of his body. Jaut's muscles tensed, and the burning anger spread throughout his veins. He slowly turned to face Linx before unleashing his rage. With his teeth pressing together, he shouted, "YOU WILL BATTLE ME NOW!"

"I-I am not claiming to be a guardian! I told them that! I am not anyone's protector!" Linx stammered. Unable to blink her wide eyes, she leaned her body back to provide more distance.

"Stand up now before I kill you where you sit! You are an intruder, and you need to leave now."

Stumbling to her feet, Linx spread her fingers as her arms dangled next to her legs. In her mind, she didn't know what to do. With no urge to fight, mild fear flowed throughout her blood—she was lost. How could she calm this guy's suspicion?

"I-I don't want to fight! Please! They held me captive in Crystal Woods, and I needed to leave. I am not claiming to be a guardian—I just need refuge." Her eyes locked onto his.

"You are not welcome here." Jaut swiftly gripped his sword, running in her direction.

Taken aback, Linx panicked. She didn't know his status or whether she should fight back. Hoping he was merely threatening her, Linx took a deep breath as she continued to stare into his eyes. His pain, frustration, and loss washed over her, seeping into her skin. Fighting him would not bring the resolution she needed—guardian or not. Before she could think of a plan, he brought his sword up, barely slashing her stomach.

"Ah!" Linx gripped the minor wound as blood lightly coated her fingers. "I am not your enemy!"

"You are a trespasser, and you do not belong here," Jaut shouted, driving his sword toward her shoulder.

Before she could react, the blade sank through her clothing and into her skin. Gasping for air, she dropped to the ground, holding her shoulder. Her head became foggy as she came to terms with the pain.

Jaut stood above her with his sword pushing into her cheek. The stinging of his blade that separated the skin on her face reminded her she was not welcome to stay. "Here is your chance to leave with your life. I don't know why you're here, but if you choose to stay, I will kill you."

Looking into his eyes, she whispered, "I have no reason to stay."

"Yes, you do! There's a reason why you came here. We need your help!" Pygo shouted as he bounced up and plunged himself into the ground, sending dirt and grass into the sky.

Dumbfounded, Linx stared at the massive explosion Pygo created around him. The beautiful green grass had been singed into dark gray ashy dust, clouding the group. As Linx choked on the dust, she sat on her behind and backed away to find clean air.

"You are a puffy pest," Jaut shouted toward Pygo as he covered his nose and mouth with his arm.

"I cannot have you ruin our chance at regaining control over our land! We have suffered long enough!"

"Huh?" Linx looked over at Pygo as he puffed himself nearly double his size.

With every pointed tooth exposed, he slowly explained, "We have lost everything except what you see here. Our magic has been drained, our creatures slaughtered, and our land isolated —vulnerable to the wrath of anyone who enters Pangotha."

"Who's in charge of this attack?" Linx questioned with passion igniting in her eyes.

"I don't know. Our land is dying, my lady. I don't know what kind of dark magic the enemy uses on our land, but we are lethargic, left helpless, and angry. We were healthy and thriving before the guards intruded upon our land, and now they continue to drain us daily."

Confused, Linx tried to pull more information from Pygo. "Who are these men you speak of?"

"We don't know for sure, but I have my suspicions. I wouldn't be surprised if Crystal Woods was the kingdom behind this. It wouldn't be a shock if they wanted to take over more land." Pygo licked his teeth as he bounced to look at the ecknids. "Many of those who live here really have no power to do anything against the enemy. They are now severely weak, and when their power begins to recharge, the enemy sends out these pulsating waves that suck everyone dry again—and it repeats."

"That is awful. I—" Linx began.

"Yes, indeed it is. The worst part came when some tried to stand up against the guards."

Linx stood silent as her gaze fell to the ground. She could only imagine what Pygo would say next.

"My lady, look around you. There are quite a few ecknids that surround us, aye?"

"Yeah . . . there are a lot."

"My dear, not as many as we once had. Their kind nearly spanned twenty times what you see now, and their colors were magnificent. But the ecknids rose against the men—they had enough. They couldn't take the torture and refused to see their friends and family abused. So they went to destroy the men, but they weren't prepared for what would happen. The enemy found a quick way to kill ecknids." Pygo shook his head, thinking about that dark, painful time. "They ignited all the ecknids at a glance with a magical ball of fire. Their ashes continue to blow in the wind on the mountains. The ones still alive haven't left the valley here in a very long time."

Tears formed in Linx's eyes as she was in complete disbelief. Without hesitation, she uttered, "I'm in. I will do whatever you need to restore your land."

CHAPTER 7

With a jolting growl, Jaut faced Linx while gripping his sword. "You will leave—now."

"Look, I don't want to fight you, but I have to stay—to free all the creatures tormented by twisted enemies. If Crystal Woods is behind this, I would be more than happy to fight for justice. It was ruled by a troubled woman who sacrificed everyone else to get what she wanted. I wouldn't be surprised if the current regime has similar values!" Linx huffed as her cheeks blushed.

"My lady, have you ever met the queen?"

"More than met her—the whole kingdom believes I killed her."

Pygo's deranged smile grew before flinging himself into a backflip. He spun to face Jaut while licking his lips. "See? You bumbling fool! She is our guardian, our savior!"

"I'm the fool? Says the one believing these stories!" Jaut challenged. He stepped toward Linx, wielding his sword. "Leave now. This is your last warning. There's too much at risk to have some stranger destroy the little chance we have to regain our land. Leave!"

Widening her stance, Linx held out her arms as sparks shimmered off her fingertips. "No. I'm not going anywhere, Jaut."

Jaut shook his head and scoffed. "What a fool you are. You're willing to battle *me* for creatures you don't even know."

Raising her piercing eyes to meet his, she sighed. "I guess that's my flaw."

Gripping his sword with both hands, Jaut spun around, dipping his sword down and yanking it toward the sky to slash at Linx's throat. Before he had a chance to succeed, Linx summoned a fireball in each hand the size of Jaut's head. She whipped one at his knee and threw another at his chest. As the impact occurred, Pygo comfortably rested up against an ecknid, smiling as the duel took place. The setting sun bounced off of his teeth as he enjoyed the chaos before him.

Sweat poured from Jaut's forehead, dripping down his chiseled jawline. Although he never lost a one-on-one battle, this one seemed like it would be close. Every hit he tried to make, she countered with a stronger block and strike. Jaut felt Linx could not only hold herself well, but she effortlessly anticipated his every move. Why did she let him stab her earlier if she was a successful fighter?

Linx gathered power to aim and shoot a massive ball of energy at Jaut's head. Fearing for his life, he dove on the ground and rolled out of its path.

With a quick smirk and a wave of satisfaction, she yelled, "Had enough?"

"When I am dead!" Jaut huffed.

"Very well then." Linx hurled another toward his stomach, barely showing her true strength.

He picked up speed with each hit. His blade slashed at her ankle and then her arm, each time merely scratching her clothing. Glancing up into her eyes, Jaut sensed a fire inside her—one he was curious about. Something ignited her anger and passion—but what?

"Are you sure you haven't had enough?" she shouted behind a blazing ball of energy surging toward Jaut's face.

As she waited for a response, her ball of energy skimmed past his head and slammed into a nearby rock, causing debris to fall everywhere. Looking around, she couldn't see what happened to Jaut. Where did he go? Linx glanced over toward Pygo, who creepily stared back. His black eyes sucked the life and comfort deep from within her bones as she widened her eyes. Gazing into his eyes, her senses heightened. A strange vibration made her skin tingle on her right arm. *Weird.*

Linx scanned the area near her right side, but she couldn't see anything at all. As she observed one of the ecknids, something appeared off. Something about its aura did not seem like the rest.

Her thumb grazed each fingertip firmly. Raising her eyebrow, she confidently inhaled cool air down into her belly. They were testing her, and she agreed to take on the challenge. She survived throughout her time on the sirens' ship, in the Inferno, during the journey through Dark Woods, and during her darker time in Crystal Woods. Linx had no interest in fighting to be a guardian, but this challenge was nothing. The silly bunch thought they were clever.

She turned to walk away when she heard Pygo say, "My lady, where are you going? But you haven't found the fool."

"I did, but I didn't want to embarrass your fool."

With a swift spin, Linx shot a bright burst into the side of the nearest ecknid. In an instant, Jaut appeared, rolling on the ground in pain.

Pygo shook his head with a laugh. "He ain't my fool."

Looking down at Jaut moaning while holding his chest, Linx rolled her eyes. "Impressive, really."

Releasing a sharp grunt, he smirked. "Thank you."

"Now, will you leave the poor girl alone?" Pygo shouted, making his way over to Linx.

Rubbing his face, Jaut pushed himself onto his knees and stood up to brush the dirt off his pants. Though she defeated him, his dark eyes brightened with amazement. Maybe Pygo was right, and dare he say—the Gemenii. Deep inside, he hoped there was energy somewhere to help shift their luck and skill when fighting this enemy. So many have died, while others awaited the day they could reclaim what was once theirs. They were forever stuck on a land that literally drained every ounce of their being—day after day.

Jaut knew it was coming. He felt the energy bubbling within the core of Pangotha. This was the worst part of it—the suspense. They knew the wave would happen. It always did. Right as he envisioned his fate, the loud vibration echoed throughout the trees. The noise triggered a painful spike of anxiety that prickled across his skin before the draining even occurred.

It won't hurt this time. I won't let it hurt this time, he repeated in his head.

Linx looked over, lifting her eyebrow. "What's going on? Are you okay?"

In that second, she witnessed them all drop to the ground,

writhing in pain. Confused, she noticed a thin, light blue line surging through the land. Right as she saw it, the line passed through her, sucking every drop of life from her soul. Her mind grew foggy as her lethargic body failed to stand up. Falling to her knees, she transformed into the shell of herself with the feeling of her internal organs melting into a goo and pouring onto the soil.

Her energy had shifted from powerful and confident into something she had never experienced before. Even on the sirens' ship or in the Inferno, she had a touch of energy to exist. But now—nothing.

Fighting the urge to lie flat on the ground, she mumbled inaudible words as she finally succumbed to her body's request. With her palms pressing against the soft grass, her forehead rested on the ground like a heavy stone. *What happened?*

Pushing her head to roll on its side, it took her mind a minute to register her surroundings. Just taking a mere breath exhausted every inch of her body. Linx forced her heavy eyelids open and noticed that everyone was suffering around her. Pygo looked like a deflated ball of fur, rolling from side to side. Once his face pointed toward the sky, his skin fell back, revealing his massive sharp teeth. Disturbed, Linx peered over at the closest group of devastated ecknids. Their bark chipped, their branches grew brittle, and their bodies wilted toward the ground.

Rocking her head back in line with her body, Linx's forehead nestled into the ground as the high-pitched ringing deafened her temporarily. Her mind throbbed as the pressure increased inside and against her skull. Would this feeling go away? Concern overcame her. With an exhale in a groggy daze, she tilted her head in the other direction.

While she fluttered her eyes, Jaut clenched his teeth together, flexing his jaw while he endured something similar to her. As Linx faded in and out of consciousness, Jaut opened his dark eyes, glancing her way. Based on her resistance, he could tell she was lucky enough to have never experienced this before. Reaching his hand out to cup hers, Jaut gripped her delicate fingertips, reinforcing that she wasn't alone.

"It'll be okay," he whispered with a grunt.

He's lying! He has to be lying! How can this get better? Linx rejected his false hope. *How can something so intense and painful be okay?*

Squeezing his hand tighter around hers, he uttered, "I promise."

Curling into a fetal position, Linx inhaled slowly, holding in the healing air and slowly releasing everything that took up space in her lungs. Focusing on her breath, she attempted to heal herself to the best of her abilities. Despite putting in all of her effort, her body succumbed to immense fatigue.

After what felt like a lifetime, every creature painfully strained to pull themselves up and continue on with their night.

"I wish they would just kill us already," Jaut complained, firmly rubbing his face. "This is getting unbearable."

"Our guardian has fallen!" Frowning, Pygo slowly bounced over. "My lady! Are you okay?"

Completely drained of any energy, she had no enthusiasm to speak. Linx fell to the ground while continuing her deep breathing. She had no ambition to move forward. With her face pushing into the ground, the soil rudely muffled her words. "I am not your guardian."

"I couldn't hear you, my lady."

"Why must you keep calling me that? I am no one's guardian —and I will never be."

Pushing himself up on all fours, Jaut let out an annoyed exhale. "Look, what's your name?"

Narrowing her eyes, she said, "Linx."

"Well, Linx, I hate to admit when I'm wrong, so I never do. That being said, it's quite impressive to see you fight—"

"She annihilated you!" Pygo piped in with a laugh.

Rolling his eyes, Jaut continued, "However you want to put it, you're skilled. We need skilled fighters to go up against whoever is behind this. Know that we cannot force you to help us, but what you just experienced, we live with daily. Every . . . single . . . day, we have to go through the draining. Every day, we're thrown to our knees as this leach sucks our powers and energy dry. We cannot let our people suffer through this for the rest of their lives."

With a hopeful smirk, Linx looked up, slightly raising her head from the ground. "At first, you were kicking me out. Now, you're begging me to stay."

Trying to use humor to push through the pain, Jaut said, "Well, I wouldn't say beg . . ."

"You better beg," Pygo quietly said, "or I will."

With a fading smile, Linx let her head drop and bounce off of the ground again as she tried to figure out how to muster up enough energy to do anything. Closing her eyes, she mentally fought her body's urge to fall asleep.

Jaut gently smacked the side of her head. "Linx! You need to push through it. We have to be careful. I don't know what kind of twisted game they play, but they send out men to capture the weak. I don't know why or what they do with them. We need to hide—now."

Squeezing her eyes tight to create some flow of lubrication, Linx pried her eyes open and pushed herself up to her feet. Slight vertigo overcame her, spinning the inside of her head around and around. Linx couldn't tell how long she'd be able to focus, but her eyes searched for Jaut.

Because of the contrast between the bright green grass and his outfit, his location popped with minimal effort from Linx's waning vision. Fighting the urge to pass out, Linx stumbled over toward his aura. Holding out his arm, Linx firmly dug her fingers into the fabric on his sleeve.

Pulling her against his side, he whispered, "Slowly, your energy will start coming back to you. We just need to hide while we wait."

Linx's heavy eyes refused to stay open, but she persisted. "Okay. Which way should we go?"

"How about we crawl into that cute hole you made? It was quite an entrance—really."

Lamely shaking her head with amusement from side to side, Linx tried to entertain him. "All right. Let's go."

Jaut wrapped his arm around Linx's back and under her arm to help hold her upright as they crept toward the cave opening. Intense fatigue swept over Linx's body and face as she held in her urge to vomit. She couldn't believe that these creatures experienced this feeling daily. What kind of sadistic group, kingdom, or enemy would do that?

As Linx stumbled over a branch, Jaut fought to hold himself up while helping her. Despite doubting her earlier, he sympathized with Linx. It felt like yesterday when he went through the draining for the first time. The pain intensified so much he convinced himself he was going to die.

"Watch yourself over here. There's a dip in the ground, but

we have to move quickly." Jaut pulled her closer as they attempted to pick up speed.

Pygo and some ecknids followed immediately behind, taking momentary breaks to gather themselves. Once they reached the cavern hole, Linx, Jaut, and Pygo climbed into the dark crevice. As Linx peered through the hole, she noticed, one by one, the ecknids stood in place and dug their sharp roots into the ground.

"What are they doing?" She raised her eyebrows.

Jaut looked over. "Oh, they'll be fine there."

"They'll be fine? I thought the men always came out to gather the weak. I thought everyone needed to hide?"

Jaut dismissed her with his hand. "They're idiots. They can't tell the difference between ecknids and old trees scattered throughout Pangotha. Plus, the ecknids are too big to be transported anyway—at least for now. It was when they lit the forests on fire and the ecknids tried fighting back that so many sadly passed away."

"Oh," Linx said. "Have the guards ever done that again?"

"Luckily, no."

She observed these incredible creatures congregating in front of the hole, providing an elusive natural barrier and disguising it from the men. In a matter of minutes, the ecknids transformed that portion of land into an incredible forest.

"But don't the men realize the land changes every time they walk through it?"

"Yes, and it makes them so angry!" Jaut laughed. "Like I said, idiots. You'll see. Just be careful. You don't want to be seen, especially if your powers aren't back to normal. They've only succeeded thus far from draining us for everything. If they never discovered that, they never would've made it out of here alive."

Linx slid down the wall until she sat on a mound of lightly dampened pebbles. She vigorously rubbed her face, hoping to wake from this bizarre state of being. As the makeshift room darkened, Linx could still peek through a few of the ecknids to see if anyone was approaching.

At that moment, she desperately wished she could shrink into a safe pod to sleep in for the night, but she didn't have even a quarter of the energy. So Linx ended up trying to make herself comfortable where she sat—which seemed impossible with this cape attached to her. Luckily, the pain had subsided from where it adhered to her upper back, but it remained a strange and eerie feeling to have a deceased troll's cape on her back.

This night reminded her of one not too long ago. Sadness swept over her as she thought about the night with Raza and Carter, hiding in the cave from the Cerberus. Filled with abandonment and missing what once was, Linx's soul felt lost. They all were supposed to be members of a great team—one that would change many lives. Instead, she found herself in a group of frauds swayed by power. A tear dripped from the corner of her eye, falling on her thigh.

CHAPTER 8

"Oye! Do you see any over there?" a voice shouted in the distance, abruptly waking Linx in the early morning.

Rushing over to the thin opening between the ecknids, she saw five figures dressed in metal armor and helmets almost covering their entire faces.

Releasing an audible sigh, she rubbed her hand over her eyes and forehead before combing her fingers through her delicate hair. Despite regaining some energy, Linx still did not feel like herself.

Jaut whispered in Linx's ear, "Hey! What do you see?"

Staring outside of the hole, Linx shrieked, "Wow! Don't do that again! You spooked me!"

With a slight smirk, Jaut laughed. "Didn't mean to scare you."

"I see five helmets creeping around down there. They're looking for—us—I guess. I hope they leave."

Shrugging his shoulders, he said, "We'll be fine. Just like I said, they are like a box of rocks. Nothing to worry about, as long as you aren't in plain sight."

Her bright green eyes scanned the figures. "Um, what are they holding?"

Flipping his hair out of his face, Jaut stealthily crawled over against Linx. As he looked out, concern grew on his face. Some figures carried a thin staff with a minuscule orb resting on each one.

Throwing his hands in the air, Jaut yelled, "I have no idea!"

"I thought we had nothing to worry about. I guess you were lying?"

Pygo rolled over toward the pair and said to Jaut, "Looks like you're the fool! So quick to make fun of everyone else."

"Every other day, around two guards come out to drag any weak creature back. But what is this? What are those sticks supposed to do? Poke us to death?" Jaut rolled his eyes.

A strange sensation overcame Linx. "I wouldn't be so quick to joke, Jaut. I sense power. Be careful."

"Look, you're the new one here. I don't need to hear your suggestions." Jaut squinted his eyes.

"What's your problem?" Linx asked.

Vigorously rubbing his eye sockets and cheekbones, he sighed. "I don't know! I don't know! I can't handle living like this anymore! It's driving me crazy."

The corners of Linx's mouth sagged. Her heart sank for him —and for the others who have endured this treatment. Looking through the thin opening, she saw the five men had their sights on some poor soul. One pointed forward, so the others followed close by. Linx jammed her head into the crevice to see where they were headed.

"Oh, no!" Linx cried.

"What? What do you see?" Pygo asked, perking up with intrigue.

"I see some . . . some creature lying next to one of the ecknids." Linx hung her head for a moment.

"See? She can at least tell the trees and ecknids apart. How come those—"

"Hold on!" Linx shouted.

"Wha-what? What's happening?" Pygo chimed in.

She asked, "Pygo, do you have other family members or friends around here?"

"Huh? What are you talking about?"

"That creature looks kind of like you! They are purple, though."

"That's impossible!" Pygo pressed his face into the wedge. "No! No, no, no!"

"Pygo! Who is it?"

Anxiously bouncing in a line, Pygo said out loud to himself, "No, no, no. Why? Why would she come out? What do I do? If I try to save her, I might jeopardize the Gemenii's premonition. But I can't leave her to die!"

"Pygo!" Linx shouted to get his attention.

He turned to face her. "That's my partner, Rena. I don't know why she came out of our hideout, but I must try to save her. We don't know what happens to their prisoners, and I can't chance it."

Within that moment, Linx saw another similar creature hop out of the bushes to distract the five men. They bounced and ran away as quickly as possible, darting behind other trees and ecknids along the way. "Uh, Pygo?"

Although flustered, Pygo asked, "Yes?"

"They're chasing someone else!"

"Huh? Who?"

"I'm not sure. They look like you, but they're blue."

Hopping back over to the crevice, Pygo peered through while Linx looked through the opening above him. "No! Ligor!"

As soon as Ligor's name left Pygo's mouth, a guard raised his staff and pointed it directly at the back of Ligor's head. With an upward swing of the staff, a gray ball of energy shot out, flying in Ligor's direction. In a matter of seconds, Ligor disintegrated into thin air.

"Holy—" Jaut nearly choked on his spit.

"No!" Pygo screamed as his eyes filled with tears. "I need to get out there for Rena! Ecknids, please let me out of here!"

"You're going to bring attention to the ecknids!" Jaut argued. "They will slaughter them too!"

"What do I do then? If you have all the answers, give me one of your brilliant ones now! Do I leave my partner to die?"

"Yes."

About to jump at Jaut's throat, Pygo said, "Why you worthless piece of—"

Attempting to show peace, Jaut held his hands in the air and elaborated, "Think about it, though! You'll risk the entire ecknid species, the Gemenii's premonition, Pangotha's future, and the guardian for the slim chance to save your partner?"

"YES! You fool, I would risk anything to save her! She's my everything, and she deserves the chance to survive. I hope someday you'll understand." Pygo immediately squeezed through the small crevice between the ecknids, making his way outside the cavern.

"Pygo!" Jaut whispered loudly. "Hey!"

"What?" Pygo snapped back.

"I'm coming." Jaut squeezed through the ecknids.

Taking a deep breath, Linx shouted, "Wait for me!"

With a giant grin growing larger, Pygo rushed down the side of the mountain. "I'm coming, Rena!"

A guard turned and raised his staff toward Pygo, blowing up a tree next to him.

"Watch it!" another guard shouted to the first. "Watch your flippin' aim! You almost blew me head off!"

"Get that pink thing!" the first guard yelled to the second.

Luckily, they didn't notice Jaut. He stood camouflaged against a tree, ready to attack. Meanwhile, Linx crouched down behind an ecknid to avoid attracting any attention. Pygo had to give it his all. Three of the men spotted him, and they called the others to follow.

One of the distant guards yelled, "You get the pink one! I've got my eyes on the purple."

Pygo turned to stare into Linx's eyes. *My lady, I know you can hear me. If you are the true guardian . . . you can hear me. I'll do my best to distract them. I need you and Jaut to save Rena. Don't worry about me. Please, just protect her.*

A sad heart consumed Linx as she watched her new friend exchange his life for another's. His eyes begged for compliance with his idea. With a gentle nod, Linx quickly agreed to Pygo's plan. She needed to grab Jaut's attention while the guards focused on Pygo and Rena. She developed a thought in her mind but didn't know if she could pull it off.

Sliding to the next ecknid, she flicked her finger, sending a minuscule bubble plummeting into Jaut's neck. He immediately slapped his neck, almost flinging himself to the ground. Linx had to keep herself from laughing to gain his attention. She waved her hand when he glanced around, and their eyes locked.

As Linx motioned to walk toward Rena, Jaut raised his eyebrow and nodded.

Once they met at a nearby tree, they noticed two guards heading toward Rena. She appeared to be injured or severely drained from the pulse earlier. Rena barely moved and made no sound. To Linx's surprise, her bright purple had drastically faded to a lavender-tinted color.

"I hope we can pull this off," Linx said. "More importantly, I really hope we can figure out a way to keep Pygo alive as well."

"He's a smart—and fluffy—death ball. I am not worried at all." Jaut refused to make eye contact as he confidently announced his thoughts. Linx didn't know what to believe.

As she turned her attention to the guards hunting Rena, Linx detected a vulnerable portion of the guards' necks exposed on the back of their heads.

"Jaut, look at the back of their helmets! If we hit them there, we have a chance."

"Let's do it."

They stealthily pursued the guards. Every moment possible, Jaut camouflaged himself into a tree or ecknid while Linx quickly darted behind anything she could to get close enough to the guards.

"Are you ready?" he whispered into her ear.

"Yeah, I'll get the one on the right."

"Good luck, guardian fairy."

With a smirk and a narrowing of her eyes, she rose from the ground, igniting a bright white fireball in her hands. Completely unaware, the guard continued onward while the burst of energy flew directly into the back of his head, charring his skin. The guard fell facedown before his head detached and rolled onto the feet of his comrade.

Looking at his feet, the guard didn't recognize what bumped into him. When he nonchalantly kicked the charred ball, he noticed his friend's head rolling away. "Oh, my—"

Before he could finish his sentence, Jaut skewered the other guard with his sword through the back of his neck. Pulling his sword out of the body, he saw Linx diving to her knees to rescue and comfort Rena.

"Rena, my name is Linx. I am a friend of Pygo's. Are you okay?"

As Linx reached for Rena, an unsettling gurgle came from her body. Although Rena didn't appear responsive, Linx had to do whatever she could to help her—especially for Pygo's sake. When Linx caressed Rena's soft fur, a bizarre and erratic movement caused Linx to jump back a bit. She wasn't familiar with this type of creature, but Linx didn't want her to die. With her fingers gripping Rena, she lifted her up from the ground. When Linx thought she felt oddly light, she noticed that only Rena's skin rested in her arms. Glaring at the ground, the life left Linx's soul as familiar bright yellow eyes looked up and winked.

CHAPTER 9

"Everything okay?" Jaut shouted as he sprinted toward Linx.

Shaking her head in disbelief, Linx could only stare back at the tiny goblin before her. Quickly, her memory bounced to the moment in the forest where they dug their nails into her flesh, barbarically tearing her to shreds. The fire of pain washed over Linx as it hypnotically stared back. She vividly remembered the feeling of their teeth sinking into her skin, peeling off what they could.

"Linx! Li—" Jaut stopped when he saw this small, eerie creature standing in front of her.

His yellow eyes were massive with thin pupils keeping her in a trance. The goblin's long, narrow ears pointed outward while his sharp claws moved subtly. Short fur coated the creature, fluffing around the ears and jawline.

Never seeing this creature before, Jaut blended into the nearby tree, hoping to sneak up on it. As he snaked around the trunk of the tree, he moved so quietly that no one could hear any footsteps.

Linx continued to stare into the goblin's eyes as she tried to figure out what to do next. Noticing his claw slightly twitch, she prepared herself for him to launch on her head. Her agility could match anyone, but they had such a wild nature that their actions were unpredictable.

"What do you want?" she asked in a monotone voice.

With a low growl, an almost inaudible voice said, "Home."

Confused and surprised the goblin had spoken, she asked, "Home? With Carter?"

The goblin nodded with a grin, proudly displaying the tiny spikes in its mouth.

"Why are you here, then?"

The goblin creepily pointed one of his sharp fingernails at Linx. "Master said follow."

"Carter wanted you to follow me? Why? Why would he send one of his goblins to follow me here?" Unsettled, she squeezed her fists closed to rub her fingertips together.

"Protect," he said before letting out a high-pitched laugh.

Linx didn't know what to think or how to feel. Why would he think he could send a goblin to protect her? And now, what does she do since he killed Rena?

Ignoring his statement, she shouted, "Why did you kill her? She was a friend!"

Shaking his head, he said, "No kill."

"You didn't kill her? Was she dead already?"

Nodding his head, the goblin licked his lips with a long, skinny tongue.

Perplexed, Linx asked, "What were you doing then?"

The goblin rubbed his belly. "Hungry."

Nausea surged through her body, and she quickly brought her hand up to her mouth. "What am I going to do?"

As the goblin waited, a light wind blew past Jaut in the direction of the goblin. Spinning its body around, the goblin somersaulted toward Jaut and violently slashed his calf muscle.

"Argh!" Jaut moaned, swinging his sword toward the goblin's head.

The goblin rapidly backflipped away from him and spun up a tree, disappearing from sight.

"What the hell was that?" he shouted.

Linx whispered, "A goblin."

"Great! So it's a goblin. Why were you talking to a goblin? Why didn't you kill it?" he yelled at Linx.

With two fingers pressing on her forehead, she said, "I-I don't know. My relationship with the goblins is very complex. This one was sent to protect me by a friend from the past."

"Um, well, that's nice—I guess. I'm sure that Pygo will find that very reassuring." Disgusted, Jaut turned away from her.

"Look, I don't know what to say!" she said, leaning against a tree.

"Me neither." Jaut continued to walk away without looking back.

Distraught, Linx stood alone—again. The wind blew through her delicate hair as she briefly thought about the chaos constantly following her. She knew she had to help Pygo though, so she brushed her woes aside. Keeping some distance from Jaut, she gathered some strength and sporadically transported herself in the direction of Pygo.

As she ran, the vibration of a distant boom rumbled beneath her feet. Was that Pygo? Linx picked up the pace, but she couldn't find him. Looking over to see where Jaut was, she couldn't find him anywhere! She scanned the dense bushes and thick trees. *Where did he go?*

Leaning against an ecknid, Linx inhaled a deep, cool breath as she attempted to hone in on where Pygo's energy could be coming from. Another rumble shook the soil and vibrated into her bones. The wind blew musical words through her hair. "Fear not, my lady. We will rescue the pink one."

With prickles traveling up her neck, Linx looked up to see two giant, hollow eyes staring down at her. The ecknid remained motionless as it waited for Linx to respond.

"How?" Linx forced out.

"Hold on tight," the ecknid said, yanking out their roots from beneath the soil.

A small mound of soil formed above each root before the tiny ends poked out, raising the ecknid out of the ground. The moans and groans of their wooden body lifting from the damp dirt sent a chill down her spine. Carrying Linx high into the air, the ecknid crunched its roots on top of the bushes beneath them.

"I cannot see him anywhere," Linx said, peering through the woods. "Wait! There he is! And Jaut, too!"

As Linx pointed to a distant opening, the groaning ecknid swiftly stabbed its branches into the ground to quicken the pace. A tingling sensation wrapped around Linx's throat as she contemplated what to do until she saw more guards step out from behind several trees. From roughly twenty feet away, Jaut observed the scene before camouflaging into the surroundings. Pygo desperately looked around, noticing he had nowhere to turn. With an expressive grin spread across his face, he bounced into the air and slammed into the ground, sending guards flying into neighboring trees. Clanking and crashing into the ground, they fumbled to stand up, pushing each other out of the way. Without hesitation, Jaut ran behind one, stabbing the guard in the neck.

"I'm sorry," Linx whispered to the ecknid. "There's not enough time. I must go—now."

Focusing on Pygo, she closed her eyes to transport herself nearby. Within a blink of an eye, she was gone, leaving the ecknid running alone.

Stopping in its tracks, the ecknid lifted its deadly branches in the air as it curled itself into a ball of knives, rolling toward the chaos. "Suit yourself."

As Linx appeared near the fallout, she quickly darted behind a tree and dove to the ground to assess who she should attack first. Glancing from one guard to the next, Linx couldn't believe how she ended up in this situation. And now, because of Carter's goblins, she had to face another battle if they made it out of this mess. How was she going to explain to Pygo that his partner's deceased corpse had been consumed by a miniature devil? The thought made her nauseous. He trusted her—he didn't even know her, yet he trusted her. This creature was guided to believe she was his guardian, but she was too late to protect the one thing most precious to him.

Scrunching her forehead, Linx exhaled acceptance of purpose. She failed him once, and she would never fail him again. With fire racing through her body, her soul awoke, guiding her to lead and embrace the unknown. Balls of energy expanded between her fingertips as her focus locked on two targets. In a matter of seconds, Linx fiercely pressed her hand forward, releasing a deadly ball. The bright light hurdled through the air, blowing right through a guard's metal armor. Scalding liquid from their melted body pooled beneath them before their chain mail suit hit the ground. The other guards spun around to see where the attack originated from, while stepping over their peer's carnage.

Sending the second bright ball toward its target, Linx saw Pygo stare at her. Initially, his gaze widened with excitement as he smiled, content knowing Rena awaited them in a safe location. However, when Linx did not return his happiness, Pygo's smile quickly faded as she abruptly looked away. He raced in her direction, slamming his body off of the ground—jolting everything connected to the soil. The closer he traveled, the more intense his bouncing became, almost knocking Linx off of her feet.

A guard stepped out in front of Pygo, pointing his staff directly between his eyes. As the staff lit up, Pygo's fur started tinting a deep red, and his smile turned dark and sinister. With a rapid hop high in the air, he glanced down at the guard and opened his gigantic mouth. Upon his descent, his mouth wrapped around the guard's head, sinking his teeth around the guard's neck. With a smooth tug, Pygo tore the head off of the guard's shoulders before his body collapsed on the ground. Spitting out the guard's head, he continued onward toward Linx.

Slaying one guard and another, she deliberately avoided eye contact with Pygo. Anger, confusion, and sadness swirled in her head. *How could she tell him?*

"My lady, where's Rena?" Pygo shouted.

Ignoring his question, Linx acted as if she couldn't hear him.

Once close enough, Pygo jumped in front of Linx and bit the head off of the guard she was fighting. "My lady! Didn't you hear me? I asked about Rena. She's safe, right?"

Inhaling deeply, she formed a flaming ball of energy and

sent it toward a lone guard—instantly pulverizing him. "Pygo, I couldn't get to her in time. I'm sorry . . . she's gone."

"I see," Pygo said, zoning out while in his new world of solidarity. "My lady, if you wouldn't mind, I'd like some time to think—by myself."

Several ecknids rapidly crawled up to spear the remaining guards that lingered.

"Of course, Pygo! Like I have said countless times, I'm not anyone's guardian," she said, shaking her head. "You don't need any permission from me. Take care of yourself. Let me know if you need me."

With a quick nod of his drooping head, Pygo spun around and launched himself into the woods. As anxious air exited her nostrils, Linx's gaze dropped to the mossy forest floor. Although guilt trickled into her mind, she believed Pygo's heart could only handle so much. There was no need to give him the gory details—unless he asked.

A strange, warm sensation radiated over the skin on her back. The unnatural feeling alarmed her as she cocked her head to the side. Before Linx could see anything, she heard a sword plunge through something behind her and a man moan before falling to the ground.

Twirling around, Jaut stood almost toe to toe with Linx. His jaw clenched tightly as his sword dripped with dark blood. Raising his eyebrows and holding a scowl, he said, "So . . . you gonna tell him?"

"I did." She hung her head.

"No." He wiped his blade with a scrap of cloth. "No, you didn't. You told him just enough to keep yourself innocent."

"I didn't do anything wrong! I didn't kill her nor did I allow her to be shredded to death. What's your problem? I was just as upset as you. Do you think I want to see someone's loved one dead—when they trusted me most? Look, I didn't ask for this—no one did. I will avenge her death."

"I see." Softening his face slightly, Jaut narrowed his eyes. "You're welcome, by the way."

Crunching her boots on dried vines and twigs as she moved forward, Linx rolled her eyes. "I'm sure the favor will be repaid—sooner rather than later."

Jaut laughed, puffing his chest in the air. "What's that supposed to mean?"

"Ha! Nothing. Nothing at all."

Shrugging his shoulders, he asked, "So now what?"

She spun around, observing her surroundings. "I want to meet the one you call the Gemenii."

"Ugh, why? They just tell stories. There's nothing to believe about what they say."

"That's fine. I'd still like to speak to them. Pygo was convinced that I was someone special, and I'd like to know why."

Jaut sighed, arching his back. "I say this in the kindest way possible, but Pygo is a fool for listening to them."

"Why are you irritated with the Gemenii?"

"Because they like to plant seeds of fear and then disappear. No one knows if there's any merit to what they say."

"Interesting." Linx rubbed her fingertips across her lips. "Take me to the Gemenii."

"But—"

"Either you're with me or not. Regardless, I'm going to find the Gemenii."

Shaking his head in disapproval, Jaut mumbled, "Fine. Don't blame me for wasting your time. I warned you. Follow me."

CHAPTER 10

"Come on." Jaut stepped down on some rocks near an opening in the woods. He hopped over some flat stones that passed through a nearby creek.

Light peered through the top of chattering trees as leaves shuffled together in the mild breeze. A sweet fragrance tickled Linx's nose as she followed Jaut. He picked up the pace to enter the clearing.

Once close enough, she asked, "How far is it to get to the Gemenii?"

Pointing ahead, he said, "We're taking a shortcut through this field to get to that cliff. Does that work for you, *mighty guardian?*"

"Do you think you're funny?" Linx hissed, placing a hand on her hip.

Giving a deep chuckle, he replied, "Yes."

"Well, I'll have to come up with a name for you then. But trust me, it won't be so lovely." She grinned while obnoxiously fluttering her eyes.

"My apologies. I thought you missed the pompous flattery."

Looking Jaut in his eyes, all the laughter left Linx's voice. "Guardian or not—you, your friends, and this land need help. If the Gemenii, or Pygo, thinks I am the one to help, I want to know if they have any insight into how I should do it."

"Fine, I'll humor you. We need to reach the cliff and shimmy to the side of the mountain. Deep inside a cave, we *should* find the Gemenii."

Squinting her eyes, she asked, "If they are that easy to access, why haven't the guards gone after the Gemenii?"

"Oh, my dear. I say that lovingly, by the way. Looks can be deceiving." Jaut let out a slow exhale.

Linx couldn't understand what Jaut meant—maybe there was a force field or something else. Regardless, she had to find them to hear their vision. She also secretly hoped they knew how to remove the cape so she could return it back to the Violet Woods. Not to mention, the relief of not having it crush her wings would be incredible.

Stepping onto the field, the tall, wispy grass covered her waist and thighs. Continuing through the vegetation, memories from the past trickled into her mind. She could hear Lyla's voice singing, *Linny, want to go out? The sun is so bright and warm! It's beautiful outside!*

Linx wondered why all these wonderful thoughts came now. What changed?

"So we need to get to the other side by the time daylight falls, okay?" he asked Linx.

Analyzing the massive field, she said optimistically, "Of course, it doesn't seem too far."

Jaut chuckled. "Remember, looks can be deceiving."

"Yeah, I know."

As they walked in silence for a bit, Jaut looked over and bluntly said, "Tell me about yourself."

"Huh?" Linx glanced over, breaking her concentration on the earth beneath her.

Running his hand through his hair, he admittedly said, "Well, we really didn't have a great introduction, and we have quite a way to go."

"If you didn't try killing me . . ."

Jaut interrupted her to say, "If I wanted you dead, you'd be dead right now. So tell me—what's your story?"

"I'm sure," she said, rolling her eyes. "Honestly, up until recently, I didn't know. Here, I had always been a lost fairy. I was held captive by siren pirates, and then I tried helping someone who I thought was a friend—until they betrayed me."

"Siren pirates, eh? That must've been an experience." Jaut lifted his eyebrow and smirked.

Dumbfounded, Linx asked, "Seriously?"

Holding his hands in the air, he chuckled. "Look, I'm sorry. I've encountered some, and I almost hopped aboard. Damn my friend for making me leave."

Linx looked at him with dead eyes. "They eat men."

"Huh? Wha-what? Wow, I guess I owe Palion an apology. I chewed his ear off for a long time after that one." Jaut pushed his hair to the side.

Shaking her head, she said, "You're unbelievable."

"What do you expect? They were gorgeous!"

"Of course they were. How else do you think they would prey upon their victims? They would also kidnap and sell them to Donem."

Stepping over a fallen branch, Jaut sighed. "Now, that's one messed up fellow."

"No kidding." A thick sweat traveled from beneath her hairline and down her neck.

Observing her body language, he noticed her hesitation before intentionally avoiding more discussion about Donem. Jaut asked, "So, what brought you to Pangotha?"

"There was someone who I helped, and something horrific happened," she said with a painful gaze forming within her eyes. "He wouldn't believe that I wasn't involved, so I had to leave."

Jaut sneered. "It seems like trouble *follows* you everywhere, huh?"

"Are you mocking me?"

"Not at all!" Jaut teased.

Staring at him without blinking an eye, she whispered, "I was accused of murdering a queen. It's nothing to laugh about. I was about to be put to death because no one believed me."

Jaut raised his eyebrows. "It certainly does seem like trouble follows you wherever you go."

As they continued on through the vast field, the journey was quiet. For Linx to have a moment to just walk felt strange. She observed random little creatures running by and magnificent ones flying across the sky. It's been a while since she had time to breathe. Nevertheless, she knew they soon had to worry about the inevitable shock that surged through the land.

"Jaut, when does that shock wave go through the land?" she asked.

"Probably within an hour or so. We need to make sure to find a secure location. Why do you ask?"

Linx whispered in a low tone, "I wanted to try something the next time it happens."

Laughing, he sarcastically said, "What are you talking about? There's nothing you can do to stop it."

"Do you have fairies here or any creatures that can manipulate or create energy to form protective bubbles?"

Scratching his head, Jaut said, "I really don't know. Why?"

"Well, I can create a force field that may protect us from anything outside."

Jaut tilted his head, suspiciously looking at her.

She continued, "At least, it should for a little while."

"To be sure, we can hide out somewhere safe. I'll help get us somewhere no one will think to look," he suggested.

"Okay, that works. Just let me know when you think it will go off. I don't want to waste extra magic, especially if I don't have to. There's no telling what will happen."

"Sounds good. Let's go this way."

After some time, they got closer to the end of the field. As the sun crept down beyond the mountains, they rushed to find safety. Linx followed Jaut as he dipped under tree branches and sprinted around bushes, ecknids, and boulders.

"Right up here," he shouted to her, pointing up into a cavern. "Hurry, we don't have a lot of time."

"Okay, I'm right behind you."

Jaut and Linx scanned the giant cliff, planning how they would ascend it. Jaut glanced toward her. "I'm not sure if we can make it in time."

"I'm going to use my magic to get us up there. I just don't know if I'll have enough to form the bubble."

"As long as we're up there, we'll be safe. Those idiots won't be able to climb this in those pathetic metal uniforms."

Linx sighed, reaching out her hand for his. "All right. Let's go."

Firmly grabbing her hand, Linx and Jaut teleported inside the quaint cavern nook. They looked around to make sure there were no surprises, but everything appeared safe.

"Okay, let me seal the cavern closed and form this bubble around us. I really hope this works."

Jaut quickly nodded while watching Linx manipulate the environment right in front of him. "Yeah, me too."

Closing the bubble under their feet, she said, "I don't know how long this will hold. I'm used to just sealing off a wall, not encasing people inside a full bubble."

"I think it will happen soon. You can hear the vibrations as the surge blankets Pangotha."

"This is insane. I've never heard of someone draining so many people of their powers. And why would they kill or capture those who provide the power?"

Jaut rolled his lips together and shrugged before saying, "It's said they essentially keep the power from those they kill. I don't how it really works—that's just how some interpret it."

With big doe eyes, Linx stared at him in disbelief at what he said. How could someone create such an intense and evil plan? She thought Carter's mother possessed ridiculous powers, but now this? Staring into his eyes, Linx tried to read beyond Jaut's lips—into his mind and soul. It was difficult to gather his true thoughts. Surprised, she didn't expect him to be strong himself. No matter what she tried, she could not access his mind at that moment. *Interesting.*

As she found herself obsessed with figuring him out, she heard the vibration echo throughout the land. Both of them stared into each other's eyes. They didn't have to read minds to know the fear they wore on their faces. If this didn't work, the pain would shock every cell within their bodies.

"It's all or nothing," Linx whispered, closing her eyes to focus on any positive thought she could.

Jaut reached out his hand, interlocking his fingers with hers. With a firm grip, he squeezed her hand as they waited to see if they had escaped the torture that every other creature would endure.

When nothing happened after a few moments, they opened their eyes and looked at each other with excitement. Overcome with joy, Jaut smiled at Linx. "You did it!"

"Are you sure?" She didn't want to get too excited, in case it didn't reach them yet.

"Yes! You did it! I haven't heard of anyone who could escape that wicked thing. I can't believe you did it!" Jaut fiercely rubbed his face with his hands. "There's hope."

Holding her shaking hands out, Linx said, "I'll leave it up for a few more minutes just in case."

Jaut softly sat down. "Do whatever you like! I can't believe it. There is no way I can describe how grateful I am. Every single night, for the past—however long—I just sat there waiting for the most intense pain to overcome my body. For so many nights, I just wanted to die as the stinging and stabbing flooded my head, chest, and stomach. I watched so many friends keel over from the pain."

Witnessing Jaut's happiness, a warm feeling blanketed Linx's arms, chest, and neck. She hadn't felt this accomplished in a long time. An innocent smile formed as she lowered her hands and disintegrated the bubble.

After several moments of hearty deep breaths, Jaut angled his head to glance at Linx. "I'm sorry."

Curving her eyebrow, Linx questioned, "About what?"

"For doubting you."

"Well, you didn't know me . . . and you barely do now. I don't take offense to that." She shrugged her shoulders humbly.

"Maybe Pygo was right about you."

Scoffing, Linx looked away. "That I'm a guardian? Don't be ridiculous. I just showed up at the right time with helpful skills. We haven't even made it to the Gemenii yet. I'm interested to see how that goes."

"All I can say is that you may turn me into a believer."

"Okay, now you are being a little much." She lightly laughed.

"My point is that no one has ever been able to do what you just did. Some have tried to evade the shock, but it ended in embarrassment and pain. Nothing was successful in preventing their powers from being drained. If you can do that, there's no telling what else you can do."

Running her fingers through her hair, Linx asked, "Where do we go from here? Should we stay a while or be on our way to find the Gemenii?"

Standing up to brush off the dirt from his pants, he suggested, "We could get a jump on the guards. I'm not sure how many they have, but we might make it to the Gemenii before they even reach us."

Linx agreed. "Yeah, let's do it. If we need to stop on the way, we can try to find another hiding spot somewhere."

"Or we can just kill 'em."

"Ha! Or that too."

As they stood looking down the steep cliff, she asked, "So where do we need to go now?"

"If we shimmy to the other end of this little ledge, it will take us down the path to find the Gemenii. Most have opted against it due to the risk of falling down the cliff, but others have tried."

"And did they make it?" Linx's eyes widened.

"Eh . . . to the opening. Beyond that? Not so much."

Stretching her neck out of the cavern to scope out the ledge, she asked, "What do you mean?"

Patting her back humorously, Jaut said, "There are some booby traps even after you make it across the ledge."

"I hope it's worth the risk."

"That's what I kept telling you, but you can poof us across there, right?" He smiled, nudging her playfully.

Sighing, Linx said, "Um, not really. I mean I could, but it's not safe. I can't see the opening, so it might get sketchy as to the accuracy of where we'd appear. I can always really focus, but I don't want to risk your safety."

"Ah, yes, let's not do that. I prefer to be alive, at least for another day or two! We'll just have to take it slow while crossing the ledge. It is very dangerous, but I've done it before," he said, warning her.

"Okay, I'm ready."

Keeping as close to the wall as possible, Jaut slowly started shuffling across the ledge. Quickly glancing down the cliff, Linx found herself a little overwhelmed while thinking about the long fall. This was never an issue before, but she couldn't fly properly ever since the cape attached to her body. She hoped the changes were temporary, but only time would tell.

"You okay?" Jaut checked in, effortlessly sliding across the ledge.

"I-I'm feeling great. Haven't felt this alive in a long time," she said. "How about you? Can you see the opening yet?"

"Ugh, not yet. The opening should be around the bend here. I think I'll see it soon."

The warm wind whistled past the jagged cliff, gently greeting their cheeks with a tender kiss. As Linx looked out over the land, she was tempted to glide over the treetops and skim the water. Several waterfalls accented the mountains with their blueish-white colors against the deep brown and gray rocks. With the sun almost set, orange and purple streaks faded into the night. Pangotha reminded her of Violet Woods, enchanting and beautiful—something she had missed for quite some time.

"We're almost there, my fiery friend," Jaut said with a hearty chuckle.

"Trust me, I would've transported myself in a heartbeat, but even I can admit the view is breathtaking!"

Snagging a steady rock, Jaut hoisted himself onto the firm platform. "Yeah, I know. Even if I could leave, I don't know if I would."

Reaching out, he gripped Linx's hand and wrist. Pulling her next to him, they overlooked the land that appeared so peaceful and serene. As they got caught up in the beauty of Pangotha, the sounds of guards yelling in the distance awakened the fire in their bodies. They needed to find the Gemenii before more destruction occurred. No one knew how many creatures would suffer from the chaos below.

Looking down the dark path traveling inside the mountain, Linx asked, "Is this where we need to go?"

"Yes."

"I know that crossing the ledge isn't the safest route, but how haven't the guards captured the Gemenii yet?"

Jaut inhaled a deep breath while rubbing his neck. "You'll

see soon. I won't spoil anything yet, but I've also heard plenty of stories."

For someone who dripped with confidence and superiority, Jaut's facial reactions created dread in Linx's stomach, haunting her body. An uneasiness filled his eyes, and apprehension cemented his boots to the ground.

"How many times have you seen the Gemenii?" she asked him.

Without looking away, Jaut continued to stare into the darkness. "None."

Linx scratched her head, placing all of her weight on her heels. "Huh? Then how do you know if we are in the right place?"

"Come over here. You'll feel the energy. I tried once, but it was an unsuccessful attempt."

Walking over to stand beside him, Linx stared into the endless darkness, not one speck of light to be seen within. A wave of energy, calling her and tempting her to enter the darkness, emitted from the cave. "Jaut, whatever is inside . . . is too powerful."

"When the enemy came, the Gemenii retreated. It's been said their power has been abused by many in the past, and they wanted nothing to do with the leadership within the lands. Instead, they essentially created a journey of fears to access them. If you make it through, they said they will be waiting . . . and maybe their knowledge will be worth your time."

Placing her hands on hips, Linx furrowed her brows. "I find it hard to believe that no one has ever tried to go through and successfully find the Gemenii."

"Ha! Of course, some tried to go through. They either came running back out like snibbling babies or . . . never came back out at all. After so many times of that happening, many stopped going. They kind of saw it as a sign the Gemenii didn't want anyone to find them anymore."

"Well, do you believe in the Gemenii? Do you think there's going to be a creature waiting at the end of the path?"

Jaut snickered, shaking his head. "It's not a matter of *if* they exist—because they do—the question is whether we'll make it out or not."

"Wait . . . I'm confused. You made the story seem like it's a bunch of garbage that shouldn't be entertained." Linx narrowed her eyes.

"No kidding! Because I'm not a bloody fool! Who, besides yourself and Pygo, would want to willingly go through it?"

"You're seriously scared of going in?"

Jaut finally turned his attention to Linx. "And you're not? I can control my fate out here, but in there, I'm not so sure."

"Should I try to create a bubble before we go in? That way, most things won't be able to attack us," Linx said.

"I don't think that'll be very helpful. No magic allowed."

"What are you talking about?"

Jaut sighed and motioned for her to go first into the cavern tunnel. "Go ahead. See for yourself."

"What? Why do I have to go first? Well, forget about it. Fine, I'll go. I'm not afraid." She stood tall, rolling her eyes.

Forming a massive bubble around them, Linx started walking toward the entrance. Interested to see what was going to happen, Jaut followed closely behind.

Stepping inside the damp tunnel, the force field around them suddenly popped. Turning to Jaut, Linx's bright green eyes looked as though they almost fell out of her eye sockets. "What the—"

"Told ya." Jaut shrugged. "Looks like we're going in with no magic."

Linx slowly shuffled forward. "How can magic be banned from this area? I've never heard of that before. Yes, I've had my magic drained from being far away from my land, but I never had this happen before!"

"The Gemenii wants someone to be worthy of finding them. If they didn't do this, anyone could find them. I can really see that you never heard of the Gemenii."

"No! No one in the Violet Woods ever spoke of the Gemenii —not even the pirates." Linx couldn't believe that she had never heard a soul speak about the Gemenii.

"Well, maybe that was on purpose. Many, many people would try to travel here to speak with the Gemenii. They could see into the future, predicting things no one else ever detected. The Gemenii always tried to hide so they wouldn't be used as a fighting tool amongst other lands, or so I've been told by others," Jaut whispered in her ear.

"Okay, but what makes you think that we'll be able to find them?"

Jaut lightly laughed as the darkness consumed them. "I never said we would. I didn't want to come here. You did."

CHAPTER 11

As their path inside the tunnel narrowed, Linx could feel sharp pains squeezing her heart. Heat exited her pores along the hairline of her forehead and down the nape of her neck. The endless darkness provoked the intrusion of thoughts from her past, like fresh hell revisiting her mind. With Jaut maintaining his silence, she only heard his breath deepen as they continued on. Voices started swirling in her mind. Soon, she couldn't decipher what was real or fake.

Linny, why did you have to come out here? All you had to do was stay home with Lyla, and nothing would've ever happened. We would've moved on, happy as could be. Now, I guess it's just going to be me and Lyla from here on. I'm sorry, Linny. I gotta do this. I really liked ya a lot. You brought so much to our family. I know Lyla's gonna miss ya. I will too.

Fingertips slowly wrapped around her throat, squeezing her esophagus closed. She began to panic, slamming herself back against the wall.

"Linx, what's going on? Are you okay?" Jaut shouted.

Releasing high-pitched gasps, Linx rolled herself on the wall while gripping her neck.

Jaut couldn't see anything, but he felt the thick cape brush past him. Reaching out to pull her close, he said, "I've got you. I've got you. You'll be okay. I promise."

Breathing heavily, she hugged him tightly. "I-I feel like I can't escape it. It feels like he's here with me."

"Who? What are you talking about?"

"My father."

Confused, Jaut said, "No one's here. It's just us."

Stopping for a moment, she stayed in his arms until she caught her breath. "Before this world, I lived with my mother, father, and little sister—Lyla. We didn't have much, but I was happy. We were all happy together. Life was simple and perfect."

Jaut held his breath, waiting for her to continue. Chills covered his body as he feared what she would say next. An ever so slight shudder rolled over her body that caused Jaut's stomach to turn.

After exhaling a sharp puff, Linx whispered, "One night, I tried to find my parents in the woods behind our house. My father was late for dinner, and my mother went to find him. Well, I guess he accused my mother of being unfaithful, but she wasn't, to my knowledge. And he . . . he savagely murdered her and another person. Then once I stumbled upon her body tossed across the forest floor . . ."

Burning droplets fell from Linx's eyes, dripping on Jaut's hand. He refused to wipe them away.

Linx broke down with a waterfall of tears. "When I found her, he had made her body almost unrecognizable. I don't understand what happened, but there was no stopping it. When he saw me there, he grabbed my throat and squeezed hard—so hard. He said he was going to miss me before squeezing more. I-I couldn't breathe anymore, and I can't remember anymore."

Jaut couldn't believe what he heard. Rubbing her back, he whispered, "I'm so . . . so sorry that you went through that. You don't have anything to worry about. I'm here with you. He's not here—it's the Gemenii. They have this whole place cursed. We need to work through it to find them."

Attempting to calm herself with controlled breaths, she slowly explained, "I-I know. It's just . . . too much. For so long, I could never remember my past. I was always told by others here that fairies were orphans, but no one said anything else. I just accepted this label and moved on. When I entered the cave leading to Pangotha, I started to see my past. It felt so real when my past filled my mind—I felt like I was reliving it again."

Giving her a final comforting hug, Jaut said, "I am here with you. We'll get through this and find Pygo. Everything will be okay."

"I hope so."

"Do you want me to go first? Then we won't have any surprises. The darkness is something I embrace . . . at least for now."

"Sure." Quickly nodding in the shadows, Linx agreed to let him pass her.

As he slid by her, she felt a sense of safety—something she rarely experienced for long. Even though Carter had been a friend to her, she no longer knew if she had anyone else to call a friend. Despite Jaut's skepticism when they met, he had a loyal, powerful aura cushioning his presence.

"Linx! I see a stream of light up ahead! Hold on, we're almost there! Grab my hand, we'll try to move swiftly."

Stretching out her fingers, she felt Jaut's rough fingertips as she clasped his hands. The stinging sensation that overcame her stomach started to fade, and Linx soon saw a few specks of light ahead. Letting out a giant sigh, she hoped they would be okay.

"Thank you . . . for being so understanding," she whispered.

"Oh, that's nothing. Don't worry about it. We all have a past, many of which aren't pretty. That's how we all got here, right?" He calmly chuckled.

"I know." Shaking off the weight on her shoulders, she asked, "What's your story?"

"My story? Ha! It's not quite that interesting."

As light trickled to the floor, Linx could see a small puddle of water ahead. "I doubt that it's not interesting. If you don't want to talk about it, it's fine."

Rubbing the back of his neck, he said, "It's not that I don't want to talk about it. It's that, well, I haven't talked about it to others. If you really want to know, I can tell you. I was in the military in my past world. There was always a war to fight, and they always needed men. I was young and needed to find myself and challenge myself, so I decided to enlist. They actually paid quite well, so it made life a little easier at home."

Linx studied his face through the shadows, watching small smirks appear and then fade. "You had a family at home?"

"Yes." The creases of his lips rose again. "I had a big family of brothers and sisters. I don't know how my parents put up with us. They were saints raising us. My mother was a doll. Some called me a mama's boy. I didn't care. They called me that, and I called them jealous. I had it all, and I loved every second of it."

"Why did you leave then?"

"I wanted to make them proud. I had a beautiful life at home, but I never could find something that would hold my interest. Growing bored as I got older, I knew that I had to find something stimulating. In my heart, I understood my purpose—I had to protect the ones I loved."

Jaut led Linx to a few rocks neighboring the puddle. Sitting on a giant rock slab, he scooched over a bit, allowing her space to sit as well.

"You know, I'm jealous of you too! I wish I had a truly happy family. I mean, I had it, but nothing lasted forever."

"Nothing lasts forever. In my heart, I know they loved me, but I know that part of my life is over."

Looking down at the ground, Linx nodded in agreement. Jaut had a good point. She always longed for a family here, but she did have one long ago and some caring creatures in Violet Woods. Maybe some relationships wouldn't last forever, but they did care about her at one time.

"It's not good to dwell on our misfortunes and woes. You'll never see the beauty and the life that surrounds you daily if you're only focused on the flowers—a temporary beauty that comes and goes."

"Ugh, I guess you're right. I don't know, though. I hate being alone."

Jaut nodded. "Me too. I soon felt that when they shipped us off to fight. I was surrounded by so many people, but all of my friends and family were home. It's not that I regretted my decision, but I did feel lonely. After some time, I made lifelong friends on the field though. Some I would've died for, and some I did die for."

Pulling her silky hair over her shoulder, Linx looked over. "Is that where you—"

"Yep. I was on the battlefield with a few of my buddies. We had a prime spot to avoid enemy fire, but we had a clear view of their bunker. Excited, we thought we were going to do big things. Can you imagine if we would've captured that piece of garbage and his men? That scum was responsible for thousands of lives and potentially thousands more. Well, my buddies and I were going back and forth with what to do when we heard gunfire. Looking around, we didn't know who was shooting until I looked out at the field." Jaut let out an exaggerated exhale as he paused for a moment. "My buddy, Miko, was holding his thigh as blood covered his fingers. Miko was one of the first guys that made military life click for me. We trained together, fought together, and had a bunch of similar interests. He was a really good guy."

Linx twisted her hair as he prepared her for the uncomfortable details.

"He," Jaut said, "couldn't move fast and was a giant target. We yelled over to him to stay low, and he yelled back, making sure that we didn't come out for him. He told me to let his wife know how much he loved her. How could I tell his wife that I just watched him die out there? I couldn't let him die alone. I grabbed a shield and sprinted like hell. Once I got him, I pulled him toward our spot as quickly as I could. Holding my breath, I remember the adrenaline rushing through my body. I almost got him all the way to safety, but then they clipped the side of my face with a bullet. I remember going in and out while surrounded by comrades. They were frantic, but I was just happy that I got Miko back with them."

With enormous eyes, she said, "You sacrificed your life to save him."

"I hope I did, but I'll never know. I try to think he is living his best life with his lady. Would I do it again? You bet your ass I would." Smiling, he patted Linx's knee as he stood up. "Now that story time is over, you ready?"

"I don't know how you can move on so fast from that story." Linx pushed herself up and wiped her eyes, walking beside him. "Where do we go from here?"

"My dear, we don't have time to dwell." Jaut placed his hands on his waist as he looked down. "Ready to take a dip?"

"In a puddle?"

"It's a lot deeper than what you might think."

Melodically laughing, Linx brushed her hair over her shoulder. "Um, no. No, no. I'm good, but thank you."

"No?"

As her laugh faded, Linx said, "Definitely not. Fairies don't do well in water."

Bewildered, Jaut asked, "Is that so?"

"It's not a good combination. Once our wings get wet, we pretty much drown. Not to mention, I have this thick cape that will make things much worse."

"Take it off."

"I can't take it off. Even if I did, my wings would still pull me down. Why are you so curious about—" She stopped, realizing why he was being so persistent. Taking a deep breath, she froze in front of him.

With an unamused smirk, he leaned his right ear toward his shoulder, stretching out his neck. Tension tightened his back as he knew that this would be another tough one for her.

"Please don't say that we have to go in there."

"You don't *have to* do anything. If you want to find the Gemenii, then this is the route to take."

Pacing in front of the boulder, Linx had chills crawling up

her arms. Stopping in front of Jaut's toes, she dropped her hands to her waist. "I don't know what to do."

"Well, I can swim and navigate the route. Can you at least hold on?" Running his hand through his hair, he tried to figure out a plan.

"I can try. Oh man, what choice do I have? How far is it?"

"I don't think it's too far, but it has been a long time since I tried."

Intrigued by his previous experience, Linx asked, "So what was the worst one for you, or don't I want to know?"

"You'll be finding out rather soon. Why ruin the surprise?" Jaut joked with a sigh. "You ready to do this?"

Standing next to him, Linx wore a heavy frown as she feared what was to come. "Better now than never. What have I got to lose?"

"Okay, I'm going to need you to focus on me, all right? Don't worry about anything else. I refuse to let anything happen to you."

With a bit of doubt, she asked, "How can you promise that?"

"Just do it, okay?"

"Okay."

Taking a deep breath, Jaut stepped into the puddle and rapidly sank inside the small opening. Linx hesitated for a moment, but she couldn't let him go in there alone at her expense. Forcing herself not to put any more thought into it, she filled her lungs with fresh air before jumping into the puddle.

CHAPTER 12

Although Linx had a strong fear of water, falling into the unknown mentally consumed her. Prying her eyes open, she desperately searched for Jaut. The only thing she could discern within the narrow tunnel was a shadow moving beneath her. *Please, let that be Jaut.*

The weight of Poba's cape pulled her backward, almost flipping her upside-down. Oh, how she wanted this horrific thing off of her. Just thinking about it made her skin crawl. Deeper and deeper, she sank into the tunnel, but the murky waters prevented her from seeing anything more than shadows beyond her hand. Surprisingly, she couldn't see Jaut anywhere. Where did he go?

Pressing her hand against the wall to slow her descent, Linx's fingertips grazed the bumpy and slimy stone. Trying to grip the minuscule indents, she stretched out her other arm to find the wall behind her. Every inch of her body needed the reassurance of stability. She wriggled her fingers to feel anything behind her. Extending as far as she could, the sinking awareness of vulnerability rolled throughout her body. Nothing was there but unknown, dark, open water.

A slight stream of light neared her toes as the stone wall ended, transforming into the edge of a ceiling for another room. The top of her feet hooked on the edge, and she gave herself a sturdy pull to propel downward. Gripping the base of the wall with her fingers, she pulled herself down, flowing into a new area or room.

Where is Jaut?

Trying to peer around the murky waters, Linx couldn't make out any shadow that resembled Jaut. Losing the ability to hold her breath, prickles covered her body as she sank further. Unsure if her lungs would burst, a burning rush of panic swept over her chest and up though her throat. Right as she anticipated the water pouring into her nostrils, a shadow brushed past her, dragging her backward through the underwater hallway.

An indescribable and intense stinging pulsated from her back before Linx bounced up to hit the stone ceiling. Dark water mixed with a faint ray of light, swirling around her head and wrapping her hair around her face. Linx attempted to grab onto anything to stop her from moving. As her shoulder grazed a rock, something pulled at her arm, yanking her head up into fresh air. Discombobulated from the cold air spreading over her skin, Linx coughed up water that had leaked down her throat. Wiping the hair off her face, Linx scanned the area several times before realizing she had been rescued.

Sitting on a rock that bordered the water, Jaut swiped his hair out of his eyes. Collapsing on his lap, Linx whimpered as she tried to calm her breathing. The whirlwind knocked some sense out of her head, sending Linx into confusion.

"You okay?" Jaut asked after a few moments.

"Yeah. I think so." Blinking quickly, she forced out a heavy cough from her chest and released a sigh. "Honestly, I don't know what happened. One moment, I was sinking, and the next, something dragged me backward and tossed me around like nothing. Now, my back is killing me."

Jaut slowly helped pull Linx out of the water, sitting her beside him. As she slid back, she reached her hand down to rub the throbbing area from earlier. Looking down, Linx noticed teeth indents in the corner of Poba's cape.

"What?" she whispered.

"What's the matter?"

"I-I don't understand. Something attacked me in the water, and—"

Shaking his head, Jaut rubbed his eyebrow. "Yeah, you're lucky it didn't kill you."

"That's not it though."

"What are you talking about?"

Grasping the bumpy cape, Linx sulked. "I can feel where the animal bit the cape."

Jaut squinted his eyes with a raised eyebrow, unsure what to say.

"I didn't think it would become a part of me. I want it off—now!" Overcome with disgust, an anxious wave washed over Linx.

"What's your deal with that cape, anyway?"

Letting out a grunt, Linx said, "Don't worry about it. It's a long story."

"Well, what better time than now?" He smirked.

"Look, I don't know what's so funny."

Resting his hands on his hips while pulling back his shoulders, Jaut rolled his eyes. "Linx, if you don't want to tell me, fine. It really doesn't matter to me. I only asked because it seems to be bothering you. I thought it could help by talking about it. If you don't want to, then we can continue on our way."

Linx sulked, thinking about how she always pushed everyone away. How could she trust anyone in this world? Even those in the previous world did enough damage to trickle the fear into her next life.

"Ready to go?" Jaut held out his hand, pulling Linx up to her feet.

"I will tell you, but you have to promise not to say anything . . . to anyone."

With a sly smirk, he said, "Who am I going to tell, my dear? The demon in the corner of the room?"

"The what?" She spun around, looking all over the dark room.

"Ha! I was joking—at least for now." Jaut winked. "My point is that I have no one to tell anyway, even if I wanted to—which I don't."

"What I'm wearing right now will tear kingdoms apart."

Jaut's eyelids opened so wide that Linx thought his eyeballs would roll out. "That right there? This cape would tear kingdoms apart?"

Pulling her hair over her shoulder, Linx stood in silence as Jaut digested the strange statement.

"I'm not saying it isn't nice or unique, but I don't really understand why it'd matter. Was it a king's favorite cape?" Jaut asked, chuckling.

"It was stolen after being sawed off from a brutally murdered troll. So, no, it didn't belong to a king—just a kind troll who didn't deserve the death he experienced."

Staring in disbelief, Jaut's mouth hung open for a moment. "You killed a kind troll for his cape? Who are you? You're ruthless."

"No!" Linx rubbed her eyes aggressively. "I rightfully stole it from the kingdom of Crystal Woods. It belongs to the trolls of Violet Woods. I did not kill anyone for it . . . except an elder . . . but that's beside the point."

Looking at Linx, he snickered, shaking his head. A charming snaggletooth poked out as he uttered, "Ruthless."

"Can we please continue through the tunnel of horrors? I'd really like to get this over and done with." Linx anxiously exhaled, observing the dark room they sat in.

A deep glow from the water lit the room just enough for the pair to see each other and the walls curving around them about twenty feet away. Although her eyes tried to focus on the domed ceiling, she couldn't see anything at all. The presence of a powerful aura rested above her body. As she looked forward into the only walkway connected to the room, the pressure of darkness seeped into every pore of her body.

"You ready?"

"Do I really have a choice?"

Shrugging his shoulders, he said, "You can always turn back."

Linx rolled her eyes. "Seriously? Do you think I'm doing this for fun?"

"How would I know? I mean, if you find killing your elders entertaining, then—"

"What are you talking about, you fool?" Linx hissed. "Have

you ever heard of an elder? They are very powerful and manipulative creatures."

"No, I haven't. I see that I'm missing out." Unable to hide his grin, his lips parted ways, revealing his unique teeth yet again. It was clear as day that he was getting pleasure out of taunting her.

"What's your problem?" she shouted. Furrowing her brows, she tilted her head out of frustration.

Jaut released a slight smirk. "It's hilarious."

"What's hilarious?"

"Anytime you get annoyed, the gems on the cape glow."

Grabbing the edge of the cape, she glanced over the gems. "Huh?"

Jaut chuckled, stepping closer to her. "Watch. I'll show you what I mean."

"What are you talking about?"

He said, "Here, I'll show you. All I need to do is mention how you murdered a troll for his cape, and BOOM!"

"What's the matter with you? I already told you I didn't murder any troll!"

Right as a wave of irritation spread over her body, Linx noticed a slight glow shining from the gems on the cape. Jaut was right!

"See?"

Staring at the cape, Linx couldn't believe her eyes. "How can this be? How long did you notice this for?"

"Not long at all. It just started when you told me about how you murdered the troll and elder."

"I wonder why this is happening."

Jaut shrugged his shoulders. "Revenge?"

"Will you please stop? I'm serious. This hasn't happened to me before. And I thought there was no magic allowed in here."

"I'm not sure. I don't make the rules. Maybe it's just in the beginning. Test out something else."

Curiously holding out her hand, Linx ignited an energy ball above her palm. "Thank goodness. I didn't like the feeling of having absolutely no protection."

"Well, since you're our little nightlight, you can go first through the tunnel." He laughed, pointing to the dark path ahead.

"You're out of your mind if you think I'm going first!"

"I won't be able to see anything!"

"What did you do the last time you came? I have no way of knowing what's going to happen. Plus, I wouldn't be able to see anything anyway if the cape was behind me. And . . . how would it stay lit?"

"Oh, I have some random topics that will keep that cape lit."

Linx's amused demeanor shifted to a suspicious one. "What's that supposed to mean?"

"Care to talk about Carter?"

Linx stood speechless as her bright green eyes locked on Jaut. "How do you know about—"

"Linny, there's a lot I know."

Shocked, Linx stood still and tilted her head. "What did you just call me?"

"Huh?"

Looking directly into his eyes, she asked, "What did you call me?"

"Um, I don't know. Linx?"

Squinting her eyes, she said, "But I thought you said—"

"What?"

"Uh. Oh, forget about it." Linx shook her head.

Before she could interrogate him any further, he shouted, "Watch out!"

Pushing her out of the way, two massive flying creatures swooped down from the ceiling, gliding through the narrow path ahead.

"What was that?" Linx shrieked.

"Imps."

"Uh, what? No way! I've seen imps before. Those were huge!"

Looking around for other unexpected creatures, Jaut whispered, "I don't know what to say other than welcome to Pangotha."

"Are they dangerous here?"

"Eh, if you get in their way. Overall, they like to be left alone though."

"It's crazy how different they are compared to the ones at the Inferno."

"Ah, those poor souls."

Floored by the sympathy, Linx stood almost speechless. "Poor souls? Are you serious? Those little devils will try to rip the skin right off your face."

"I'm really not trying to pick sides, but anything under Donem's rule isn't going to be kind. It's not a surprise. Any creature serving him isn't living their best life. They're all slaves to a monster." Jaut shook his head before running his fingers through his damp hair.

Sadness twirled in her gut. As much as she didn't want to admit it, he had a point. Any creature that lived in the Inferno was not there by choice. Tortured and held captive, no one had a chance to thrive.

"Anyway, I don't know how you know about Carter, but I don't feel like talking about him right now. Sometimes things just happen."

"Linx, take a moment to think."

With the cape gems igniting, Linx waited to hear the riveting words that Jaut would provide. "Enlighten me."

"My dear, most things are calculated—whether it's consciously or subconsciously. Rarely do things happen in relationships out of mere chance—even with you. Go ahead and try to pretend that it's not true, but I can guarantee it is."

"Are you serious? Everything is calculated? Yes, because my goal was to end up in a deadly cave game with a stranger."

Shrugging his shoulders while flipping his hand in the air, Jaut said, "Well, it seems that it was."

"What the hell are you talking about? Should I leave? I'm getting a little concerned."

Letting out a high-pitched laugh, Jaut grabbed his stomach from chuckling so hard. "Now? Now you are concerned? How far would you go, Linx? How far would you go to find your answers?"

Staring at the absurdity unfolding, Linx remained silent.

Jaut continued to say, "How far would you go to find acceptance and tranquility?"

"You haven't answered me! What are you talking about, Jaut?"

"How far would you go to find someone who you could call a friend? Honestly, that's a literal and figurative question."

"Will you stop it? You're not making any sense! Why are you doing this?"

Jaut brought his face closer to hers. His eyes displayed a tiny sparkle that kissed his irises. "How far will you go to be loved?"

Tears flooded her eyes, rolling down her cheeks. Suddenly, the hollowness of her reality spread throughout her body. Hanging her head, she cupped her face, trying to catch all her burning tears.

Rubbing the side of his face, he said, "Linx, I don't say that to hurt you, but you need to realize every action has a consequence. With each decision you make and every direction you turn, you have substantial control over it. You are so driven to appease everyone else that you push beyond your own limits, sacrificing who you are to make everyone else happy."

"How dare you? You know nothing about me."

"I know enough that it bothers you."

Wiping the tears from her eyes while dabbing her nose with her arm, she looked away. "Why would you say those things? You don't know anything about my past and the reasons for my actions."

"Allowing the world to know our vulnerabilities is something that many people fear. It can be the end to us—both physically and psychologically speaking."

Turning around to face the dark tunnel, Linx took a step forward. "How do you know this?"

Hesitating to answer, Jaut said, "I guess it's my turn to be vulnerable soon. Just so you know, I've been in your shoes, and it's a hard lesson to learn. We can talk as we walk. Are you ready?"

Looking down the dark pathway and back toward Jaut, a numb and cold feeling washed over her body. "Yeah."

CHAPTER 13

A dim light radiating from Linx's cape gently highlighted the tunnel walls. Her sense of comfort with Jaut quickly became tainted by his sharp tongue. Why would he say those things? Regardless, if they weren't true, why would she be so bothered?

"You might want to pick up the pace a bit."

Scowling over her shoulder, Linx asked, "Why's that? I can barely see. I'll have to create more light."

"Unless you're a fan of maacrubs, we need to move through here as fast as we can."

"Huh?"

"They're parasites that find their victims through vibration. Maacrubs are little blind buggers, but they're speedy things. Once close enough, they enter your skin and slide into your body. They leave pretty nasty holes in the skin. It's quite gross."

"Yuck! Luckily, my feet are covered."

Jaut sighed. "Unfortunately, my friend, that doesn't matter.

Their saliva is very acidic, eating through boots and skin in a matter of seconds. They come in droves too. Just keep moving."

With raised eyebrows, she asked, "Have you ever been bitten?"

"Me? No, no. I was lucky, but my friend wasn't as fortunate."

"What? Really?"

"That's what actually made us turn back here. We didn't realize some crawled on the back of his boots. As we walked, he noticed a burning sensation in his right calf muscle. He swatted at his leg and saw three burrow in. It was hell trying to help him swim back and get them out. He has had a limp ever since. You can't even get him to go near this area after it happened."

Shuttering at the thought of giant holes covering her body, Linx swiftly lifted each foot and slammed them to the ground. With a flick of her wrist, she lit an immense fireball in her hand that illuminated the tunnel. "I will cook anything that comes near me."

"Ah, yes. Makes your skin crawl, doesn't it?"

"One of many things." Linx felt his eyes burning through her as they marched through the darkness.

"Oh?" The right corner of Jaut's lip slightly lifted, finding amusement in Linx's response.

"You called me Linny before. Why?" Linx spun around, lifting her hand to light the space between them while her piercing green eyes locked onto Jaut's.

His dark, chiseled face rose above hers. Gazing down at her, his smirking soon faded to an expressionless stare. "Do you really want to know?"

Gulping the little liquid in her mouth, Linx inhaled deep into her stomach. "Yes."

"I can camouflage into my surroundings and fight well—

which I quite enjoy. Another ability I have is not as convenient sometimes."

"What do you mean?" She studied his face as he continued.

Jaut sighed while running his hand through his hair. "I am considered a protector of Pangotha as well. With that responsibility, I can see many things others cannot."

Intrigued, Linx perked up to learn more. "Like what?"

Jaut looked around hesitantly, avoiding eye contact with Linx. "I've never discussed this with anyone before."

"Honestly, Jaut, you did this to yourself. Had you not referred to me as Linny, I wouldn't have asked it."

With a charming smirk displaying his snaggletooth, Jaut pulled his shoulders back. "I know. It was too hard to resist, though."

"Well? Are you just going to keep me in suspense? If you won't tell me, we can continue on our way." As impatience tingled in her knees, a tinge of pink dusted across Linx's cheeks.

Gently pinching his thumb and pointer finger on the bridge of his nose, Jaut lowered his head while closing his eyes. "Sometimes, I can see a person's thoughts."

"Oh, really? So can I!"

Letting go of his face, Jaut looked up and stared into Linx's eyes. "You see them too?"

"Not all the time, but yes, I can read minds and see snippets of the future."

"So you can see them there?" Jaut asked, gesturing toward the area beside her. "Why are you ignoring them, then? I mean . . . I shouldn't say why because I can see why, but I don't know how you can. You must have strong willpower to ignore them."

"Huh? What are you talking about?"

"Well, I'm no one to judge, but it would drive me crazy with them gabbing like that."

Linx paused as she attempted to rewind what Jaut said. "I have no idea what you're talking about. Who's gabbing?"

Squinting his eyes and tilting his head, Jaut said, "I thought you said you can see people's thoughts too? Is it just your own you can't see?"

"I can see thoughts if I touch the person or something. I haven't tried working with my powers too much, so I'm not sure how much more I can do yet."

Jaut's eyes widened, raising his eyebrows. "Ah, I see. I don't mean reading someone's mind or transferring their thoughts into your mind. I can see people standing next to you—people you are thinking about, people you wronged, people who wronged you."

"I, um, what? Seriously?"

"Yes, I can see strong thoughts that pass through your mind. If it's enough to shake your nerves, I can see them. It's quite helpful when meeting new people, such as yourself."

Blushing and turning away, Linx asked, "What's that supposed to mean?"

"Don't worry. I can see them no matter if you look away."

Spinning back to face him, Linx jammed her hands against her hips. Letting out a huff, she asked, "Well, what do you see?"

Leaning toward her, Jaut said, "You mean who?"

Squinting her eyes and puckering her lips to meet her nose, she tried to hide her embarrassment. "Look, if it's Carter, I'm sure everyone in this land and beyond would understand why he'd be on my mind. Wouldn't you think about someone who crossed you in the worst ways?"

"While I don't disagree with you, it's not Carter who I see right now."

"Ah, so that's what your little episode was about before. You saw my thoughts about Carter and couldn't resist. Well, who do you see?" Exhaling, Linx felt her blood pressure increase as she rambled off names of any person she thought Jaut could see. "An elder? A troll? Donem? A siren?"

Jaut rolled his eyes out of disappointment. He didn't know if she was this disconnected or was attempting to deceive him.

Following behind, Linx shouted, "Are you sure it's not Carter?"

"Nope. Not them."

Scuffing her feet into the dirt floor, Linx pleaded, "Jaut, can you just tell me who you see? Please?"

Stopping dead in his tracks, Jaut asked, "You truly don't know who's beside you?"

"No, I don't have an idea. I mean . . . so much has happened recently. In my head, it could be anyone."

"Anyone? You made it seem so odd that I called you by your nickname, Linny."

Tightlipped, Linx felt tingles roll up her back and cover her neck. Another flush of warmth ignited her cheeks to a bright pink. The only ones who would call her that—

"Yep. There we go. I see the wheels turning in your head now."

"Say their name."

"Names."

Linx sighed, closing her eyes. "Please, Jaut. Say their names. I need to hear them. I've never spoken their names since I arrived. My ears need to hear it."

Walking a few steps toward Linx, Jaut gently placed his hand on her face. "There is a man named Rydan."

Instantly, Linx tensed as her body filled with rage that broke once he mentioned the other name.

"I see a girl—Lyla."

Tears trickled down her face, curving over Jaut's fingers. A heaviness in her heart restricted her breathing, and she squatted down to cover her face.

"Are you surprised?"

"I don't know if I didn't believe you or . . . I don't know. They've been on my mind so much lately. I'm confused and angry with my father. But Lyla—oh, how I miss her so much. I feel like I failed her in so many ways. The worst part is that I don't know what happened after . . ."

Despite believing he already knew the answer to his question, Jaut wanted to give Linx the ability to tell her story. "After what?"

As all the air left her body, Linx couldn't inhale anymore. Her body froze as some memories flooded her mind. She dropped the remaining few inches to sit on the ground as she dug her fingers into the dirt and pebbles. Rocking back and forth, she began hyperventilating as she felt Rydan's hand gripping her throat.

Quickly kneeling before her, Jaut grabbed her hands. "Breathe. Linx, breathe."

Sweat formed on the edge of her hairline, and she bent forward into a ball. Gasping for air, her hands grew clammy while tears cascaded down her face.

"Breathe. I'm here. No one else is with us. Take control and breathe!"

Inhaling fresh air into her lungs, Linx wheezed as she fell

into Jaut's arms. Panting, she tried taking longer breaths to slow her heart rate. "I . . . don't know what happened to Lyla after my father tried strangling me. I can't remember if that's how I died or if something else happened. If he hurt her, it's all my fault. She didn't want me to leave her, but I did. Why didn't I stay with her?"

Jaut sat patiently with a kind hand resting on her shoulder. Silence cushioned them as Linx revealed the dark thoughts consuming her. Jaut didn't dare to speak until Linx needed him.

Linx exhaled a giant breath, pursing her puffy lips. "I just wanted to find our mom. It was dinnertime, and she hadn't come back home after searching for our father. Lyla didn't want to be left home alone, but I told her I would be right back. I don't know what I expected to find. I thought I would find them talking or picking extra fruit. It was so late—I should've known better. I was so naïve."

"You should've known what?"

"I should've trusted my gut. Father normally was home well before dinnertime, and then mother left—but she never came home. Our tummies burned from waiting so long. We should have waited or gone to find help."

Jaut shook his head. "Linx, how would you know any better? Your parents made dinner and never came back. I'm sure plenty of children—no matter the age—would search for their parents."

"I wish I hadn't. If I waited about a half hour more, I might've survived. We could've tried to dish out our own soup, and he would've walked back into the house with some lie about what had happened. If I did that, I never would've seen my mother's remains sprinkled throughout the woods, and I'd be sitting right next to Lyla now."

"Are you so sure about that?" Jaut challenged.

"I don't know. I'd like to think so." Her teary, red eyes raised to meet his.

"Even you seem unsure if that's how you died. Give it some time. After denying and ignoring your past, it will take time for the pieces to fall back into place."

They absorbed each other's presence as Linx's sniffles finally died down. It was a much-needed pause for both of them.

Looking beside Linx, Jaut noticed the male figure begging for forgiveness while reaching for her throat. He didn't dare explain what he witnessed, but he was curious. "If you don't mind me asking . . ."

"It's okay. Ask whatever you'd like. Regardless if I cry, it doesn't change anything about the truth."

"W-why did he kill her again? Did you say she cheated on him?"

Shaking her head, she said, "I don't know. He mentioned she had been cheating on him."

"Do you think she was?"

"I'm not sure."

"No?"

Linx gently wiped the burning tears from her cheekbones. Running her fingers through her soft hair and twirling it around her fingertips, she sighed. "I don't understand how it would've been possible. She was always with at least one of us. Plus, she loved tending to the family. Why would she jeopardize that?"

"I'm sorry that you witnessed what you did."

Lowering her eyes, the gruesome crime scene flashed across her mind yet again. Linx never had a moment to absorb nor reflect on her previous life. Honestly, she didn't remember the details until she walked through the tunnel into Pangotha.

Once she gathered her thoughts, she raised her head to meet Jaut's eyes. "To be transparent, nobody wants to die, but that wasn't the worst part of it. It's wondering if someone you love is in the hands of a monster and has no one to protect them. I think that's the hardest pill to swallow. At this point, I just wish I knew if she was okay."

Looking over, Jaut noticed the young female figure next to Linx, tugging on her. Lyla whined, "How could you leave me? Why did you go?"

Jaut's heart dropped as he observed the eerie images surrounding Linx. How could he tell her? He couldn't. There was no digestible way to approach this type of thing.

Sometimes seeing these conscious and subconscious thoughts helped him assess whether the person had good intentions—especially in Pangotha. Nevertheless, there were plenty of creatures that were exceptions to the rule.

Linx clenched the soil beneath her, pushing her body upright. As she raised her head, she noted Jaut's strange facial expression as he stared just beyond Linx's presence. He appeared entranced and intrigued by something—or someone.

"What do you see?"

Pressing his lips firmly together, Jaut broke his gaze from Lyla to acknowledge Linx. He noticed that the red surrounding her irises had brought out a new depth to her green eyes. Jaut parted his lips to inhale a deep breath, filling every inch of his lungs.

Linx whispered, "Please tell me."

Digging his fingertips into his eyelids, Jaut said, "Lyla was—"

With her eyes widening, she asked, "Lyla was what? I don't know what you are seeing, but I need to know."

"She was upset."

Sulking her head, Linx buried her face in her hands. Her shoulders dropped as her body convulsed from the double breath after her sobbing.

"Linx, I'm only going to see what's haunting you. I don't see the truth of the situation. She may very well be living her best life while surrounded by all the riches of the world. You need to find a way to forgive yourself."

"I don't know if I ever can."

Pushing off the ground to stand, Linx brushed the dirt and pebbles from her clothing. Lifting the back of her hand, she smeared the tears from under her eyes.

"I'm not sure if this helps, but I don't think you are a bad person at all. You did the best that you could in a horrific situation. There was no point in your story where you intentionally put Lyla in danger. You tried to keep her safe by having her stay home. You were a wonderful sister to her."

"I wish I felt the same."

With the corners of his mouth curling downward, Jaut nodded as they advanced through the tunnel. Continuing into the darkness, he noticed Lyla and Rydan slowly fade away.

CHAPTER 14

After trekking through the tunnel for several hours, Linx released a dainty yawn that almost slipped past Jaut's attention. Smirking, he kicked some pebbles her way.

"Hey! Knock it off," she complained.

"You all right there? It seemed like you were going to fall asleep." He smiled.

"Honestly, it wouldn't hurt if we found a spot where we could safely rest. What are your thoughts?" she asked.

Rubbing his chin, Jaut looked ahead and behind them. He dropped his shoulders and shook his head. "Well, since we have no idea how long this part will take, why not?"

"I see. Well, do you mind if we take some time to rest?"

Jaut shrugged his shoulders. "I won't fight taking a break. I just don't know where would be a safe place to rest."

Touching the tunnel walls, Linx gently closed her eyes. "I'll create a protection bubble for us while we rest."

Brushing past Jaut, she walked about fifteen feet down the

way they came and held up her hands. Bright lights swirled from her palms as an energy wall formed. Jaut stood in amazement with his arms folded in front of his chest as he witnessed her impressive skills. Once she sealed off the first end of the tunnel, Linx walked past him again to secure the other side.

"How are you sure this can withstand another creature—especially while you sleep?" Jaut tightened his eyebrows, creating two deep lines between them.

Rolling her eyes, Linx said, "Relax. You'll be fine."

"Fine? This may be a joke to you, but I'd really like to be alive after this."

"This force field can withstand quite a bit. You'd be surprised." Linx grunted as she waved her hand over the last open area.

"Is that so?" Jaut widened his eyes, trying not to let his doubt shine through.

"Well, based on experience, it can at least hold back a Cerberus. Are there stronger creatures here?"

"A Cerberus?" Jaut whispered, throwing his hands out in front of him. "Are you serious? Where do you even find a Cerberus?"

"On our journey, there was a cave between Dark Woods and Crystal Woods. The beast was huge. But yes, my force field performed nicely—if I say so myself. Um, where would you like to rest? I was hoping to sit on this side if that's okay with you." Linx pointed to a spot that had a comfortably curved wall, perfectly fit for her back.

"The choice is yours, *my lady.*"

"Knock it off."

Unfortunately, the narrow tunnel prevented them from completely stretching their bodies out, but at least they had a safe spot to rest. Linx nestled her back gently against the wall as Jaut debated on which spot he should claim.

"Wake me up if anything weird happens." Linx smiled as she lightly closed her eyes.

"Very funny. Don't worry. I won't," Jaut sarcastically said.

CHAPTER 15

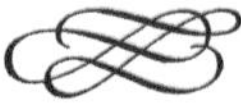

As her consciousness faded into lower awareness, her reality shifted into a distant yet familiar setting.

"Rydan! Rydan! Get away from her!" an older, shaky voice shouted from several yards away.

Twigs snapped in the distance, and the vibrations from someone stomping on the soft dirt floor grew stronger. Linx felt her body jolt as wrinkled hands gracefully caressed her cheek.

"What in the hell is going on here, Rydan?"

Linx opened her eyes to see their neighbor, Mr. Nelson, hunched over her body, protecting her from Rydan's next move. It was quite some time since she had seen him. Her eyes studied his sagging face and his trembling jaw. White and silver beard hairs poked through his tannish skin, burned from the years of farming under the sun.

Backing away for a moment, Rydan stood in shock as he was unexpectedly interrupted.

"Rydan! Answer me! What were you doing to your girl?"

Looking through hollow, dark eyes, Rydan remained silent with his eyes fixed on Mr. Nelson's close placement to Gaela's severed arm.

"Answer me!"

Deepening his gaze and squaring his shoulders, Rydan demanded, "Albert, go home."

"Excuse me?" Mr. Nelson looked slightly offended that Rydan would speak to him in that manner.

"You have no business here." Ryan clenched his hands into tight, solid fists.

"I am going nowhere, damn it! You had your hands on a little lady. There is nothing she could've done that would warrant that. Act like a true man—not a vicious animal!"

"You want me to act like a man, Albert?" Rydan mocked while tightening his biceps. His face grew red as veins popped from his neck and forehead.

"What has gotten into you, Rydan? Look, I don't know about your home life. Everything may be different behind closed doors. People can be different too. But I understand that providing for a family is hard, grueling work. You're talking to a guy who never took a day off in forty years. I love what I do, but it's not for the weak. It's long hours and work that destroys any man's body after the years I put in. I got to do it though. If I want it to work out, I have to. Hell, no one will care about my farm as much as me. Whatever is going on, though, it's not right to take it out on a kid. Yeah, they have ways of riling us up. You'd swear that it's in their DNA, or whatever you call it, to push your buttons. I get it."

Rydan looked him up and down. With a smirk on his face, he shook his head and chuckled. "I'm warning ya, old man."

Turning toward Linx, fear bled through Mr. Nelson's hazel eyes. He quickly whispered, "Linny, you need to run. Run as fast as you can. Head back to my house. Tell Edith what happened and that I love her."

Pushing herself off the ground, Linx looked up with innocent eyes. Confused about what she had witnessed, fear held her in place.

"Go now!"

Without another thought, Linx took off running toward Mr. Nelson's home. Kicking dirt up from under her shoes, she held her breath, running for her life.

Walking in Linx's direction, Rydan shouted, "Linny, you better not leave. You hear? Cause I'll find you. Papa will always find you."

Mr. Nelson stepped in front of Rydan, placing his right hand against Rydan's chest. Blocking him from moving forward, Mr. Nelson looked him dead in the eyes. "Rydan! Come to your senses!"

"Out of the way, old man!" Rydan shoved him into a nearby tree.

Falling into the trunk of the tree, Mr. Nelson barely caught himself. Taken aback by the chaos, he gave himself only a split second before turning around to run toward Linx. He weaved as quickly as he could through the trees before something caught his eye. Doing a double take, Mr. Nelson saw Gaela's face covered in blood, resting near a tree.

"Ga . . . Gaela!"

Hearing her mother's name, Linx turned around, fearful of what would happen to Mr. Nelson. Hiding in a thick bush, she peered through its branches, hoping he would get himself to safety. Linx saw him reach out his hand to see if her mother was okay.

"No, no!" Linx whispered to herself. "Please go!"

Searching for her father's location, she panicked. Where could he be? Without inhaling or exhaling another breath, she dipped as low as she could to the ground, looking for his boots nearby. Once the coast was clear, Linx slowly exhaled as she attempted to get a glimpse of Mr. Nelson. She spotted him stumbling backward, unable to make sense of the horrific scene he had come across. The fading stream of light bounced off of his pale, wrinkled face.

In a matter of seconds, Rydan appeared from the shadows. Leaning toward his right side, he gripped a long wooden handle. As he straightened up, a flicker of light reflected off the blade of his bloodied axe.

As he swung the axe up slightly behind his back, Rydan said, "You just couldn't go away, could ya?"

Tears streamed from Linx's eyes as she forced herself to flee. Running on trembling legs, she tried to focus forward on the path toward the Nelson's home. Only a few steps in—she heard it—the thud of the axe and the cries of Mr. Nelson. Holding back the screams she wanted to release into the sky, her chest convulsed as she continued running. If she stopped, she knew what her fate would be.

With each thud, she briefly pulled her shoulders up to cover her neck while gruesome and bloody images infiltrated her mind. Mr. Nelson's muffled sounds punched through her ears and dove down her spine. As the moans sadly faded, Linx could not suppress the violence in her stomach any longer. Jumping behind a tree, she held onto the trunk as bile spewed from her mouth and mucus dripped from her nose.

"W-what do I do?" Linx sobbed into the side of the tree.

Almost paralyzed, she hugged the rough tree tightly. The bark scratched her forehead and cheek while she tried to steady her mind. Linx feared that if she ran to Mrs. Nelson's house, then her father would follow. But what would happen if she ran toward the next town? Would he still go to Mrs. Nelson's?

He probably would. Papa would go straight to her door and kill her without saying a word. He might even know that Lyla was there.

There would be no way she could live with herself if she left. Linx sprinted through the trees to reach Mrs. Nelson's back door. She felt like she was almost flying as she put every ounce of energy into reaching the back porch. As she sprung up the stairs, Linx tightly gripped the doorknob and barged through the doorway into Mrs. Nelson's kitchen.

"Linny? There you are! Lyla and I were worried sick!" Mrs. Nelson held her heart as she stood up from the kitchen table.

As Linx quickly slammed and locked the door, Mrs. Nelson realized her husband wasn't right behind Linx. Before she could say anything, a disconnected look overcame Linx's face as her skin turned a pale white.

"Sweetie? Where's Albert?" Mrs. Nelson asked cautiously.

When Linx stood there, absorbing the temporary safety that Mrs. Nelson's home provided, it took her a moment to gather herself before saying anything. Mrs. Nelson gently wrapped her warm arms around Linx. Instantly, Linx felt so protected she broke down in tears. Mrs. Nelson had a soft face decorated with silver hair and big brown eyes. With her unconditional kindness, she was known for being everyone's grandmother.

"He's gone."

Shocked by the unexpected remark, Mrs. Nelson held Linx

at arm's length to study her face. "My dear, what are you talking about?"

Sobbing uncontrollably, Linx shouted, "Papa killed everyone!"

Mrs. Nelson stood in disbelief as she attempted to process what Linx said.

Crumpling the front of her dress in her hands, Lyla quietly asked, "Papa hurt people?"

"Papa killed Mama, Mr. Nelson, and someone else!" Linx sobbed. "And he tried to kill me too! He is probably on his way here now! We need to call the police!"

Mrs. Nelson held her composure as she cupped Linx's face with her hands, glancing at Lyla. "I need you to take Lyla down into the basement. Under Albert's desk, there is a hidden crawl-space. No one will find you there—I promise. Stay there until you hear me or the police officers calling for you."

"The basement?" Linx shuddered.

"Go!" Mrs. Nelson ordered as she ran to her phone on their desk.

Never hearing Mrs. Nelson yell before, Linx's stomach violently sloshed around. The unspeakable and unpredictable events threw Linx into autopilot mode, causing her to focus only on the instructions Mrs. Nelson gave. Lyla slid off the wooden kitchen chair to follow Linx closely. They swung open the creaky basement door and carefully made their way down the uneven and warped stairs. The rotary phone swooshed as Mrs. Nelson dialed the local police station.

"Hold on to the railing," Linx whispered to Lyla.

"But, Linny, I don't want to go down there! It's so dark. What if there are spiders?"

Turning to Lyla with a straight face, Linx whispered, "If you saw everything that just happened, you would dive down those stairs."

Lyla stared at Linx with huge eyes, making Linx feel bad for expecting her to understand. Hugging her little sister, she said, "Look, I will make sure that nothing bothers you."

"You promise?"

"Yes!"

The girls descended the stairs as quickly as possible, and they heard Mrs. Nelson speaking to someone on the other line.

"Hello? Hello? We are in danger! My young neighbor said her father killed my husband, his wife, and someone else in the woods. Can you please send someone . . . anyone? Please, we need help! I have her and her little sister with me. I'm sending them to hide in the basement," Mrs. Nelson rattled off.

Just by her tone and speed, Linx could tell that Mrs. Nelson didn't know how much time she had left. Linx sighed, trying to shake the jitters off. Running over to Mr. Nelson's desk, Linx crouched down to find the door to the crawlspace.

"Over here! I see it," she said to Lyla.

They slid a dusty box out of the way so they could open the door wide enough to squeeze through. After Linx motioned Lyla to go in, the sound of pounding on the kitchen back door caused them to jump.

Terrified, Lyla looked over at Linx. "Is that Papa?"

Linx swallowed a loud gulp. "I don't know. Hurry up. Get in."

"Are you sure?"

"Lyla, get in now!"

"Okay," Lyla whispered, squirming under the desk and into the crawlspace.

Linx followed right behind her and quickly backed into the

space. Before closing the door, she pulled the box close enough to block the front of the door and then shut it.

"Open up, Edith! I know you're in there!" Rydan's deep voice yelled outside.

Mrs. Nelson refused to acknowledge his presence. Linx didn't know where she was hiding or if she was still on the phone. All they could do was listen to their father terrorizing one of the sweetest ladies Linx ever knew.

"Edith!" Rydan shouted through the door. "Where are my girls? You can't keep them locked inside forever!"

Shuddering at her father's voice, Lyla whispered to Linx, "Is it true?"

Softly glancing toward Lyla, she asked, "Is what true?"

"Did Papa kill Mama? And Mr. Nelson?"

Inhaling slowly, Linx felt horrible about what she would reveal—forever altering her sister's understanding of their father. Wringing her hands, she quietly said, "Yes. It's all true. I went to find Papa. Instead, I saw Mama. It was—I don't even know how to put it into words. I couldn't breathe. When I turned around, Papa was there. He grabbed me by my throat, and he . . . tried to kill me. Mr. Nelson heard and tried to save me, but Papa killed him too. I didn't see it happen, but I heard it." The memory of Mr. Nelson's cries and thuds from the axe echoed in her mind.

Muffling a blood-curling shriek, Lyla trembled with fear while pushing herself up against Linx. Delicate tears fell from her eyes. "Why would he do such awful things?"

"I don't know." Linx shook her head while looking at the ground. "He said Mama . . . loved someone else."

"That's not true!" Innocently pausing, Lyla asked, "Do you think it was true?"

"I'm not sure. There was another person with her there." Linx's mind flashed to the blood and carnage that coated the woods. "Let's not focus on that now. We need to survive. We will survive, you hear me?"

"Yes, Linny."

As they both exhaled together, a sharp whack made them jump out of their skin. Two more strong whacks shook the back door violently.

"If you're not gonna let me in, I'll let myself in!" Rydan grunted as he swung his axe into the door.

Linx and Lyla heard light footsteps moving across the house. They knew it was Mrs. Nelson trying to find a safe place to hide. Linx started shaking her ankle beneath her as she anxiously waited. With one more swing, several chunks of wood flew across the floor. Rydan peeled off another piece of wood to bust his hand into the house and unlock the door.

"Oh, no!" Lyla shrieked.

"Shh!" Linx held her finger up to her mouth.

Heavy footsteps stomped through the kitchen. With the boards threatening to snap beneath his boots, he asked in a taunting tone, "Edith! Where are you, my dear? You know, it's not nice to ignore guests!"

The house went completely quiet.

Lyla and Linx looked at each other in the darkness. Barely able to see each other's silhouettes, they did the only thing they could do—wait.

Dishes and glass smashed on the floor above them as Rydan slid his axe over the countertop. "Awe, Edith! That was your favorite teacup!"

"Linny, why is he doing this? What's the matter with him?"

"I . . . don't know."

More dishes came crashing down on the ground, and the noise from the sharp axe scratched across Mrs. Nelson's table. While Rydan destroyed the kitchen and dining area, Linx heard rustling on the other side of the house. Their eyes bounced from their father's location to Mrs. Nelson's. Like a stroke of bad luck, after Rydan swung his axe against a glass vase, something fell to the ground near Mrs. Nelson. Linx and Lyla froze, grabbing each other's hands.

Slow footsteps walked toward the noise above them.

"Oh, no! Oh, no! Mrs. Nelson!" Lyla cried.

"Shh!" Linx said, nudging her with her elbow.

Suddenly, the footsteps stopped. Linx didn't know what to think. *What is he doing? Did he see Mrs. Nelson?* Before another moment passed, the basement door creaked open. Linx grabbed Lyla's arm and squeezed tightly. A thick sweat formed on Linx's forehead and along the back of her neck as footsteps went down the stairs one by one. With each step closer, it became increasingly difficult to breathe.

"Hello?" Rydan's deep voice taunted. "Linny? Lyla? Come out, girls. It's Papa. I won't hurt ya."

Linx squeezed Lyla's arm tighter, reminding her not to move. His grunting traveled closer before the soles of his boots shuffled to another area of the basement.

"I'm up here, ya fool!" Mrs. Nelson's high-pitched yell echoed from the top of the stairs.

Burning tears rolled down the girls' cheeks as they knew the sacrifice Mrs. Nelson had just made. Rydan chuckled, turning around to head up the stairs after Mrs. Nelson. Climbing the stairs two at a time, he quickly reached the top.

"Edith! I'm not playing games!" he shouted, smashing his axe into the furniture above. "Ah! Just the lady I was looking for!"

"I'm not afraid of you! You're a coward."

As his footsteps followed her, Linx said quietly, "Lyla, I need you to cover your ears. Okay?"

"Why?"

"Whatever is happening up there, no good will come out of us hearing it."

"Okay," Lyla whispered, bringing her hands to her ears.

Muffled shrieks, pops, and thuds swirled around them as they pushed their hands harder against their ears. What felt like a lifetime of chaos finally broke into silence. Once Linx heard nothing, she released her fingers from her head.

As her heart settled for a split second, stomps entered the back door. A rush of nausea overcame Linx as she rocked back and forth. Footsteps walked across the floor, and the basement door swung open. The moaning of the basement steps brought a wave of heat and sweat across her face. Clenching to Linx, Lyla buried her head into her neck.

The footsteps stopped in front of Mr. Nelson's table. "Linx? Lyla? This is Officer Williams. Edith told me where to find you. You're both safe now. You can come out."

With a giant sigh of relief, Linx's dream temporarily faded into a dark cloud. As she tossed and turned on the cave floor, her mind jumped to another memory. Once the fog cleared in her dream, Linx found herself surrounded by familiar, tan, institutional walls. The black sneaker scuffs on the floors and lower walls quickly brought back memories of the other children who used to fill the room with laughter.

"Linny! What are you doing?" Lyla asked.

"Just looking out the window."

"Linny, you don't have to keep worrying about him. I don't even think he knows where we are."

Glancing over toward the sidewalk, Linx's eyes noticed the rust forming on the signage on the front lawn. When she read the name of the orphanage, a deep knife twisted in her stomach. Sacred Heart Orphanage became the new norm after the incident in the woods.

"Linny? Can I talk to you?"

"Of course."

Looking to the side, Lyla took a deep breath. "Miss Rylie said that Mr. and Mrs. Widener want to adopt me."

A stinging sensation danced across Linx's heart while tears overwhelmed her eyes. "That's wonderful!"

Staring at the floor for a moment, Lyla's eyes met her sister's. "Linny, I don't know what to do."

"What do you mean? You have to say yes!" Linx held Lyla's arms.

"I know, but I can't leave you!"

"Lyla, they said our chances here are higher if we are adopted separately."

"I know," Lyla said, shaking her head.

Linx gently held her sister's face close to hers. "Then you have to. For all we know, I can be adopted soon. Can you imagine if you turned down Mr. and Mrs. Widener? They are perfect!"

A stream of tears curved around Lyla's nose. "I'm going to miss you so much, Linny."

"We will always be sisters. No one can ever take that away."

CHAPTER 16

Falling into a deeper sleep, Linx's mind wandered to the last day she had seen Lyla. The warm sun greeted everyone, especially Lyla. The Wideners gracefully strolled into the orphanage with arms outstretched as Lyla sprinted over to them. Linx stood against the wall with a forced smile and her head tilted down. Her twiddling fingers were a gateway into her breaking heart. Although she wanted the best for Lyla once she was gone, Linx could no longer protect her.

After Lyla ran over to the Wideners, she looked back with sparkles in her eyes, but she refused to smile. Turning to ask them something, Linx saw Mrs. Widener smile and nod.

Lyla ran over, giving Linx the biggest hug of her life. "I love you so much, Linny."

"Oh, Lyla. I love you too." Linx held back her tears as best as she could.

Lyla said, "I know that their house is—"

"You mean your house?" Linx smiled.

Bashfully bending her head, Lyla continued, "Yes, I guess. It's kind of weird saying that, though."

"Lyla, don't be embarrassed! This is an amazing thing for you. I'm so happy for you!"

"Well, I guess they said that although it's a far drive, we'll be coming to visit the first weekend of every month!"

"Really? Oh, that is wonderful news!"

"I know! They also bought this for you." Lyla handed Linx a wrapped box.

Lyla and Linx hugged once more before she ran back over to the Wideners. They all smiled and waved as they walked outside toward their beautiful car. Linx stared out the window, watching the last piece of her family and her life disappear. Despite feeling sad, Linx was truly happy for Lyla. She knew Lyla was safer away from this area, mentally and physically.

"Linx!"

Spinning around, she couldn't see who called her name.

"Linx! Linx! Wake up!"

Ripping her eyes open, Linx found herself back in the cavern tunnel with Jaut. Rubbing her face and eyes, Linx remained quiet for a second, hoping the jarring feeling would subside.

"I'm sorry to wake you. I thought I heard something, and I didn't want you to be caught off guard."

Groggy, Linx shook her head. "No, don't worry about it. Honestly, I'm glad you did."

"Really? It looked like you were happy."

"At that moment, I was. But more of my memory is coming back to me now. How much were you able to see?"

"Most of it. I'm sorry, but I tried to look away for some."

Linx shrugged. "Don't be sorry. It saves me time trying to explain it."

"Was that around the time that you—"

"Died? Yes." Linx remained still for a moment as she allowed the truth to sink into her soul for the first time. "About two days later, a fire broke out in the orphanage. I was trapped in my room and couldn't get out in time."

Reaching his hand out to her shoulder, he quietly whispered, "I'm so sorry."

"Stop saying that. We are all here because we died somewhere else."

"That's true, but some went through more traumatic times than others. What you experienced with your father, no child should ever have to go through that."

Standing up while pushing against the wall, Linx didn't say anything. She brushed off the dirt and looked at Jaut.

"You want to keep moving? I don't think that noise was anything to worry about."

"Sure," she said, dissolving the force field. "I'm so thirsty, though. I need to find something to drink."

Pulling out a small canteen attached to his waist, Jaut passed it over to Linx. Her eyes grew wide with delight as she unscrewed the lid.

"We need to make it last, so don't drink it all," he warned.

"Okay, I won't." She gently placed the opening of the canteen against her dried lips. Carefully tipping it up, she felt a cool sensation rush over every inch of her mouth. With two conservative swigs, she tightened the lid and handed it back to Jaut. "All right. Let's go."

Heading down the path, neither spoke for a while as they focused on the darkness ahead with an occasional glance over the shoulder. Luckily, they didn't encounter any creatures. Linx had no idea what to expect. After her vivid dream, the prickles of anxiety covered her stomach and traveled down her legs.

Jaut needed to break the silence. "Can I ask you something?"

Without looking his way, Linx said, "Sure."

"What was the gift?"

"Huh?"

"The gift that Lyla's new parents gave you."

Taken aback, she asked, "You saw that part too?"

Jaut shrugged. "I can't control these things."

"I understand. I don't see thoughts, but I can hear and read them—for the most part. I've also had premonitions come true, but I have no control over that either."

"It just seemed sweet. I didn't know if it truly was a nice gesture or not."

Linx's face glowed. "It was very sweet. I ran into my bedroom at the orphanage to open up the box in privacy. I shredded the paper and found a note and a beautiful heart necklace inside."

"Oh, wow."

"Yeah, it was gorgeous."

"What did the note say?"

Looking up at the curved arch of the tunnel, Linx sighed. "That they gave Lyla the same one. They never wanted us to forget each other. I'm not sure why it took so long to remember what happened, but it's nice to finally get those happy memories back."

Jaut kicked a rock out of the way. "Not to mention, you can hopefully go a little easy on yourself now."

"What do you mean?"

"You blamed yourself so much with Lyla, but it seems like

you did everything in your power to give her a better life. Hell, you even saved hers."

Confused, Linx looked over with a sad, innocent gaze. "How so?"

"If you didn't let her go with her new family, she would have perished in the fire as well. You never know, she might be living her best life right now."

As she pictured Lyla happy and surrounded by others, a heavy weight lifted off of her chest. Jaut was right. Linx guided Lyla toward the best path she could have taken. Now it was time to focus on herself and finding the Gemenii.

"Thank you," she said to Jaut.

"For what?"

"Helping me to release these demons that this place brought back into my mind."

Tipping his head, he smiled. "Anything for the guardian of Pangotha."

Linx rolled her eyes as she smiled back.

"You good?" Jaut nudged his head to keep walking.

Nodding, she said, "Yes."

After walking for a while longer, a flicker of orange and yellow light whipped around in the distance. Shadows danced against the walls of the tunnel. Jaut and Linx slowed their pace as they each inhaled a deep breath.

"Almost there, Linny." Jaut gave Linx a warm smile.

"Oh, you think you're funny?"

Bumping her shoulder in a friendly manner, Jaut said, "We got this."

"If things get too crazy, I can try to create a protective bubble around us. I hope the Gemenii is close."

"Me too. Watch your step here."

Climbing up chunks of loose rock, they crawled through an opening that led them to the flickering light. Jaut volunteered to go first, hoping to warn Linx of any danger that awaited. As he pulled himself through, he stood almost paralyzed. His eyes darted all around before dropping to the ground.

"What do you see?" Linx asked, pulling herself up the rocks.

With a dry mouth, Jaut whispered, "Holes."

"Huh?"

Stretching his neck down to gather himself by focusing on his shirt, he repeated quietly, "Holes. Large holes everywhere."

"What are you—"

Once she pulled herself through the opening, Linx glanced up to see the overwhelming and eerie sight Jaut so vaguely described. In front of them was a giant and spherical room filled with massive holes, and in the middle of the room, steps led to a thin walkway suspended in the air. Holes, roughly twenty feet in diameter, covered the ceiling, walls, and floor in such a pattern that gave Linx intense goosebumps rolling from her neck down to her legs. One flickering light rested in the middle of the walkway, faintly illuminating the room. Reluctantly walking forward, they entered the uninviting room, resembling the structure of an enormous beehive. As Linx and Jaut glanced at each other, a thick draft crept in, hugging them tightly.

"What do we do? What do we do?" Linx whispered quickly.

"I have no idea! Leave?"

"You're not helping!" Linx scolded.

Whispering loudly, he said, "Look, I don't know what to tell you. Despite my suggestions, you *had* to find the Gemenii, and now look. Do you really think I'd have good guidance for how to maneuver a giant, domed, hole room? No, this is insane. Who knows what lives in each one."

Stretching out her arms and backing up toward the entrance opening, Linx realized she hadn't thought about what could be living in each hole. Hypnotized by the bone-rotting dread the holes evoked, her legs froze in place. "What do we do?"

Touching the handle of his blade, his gaze bounced from one spot to another. "I'm not sure."

"Should we head over to the light?"

"Of course not! Why would we do that? That's exactly what we shouldn't do!" Jaut snorted as he rubbed his face.

"Well, unless you have any better ideas, it seems like we have no other choice. I can transport us there, or we can try to fly together while I hold your hand."

"Our luck, this place is booby-trapped. I'm not sure if flying through here is a good idea."

"Fine, we can walk over slowly."

Jaut clenched his jaw while squeezing the sword's handle. "If I die, it's your fault. Just remember that."

Linx smirked as she gently patted his forearm. "I'll go first."

Carefully, she stepped down on some slippery rocks and pebbles, being aware of the open pits from the holes on each side. Between each hole, the path widened and then eventually shrunk in the middle. They became so small they could barely fit Linx's tiny footsteps. Trying to face forward, she could see several enormous holes above her head. A burning sensation overcame her knees and traveled down to her calves. Although the intimidating feeling of unfamiliar, dark, open spaces above her made her queasy, she peered over her shoulder to see Jaut in a worse condition than her. "Are you okay?"

With an unamused frown and furrowed brows, Jaut said, "Yes—just never have been a fan of holes."

"I never put much thought into them, but I can see why. As we make our way over, I guess just try not to look down . . . or in any direction." Linx lightly laughed.

"Thank you. That was very helpful."

"I'm sorry. That didn't come out the way I had hoped. Should we hold each other's hands to stabilize our balance while we walk?"

Jaut's brown eyes almost popped out of his skull. "Um, no! I'm good, thank you. I don't want to be responsible for your death."

"Ha! Well, once we cross this one here, there are stairs just ahead."

"Keep it moving! I'm trying to focus on the path and not . . ." Jaut trailed off. "Ah! I looked down! Whatever you do, Linx, don't look down! You think it can't get worse when you enter this room, but then . . . you look down. There are endless dark holes—on both sides of us. If we ever get out of here, I'm never coming back. You couldn't pay me enough."

"Jeez, settle down! What would you have done if there wasn't a walkway?"

"Uh, I don't know. Can we keep moving, please?"

Right as Linx was about to joke with him, her left foot slid down the side of the hole. As her balance gave out, she slipped backward and dropped on her right shoulder. Falling into the gigantic hole, she desperately tried to grab onto anything while attempting to fly. As the cape pressed against her wings, Linx's heart sank to her stomach as the darkness consumed everything beneath her feet.

Frantically crouching and reaching for her, Jaut managed to grab Linx's arm and pull her up. "Linx! I got you!"

Linx sat on the narrow path, straddling one leg on each side. Closing her eyes gently, she didn't move while breathing slowly. "I'm almost ready to keep going. I thought I might've been a goner. When I fell, I hit my shoulder and couldn't grab onto anything in time. Thank you."

"Of course. And take your time. The view is to die for," Jaut said, shuddering as he looked around.

Delicately standing up, Linx found her balance as they shuffled the rest of the way to the stairs. They climbed three steps to reach the walkway that crossed over one of the vast holes. She couldn't tell if some of them were tunnels, but she definitely didn't want to find out.

"Ugh, I don't know if this walkway is going to be any better."

Thin slabs of old wood were placed one in front of the other while thick vines lined the sides of the walkway, acting as a decorative handrail.

"Careful," Linx warned, wrapping her fingers around the vine.

"Linny, you better watch yourself!"

"Will you stop calling me that?"

Shrugging, Jaut asked, "You don't want to be called that anymore? I think it's cute. I can stop if you'd like."

"Fine. Just don't start saying it in front of everyone. It's been a long time since I heard that name. It's going to take a little while to get used to."

Rolling his eyes, he followed her across the bridge. Once they were about halfway through, a rumble shook everything from side to side.

"What was that? Let's book it to the other side!" Linx shouted.

"Okay, go!"

Barely on the other end of the bridge, chunks of rock fell from the ceiling. A heavy wind started to swirl from the massive holes, causing more debris to whip around. Linx focused on the ceiling and noticed a portion was barely attached to the rest of the rock. As the wind increased to an aggressive speed, Linx and Jaut tried to find the safest spot near them.

"Should we try to take cover in one of the holes over there?"

"We can try. I don't know if I should just try to transport us out of here instead."

Afraid they would get hit by something, Linx opted to create a protection bubble to surround them.

"We should be safe in here," she shouted over the whipping winds. "Do you want to wait this out or leave?"

Jaut shook his head. "Linx, we can't leave now. We've come so far, and it's not getting any better out there. We need to find the Gemenii."

"I hope we can!"

"We will."

Overwhelmed by the winds, Linx placed all of her power into reinforcing the bubble that protected the two of them. She added what magic she could to assist if anything fell on their heads.

"I wish I could help," Jaut yelled.

"You can! Stay close. It'll be less energy for the force field."

Jaut and Linx huddled together as Linx finished adding to the bubble. Right as Linx released her hand for a moment, something caught Jaut's eye. It appeared to be two enormous sticks poking out of a distant hole. Confused, he stared for a moment to observe what it could be.

"What is that? Were those there the entire time?" he asked.

"Huh? What are you talking about?"

Pointing to a hole across the room, Jaut said, "Look at those two sticks over there, curving at the ends. Were they there before?"

"Um, I really don't know, Jaut. I didn't notice them. Why?"

Jaut shuddered. "It just seemed like it came out of nowhere. I don't remember seeing it before."

"Not to be mean, but you freaked out when we came in here. I'm sure there are a lot of things we didn't notice."

As the wind increased, Jaut hypnotically stared into the hole. Before he had a chance to get a good look, an immense gust pushed through the holes, carrying the bubble up off of the ground. Jaut and Linx whirled high in the room, dropping every few seconds. Clinging to each other, they closed their eyes as the bubble began to spin.

Swirling in the chaos, Linx shouted, "I think I'm going to be sick."

"Hold it in, Linny!"

With a quick spin, the bubble was violently sucked into one of the holes in the ceiling.

CHAPTER 17

Once the madness settled, Linx cautiously released the force field. They stood up to assess where they had ended up. Observing their surroundings, they looked around to see only walls and a ceiling in the tiny room. The bubble had entered through a hole in the bottom of the room. Despite some minor rubble in one corner, the room was oddly bare.

Jaut walked up to each wall, knocking and trying to feel what they were made of. With his curiosity peaked, Jaut placed one ear against a wall while he continued tapping.

Perplexed, Linx tilted her head and scrunched her eyebrows. "What are you doing?"

"Something appears to be different about this wall. I want to try knocking it down. Seems like it was recently rebuilt."

"Huh? Are you sure?"

Without a second thought, Jaut pulled out his sword and firmly whacked the pommel against the wall. Slowly, he started chipping a hole through the dried mud. Busting through the barrier, Jaut felt an open area on the other side. He kicked it several more times before pulling chunks out of his way.

"Can you see anything? It looks dark in there," Linx said, crouching to peer through the hole.

"Nah, I can't see much of anything. There might be a stream of light in the distance, but it's not close enough for me to see anything." Jaut wiped the sweat off of his face using his forearm.

After a few minutes of breaking down more of the wall, Jaut tried to slide through the hole. His shoulders got stuck between jagged spots in the opening as he pushed forward. Snaking his way back out, he kicked off the wall to free himself.

Brushing off his arms, he looked over at Linx. "It may take a little time to get the hole big enough for us to enter—or at least you. I'm not sure if I can get through."

"I don't think it's a good idea to separate from each other. I can wait until we both fit through."

"All right."

"Do you want me to help? I can try to bust down the wall with a ball of energy. It would only take a couple of seconds," Linx offered.

"Normally, I would say yes. I just don't know what's in there. If it's the Gemenii or an enemy, I'm not sure how anything will react to an explosion."

Rolling her eyes, Linx stepped back to let Jaut finish. "Okay, fair enough."

Continuing to chisel a hole for a while longer, he finally created an opening large enough for them to move through. Sliding his sword back into his scabbard, he climbed onto the ledge and slipped into the neighboring room.

"Can you see anything?"

Holding out his hand for Linx, Jaut whispered, "No, not yet."

Gently gripping his fingers, Linx stepped through the hole and jumped next to him. She brushed the hair away from her face, squinting her eyes. As they maneuvered through the poorly lit area, they noticed the right side of the room opened up into a larger area than what they could see before. Walking forward, Linx saw a statue resting in the center of the dark room with four large candlesticks surrounding it.

Slowly approaching the smooth gray statue, Linx lit a flame in her hand. Studying every inch, she was amazed by its beauty. Two women sat cross-legged and back-to-back, each with magnificent crowns sitting gracefully on their heads. Their hair was braided together, merging the statues as one. Holding each other's hands on each side of the statue, their palms rested one on top of the other.

"What is this?" she softly asked.

Jaut said, "I-I have no idea. I wonder if it's—"

"The Gemenii?" Linx whispered.

"Maybe. I'm not sure what the Gemenii looks like."

The more they analyzed the unique statue, the more intrigued they were. As they circled the sculpture, Linx's eyes met Jaut's gaze. "Something is missing."

"What do you mean?"

"It looks like there used to be a ring of some sort here." Linx's fingertips grazed over the indent on a hand where a ring once sat. "That's strange. Do you think that someone stole it?"

Coming over to see what she was talking about, Jaut said, "It's almost unbelievable. Look what we traveled through to get here. But something seemed off about that wall."

"If this is the Gemenii, what should we do next? I guess I expected to speak with someone. I didn't realize they might be a statue. I'm so confused." Linx stepped back to look at the sculpture from afar.

"You and me both. Others view the Gemenii as a goddess who protects nature and vitality within Pangotha, but that's all we know. Some claimed to speak in the name of the Gemenii, like Pygo. However, nothing could be proven or disproven. The people always passed down the knowledge of serving the Gemenii and protecting Pangotha."

"Hmm. Interesting." As Linx carefully circled the statue once more, walking past a candle, a burst of wind lightly bounced the flame from Linx's hand to one of the candle wicks. Looking at Jaut, her jaw almost fell to the floor. "W-what just happened? I didn't do anything! I swear!"

"Linx!"

"I-I'm sorry! I didn't do anything . . . or at least I didn't mean to!"

"I don't think that matters now." Jaut pointed to the flame, which turned a bright green and fading to blue near the wick.

"Should I light the rest?"

"Oh, man. I don't know. This will go one way or the other. What if this isn't the Gemenii, and we release a plague?" Jaut stretched his neck back to look at the ceiling.

"I take it as a sign the first candle was accidentally lit. Why not light the others? If nothing happens, at least we can get a better look at the statue."

Rubbing his face with both hands, Jaut grumbled loudly. "Fine. But I want it noted that it wasn't my idea."

"Noted." Linx rolled her eyes.

She swiftly walked from one candle to the next, quickly lighting them with her hand. Once she lit the last one, Linx stepped back next to Jaut.

"I'd be more comfortable if you stood on the opposite side of the room in case you pissed something off."

"Oh, will you stop?"

They stood still, staring at the candlelit display for several moments while nothing happened. Looking at each other a bit underwhelmed, Linx and Jaut were disheartened at the thought of continuing the search throughout the deathtrap of a cave. They didn't know how long it would take—if ever—to find the Gemenii. Releasing a giant sigh, Linx approached the marvelous masterpiece and knelt before it. Sitting on her feet, she scanned all the immaculate details incorporated into the statue. The big eyes appeared to kiss shut while their full lips rested comfortably beneath a perfect, broad nose. Each side had their nose pierced—one with a ring while the other had a stud.

Small flowers were woven into their braids, and the women wore a flowing, strapless dress that complimented their curvaceous figures. *Whoever created this sculpture exhibited incredible talent,* Linx thought to herself. As her eyes rose to admire the tall crowns resting on their heads, something strange caught her eye. *Did something move?*

Turning her head to face Jaut, Linx asked quietly, "Did you see that?"

"Huh? See what? I don't know what you're talking about."

"Never mind." Linx wondered if she was seeing things.

As she brought her attention back around, the sculpture welcomed her gaze with haunting, open eyes. Linx nearly flew back while the statue's bright yellow eyes glared at her. Tiny explosions of lime green accented her eyes as she looked directly into Linx's. "We've been waiting for someone like you."

"I don't know what to say," she said, bashfully looking toward Jaut.

He shrugged as he stepped back farther. By no surprise, Jaut's widened eyes locked onto the intimidatingly beautiful sculpture. Perplexed by what he was witnessing, he rubbed his eyes with his thumb and pointer finger, hoping he was just seeing things.

"A great injustice has occurred, and we think you can help us."

Raising an eyebrow while massaging the back of her neck, Linx listened intently.

"Are you . . . the Gemenii?" Jaut blurted out.

The statue momentarily glanced toward Jaut and then eerily back at Linx. "Yes."

"What happened?" Linx curiously asked.

"A group of men came into Pangotha and kidnapped a royal Pangothian child along with an ancient ring. Now, they're using them as leverage against our land."

At this point, Jaut stepped forward to listen to what had happened. The situation made him nervous, yet he was mesmerized by how the Gemenii spoke. The Gemenii's voice eloquently and calmly delivered devastating news.

"These monsters took Zalia, using her to harvest power from the residence of Pangotha. Each night, the surge that ripples throughout our lands originates from her, sucking intense power back to her captors."

Linx and Jaut stood dumbfounded, staring at each other for a moment.

The Gemenii continued, "They were cowards."

"So . . . how can I help? Do you need us to find them? I mean, I don't mind helping, but I'm not familiar with Pangotha."

The Gemenii smiled, revealing stone-gray teeth. "They are

not in Pangotha. They would've been fools to stay. The ecknids would've destroyed them all."

"Well, where are they then?"

"A place you are familiar with—Crystal Woods."

With her jaw falling open, Linx shouted, "Huh? Wait, what? I'm not going back there!"

"You can help our land," the Gemenii politely said.

"How do you know I am familiar with Crystal Woods anyway?"

"Your cape, my dear. The cape you wear has been a very popular topic amongst those with dark motives."

"What do you mean?" Linx asked.

"The group wanted it, along with the rings, to overthrow the monarchy. With the cape's defense combined with the ring's unlimited power, it would be effortless to take over Crystal Woods—and potentially beyond."

"Did they come here for the cape as well? The cape was in Crystal Woods the whole time."

The Gemenii gently glanced from Linx to Jaut. "The men were aware of that, but they also knew they'd be targeted since no one could get it off. They wanted to harvest power to have the ability to remove the cape when necessary."

Linx looked around, thinking about the burden the cape carried. "I see."

"Fortunately, they only found one of the two rings," the Gemenii confided, slowly rotating and grinding their bare stone hand.

"They found you in here?" Linx asked.

With a solemn face, the Gemenii said, "They stuck a sword right through the stomach of Zalia's main caretaker—as she stood watching. Then, they threatened to do the same to another beloved caretaker unless she helped them locate the rings. She led them through the tunnels to me."

Interrupting, Jaut asked, "How the hell did a little girl make it through that labyrinth of death?"

"Since she is destined for the throne, she has unlimited access to me. The tunnels are safe for her to enter." The Gemenii smiled slightly. "She could come and consult with me at any time to prepare for becoming a ruler."

"When was she supposed to become the ruler?" Jaut asked.

"Once she reached maturity with her magical strength. Pangotha needs strength, patience, and a leader with magical maturity. That is why she was supposed to wait before accessing the rings. Although they only found one ring, she was never supposed to wear any until she was ready. They forced her to put it on and touch the ground. Instantly, Pangotha became nothing of what it once was."

Standing momentarily, Linx took a deep breath as she thought about how scared the poor girl must be. Disgusted with the horrendous lengths Crystal Woods had gone for power, she was glad to have left. Carter and his minions—or, truly, the lords and their minion, Carter—did Linx a favor by pushing her to her limits. She couldn't comprehend how scared a little girl would be in a prison cell.

"Where is the other ring?" Jaut asked. "Unless that's a secret."

The Gemenii chuckled, opening and closing their vibrant eyes. "I'm glad you asked. Slide out the ring in my nose."

Linx and Jaut turned to each other, looking to see who would volunteer first. The idea of reaching toward the Gemenii's face was unnerving. When Jaut didn't budge, Linx faced the Gemenii again. "Okay, um, I need to remove your nose ring?"

"Don't worry about anything. It slides down."

Reaching her hand near the Gemenii's face, Linx paused. "Wait. Will anything happen when or if I grab it?"

"No, my dear."

"I didn't know. The last thing I want to do is cause more chaos or destruction, like those who are abusing their power with the other ring."

The Gemenii nodded. "Luckily, the surge occurs every night, but everything resumes its natural course of things by morning. That is not by coincidence. The ring Zalia is wearing draws in the power, but it can't store it. So after several hours, the magic begins to dissipate."

Linx pinched the ring between her thumb and pointer finger with a shaky hand and gently pulled it down. At first, the jewelry felt as though it was stuck inside the Gemenii's face. She hesitated for a moment before it released from the Gemenii's nose. Once Linx pulled the ring out, she saw something very interesting. "Wow! I didn't realize a gem was hidden inside!"

Examining the jewelry in her hand, she didn't expect to see a beautiful ring with a unique blue gem. As she studied it, the gem was in a squared "U" shape. Impressed by its beauty, her eyes lit up.

"This is an exceptional ring. It goes hand in hand with its sister ring."

"Sister ring?"

"Yes, the ring Zalia has is its sister ring. The thieves stole a green ring that fits right inside the blue gem. Once they are combined, the power is unmatched by most. Separated, the green gem harvests power from the soil and Pangothians, and the blue gem can transfer power from the host to the recipients."

"Oh, wow!"

"Yes! The blue gem can be beneficial during battles when a friend has been attacked. The host can transfer power, and the friend can utilize it as their own—temporarily."

Jaut stepped over to analyze the ring in Linx's hand. "That's incredible."

The Gemenii glanced at Linx with a smirk. "Go ahead. Put it on."

"Huh?" Linx's bright eyes grew with confusion.

"You feel it, don't you? The pull, the allure—it's hard to resist."

"Is that a bad thing?" Linx inquired.

"No, the power knows how to get the other ring back. And that's with you."

Linx sighed, shaking her head. "I really don't know what to say. I can't promise that I will ever return to Crystal Woods. It's basically a death sentence if anything goes wrong. They wanted me dead before. I'll be a walking target now that I'm wearing Poba's cape."

Releasing a heavy exhale, Jaut swayed his body from the ball of his foot to his heel. Without making his wishes known, he secretly hoped Linx would have said yes to the Gemenii. He knew what this world was like before compared to now. The residents of Pangotha wandered like shells of what they once were. Yes, they eventually got their power back for a bit. But going through a perpetual loop and anticipating the severe daily fatigue and helplessness spirals even the strongest creatures into a suffocating depression.

Turning to Jaut, Linx looked at him with pained eyes. "Do you think I'm a coward?"

"I-I, um, why would you ask that?" Jaut asked, shocked by her question.

"Just like you see my thoughts, I can hear yours. Do you think I am a coward?" The corners of her lips fell, curling into a frown, as tears formed in her eyes.

Closing his eyelids to gather his compassion, Jaut held out his hands to hold hers. "Linx, just as you can hear my thoughts, I can only see a portion of what you went through. I'll never know the depth of pain you experienced, just as you'll never know what Pangotha was. Lands blossomed, creatures flourished, and it was known as a land of healing. Look at us now."

Linx's gaze fell to the floor as Jaut looked toward the room's ceiling.

He continued, "All creatures from different backgrounds could be in each other's company, absorbing the warmth from the sun and meditating in the flowers. Now—we hide. I'm not sure who's even alive and if they're hiding in the ground or caves."

"That's crazy to comprehend. Pangotha looked so beautiful when I arrived. I can't even imagine what the Pangotha you remember looks like."

"Linx—"

"I don't know what to do," she interrupted, falling to her knees.

Crouching near her, Jaut said, "Linx, you need to make whatever decision you feel is best. But if you decide to go, I'll be right there beside you."

Resting her face in her warm hands, she remained silent as a stampede of questions bombarded her mind. What if she was caught by guards? They would never let her go. Worst of all, how could she face Carter again? What would she say to him? But how could she turn her back on the Pangothians?

Rubbing his hand on Linx's back, Jaut whispered, "I will be by your side as a warrior and friend. I know this is a lot to ask."

The Gemenii calmly said, "Fate brought you here to me. My power can only do so much, but you came to Pangotha, met an incredible adventurer, and completed your way through a maze intended only for someone special to succeed. Had you fallen into any of those holes, they could've easily killed you. We cannot force you to sacrifice your life to help this land, nor would we want to do that, but I am grateful that you are considering it."

Releasing her head from her hands, Linx sat back on her ankles. Swallowing the flutters that tried escaping her throat, she closed her eyes. "I will retrieve Zalia and the ring."

"What?" Jaut raised his eyebrows.

Squeezing the ring in her hands, Linx softly said, "I'll help free Zalia and Pangotha by returning to Crystal Woods."

"This is wonderful news, my dear!" the Gemenii said with a gentle smile. "You will have an army that can support you."

"They'll be up against a very powerful force. I should say . . . we will. Their new king, Carter, has this incredible ability to summon waves of goblins that ravage everything in sight. I was . . . I was on the other end of their devastation, and they can be ruthless."

"Was that the thing you saw in the woods earlier? A ravenous goblin that you let run free?" Jaut didn't try to hide his irritation.

"Look, it's something that even I can't explain because I don't understand it."

Jaut smirked and rolled his eyes, sarcastically saying, "Why, let me take a guess. Is it because that by killing a goblin you feel that you're killing him?"

With a gust of life, Linx looked into Jaut's eyes, down to his mouth, and back up into his gaze. Without skipping a beat, she whispered, "Yes."

Clenching his jaw, Jaut firmly blinked his eyes, reopening them without uttering a word. Annoyance burned through his veins as his mind replayed the chaos that ensued because of the demonic creature.

The Gemenii stared at Jaut. "My dear, this is not your battle to fight now. Some struggles need your presence, and others suffer because of it. We all have demons we nurture or struggle to combat. Hopefully, we can look back someday and appreciate the growth we've endured. Don't worry, justice will be served."

With a warm heart, Linx found comfort in the Gemenii's words. "Thank you."

"No, thank you. Our people will be eternally grateful for your help."

Examining the palm of her hand, Linx tilted the ring from side to side. "I just hope that I can help."

"You will be of great help. Keep in mind that one of you must wear the blue sister ring throughout your journey. The last thing you want is for the ring to fall into the wrong hands."

Without a second thought, Linx slid the ring over her finger. "I will do my best."

"We'll figure it out together." Jaut nodded with a solemn face.

CHAPTER 18

Looking deeply into the Gemenii's eyes, Linx asked, "Once we locate Zalia, should we immediately escort her back?"

"Yes. Make sure she is safely returned to Pangotha."

"And what about the ring? Should I give her this one? Or should I keep it on until we get back?"

The Gemenii sat still, not responding for several seconds. "I have concerns about Zalia having full access to the rings. Refrain from giving her the other ring. When you're in Pangotha, you must return the rings to me. In the meantime, be mindful of where you send your energy. This ring can send it to anyone—even your foes. If you need to send your power to someone, shift your focus to them and only them. It's easier said than done."

Slowly nodding in agreement, Linx peered over at Jaut. "Are you ready?"

As Jaut exhaled, preparing to leave, the Gemenii said, "Before you leave, come to me."

Standing before the Gemenii, Linx and Jaut awaited their next instruction. The crushing stress of returning to Crystal Woods knotted Linx's stomach. She tilted her right foot from side to side, bringing her ankle near the cold floor. *This journey will be for all the innocent creatures. Breathe.*

"I'll provide you with something special to leave and reenter these tunnels most efficiently. Rest your forehead against mine." The Gemenii closed their eyes.

Jaut stared at Linx, his eyes slightly bulging from their sockets. He whispered, "What?"

Linx shrugged her shoulders as she waved him forward.

He continued, "There's no way I am putting my face against—"

The Gemenii interrupted, "Well, if you'd like to squeeze your way through the beehive, squishing against angry bees, *be* my guest."

Jaut aggressively rubbed his neck. "Huh? Are you serious? Oh, man. I knew it! I knew there was something there."

Laughing, the Gemenii said, "I'm teasing. They are my favorites. They take care of me. Once you leave, they'll patch up the hole you entered through with such talent."

"Oh . . . how cute." Jaut stood in place, itching himself from the thought of going through a beehive.

"They'll guide you to the closest exit. Whenever you need to return, every creature will know you are invited."

Linx's face relaxed as a slight smile formed. "Oh, that is wonderful. I do wonder, though, if we were able to reach you now, what difference would this make in the journey?"

The Gemenii kindly smiled. "Depending on where you are

and what entrance you take, it can be very beneficial. I try my best to be aware of who's entering the tunnels, but even I cannot see everything. In the worst case, if something happens to me, you could still access the tunnels safely."

"I see. Well, thank you." Linx nodded politely.

"Yeah, sure. I think you forgot about the *beehive,* Linx."

Rolling her eyes, Linx sighed. "What other option do you have?"

"Fine." Jaut adjusted his shoulders and hesitantly walked up to the Gemenii.

"Place your forehead against mine."

Reluctantly, he pressed his face firmly against the Gemenii's. Holding still, the center of his forehead tingled with a slight burn. "W-what's happening?"

Once the tingling faded, Jaut stepped back and looked into the Gemenii's eyes.

"You are now marked as an ally of mine." The Gemenii smiled. "If the other creatures here see the symbol, they won't attack you. This will also help you see who's an intruder."

As he turned to face Linx, her eyes widened, and her bottom lip dropped in shock at what she saw. A glimmering symbol glowed from the center of Jaut's forehead. "Wow! Jaut!"

Touching his forehead, he looked up. "What?"

"Do you feel any different?" Linx curiously asked.

"Um, I don't think so."

"That looks so cool!"

The Gemenii asked, "Are you ready, my dear?"

"I am." Linx gracefully approached, placing her forehead in place. A surge of energy flashed between the Gemenii and Linx. The tingling cupped her face as it wrapped around the back of her head.

"Now, you are welcome here as well."

Linx bowed her head. "Thank you."

As she stepped away from the Gemenii, Jaut's fingers grazed his forehead again before pointing to her. "Linx, your forehead is glowing!"

Raising her eyebrows, Linx laughed. Her demeanor exuded confidence, and a feeling of purpose washed over her. With this journey becoming a new distraction from her woes, she began to welcome the challenge. Nevertheless, something popped into her mind. "Before we go, is it true? Can the rings help get the cape off? If I could get this off, I would be less conspicuous . . . and more comfortable."

"The short answer is no."

With sinking shoulders, Linx frowned. A loud exhale escaped her lips as she stared at the ground.

"I'm sorry that wasn't the answer you were searching for."

Leaning up against a pillar protruding from a wall, Jaut stood in shock as he glanced toward Linx. Her glow faded for a moment as reality sank in. The Gemenii didn't have to elaborate on the high stakes. He pictured them immediately. Pangothians would suffer immensely if any enemy invaded their lands. *But what would she say? Would she retract her offer to help?*

"Jaut! Stop it!" Linx shouted.

Spooked, he jumped back, bumping into the pillar. "What? What did I do?"

"Of course, I will still find Zalia! I wouldn't back out solely due to the cape. What kind of monster would I be if I did that?"

Pressing his lips into a tight smile, Jaut relaxed his body and stepped forward. "Ah, Linny. That's some good news."

"As much as I would love to speak longer, we should go,

Jaut. If these men are associated with Crystal Woods, I don't know what conditions they subjected Zalia to. And that's based on experience."

The Gemenii said, "You'll have access to your magic in most of the areas as you exit. Just be mindful of who sees where you leave from. I've been trying to minimize the visitors since Zalia's disappearance."

Linx raised her eyes to meet the Gemenii's. "Thank you for everything, and I will do whatever I can to save Zalia. You have my word."

"Do you need anything before we leave?" Jaut asked, stepping over some rubble.

"No, thank you. Follow the tunnel out, and someone will be waiting to guide you."

Closing his eyes firmly, Jaut shuddered. "Ah, yes. The moment I have been waiting for."

Linx climbed over the wall and into the neighboring room as Jaut dragged his feet behind. Turning her head to the left, Linx saw the tunnel opening, and something caught her eye to the right. Jumping down from the ledge, her feet slid on the bits of debris from earlier. With her legs trembling, she quickly stepped backward before freezing in shock.

"What's the matter?" Jaut crouched through the opening.

"Um," Linx whispered. "You have to see this."

"Based on your face, I don't know if I want to," Jaut mumbled. Taking a deep breath, he hopped down to see what Linx was hypnotized by.

A massive bee towered over them, waiting for Linx and Jaut to exit the Gemenii's chambers. Light fuzz surrounded its two dark compound eyes, and two long, thin antennae stuck out of the sides of its head. Once Jaut stepped away from the hole, the bee crawled over to seal up the wall, buzzing about while gathering mud from the corner of the room. Jaut nearly crumbled to the ground, watching the bee before motioning toward Linx to leave.

"Where should we go? We have no idea how to get out of here. Even the Gemenii said that a bee will help us leave. What if this was the bee?" Linx played with the ring wrapped around her finger.

"We have to get out of here—now. I don't trust these things."

Opening her eyes wide and rolling them to the side, Linx shook her head. "This is ridiculous! I'm not thrilled about this plan either, but we need the bee's assistance to escape! I refuse to waste more time in here. Think about Zalia and the other Pangothians. They need our help."

Rubbing the side of his head while clenching his jaw, Jaut slowly walked toward the tunnel. "Linx, I said I would help you —I am not a liar. But please understand, I had a horrible experience a long time ago. I cannot even explain what it does to me when I see them. If I could, I would peel off my skin."

"Wow. Okay, okay. I'll stand closer to it, and you can keep your distance. I just want to ensure that we don't lose track of where it goes. Does that work?"

Watching the bee construct the wall, Jaut whispered, "Fine."

When the bee finished its task, it stared at them before coming closer. As goosebumps tickled his back, Jaut brought his shoulders up to his ears and stood behind Linx. Sticking out its smooth forearm, barely covered in fuzz, the bee attempted to touch Jaut's face. Letting out a high-pitched shriek, he rushed into the tunnel to escape the bee's touch. Unsure of what to do,

Linx patiently yet nervously waited as the bee examined her. Gently tapping her forehead and cheeks, it swiftly moved on to fly down the tunnel toward Jaut.

"Oh, no! No, no, no! Get away!" Jaut's screams echoed throughout the tunnel.

Rushing to console him, Linx found herself filled with more energy than ever. Was she thriving off of others' need for her? Regardless, fulfilling bursts of power surged through her body. "Jaut, hold on! Stop running! It only checked my forehead for —" Linx panted.

Stopping in her tracks, she witnessed a version of Jaut she never thought existed. Curled on the ground, Jaut began breathing heavily as he kept his eyes tightly shut. His fingers gripped the ground, but his elbows appeared weak—shaking with fear. Thin streams of sweat covered Jaut's body. Sprinting over to him at the end of the tunnel, she soon understood what triggered his freeze response. Linx was dumbfounded as she witnessed hundreds of enormous working bees flying in and out of the holes within the room they passed through earlier.

"What the . . ." Linx trailed off, watching several bees zip right by. "I can't believe we're in a giant hive."

Between strained breaths, Jaut shouted, "Linx?"

"Yes?" Linx dropped to her knees and placed a hand on his back.

Sweat dripped from his hair and nose, splashing on the ground as he paused. "You aren't helping."

"J-Jaut?" Linx cautiously questioned. "Are you okay?"

Almost losing his head, Jaut yelled, "Am I okay? Am I okay? No! I'm not okay! I have an extreme fear of bees. And now, I am surrounded by countless mammoth bees. How do you expect me to be okay?"

"I-I'm sorry! I was hoping, by talking about it, you would feel better. How can I help?" Linx rubbed his back while observing the room.

Racing over, a different bee landed nearby to get their attention. Linx calmly closed her eyes as she tried to develop a plan that Jaut would agree to. The buzzing intensified, almost to a deafening level, when she had an idea. "What if I try to create a protection bubble for our journey out of here? Would that help?"

Exhaling loudly, Jaut sat up, turning away from the overwhelming view. He slowly blinked as he considered her suggestion and offer. "I don't think we have a choice. Let's give it a shot."

When Linx lifted her hands, a bright light formed around her fingertips. As the spark grew, the light caught the attention of a nearby bee. Cautiously observing, Jaut witnessed the bee frantically flying toward Linx, extending a giant stinger from its abdomen. With a swipe of her palm, Linx started constructing the protection bubble.

"Hey, Linx! What's going on with that bee?" Jaut shouted.

Turning her head to identify the commotion, Linx spotted the massive bee flying her way. Quickly finishing the protection wall around them, Linx covered herself and Jaut before the bee arrived. Like a chain reaction, others immediately joined, swarming around the bubble. The buzzing vibrated within the cave tunnels, shaking bits of rock and dirt over the top of the force field. Jaut's wide eyes scanned from one side to another as countless bees tried stinging the barrier between them.

"What do we do?" he shouted over the buzzing sound.

With her hands on her head, Linx said, "I don't know. I'm

not sure what to do. Why are they attacking us? I thought we were supposed to be protected by the Gemenii?"

Overwhelmed and perplexed by the situation, he stared at the chaotic mess of bees attempting to pierce the bubble. The swarm jumbled together as they began pushing past each other. Layers of wings and legs covered the bubble, preventing dimmed light from getting through.

A muffled female voice shouted from a distance, "Take down your shield!"

Barely able to hear what was said, Linx paused. "Huh?"

"Take down the force field," the voice shouted again.

Linx and Jaut looked at each other in confusion.

"She wants me to take down the barrier? Is she crazy?"

"I . . . I have no idea why she would say that. I just want to get out of here!"

The woman yelled through the waves of bees, "Can you hear me? You must take down the force field!"

"Are you mad? You must be out of your mind! There's no way that's happening! You think we want to die?" Linx demanded.

"You have to! They can't see that you're protected! If they think you're an enemy, they'll try to suffocate you to death!"

"Oh, I don't know what to do." Thoughts flooded Linx's mind.

"You have to trust me! I can get them away from you for a short time. But you must bring down the shield! Okay?"

As her insides tightened, Linx stood silent for a moment, thinking about what her options would be.

"Okay?" the woman shouted.

"Yes!" Linx raised her eyebrows while looking at Jaut.

Within seconds, the force field rocked from side to side as Linx and Jaut waited to see what to do. The pressure forming within the cave almost pushed them into a nearby hole. One by one, bees blew off the bubble, finally allowing them to see beyond the barrier. Several feet away, the silhouette of a slender figure moved her hands in the air.

"Take down the force field!" the woman yelled, holding her hands firmly toward the bees.

Releasing air from her nostrils, Linx's shoulders dropped as she dissolved the barrier between them. Glancing over at Jaut, she noticed he remained calm while discretely fidgeting his hands. Linx looked toward the distant figure, mentally scanning the woman's marking on her forehead.

"Hmm. It appears she has met the Gemenii as well."

"Oh, yeah?" Jaut squinted toward the silhouette.

"Thank you!" Linx shouted to the woman.

"You're welcome. Hurry, though. Head down the hole near your right. They'll follow you until they know who you are. At least there is only enough room for them to be single file rather than swarming you."

"I'm supposed to be happy about this?" Jaut asked sarcastically.

"Look, I'm trying to help you. If you wait too long, they will emerge through other holes. You need to go now."

Shuffling up to the massive hole, Linx heard Jaut frantically mumbling under his breath. "Are you okay?"

"No! How do we get down from this thing?"

"Look! There are some rocks protruding from the side. Let's go!"

Carefully sliding down the side of the hole, Linx planted her foot on a rock before descending all the way in. She found the stones were perfectly placed, missing only a few chunks here or there. Quickly following behind, Jaut scrambled to find a rhythm to increase his speed into the cavern tunnel. Linx hadn't witnessed him move so fast throughout their adventure thus far. A vibration trembled through the tunnel, rattling the dirt and pebbles surrounding them. Linx squinted her eyes as the dust swirled within the spiraling winds. As the tremors grew, the figure appeared at the opening. The woman looked behind her before jumping into the hole. Surfing on a slanted portion of the wall, she hopped from one rock to another.

Impressed, Jaut asked, "How do you make that look so easy? I'd break my neck if I tried that."

She nonchalantly said, "Practice."

Pulling the corners of his lips down while raising his eyebrows, Jaut tilted his head in agreement. He paused for a moment and analyzed the distance from himself to Linx.

Effortlessly passing Linx and Jaut, the woman's long braided hair floated above her head. "You both need to move faster, or you *will* die."

"Easy for you to say!" Jaut shouted back.

"Look, I'm not trying to be rude, but they're on their way to find the intruders—you."

"I thought we weren't supposed to be attacked? The Gemenii explained that these *fancy* markings will protect us." Jaut pointed to his forehead, shrugging his shoulders.

Shaking her head, the woman continued sliding. "Exactly. They'll prevent you from being attacked, not falling to your death when the bees charge down here."

"Oh," Jaut said, speeding down the rocks. "Come on, Linx. Move it."

"I'm going as fast as I can! Knock it off, or I'll stop dead in my tracks."

"I swear . . ."

"The Gemenii granted access to you? I don't understand it, but it's not my call. Careful as you approach this bigger rock. The landing is just below," the woman yelled up.

As she quickened her pace, Linx heard the thump from the woman beneath them. *She must have jumped to the floor. Thank goodness that we're so close.*

"Can't you fly down or something? They're coming!" Jaut shouted.

"Won't that irritate them?" Linx gripped the rocks tighter as she scaled down the tunnel.

"Gah! I can't do this. I'm trying her route." Jaut hopped over to the side of the rocks and quickly slid down the dirt wall. "Ah! How . . . did you do this? I'm gonna die. I'm gonna die!"

As her heart sank, Linx heard Jaut tumble onto the floor, moaning in agony. "Are you okay?"

"Ugh, I'll be okay. I just landed on my shoulder. Hurry up!" Jaut groaned.

Leaping onto a stone sticking out from the wall, Linx jumped from rock to rock until she met them below. "Thank you again for helping us."

"You're welcome," the woman whispered as she disappeared before them. "Keep moving. They're coming."

"Wait! Where'd you go?" Linx looked over at Jaut to see if he knew where the woman went. "Hello? Where are you? I don't even know your name!"

Shrugging his shoulders, he glanced around quickly, but nothing stood out. As his attention focused above their heads, several antennae poked over the edge of the tunnel. Standing against the wall, Jaut said, "Oh, no. Linx!"

"What?"

"Look up!"

One after another, giant bees poured into the tunnel, charging down to identify whether they had intruders or not. As they crawled quickly in his direction, Jaut felt a rush of sweat coat his back. His breath shortened as he tried to figure out what to do. Every inch of his body wanted him to run. But he found the longer he stood there, the harder it became to convince his brain to move.

Shaking his arm violently, Linx's breath sounded heavier as the swarm of bees moved in closer. "Jaut! Jaut, what should we do?"

Jaut remained stuck in his head. If only he could find a way to verbalize what he wanted to say.

"Jaut! Why are you not answering me? Answer me!" Linx couldn't understand why he wouldn't say a word. Grabbing his face, she looked into his eyes to see that he was trapped within himself.

His mind wandered to a time long ago. Resting on a grassy hill as a child, his fingers combed the blades of the vegetation while quietly singing a nursery rhyme to himself. Admiring the clouds gliding across the sky, Jaut stretched on the ground. Within an instant, he rolled down the hill, giggling with delight as his body gained speed.

"Jaut! Slow down!" a young male shouted from the top of the hill. "You're going to hit a tree!"

Acknowledging his cue to stop, Jaut braced himself by stiffening his body and desperately grabbing at the land. Skinning his knee on a pile of twigs, he firmly gripped the earth. As his fingers sank into the ground, his index finger hooked inside a dirt hole. Abruptly halting his body, Jaut pulled himself up on his hands and knees while the weight of his head shifted from one side to another. The world spun around him. Once his vision finally focused on the ground, he glanced at some erratic movement near the hole. A distinct and high-pitched buzzing grew louder as a chaotic cloud swarmed around his head. Within seconds, dozens of yellow jacket wasps covered Jaut's chest and face.

Burning needles repeatedly stabbed his body as he screamed in agony. Slapping his cheeks and swatting his arms, countless wasps scraped against his stomach and chest while flying up the front of his shirt. With no other option, he ran for his life toward a nearby small pond. The intense pain traveled down to his legs as the aggressive wasps relentlessly stung him.

"Jaut, keep running! Don't go in the water!" Jaut's friend warned.

With the buzzing sound drowning out his friend, Jaut headed for the only relief he could see. Jumping into the pond, he held his breath for roughly forty seconds before floating back to the surface. As he slowly raised his face, exposing his nose and lips out of the water, several yellow jackets pierced any skin they could come in contact with. He held his breath and brought his head below the surface level again. After waiting another minute, his head emerged from the water, hoping the swarm had left. As soon as his skin made contact with the air, he was tortured by stingers penetrating his skin. Diving back down into the water, Jaut felt he had no choice other than to swim toward the opposite edge of the pond. Every time he lifted his head to welcome a breath of fresh air, a handful of wasps mercilessly attacked his face. Once his fingers touched the shoreline of the pond, Jaut gathered his strength to bolt home as quickly as he could.

Focusing on the pitter-patter of his feet, he didn't know if he had the energy to make it home. The violent swarm trickled down for the next half-mile, sending him off with a handful more jabs before turning back around. As he heard the buzzing die off, Jaut collapsed on the side of the road.

CHAPTER 19

"Jaut!" Linx vigorously shook him. "Snap out of it! You must focus on getting out of here."

She noticed his eyes looking right through her before squeezing shut. Peering over her shoulder, the bees rushed closer. Unsure of what to do, she raised her hand toward them.

The woman appeared in front of Linx. "Don't!"

"What am I supposed to do? I can't risk Jaut being attacked!"

"If you want them to trust you, you must trust them."

"I'm sorry. It's not worth the risk." Linx formed a thick barrier between herself and the bees.

Shaking her head, the woman vanished once again, leaving Linx to figure out an exit strategy. Grabbing Jaut's shoulders, she noticed his eyes finally lock onto hers. Slightly dazed, he stood up and stumbled down the tunnel as the bees slammed against the barrier.

"I thought we weren't supposed to have a shield up," Jaut shouted over his shoulder.

Throwing her hands into the air, Linx's face tinted red. "What did you expect me to do? You wouldn't move!"

"Look, I don't know what happened. This . . . all of this reminded me of something that happened when I was a kid. But once I thought about the memory, I was stuck in it. So strange."

Shrugging off his comment, Linx continued through the tunnel. "I'm not sure how much time we have left. I hope it stays, but I don't know their strength."

"All right. Let's just move."

Sprinting down the tunnel, the main path caught their attention as it split into three. The path to the right had a slow incline layered with thick cobwebs. The middle path ahead remained flat, and the option to the left had a steep decline while surrounded by damp walls.

Cursing under his breath, Jaut vigorously rubbed his face as his eyes bounced to each tunnel. "Where do we go now?"

"Left."

"Left? Are you sure?"

Linx nodded and pointed to the right. "We need to choose a path they won't travel. There's no way I'm running through those massive webs, and if water makes their wings heavy like mine, it seems risky for them to go down the left path. Let's go left!"

"Are you sure?"

"Yes."

"All right."

Sprinting into the tunnel, the buzzing intensified behind them.

"Go! Go! Go!" Jaut frantically nudged Linx to move faster.

"Look, I'm trying!"

Water dripped from the tunnel walls, puddling along the edges of the path. Their shoes lightly splashed from the ground as they sprinted through the winding tunnel. Linx looked over toward Jaut. Sweat dripped from his forehead, and his chest rose and dropped rapidly. Honestly, she had never seen him in this state before. Releasing a heavy breath, they continued onward.

After several moments, Jaut turned his head toward Linx. His distraught look resembled that of a scared child. "Do you think we lost them?"

"I'm not sure." Linx didn't know how to respond. Jaut knew about these bees as much as she did, which wasn't much at all. Seeing his frown sink deeper into his face, Linx tried to raise his spirits. "I hope so. They would've been right behind us if they were still following."

His face lightened up, and the heavy frown lifted to display a slight smirk of appreciation. In his mind, anywhere they went from here was better than being surrounded by a suffocating swarm of bees. They trudged farther down the tunnel, and relief gradually overcame them when no buzzing approached during their walk.

The path dragged on for what seemed to be a lifetime. Slowly, the ground became squishier, suctioning their feet with each footstep. Linx grunted as she pulled her foot out of the mud. "This is disgusting."

"Beats whatever our fate was with the bees." Jaut shrugged his shoulders, glancing around them.

Faint streams of light trickled over distant, thin trees and dark vegetation, leading up to their feet. Several feet away, swampy waters crawled over a smooth boulder. A foul smell lingered, exhibiting a rotten odor that comfortably sat over the land and water. A couple of insects chirped sporadically beyond a large rock, while something in the water plopped and swished closer to the duo. Scanning the area, the dim lighting and dull green vegetation made the view hard to see at first.

Linx squinted her eyes. "That's weird. Do you see anyone around here? I only see grass, trees, and some mucky ground."

"Nope. It's too dark to tell for sure, though."

"Well, something else is here, and I have no idea where to look."

"Just keep going."

"No kidding! I'm not planning on putting up a tent."

"Linx, I'm not trying to be bossy. I just don't want to be here long enough to find out what lives or hunts in this area."

"Me neither!"

When they reached the next tree, Jaut's fingers firmly gripped a branch as he focused on a tiny light in the distance. "I'm afraid to get hopeful, but I wonder if that's an exit."

"Really? Where?" Linx stood on her tippy toes, looking over the end of Jaut's finger.

"Do you see it?"

"Yeah, but are you sure?"

"No. I'm not completely sure, but I hope so."

A nearby splash, followed by three more, immediately made the hair on their skin stand tall. Turning toward each other, Linx and Jaut held the air in their lungs. Slowly blinking to adjust their eyes, their legs locked as deep grunts circled around them. Linx held out her arms, swirling her hands to form a protection bubble. As she pushed forward, nothing. Dumbfounded, Linx tried again, incorporating as much energy as possible and—nothing.

"Wha—"

Jaut interrupted, "If we are near the opening, maybe we can't utilize our magic."

Linx's shoulders dropped as a frown quickly formed. "What are we going to do?"

"I don't know," he whispered.

As the grunting approached closer, Linx's stomach felt as though it was rolling into itself, almost tying into a knot. Prickles crawled past her lungs and heart, racing up her throat. Peering to her side, she noticed Jaut's fingertips aggressively rubbing against his thumb. Swallowing the anxiety, Linx inhaled a full breath and calmly reached for his hand. Swiftly turning to her, Jaut's furrowed brows relaxed. Fire burned in her eyes, inspiring the hope that they might make it out alive.

"On three, I say we run like hell toward the light. I have a feeling we might be close to getting out of here," Jaut whispered.

With a confident smile, Linx gave a sharp nod. "I'm ready when you are."

Pulling his shoulders back and bending his legs, Jaut quietly said, "One."

Another growl vibrated the tiny hairs from the right side of her shoulder over to her left.

"Two."

Linx felt her hair clinging to her damp neck as sweat dripped from her hairline. Despite trying to calm her mind, she jumped when a twig snapped behind them. "What was that?"

"Three!"

Instantly, thuds pounded on the ground, and something

clawed at the mud and rock close behind. Jaut and Linx bolted toward the distant light. Bellowing sounds ripped through the air, threatening death at any slipup. They sank deep into the ground with each step, squishing into the mud.

"Go! Go! Go!" Jaut shouted.

Linx pushed herself to run as quickly as she could, slowly reaching the lead. Jaut maintained a distance not too far behind her, watching Linx's hair toss from side to side while they desperately hurried to find safety. The clingy mud wore down their energy as it tried to hold them in place.

Peeking over at Jaut, Linx couldn't see anything chasing them. "I don't see anything behind us. Which way should we go?"

"Up . . . the hill," Jaut said, losing his breath.

Veering left, Linx bounded up a hill of dirt and rocks. As a rock shifted beneath her feet, she held out her arms to hold her balance. "Careful."

Rushing up several boulders, they desperately crawled to the top of the rocky hill before turning around to see long, pointed, snapping jaws. Three hungry reptiles impatiently circled the base, lamely pulling themselves up on jagged rocks. As the faint light barely illuminated the inside of the cave, Linx could see that they had double rows of teeth lining their narrow mouths, poking out near their snouts. Rough scales and dark leather covered their bodies, measuring four times the size of Jaut in length. The deep bellows emitted through their ravenous chops translated perfectly to Linx as to what their fates would be. Their misery and the emptiness growing in their stomachs meant there was no doubt they would sacrifice anything to eat.

"I feared what was following us was big, but I could not have imagined this," Linx said.

"Deinoses."

"Huh?" Linx scratched the back of her head.

"An attack from a deinos is a brutal end to suffer." Jaut's eyes analyzed the distance between them, the deinoses, and the distant light. "We are close to the exit, Linny."

"Are you sure?"

"Yes, I am familiar with the area where deinoses commonly frequent. The thing is they are quick on land and water. Even if we get out of the cave, they can still chase us for quite a distance."

"What should we do? Where should we go?"

"With them chasing us, and the guards roaming, our best bet would be to get high into a tree—or an ecknid."

Relieved, Linx relaxed her shoulders. "Oh, okay. They can't climb?"

"Oh, they can!" Jaut said humorously. "They just aren't as quick going up."

Rolling her shoulders backward, Linx pressed her lips firmly together. As they briefly watched the deinoses pathetically nip at each other while slipping off the rocks, Jaut and Linx gathered energy before fleeing the cave. They observed the light fade as darkness soon set in.

"All right, so we have a decision to make. We can either bolt out now or wait."

Linx furrowed her brows. "Huh? Why the heck would we wait?"

"Linny," Jaut said with a cheeky grin, "we think it's hard now. Can you imagine running from these big guys after the wave drained your powers and energy?"

"Oh, no! You're right. I didn't even think about that. How long do you think we have before the pulse?"

"I'm not sure. I think it's getting close."

"Do you think we can survive long enough to make a run for it afterward?"

The deinoses continued struggled to climb the rocky hill, becoming more infuriated every time one slid off the rocks and landed on another.

Jaut nodded. "It seems like we should be okay for a little bit. We'll need to think quick once we leave. I'm not looking to become dinner."

Crouching close to the ground, Linx rocked her body back to sit down and rest her legs. Within a few moments, Jaut joined her. Being so close to escaping, their bodies transitioned from anxiety flooding their arms and legs to fatigue. The lack of food was taking a toll on their energy, so Jaut pulled out his canteen and passed it to Linx.

"Thank you. I'm starving and so thirsty."

He gave a slight smile and said, "I know. Hopefully, once we get out, we can meet with some of my friends and get some food in us."

"Friends? You have friends?" Linx teased.

"Yeah. Hard to believe, right?" Jaut chuckled.

"I'm joking. But I can say that a fresh meal sounds amazing right now."

They rested in silence for a bit, reflecting on their journey thus far. Nothing was promised, but Linx felt confident in her adventure while partnered with Jaut. Unfortunately, though, tension grew in her stomach as time went on.

"I just want to get out of here!" Linx said.

Jaut sighed. "I know. Hopefully, we can move soon."

"Are those things still down there?"

"Huh? The deinoses?"

"Yeah."

Looking over the edge of the rocky hill, he could only see one angrily guarding the base. "Um, I only see one. I'm not sure where the others went. They probably gave up to hunt something else."

"I'm not buying it." Linx adamantly shook her head.

Confused, Jaut asked, "What do you mean?"

"There's no way they left. They have to be waiting for us."

"Oh, yeah?"

"Jaut! What food have you seen since we've been here? There's nothing roaming around—besides us!"

"Look, I'm not saying you're wrong."

Scanning their surroundings continuously, they noticed the light in the distance grow dark. Linx slowly stood up. "Jaut, clearly I want to wait so our powers don't drain, but we won't have any light to see if it gets too dark. I think we should go now."

"All right. I'm good, if you are."

"Yeah, let's go."

Stepping to the edge, they couldn't see any deinoses nearby. Quickly, they sped down the shifting rocks toward the dimming light. It felt like an impossible mission as the stream of light reaching the cave was almost nonexistent. As they jumped off the last rock connected to the hill, their feet immediately sank into the soft ground again. The squishing sounds amplified in Linx's ears with every step. Thoughts raced through her mind. *There is no way that a deinos can't hear us!*

Their visibility continued to fade—leaving their destiny in the hands of time. Linx pressed on while hearing Jaut's heavy breathing behind her. Guilt consumed her as she thought about her speed slowing him down.

"You're quicker than me. Just go in front! I'll try to keep up."

"There's no way that I would leave you behind. Just keep going!"

The thick mud intensified the situation, refusing to let them leave. Linx yanked her legs, one by one, as the mud level rose. As they struggled, a deep bellow echoed off of the neighboring water. Whipping her head around rapidly, her eyes grew wide. A blanket of sweat covered Linx's neck and back while she frantically pulled her legs out of the mud, trying to find firmer land.

"We've got company," Jaut said quietly.

"I know! I heard it back there."

Pointing in the water, Jaut said, "No, not that one. Look!"

Following the direction of Jaut's finger, any courage that flowed in Linx's body sank to her feet. Four pairs of bright green eyes poked out from underneath the water. The deinoses swiftly swam toward their prey. Spikes from their long tails sliced the water.

"We have to hurry. They are nocturnal, so they'll have an advantage soon."

Linx looked at him with disdain. "Why didn't you mention that before?"

Shaking his head, he said, "I don't know. Just go!"

With brief, light breaths, Linx pushed herself to rapidly march through the mud. "I hope we can make it."

"We will! Keep going!" Jaut said as he yanked his left foot into the air.

Linx glanced into the water. She could almost see the deinoses smile at her. The corners of their mouths curled to form an eerie grin. Their razored teeth promised a gruesome experience if she didn't run quick enough. Once she found her footing, she rhythmically lumped herself from one side to another, shifting her weight enough to lift each foot. After several more steps, her legs burned from her calves to her thighs. Even her back ached from the workout.

"You okay?" Jaut asked.

"Yes. I'm starving, and this is exhausting. I don't know if I can make it," she said, tugging on her right knee.

"Stay focused, Linny."

Glaring at him, she shook her head and then rolled her eyes.

He smiled before saying, "We're so close. You can do it."

"I know. It feels like we've been walking forever because of this stupid mud."

"Well, if you want a shorter route, you can try going in the water."

"Yeah, a shorter route to die. Can you see them behind us? Are they close? I can't see any now after they got out of the water." She squinted her eyes, scanning the water.

"Only two. They're a ways back there, but they seem determined."

Her furrowed brows relaxed when her eyes focused on the fading light. "I think you were right, Jaut! This appears to be an exit out of the cave!"

"Let's hope we can get out before they catch up."

Luckily, the mud slowed two deinoses enough that Linx and Jaut had a comfortable lead. Although their grunts sent a chill up her spine, she knew they had a solid chance of escaping. Within several steps, Linx reached the edge of the cave. Turning around, she saw Jaut was still being stalked by the hungry reptiles.

"Come on! Come on!" Linx shouted.

"I'm good. Don't worry."

As the words left his mouth, the deinoses realized they wouldn't catch their prey, so they plopped back into the water and swam quickly toward Jaut's location. The swishing in the water intensified, causing some doubt in Linx's mind. She thought he could make it—but feared their advantage in the water might change that. Linx screamed from outside of the cave, "Hurry, Jaut!"

Finally, extending his arm out to a nearby branch, he pulled himself out of the mud. Kneeling on the dirt momentarily, his wobbly legs trembled from the strenuous journey.

"We've got to find somewhere safe," Linx said, holding out her hand for Jaut to grab.

Clasping his fingers around her hand, Jaut brought himself to his feet. Weakened from no food and constant activity, their heads felt like everything was spinning.

He said, "There! Head for that tree. We can climb up and hop over to that neighboring branch. Hopefully, it's enough to discourage them from following us anymore."

Sprinting through the woods, they passed through several thorny bushes, ripping at their clothes, before reaching the biggest tree. To their surprise, some muddy grounds spread from the cave through a dip in the woods, surrounding several close trees.

As Linx observed the area of mud around the tree, she shouted, "You've got to be kidding me!"

"Just go! We don't have a choice."

Pushing through more thorns, vines, and bushes, they sank into the mud, leading to the tree's base. Linx successfully ripped the vines off her clothing, but she noticed Jaut was entangled in a thick one that clung to his legs, digging its thorns deep through the material and into his skin.

"Do you need help?" Linx asked, igniting a flame in her hand.

"Um, I should be okay," he said, fidgeting with the painful plant.

When Linx turned to help free Jaut, the wave vibrated through the lands, causing both to fall to their knees.

"No! No!" Jaut yelled.

"Oh, no! I hoped we missed it."

Jaut tensed his fists, trying to focus on getting to safety. "Where are the deinoses?"

"Uh . . . I don't know." Linx searched around until she spotted them. "We have a little distance. They are exiting the cave."

"No!"

"What?"

"Linx!" Jaut struggled to say. "They didn't get hit by the wave. They're at full strength."

Her jaw dropped. "Oh, no. Come on! Let's go!"

"I'm trying! I'm stuck, though. The vine is caught around my leg and ankle under the mud."

Hobbling toward him, she tried forcing all her energy into her hand. If she could blast the vine, he could try pulling his leg out of the mud. Just moving in the mud was proving to be a difficult task after the wave. "I'm coming, Jaut!"

"Don't worry about me! Go! You need to get somewhere safe."

"I'm not leaving you!" Linx said.

Jaut weakly tugged at the vine, trying to snap it with no luck. The sharp thorns pierced his hands each time he gripped it. Looking up to see Linx wrestle her legs out of the mud, he heard the deinoses gaining on them. "Linx, please go!"

Ignoring his requests, she eagerly ventured on, funneling her power into her hand. Her feet felt like stone as minimal energy circulated throughout her legs. Once close enough, she motioned her hand forward, commanding a ball of energy to break the vine connected to Jaut. As her hand fell, so did her body, landing in a lump on the ground.

"Linx!" Jaut broke free from the vine, rushing to lift Linx before the deinoses reached them.

He slid his arm under Linx's legs, and while resting her head against his chest, Jaut raised her from the ground. Sloshing from side to side, his heart raced as he approached the tree. Jaut felt the deinoses close by, so he hoisted Linx over his shoulder and tried climbing quickly. With her hair and the cape draping down Jaut's back, the deinoses leaped off the ground, snapping at anything they could. Digging their nails into the bark, they fixated on Jaut, pursuing him up the tree.

With a swift snap of its long jaw, a deinoses latched onto the cape adhered to Linx's back. She moaned in sheer agony as the creature attempted to forcefully yank the cape from her skin. Jaut wrapped his free arm around a branch to secure himself on the tree. As his grip on Linx began to fail, the bushes viciously rustled just a few trees away.

Although the energy had been drained from her body, Linx screamed from the pressure of the deinos pulling on her back. Pain surged through her body, causing fear she'd be torn in half from the weight tugging down on the cape. In a fit of rage, the deinos spun its head, twisting the cape. Unsure of what to do, Jaut held onto Linx for dear life. The deinos's back foot slipped, sending it falling to the ground—and taking Poba's cape as its prize. The two creatures gnawed on the cape, ripping it out of each other's mouths.

"Ah!" Linx shrieked as blood oozed from her back, dripping onto the ground.

As the deinoses fought over who would eat the exotic snack, several droplets of Linx's blood fell, distracting one deinos away from the cape. Looking up, the deinos began the pursuit of its larger meal while the other deinos ran off, taking its reward.

Witnessing the predator climbing up the tree, Linx squirmed in Jaut's arms. Her words faded into the air as she attempted to yell, "Go!"

The deinos crawled just below Linx's foot and proudly opened its mouth. Right as it lifted its head and outstretched its neck, she heard a familiar voice.

"Hold on, my lady!"

CHAPTER 20

Delirious and disoriented from blood loss, Linx turned her head to see something vaguely moving in the distance. Feebly bouncing out of the woods, Pygo's puffy body was a sight for sore eyes.

"I thought I heard you scream! I've been searching all over for you!" Pygo's voice echoed in the woods.

Dread swept down Linx's neck to the base of her spine. Her eyes locked with Jaut's as she tried to find words.

"Relax. You'll be fine. I promise," he whispered.

"I'm not worried about me. Pygo will be shredded!" Linx shouted. "Pygo, watch out!"

Pygo quickly approached while Jaut braced their weight against the tree. Each thump from his body on the ground sent prickles surging through her body. Once close enough, he forced his body high into the air and fell with a boom, sending the deinos flying off the tree.

Landing next to her feet, Pygo looked into her eyes. "Is everything all right? Oh!"

Blood poured over her back from the open wound that spanned from one shoulder blade to the other.

Rubbing her face, she focused on the ground behind him. "Yes . . . I'm glad you found us."

Squinting his eyes and staring deep into her soul, Pygo paused before turning to look behind himself. "We best find a place to hide. The guards will be out soon."

Sliding down from the tree, Jaut carefully walked Linx over to dry land, gently sitting her down to assess her injury.

Jaut nervously asked, "Where should we go? She's bleeding pretty bad. Have you seen anyone patrolling yet?"

"No, not yet. I'm hoping we can find a safe spot. I heard guards mention that they wanted to bring back some creatures." Pygo shuddered.

Linx shrugged her shoulders before wincing from the pain. "Well, maybe we should consider taking them up on their offer."

Pygo viscously shook his head from side to side.

"Are you mad?" Jaut said. "What can possibly be going through your head to make you think that would be a good idea?"

"Well . . . we needed to go to Crystal Woods anyway, correct? This would just shorten the wait."

Jaut slammed the palm of his hand against his forehead. "I don't believe this. We need to get you taken care of before worrying about that."

"What are you two talking about?" Pygo glanced from Linx over to Jaut.

With a stroke of bad luck, a twig snapped near the group. They looked at each other in horror—vulnerable and exhausted. Immediately, Jaut bent down to scoop up Linx in his arms. Before he stood, he found himself eye to eye with big, yellow eyes and tiny, pointed ears.

"Put her down." The creature grinned as Jaut hoisted Linx off the ground.

Jaut clenched his jaw. "You're out of your bloody mind if you think I'm going to put her down."

Flicking its razored nails into the air, the creature raised its claw, threatening to slash Jaut.

"I'm not afraid of you," Jaut said, attempting to lift Linx.

"What . . . is going on? Who are you talking to?" Linx asked, looking at the ground.

Her heart dropped as her gaze met the goblin's, and her breathing rapidly increased. Tensing her body, Jaut knew he had to protect her. Pygo approached the demonic goblin with fire in his eyes. Licking his long teeth, he had to act quickly.

Sparkles danced in its irises as it crouched to the ground. Scratching its claws into the dirt, it concocted a salve, mixing mud with the juice from a handpicked plant. "I need to help her."

Skeptical for a moment, Jaut stared at the goblin and then glanced at Pygo. Surprisingly, Pygo appeared impressed by the goblin. Jaut asked, "Should I trust 'em?"

"I don't know what other option we have. It's getting dark, and the poor thing is bleeding badly. Anything might track the blood, no matter where we bring her."

Desperate to help her, Jaut rested Linx on the firm ground. Without breaking eye contact with the goblin, he warned, "If you do anything to hurt her, I will kill you myself."

Unfazed, the goblin grinned, dipping its claws into the mixture. As it carefully approached Linx, it peered in Jaut's direction. Reaching its sharp claws near the nape of her neck, the goblin generously smeared the salve over her wound. Linx hissed from the initial pain of the application and dug her hand into the dirt, but her pain eased as it set in. Stepping back, the goblin stood in place, observing the status of her injury.

Shortly, her wound stopped bleeding, and she sat up. "Thank you."

The goblin bowed without uttering a word.

Gaining some strength, she whispered, "Can I ask you something?"

Amused by her tone, the goblin stood in place, waiting for her following words.

"Do you know anything about a ring stolen from Pangotha or a girl named Zalia?" she asked bluntly.

Linx's bold and dangerous question shocked Jaut. "What are you doing?"

"What? The goblins serve Carter—who is the king of Crystal Woods. If anyone might know, it'd be them." Linx shrugged her shoulders.

Frustrated, Jaut shook his head. "But you can't just outright ask that! You don't know who's listening."

Without a sound, the goblin maintained its devilish grin while backing away from the group before somersaulting into the bushes.

"What was that about?" Jaut's eyes widened.

"Well, it had no idea what I was talking about, or it knew something suspicious."

Jaut laughed. "Way to narrow it down."

Glaring at him, Linx continued, "My guess is that it knows something. Honestly, Carter may have more control over the goblins now. I'm not sure what to think."

"Well, now that you tipped them off, we must get moving. Who knows where it's going—probably to go warn everyone in Crystal Woods."

"Look, I'm sorry. I thought it was worth a shot." Linx rolled her head to the side, leaning it against her shoulder.

Hopping over near Linx, Pygo asked, "Can someone please explain what I missed?"

Jaut sheepishly said, "Linx and I made it through the caves and found the Gemenii."

An infectious smile spread over Pygo's face. "Are you serious?"

"Yes! We finally found the Gemenii," Linx said. "I couldn't believe it, Pygo."

"Well? What did they say?"

Sighing, Linx said, "I guess the guards kidnapped a child named Zalia after killing her caregiver. They had her lead them to the Gemenii, and they stole a sacred ring. The Gemenii believes they came from Crystal Woods. I promised to help bring her back home and locate the ring as well. Hopefully, we can put an end to the draining pulse that wrecks the land."

"That's wonderful you agreed to help," Pygo said.

Jaut impatiently said, "For now, though, we have other things to worry about—including finding a spot to hide and sleep. Linx, how is your back feeling? I don't see any more blood dripping. It seems like that little devil knew what it was doing."

Standing herself up, she grunted as her hair tickled the skin on her sore back. "It feels like it's helping a little."

"Let me see your back," Jaut requested.

Pushing her hair to the side, he saw the mud had successfully coated the open wound and effectively sealed it up. Fascinated by the goblin's handcrafted dressing, he wondered what else the goblin knew. It was strange that such a feral creature would know medicinal treatments and apply them in such a gentle manner. Jaut noticed that darkness was quickly engulfing the woods, swallowing the trees and creatures within it.

"Where should we go?" Linx asked, slightly nervous that a deinos would return from the cave.

"I think I know how to get to my friend's campsite from here. They will definitely have hot food—they always do!" Jaut teased.

Linx's stomach rumbled on cue. It felt like her stomach acid was burning a hole through its lining. Various foods filled her thoughts as she envisioned herself binging on anything placed in front of her face. "Let's go!"

"Can you walk?" Jaut compassionately asked.

"Uh, yeah. I'll be fine."

Shaking his head, he lethargically approached her while holding out his arms, offering to carry her.

"Enough! Just go. I'll be fine to walk."

"Okay, suit yourself. Follow me." Jaut nodded in the direction of their route. Looking back, he noticed Pygo uncomfortably making his way ahead. "Come on, puffball."

"You best watch your tone."

Spinning around, Jaut held his finger over his lips. Linx wrinkled her forehead as she stared at Jaut.

A high-pitched male voice yelled, "Shh! I heard someone over there!"

"You heard someone? I didn't hear anyone! You're going nuts. The boss is going to dispose of you once he knows the game that you're trying to pull," a second voice responded.

"What the hell are you complaining about?"

"I'm not an idiot! Every time we approach this area, you make up some reason to go near the cave! The boss said that no one is allowed in the caves! He doesn't want anyone looking for the Gemenii. How many times do they have to tell you that?"

"Look, make jokes. At least I'm not the baby afraid to do his job!"

"Afraid to do my job? I ain't bloody afraid to do my job! I'm tired of getting stuck with you! Out of all these trips, you never do anything. I'm always stuck killin' or capturing the enemy. And what do you do? Nothing!" said the second guard.

Rolling his eyes, Jaut kept his finger on his lips while he stared at Linx and Pygo. Within that moment, he swiftly camouflaged in front of a tree. Linx attempted to follow Jaut's path with her eyes, but he was nowhere to be seen. As Pygo awaited the plan, he stood silent in the wake of the chaos before him.

The second guard complained, "I don't see anything. Let's go!"

"No way! I heard something, I tell ya!"

They quietly stood beside one another, turning their heads in opposite directions. In a matter of seconds, Linx witnessed their heads tip away and forcefully slam into each other.

The second guard rubbed his head. "Ah! You fool, what was that for?"

"Huh? That wasn't my fault! What was that?"

While his hand trembled vigorously, the first guard held a sword in the air. Swinging his fists frantically, the other spun around to see what had attacked them. Without revealing himself, Jaut kicked one guard over and elbowed the other, grabbing his sword in the process.

Stumbling to stand, the first guard said, "Show yourself, you coward!"

In a smooth motion, Jaut grabbed his head and sliced his throat. The guard's body promptly dropped to the ground and sent the other guard fleeing for his life. Linx could now see Jaut standing over the body while wiping his forehead.

"That was incredible," Linx whispered.

"I'm not done yet. I'll be right back."

Pygo anxiously hopped a few steps toward Jaut. "Do you need help?"

"No. Stay with Linx." Jaut vanished into the dark abyss.

As they waited for Jaut's return, Linx shuffled over to a dry area to rest. Cautiously kneeling to the ground, she babied her back to prevent further injury. Pygo rushed over to check on her.

"My lady—" Pygo paused.

"Yes?"

"I just can't understand how I didn't know about a missing girl. I don't recall anyone mentioning a stolen ring either."

Linx shrugged. "I'm not sure why it was kept a secret. But the Gemenii mentioned that a ring and a girl were taken from Pangotha and brought to Crystal Woods. Now, we must find them and rightfully bring them home. It's the last thing I want to do, but I have no choice. How do I leave a girl in the hands of evil monsters that plan to crush a land and its people?"

Pygo remained silent as he absorbed what she explained. As he opened his mouth, the guard's skin-crawling pleas and screams echoed throughout the woods before a slash and ting. Linx and Pygo raised their eyebrows as they stared at each other. A vigorous twisting in Linx's stomach threatened to spew out every bit of water that Jaut had given her earlier. Her body trembled as the guard's cries transformed into Mr. Nelson's screams, playing like a record in her mind.

"Well, it was either him or us!" Pygo grinned.

Speechless by Pygo's nonchalant attitude, Linx gently blinked and shook her head. "I guess I should be unfazed by now. So many things happen each day, yet I am still paralyzed by the sound of death. You know . . . the last shrill cry for help. The kind where you envision their vocal cords shredding themselves in a desperate attempt at mercy. Despite knowing that no one could logically save them, they shout out to the universe in hopes of a miracle. It's those moments that cause the hairs on my skin to raise and my stomach to turn. I don't know if that will ever change."

Linx lowered her head, staring at a few light speckles on the dark ground until they disappeared into the night. Pygo's smile transformed into a solemn line, absorbing the message of Linx's words.

"My dear, it's not that I've ever forgotten empathy or the feeling of fear, but if I want to survive, I can't ever let my mind slip to a place like that. What good will injecting a lethal amount of stress into my mind do?"

Without looking up, Linx silently sat waiting for Pygo to continue as rustling in the distance approached.

"Exactly—nothing. What it will do is make me question my actions long enough to get me killed. Just because you are forced to do something that is coined evil does not always make you bad. You are a bright soul, Linx. Remember, not everyone cares like you do. Some, just like who these men follow, actually fancy fear and death. They take solace in knowing they have enough power to make others crumble in their most vulnerable moments—physically or mentally. Don't ever give anyone that power."

Raising her eyes to meet his, Linx said, "Do you ever think about your life before this?"

As he released a sigh from his stressed little body, Pygo frowned. "Every single day."

Before she could ask more, Jaut appeared out of the corner of her eye, dragging the guard's heavy armor through a bush. In his other hand, he swung the helmet with every step. Dropping the equipment on the ground, it clanked and tinged in a pile in front of Linx.

Jaut panted, pulling back his shoulders and puffing out his chest. "Will this fit you?"

Startled, Linx asked, "Huh? What are you talking about?"

"I don't know about you, but I'm not sure if I can muster enough energy for another fight. We have quite some distance to go, and it'll be safer if we disguise ourselves. Can you fit into this suit?"

Linx shrugged. "I'm not sure. Maybe, I guess."

"I chased him down since he appeared a tad smaller than that other idiot," Jaut said, nodding toward the first guard slumped on the ground in a puddle of blood.

Linx walked up to the suit and winced while weakly lifting the armor. Blood slowly dripped from a corner, splattering on her boot. "Eh, Jaut. I don't know if I want to wear this."

Jaut yanked the armor off of the nearby guard. "What are you talking about? It's a safe option, so we can travel through the woods. No one would even notice that it's us."

"What about me?" Pygo questioned. "I don't have armor."

Jaut smirked. "Well . . ."

"Well, what?"

"Honestly, I figured that you'd essentially act as our captive."

"Captive? Captive? What kind of garbage is this?" Pygo shouted.

"Hold on! Look, it's a perfectly logical plan. Linx and I would wear the armor, disguising ourselves like the guards, and you would pretend to be our captive." Jaut shrugged. "It's not ideal, but it's a great plan—if I do say so myself."

"That is the stupidest idea I've ever heard! I'm not going to pretend to be a prisoner walking through these woods!"

"Do you have a better plan?"

Flustered, Pygo opened his mouth but didn't know what to say. Looking at Linx's repulsed face, he hoped she would quickly step in to offer another option.

"I guess not," Jaut quickly said.

Linx sighed. "Jaut, I'm not putting this on. My energy is wiped out, and I'm so hungry. There's no way I can walk around in this thing."

"Okay, suit yourself. That's the exact reason why I'm choosing to wear it," he said, slipping into the armor.

A thick branch or log cracked in the distance—followed by a howl from a distressed animal. Screams and the sharp sound of nails scratching metal sent chills across Linx's arms.

"Fine. But I want to note that this is disgusting."

"Linx, I'm not forcing you to do anything. I just want to get this on so we can go find some food."

Linx grunted as she tried turning the armor around. "I don't know how to get this on."

"I'll help you in a second."

While they rushed to dress in the uniforms, Pygo attempted to keep guard despite the lack of light. The bushes and tree leaves rustled as a light wind brushed past their faces. "I'm afraid that little beast will jump out again."

"I think it's gone—at least, I hope so," Jaut whispered.

Once they donned the suits, they quietly headed onto a close path. The scarce light from the night sky peered through the treetops, illuminating just enough to see the route. Linx and Jaut awkwardly walked on each side of Pygo. The oversized suit made it difficult for Linx to move naturally, so she wobbled from one side to another.

"Yeah, there's no way the guards will figure out you're imposters." Pygo rolled his eyes as he bounced along.

"Enough already, you ungrateful puffball! You offered no other idea. You're more than welcome to travel on your own if you don't like this plan!" Jaut snapped. "Otherwise, be quiet!"

"Oh, calm down. I'm not going anywhere. I just wanted to let you know how silly you both look before some guard does. If you want to convince them, you better be able to convince me."

Linx's chest burned while she heavily panted within the suit. Sweat glazed over her body, and humid air surged throughout the armor. "I'm trying to move the best I can. I don't feel like I can make it much farther."

"Keep going, Linny! We'll be there soon."

"Linny?" Pygo questioned.

Linx whispered, "It's a long story."

Side-eyeing them both, Pygo miserably hopped forward. What choice did he have at this point anyway? All of them had no energy to waste, let alone attempt to travel by themselves.

"How much farther do we have to go? I feel like I'm going to be sick. I wish I had enough power to transport us, but I—" Linx collapsed onto the ground.

"Linx? Oh! No, no, no!" Pygo rushed over to her side. "Jaut, you fool! This is all your fault!"

Without a second thought, Jaut scrambled over to join Pygo. "Let's get the gear off of her so she can breathe."

"She shouldn't have put it on in the first place!" Pygo shouted. "I told you it was a ridiculous idea."

Reaching for her helmet, Jaut heard stomping behind them. "What was that?"

"Huh? What are you talking about?"

"You don't hear that?"

"No," Pygo whispered.

Waiting to hear any other movement in the woods, Jaut contemplated what to do. He knew Linx needed assistance and had to be freed from the armor. But the armor was the only thing at this point protecting her from an attack.

"Well? Get it off of her!"

"Shh!" Jaut hushed Pygo, holding his finger firmly against his lips.

Distant shouts soon silenced as movement drew closer. Staring into Pygo's giant gaze, Jaut widened his eyes before propping Linx up to sit against a tree. He swiftly tilted her helmet back to pour the remaining drips of water through her dried lips and into her mouth.

"Ugh," Linx weakly moaned.

Jaut knelt beside her, trying to lift her to stand. "Linx! Linx! You must stand up. Someone or something is coming toward us, and we have to get moving."

Pygo shuffled backward while looking in the direction of the noise. "We don't have much time. I don't know what that is. Oh, it's—"

"Hey! You all right there?" a deep male voice shouted.

Startled, Pygo hopped behind Jaut and Linx to hide. Raising his head to see what the commotion was about, Jaut froze before readjusting Linx's helmet. Three armed guards walked into their line of sight. As they approached, one guard pulled a thick rope behind them. Pygo's eyes traced the rope back to a giant net containing a distraught creature soaked in blood and an indistinguishable carcass.

"You good, mate?" the guard holding the rope asked.

"I . . . uh . . . yup! We're okay! Just needed to rest for a minute." Jaut attempted to hide the conspicuous smudges of blood on Linx's helmet and cuirass.

"What happened to that one?" a guard pointed to Linx's disguised body.

"Um, we were attacked by deinoses but got away in time. We just need a minute to gather ourselves."

One guard shouted, "No way!"

"That's unbelievable. Consider yourself lucky to have survived those things," another guard said.

"Hmm." The guard with the rope peered around Jaut to see a puffy creature cowering in the shadows. "What's that ya got over there?"

"What?" Jaut asked.

The group of three guards approached closer. "There's some fuzzy thing behind you."

"Oh, it's nothing. We encountered that pathetic puffball right before the deinoses attacked." Jaut shrugged, trying to play off the situation. "We'll be fine."

"All right." The guard tugged on the rope, causing the creature to wail in pain.

As the guards started to walk by, Jaut avoided eye contact with the creature. He couldn't risk intervening or being seen.

Based on his suspicions, he knew the shredded carcass inside the net was the luckier of the two. Right when he thought they were in the clear, a guard paused. He stomped over to Linx's slumped body, squatting in front of her.

Jaut felt his heart pounding into his throat as he witnessed the guard look closer. He couldn't see what the guard was looking at. Did he realize she wasn't a guard? If so, how? You couldn't see any identifying markings giving her away. Nervously, Jaut held his breath as he watched his ingenious plan potentially crumble. Finally, the guard stood up, waving over the other guard who pulled the net.

"Huh? What is it?" he asked, dragging the net back toward Jaut, Linx, and Pygo.

"He lied to us."

"What do you mean?" Jaut felt pins and needles poking his feet and slowly climbing up his legs.

"They're not okay. There's blood all over 'em."

Jaut saw Pygo lower himself to the ground.

"Come over here, take the fuzzy thing, and put it in your net. These guys need to go back to heal. They don't need to be worrying about collecting the garbage."

"Wait, what?" Jaut forced himself to stand up. "You don't have to worry about that. We'll be fine."

The guard tugged the bag over near Pygo. "Look, we won't rat you out. Plus, I like having pets. It's fun to watch them interact."

"You have to feed pets, ya know," a guard shouted over to him.

"They do eat!" The guard swiftly grabbed Pygo while laughing. "I treat them well by giving them company, and when they get hungry, they can eat each other."

"No!" Jaut shouted.

Confused, the guards looked at him, gripping their swords. "What?"

Jaut could either try saving Pygo with the minimal energy he had or let him go and try rescuing him once they had more power. Feeling helpless, he knew all three would be at risk if he made a big scene now and couldn't fight them all off. The Gemenii made it crystal clear Linx was crucial to saving Pangotha—but at what cost? With defeated eyes, Pygo knew exactly what was going through Jaut's mind. It was too much of a foolish risk for them to try saving Pygo.

Making one last attempt that wouldn't attract suspicion, Jaut offered, "I can take him! I've fought hard so that I could be the one to bring him in."

They all looked at each other and laughed.

"Nah. I need another pet. Mine's lonely." The guard carelessly tossed Pygo into the net. He landed with a thud next to the other creature and the carcass. Thick blood soaked into Pygo's fur, clumping together with the dirt beneath him. He struggled to move within the heavy rope. As the creature growled at Pygo, the guard effortlessly dragged him away.

CHAPTER 21

After witnessing the guards brutally rip Pygo away from the group, pain surged through Jaut's heart while helplessness and guilt sank into his gut. *How could he have let that happen? Why didn't he fight more for him?* As he relentlessly tormented himself with questions surrounding his remorse, Jaut noticed that Linx eventually pulled her legs closer to her body. Sliding her helmet off and tossing it on the ground, he tried fanning air toward her face.

Rubbing her eyes, Linx whispered, "Pygo?"

Silence ruled the conversation as Jaut sat ashamed of his actions. He was happy to see she was okay, but he didn't know how to break the horrific news.

When no response was made, she repeated herself, "Pygo?"

"Linx," Jaut said quietly, "he's not here."

Tightly squeezing her eyes shut and opening them several times, Linx tried adjusting her focus. "Jaut, where's Pygo?"

"Linx—" Jaut hung his head.

"Where is he? Where'd he go? He was just here . . . then everything turned black. Why did he leave?"

"He was taken as a prisoner by three passing guards."

Looking around, Linx asked, "Are you joking?"

"No," Jaut said. "After you fainted, we tried to figure out what to do. Out of nowhere, three guards emerged. It seemed like we'd be okay, but then they saw blood on your armor. Thinking it was yours, they took Pygo and wanted me to get you help. Linx, I feel like a terrible friend. I let him down, and now he may have to pay with his life."

Completely shocked, Linx rested momentarily as the unbelievable story sunk in. "Well, he's still alive, right? Like you saw him leave? That's a good thing! We can find him."

He nodded without missing a beat, sparing her the gruesome details. "We need to get you some food before we do anything else."

"What about Pygo? He can't wait! We need to find him now."

"Linx, you won't be useful to anyone if you are weak. You need food, water, and some rest. We can't forget our promise to the Gemenii."

Rising to her feet, Linx staggered forward for several minutes until she collapsed again. "I can't function properly with this armor on. I need to get it off—now. Can you help me?"

"Yes, but we need to hurry in case anyone sees us. Let's walk over near that dense area of trees and bushes to avoid being spotted."

Walking into a secluded spot in the woods, Linx and Jaut quickly removed their gear and left it hidden in a bush. They quietly covered the gear and marked the area with sticks and rocks in case the armor would be helpful in the future.

"Where do we go from here?" Linx asked.

Pointing ahead, Jaut explained, "I know some people down this way. They can protect and feed us while we're there. We just need to be very careful. The last thing we need is to be followed."

"Okay, sounds good. Show me the way."

Moving as quickly as they could, Linx followed Jaut down a dark, windy path that curved around random large trees, twisting enough to confuse the most skilled adventurer. The night's ebony sky, lightly speckled with dim stars, made the trek even more perplexing as every tree appeared to be the same.

"Are we almost there?" Linx begged.

Brushing his damp hair away from his tired eyes, he said, "Yes, it's just right up here."

The rarely traveled path led to a cavern almost indistinguishable from the rest of the rock wall. As they pushed branches away from their faces, they carefully stepped over thick roots bulging from the soil. Jaut stood in front of the wall, and he slid his hand along the rough surface until he felt a narrow opening that could easily be missed with the naked eye. Slipping inside the slender crevice, he held out his hand for Linx to grab.

"You need to watch your step as we walk. It's unintentionally, yet conveniently, booby-trapped." Jaut shoved a rock with his foot to show a deep hole in the path. "There are a bunch of these, and you need to keep to the right. If you go to the left, you'll wind up sliding down into pits of sharp rocks."

Amazed by the details, Linx curiously asked, "How did you ever figure this out?"

Jaut chuckled. "While I would love to take the credit, some friends showed me the way through this hideout a long time ago."

"Very interesting." Linx's eyes glanced over the jagged rock walls.

While they continued through the tunnel, the dim light soon faded. Linx and Jaut found themselves at a dead end. Holding out her arm, Linx feebly attempted to create light in the palm of her hand. With only a few sparks flickering, Jaut cupped his fingers around her hand, slowly closing it.

"Don't worry about that now. Save your energy," he whispered.

Furrowing her brows, she said, "What are you talking about? There's nowhere for us to go."

"Shh!"

With a soft knock, Jaut tapped his knuckles in a pattern against the rock wall three times. *Tap-tap. Tap.* As he stepped back, dirt crumbled from the ceiling, and the wall rolled to the side, exposing a community that Linx couldn't anticipate. Moving into the giant stone room, countless creatures froze—terrified and confused. Linx admired the massive ceiling. It was so high she could barely make out the ridges above. A stone staircase looped around the room, spiraling up to a balcony. Before Jaut said a word, Linx saw creatures of various sizes and shapes spread throughout the room. Some gathered around tiny campfires, and others kept to themselves in the far corners of the room.

Strolling down the staircase, a slender woman in a green hooded dress asked, "Were you followed?"

Jaut looked toward Linx before returning to the figure. "No."

Holding out her arms to embrace Jaut, the figure breathed a sigh of relief. "Jaut! I'm so glad to see you."

"It's amazing to see you too." Jaut hugged her tightly.

Unsure of what to do, Linx stood uncomfortably, waiting to see where they were going or what they needed to do.

"I was worried when you didn't return for quite some time. We've been losing many creatures to the guards—even some to the shock waves."

The woman pulled her hood off her head, revealing long, dark brown braids and deep brown eyes. Linx was mesmerized by her beauty. She had full red lips and a charming flat nose pierced with a gold septum ring.

Jaut noticed Linx staring and realized he hadn't introduced them. He rubbed the back of his head and smirked. "Oh, I'm so sorry. Linx, this is Kateerah. Kateerah, this is Linx. I met her in the woods with—"

The guilt hit him again—Pygo. Despite trying to push his mind from it temporarily, a vigorous wave of regret crashed into him. His lack of energy, along with gravity, forcefully pulled his body to the ground. Trying to fight the urge to fall, he stumbled toward a nearby rock to sit.

Concerned, Kateerah asked, "Are you okay?"

"Yeah," Jaut said, sadly gazing at Linx and back to Kateerah. "Do you have anything to eat?"

"Oh, yes! We have some berries, bread, and salad over there. I'll go get you some."

"Thank you so much."

Smiling, Kateerah turned to Linx. "Are you hungry? I can grab some food for you as well. You must be starving."

"Yes, please!" Linx nodded eagerly.

"I'll be right back."

Linx watched as Kateerah glided across the floor and heaped generous helpings of food onto their plates. Throughout this, Linx saw that most creatures maintained distance and refused to speak with each other. *That's odd. I wonder if they are suspicious of me?* Linx thought to herself. It was challenging to focus on specific creatures to attempt to read their thoughts. She also didn't want to call attention to herself, so she lightly sighed.

Sitting next to Jaut, Linx nudged him. "Why is no one talking? It's so weird. Are they unhappy that I came with you?"

Shaking his head, Jaut said, "No, it has nothing to do with you at all. They're all terrified of what's going on. On random days, some can be more talkative than others. But this is normal for the Hideout."

"Oh, I didn't realize. That makes sense, though." Linx frowned.

"Yeah, it's devastating what this has done to Pangotha. And, truly, everything dies that leaves this spot. So they go out for maybe a few hours and rush right back. It's the unfortunate souls who are searching for someone, or something, who find themselves killed or kidnapped."

Gracefully approaching, Kateerah handed each of them a plate of food.

"Thank you," Jaut whispered, smiling at her. "I don't know how long it's been since we had some food."

Ever so slightly bowing her head, Kateerah's eyes deeply gazed at him. "Well, let me know if you need anything else. I need to go check on Rombil. He was wounded pretty badly today, but he got away from a guard."

"He's lucky he got away." Jaut shook his head, looking at the stone flooring. Patting his shoulder, Kateerah walked over to join a group of creatures several feet away.

Staring at her, Linx feasted on the delicious and flavorful meal. The group parted for Kateerah, allowing her to assist a severely wounded large bird with a broken wing. Linx assumed the creature had to be Rombil as every other being surrounded him out of concern. Assessing the progress of his recovery, her hand softly caressed Rombil's face, calming his spirit. Feeding him a light blue tonic, the corners of Kateerah's lips gently raised as she wrapped his wing.

"Poor guy," Linx said softly.

"It's awful to see anyone going through this. And now, knowing Pygo is their captive, I feel helpless. I don't know where they're taking him or how long he has to live. He was right all along. I should've listened to him—or led us through a different route." Jaut weaved his fingers through his hair, massaging his scalp.

"Stop blaming yourself. This isn't your fault. We will find him."

Shaking his head, Jaut said, "As much as I'd love to believe that, no one has ever been found once guards took them away."

"Well, where would they take them?"

Jaut threw his hands up in the air. "Who knows?"

"Do you think it would be Crystal Woods? Or do they have another area?"

Shrugging his shoulders, he said, "Maybe Crystal Woods, but I don't even know if that's where these guards were headed."

Linx optimistically said, "At least we have somewhere to start."

"Before we go anywhere, we need Kateerah to look at your back."

"Why? I'm fine."

Jaut set his plate down next to him before viciously rubbing his face. "Linx, I don't know what that demonic creature put on your back. Don't you want to make sure you'll be okay?"

Rolling her eyes, she said, "We need to rest more than anything."

"How about we talk with Kateerah first and then rest briefly?"

"Fine."

In a matter of moments, Kateerah glanced over at Jaut and Linx. She could tell something was off. Despite his typical demeanor, Jaut appeared tense—something was on his mind. Once she finished speaking to a couple of other creatures, she quickly returned to see if he needed anything else. "Jaut, are you okay?"

Opening his mouth, Jaut's mind wandered down a dreadful path. He pictured Pygo bloodied and covered in lacerations and bite marks. Sympathizing for how scared Pygo must be, a tear formed in Jaut's eye. Not knowing how long he had to live or if anyone would be able to rescue him was breaking his heart. Then a darker thought came—what if he was already dead? Jaut had been temporarily hopeful. Regardless of the thoughts of Pygo injured, they were just that—thoughts of him being injured, not dead. Tears immediately drizzled over his cheekbones and curved around his jaw. Wiping them away quickly, he shook his head no.

Hesitant to move, Kateerah rubbed her right arm from her shoulder to her wrist. Focusing on Linx, she furrowed her brows in confusion. "Do you know what's going on? I've never seen him like this before."

Solemnly nodding her head up and down, Linx inhaled deeply. "After leaving the Gemenii's cave, we—"

"Wait. You went to see the Gemenii?" Kateerah stepped back as her eyes bounced from Jaut back to Linx.

Unsure if she just opened a can of worms, Linx carefully chose her words. "Yes. It was my idea, but once we left—"

"But it was unsuccessful?" Kateerah interrupted again.

"No. We met the Gemenii."

Kateerah laughed. "There's no way that *you* met with the Gemenii!"

Annoyed, Linx crossed her arms. "What is that supposed to mean?"

"Oh, I'm not trying to be disrespectful." Kateerah shook her head. "It's just that many try . . . just to fail or die. There was one who was very close with the Gemenii, always seeking their wisdom. Once they disappeared, the Gemenii increased their security and chose seclusion."

"Well, I did." Linx didn't realize the room got quiet, and everything fell silent. Unable to determine whether they were intrigued or agitated, Linx remained quiet. She attempted to read the room, but it felt hopeless and overwhelming.

"I see. What did the Gemenii say?" Kateerah studied her face with suspicion.

"The Gemenii mentioned that a girl named Zalia needed our help."

Raising her eyebrow, Kateerah stepped closer. "What do you know about Zalia?"

"I believe I know where she is, and the Gemenii wants us to find her."

Spinning around, Kateerah walked away in long, sharp strides, pulling her hood over her head and climbing the stairs. "Follow me."

Taken aback, Linx looked over at Jaut's tired face as he refused to look up. "Jaut? Are you coming?"

Shaking his head, he whispered, "You can go. I'll meet you up there."

CHAPTER 22

As Linx attempted to keep up with Kateerah, her lungs burned. Fatigue clenched its grip around Linx's tiny body, threatening harm to her as she looked behind and back down the staircase. Lifting each leg to the following step proved to be difficult, as her body felt like goo spilling over the stone slabs. Distracting her mind, she wondered why Jaut wouldn't follow. Glancing in his direction, she witnessed him briefly bury his head in his hands before sitting up and forcing a smile at a passerby.

Finally reaching the top, the staircase opened up into a large stone balcony with a beaded curtain hanging from the arch of a connected room. Strong woodland incense danced from the room, leaving a faint floral trail in its path. Thin curves of smoke twisted and looped, escaping between the strands of delicate, round beads. The pleasant but heavy scent made Linx's nostrils tingle. The aroma conjured serenity and tranquility within her. Pushing through the smooth beads, the divine cloud of incense gently welcomed her inside. As her brain felt light and featherlike, she peered through the fog to find Kateerah. Unable to see her clearly in the dark room, Linx swatted the air and released two coughs. The smoke slowly dried out her eyes, forcing her to squint and shut her eyelids.

"Are you prepared for this journey?" Kateerah asked from the flickering shadows.

"I . . . have no choice." Linx released her shoulders with a sigh.

"Of course you do." Kateerah selected some items and tossed them into a gray mortar.

Shaking her head, Linx explained, "I don't think you understand. I don't have a choice. Yes, I *could* say no. However, morally, I can't. The Gemenii explained that innocent lives are at risk. How can I say no to that?"

Delicately lifting a pestle off a table, Kateerah began grinding the items into fine dust. She scooped out a soft line of powder and then mixed it in a mug of herbal tea. "Drink this."

Linx's eyes shifted from the mug and back to Kateerah. "What is that?"

Without batting an eye, Kateerah said, "Protection."

Quickly sipping the tea, Linx rubbed her eyes.

"You need to rest. Follow me."

"That would be great." Linx yawned, holding her hand in front of her mouth.

Motioning her to follow, Kateerah led Linx over to the side of the room where another beaded curtain hung. Pulling back half of the strands, Kateerah patiently waited for Linx to enter.

"This is normally where I sleep. Hopefully, you can get some rest. I'll have another drink for you when you wake." Kateerah kindly smiled.

Linx weakly walked over and collapsed on the bed. "Thank you so much. Is Jaut going to be okay?"

"Yes, he'll rest too, and you both can be on your way."

"Okay. Thank you."

With a gentle smile, Kateerah released the beads and walked toward the balcony. Linx quickly drifted off to sleep the moment she rested her head on the pillow.

Vibrant smears of light danced in her mind. A rich blue swirled from one side of her head to the other, while a bright green soon emerged. Deep purple and golden yellow hues splotched randomly behind the swirls. Her breathing eased as her mind gave in to the beautiful show of colors. After enjoying the hypnotic display for what seemed to be a while, a deep, muffled sound jolted her out of serenity.

"Linx! Linx!"

Gently rolling her head to the other side, Linx released an extensive sigh though her eyes remained sealed shut. Getting impatient, the male voice began desperately shaking her by the shoulders.

"Wake up, Linx! We have to go!"

Peeling her eyes open, Linx saw a blurry figure standing above her. Trying to regain her vision, she roughly squeezed her eyelids before opening them again.

"Linx, please!"

As her sight cleared up, she noticed panic lines stretching across Jaut's forehead. Quickly sitting up, Linx rubbed her eyes. "Hmm? What's going on?"

"I don't know. Somehow, they found our hiding spot. We need to go—now!"

Ripping the blanket off, Linx jumped up from the bed.

Clutching the bed, her legs buckled and almost gave out from the transition. "Where's Kateerah?"

"Over here. She wanted to give you something before we go."

Pushing through the beads, Linx found Kateerah gliding across the room to gather ingredients. Her graceful presence was fascinating to witness. She pointed to the two mugs on the table closest to them and whispered, "Hurry! Drink them before you go while I prepare something else."

Grabbing the drinks from the table, Jaut looked at Linx. "Bottoms up."

Holding the mug up to her lips, Linx meticulously observed Kateerah as she reached for a vial. Adding three drips of liquid, Kateerah used the pestle to combine the ingredients into a creamy paste. She dipped her thumb into the mortar and painted two lines on Linx's face—a vertical line on Linx's forehead and one from her lower lip to her chin. Unsure of what to make of it, Linx stood still and watched with intrigue.

"You are a warrior—fierce and strong."

Raising her eyes to meet Kateerah's gaze, Linx said, "Thank you for taking me in and preparing us for the journey."

"My thoughts and spirit will be with you as you search for our sister. Please bring her home."

"Are you coming with us?"

"I can't. They need me here. We need to relocate our sanctuary before any other guards show up."

Walking toward each other, Kateerah hugged Linx tightly. "Stay safe."

As they sprinted across the balcony and rushed down the staircase, a congregation of creatures formed a circle on the main floor. Looking closer, Linx could make out two bodies bloodied in the middle. Beneath the deep red, shiny armor lamely protected the two deceased intruders.

Dumfounded, Linx asked, "How did they find this place?"

Shrugging, Jaut shook his head. "I'm not sure. They could've followed us from a distance or might've been watching creatures here for a couple of days."

"Are there more coming?"

"I would assume so. Kateerah didn't want to take any chances, so they will take a tunnel toward another hideout."

Almost reaching the base of the stairs, a rush of dread and anger flooded her body. Looking around at the creatures collecting everything they could, her heart broke. "I will do whatever I can to make Crystal Woods pay for their actions."

"If they are the ones at fault," Jaut said.

"I wouldn't be surprised in the least if they were behind this."

Jaut solemnly nodded ever so slightly and pointed to the right. "We're going to head out a different way. This path, I think, will lead us toward Crystal Woods."

Peering over her shoulder at the chaos, Linx frowned before proceeding onward. They silently raced through the tunnel, over rocks and clumps of dirt. Compared to the tunnels near the Gemenii, it felt uneventful and calm—a breath of air before a raging storm. Once they reached the wall, Jaut tapped twice. Someone scurried by in the darkness, causing Linx to jump out of her skin.

"What was that?" she asked, panting and holding her chest.

"You mean who?"

"Yes, of course."

"They're our way out."

The grinding of rocks echoed throughout the tunnel as faint

light illuminated from an opening. Following Jaut closely, Linx scanned her surroundings to see who had opened their exit, but she couldn't see anything or anyone at all.

Perplexed, she scratched her head. "Where did they go?"

As the words exited her lips, the opening slowly closed shut.

"They're there. They're always there. Remember, everyone has learned to hide very well. Because if we don't, exactly this happens."

"Will everyone with Kateerah be okay? Since two guards found them, I hope they can escape to the new spot in time."

Holding his head high, Jaut said, "They will make it. I'm sure we'll have some casualties, but the enemy will have more. For the longest time, we didn't know who the enemy was. The people of Pangotha feared the unknown. Invaders ransacked the land at night. Many people were dead or missing every morning, and our power was constantly drained. Now that we may know who's responsible, this changes everything."

"It's so saddening to know that this is all their fault. However, it isn't surprising. Before leaving, I found out how they were also responsible for the devastation within Violet Woods."

Focusing on her for a moment, Jaut asked, "Getting there is one thing, but do you have a plan to find Zalia? I'm unfamiliar with the layout, so I don't know what to expect."

Heavily sighing, Linx replied, "The only place where they'd keep her would be in the dungeon. I was held in a cell, surrounded by many. It's awful, and all you hear are the screams of tortured souls circling around you. I just hope she's still alive."

As Jaut occasionally camouflaged into the darkness, Linx dove behind bushes and trees to hide from any guards walking by. The familiar area appeared lonelier than ever, as no creature dared to show themselves. Lightly treading on the ground, they picked up their pace to reach the cliff where Linx had met Jaut and the others for the first time.

Looking up toward the massive hole glaring down from the rocky cliff, Jaut chuckled. "Ah, perfect! Just how you left it."

Rolling her eyes, Linx gently lifted the corners of her lips. After she glared at Jaut, they climbed high into a tree to avoid being seen. The peeling bark crumbled beneath their hands as they firmly gripped the branches. They rushed up the thick tree, hoping to reach a vantage point. Boulders began to look like pebbles, and the saddening reality of the devastation Pangotha currently endured was sinking in. Linx scanned the vast land only to see the greenery she had not seen too long ago, which was now fading to brown. Once high enough, Linx rested her face against the tree as she thought deeply about why Crystal Woods wanted Zalia. Her stomach turned as she envisioned the worst. At her core, she knew they had minimal time because the last thing Crystal Woods needed was someone who could scream—bringing unwanted attention to the corrupt leaders.

Guards grumbled on the ground underneath them as they passed by. Clearly, many hated their job but felt compelled to serve the kingdom or be threatened by those in charge. Jaut and Linx exchanged humorous looks as each one ranted about the ridiculousness of the mission.

"I wish this whole place would turn to ash already." A guard huffed and kicked a tree, swinging his torch violently.

Unknowingly, the guard had kicked an ecknid. Annoyed with the unwarranted attack, the ecknid swung a sharp branch down, whipping the guard on his rear and thigh.

"Ahh! What the—"

Sighing, the second guard said, "Oh, quit your moaning."

"You know what? No! It's eat, sleep, and hunt. I'm tired of it. I didn't want to do this from the beginning. And they said that it would take two weeks max before this crappy place rotted to its core. Now look at it. We've been doing this for who knows how long, and they're still finding villages of nasty creatures. I wish they would all die so I could go home."

Slamming the point of his sword into the ground, the other guard screamed, "Will you just shut up? Whenever we come out here, you just complain and complain and complain! They ought to send you with the ungrateful, pathetic, and useless men to scavenge Dark Woods."

"You're just as sadistic as the king and his cronies. You and I know those men will never see the light of day again once they send them."

Snorting, the second guard said, "Yeah, that's the point."

"Is that so? Well, there's nothing stopping me from gouging out your eyeballs and leaving you for dead." The guard shook his torch, quickly pulling out his sword.

Linx shook her head at the exhausting conversation while Jaut was almost in tears from silent laughter. Several other guards entering Pangotha gave the two side-eyes as they bickered back and forth. Luckily, the guards scuffed farther away. The sun peered over the mountain, so Linx and Jaut knew they needed to make a run for it.

"Okay, if we go up the side of the rocks, I don't think they can see us as easily. What do you think?" Linx asked, pointing through the branches toward a secluded path around several large rocks.

Glancing at the spot and back to the guards, Jaut nodded in

agreement. "That sounds good. They're far enough away that I think we can go unnoticed."

Shifting her weight to descend the old tree, a slice of rolled bark dropped beneath Linx's feet. Her eyes widened as the chunk of bark smacked the tree a few times before finally resting on a root protruding from the dirt. Jaut deeply gasped as he turned to locate the ornery guards. Perking up their heads, the first guard pointed back in the direction where Jaut and Linx waited.

"We have to go—now," Jaut ordered.

Climbing down the rest of the tree, Linx's heartbeat increased as she feared they wouldn't reach the spot in time. "Should we just book it to the hole?"

"No, we have to go behind the rock. We won't make it to the opening!"

Linx wanted to trust his advice, but something inside of her screamed to run toward the opening of the cliff. "I'm sorry . . . I have to."

Shaking his head in annoyance, Jaut nodded while motioning to run forward. "Fine, just go!"

Desperately sprinting from tree to ecknid to tree, Jaut camouflaged when he could while Linx ducked behind anything that covered her. Despite rushing toward the opening, annoyed mumbles gradually approached. Looking up at the rest of the route, an unwelcomed wave of pessimism touched Linx's mind. Would they be killed before reaching the cave? Catching her thoughts, she reminded herself that the land of Pangotha would be doomed without them. They had to make it—they were destined to make it.

"I'm telling you, I heard something over here!"

Faster, faster, climb faster!

The other guard snarled, "Where? I don't see anyone!"

Crawling into the hole, Linx nervously waited for Jaut to catch up. The fierceness of her pounding heart deafened her head. She bent down to reach her hand toward Jaut. Observing beyond Jaut's shoulder, her eyes briefly locked onto the guard's. With the sun's rays bouncing off of her light hair and piercing green eyes, there was no doubt he saw her.

"You bloody fool. I told you something was here!"

"Huh?"

"Up there! There's two of 'em."

Breathing harder, Linx focused on getting Jaut to safety.

"Just go! Don't wait for me!" Jaut directed while pulling himself up.

"Are you kidding me? I'm not leaving you behind. If I'm making it, so are you!"

With a quick smirk, Jaut pulled himself up just beneath the opening. As the wind blew harder, Linx clasped her fingers around his hand, pulling with all her might.

Sliding into the opening, Jaut turned around to see how much distance they had from the guards. To both of their surprise, an ecknid groaned as it lifted a root from the ground, enough to trip the guard in front. Linx smiled as she witnessed the compassion from a new friend. The second guard tripped over the first, sending him to his face and kicking the torch out of the first guard's hand. The torch bounced against the ecknid, instantly igniting their trunk.

"No," Linx whispered, covering her hand over her mouth.

Concerned, Jaut asked, "What?"

Tears filled Linx's eyes as the whispered moans emanated from the ecknid's body. Knowing the dismal fate coming, the ecknid slowly rose—with fire seeping through the rings and flames creeping higher. The cracking of limbs echoed throughout the forest, and the guards looked up to see a protector of the land towering over their existence. Terrified, they attempted to squirm away like the slugs they were. But the ecknid pulled back a single limb and jabbed it forward with the last ounce of its life. Jaut and Linx were dumbfounded as the heroic act played out before them. The limb viscously impaled both guards and lifted their skewed bodies off of the ground. A second later, the ecknid crashed down to its death. A waterfall gushed from Linx's tear ducts as the ecknid turned to ash.

Jaut grabbed Linx's lifeless arm, tugging her toward the darkness. "Come! We have to go! The ecknid sacrificed its life for us. The only guards that saw us are dead! We must go —now!"

CHAPTER 23

Wiping warm tears from her cheeks, the fire for justice only grew within Linx's belly. An unnecessary life was lost, protecting others from dark intentions. Her eyes burned as she held in the urge to cry more.

Jaut mumbled, "It happened so fast, there was nothing we could do. Don't beat yourself up over it."

"I'm still in shock," Linx said.

"No disrespect—honestly—but the ecknids are the true guardians of Pangotha."

Linx barely looked up while they continued to walk. "No disrespect taken."

"I could just tell it was on your mind, that's all. They are creatures who love their land and most who roam it. They've been around the longest, so I'm sure it's hard for them to see what it's become."

Taking a moment to gather her thoughts, a sick feeling overcame her stomach and traveled up her throat. Linx envisioned what beauty the ecknids must've seen over their lifetime. She said, "Alongside the death of a child, nothing hits my heart harder than someone giving their life for another. The compassion, the love for another living being, and the love put toward a cause are incomprehensible, selfless gestures. And my heart aches for the ecknid."

Raising his eyebrows, Jaut could only nod in agreement. "Well said."

"It's funny because sometimes you could go months without crossing paths with an empathetic creature. And then, there'll be days where you forget that bad even exists."

"True. It's all who you surround yourself with."

"It is," she said. "I feel that Pangotha would've been the latter. It seemed like an incredible place to live."

As he slowly cracked his knuckles, each thumb pressing down on a finger, a whisper of emotion tried to break through. "It was."

"Well, it can be again." Linx pulled her shoulders back.

"I hope so," Jaut said, sighing. "I really hope so."

"At one point, part of me had that positivity about where I was from as well, Violet Woods. The endless feasts, the fun, and the family-like environment were all a façade. I don't know what parts of the happiness were true and what it's like now."

"That bad, huh?"

"Considering that we were led by elders . . ."

"Ah, yeah, I see."

"I just hope we can give Pangotha another chance. Regardless, I'll give it everything I've got."

Jaut patted her on the back. "That's all we could ask for."

As they traveled through the darkness, Linx raised her hand to light their path. Returning to the same route she traveled not too long ago was a strange feeling. She barely recognized anything this time.

Curious, Jaut asked, "So, where does this lead us exactly?"

"This path will take us to an area very close to Crystal Woods."

"Good. Hopefully, we have no one waiting to greet us."

"Oh, I doubt it." Linx thought about the last time she saw Carter's face. He looked sad and lonely, but it didn't matter anymore. He had his chance to do what was right. Instead, he listened to the fearmongering.

Jaut watched Linx's face as she battled herself through internal dialogue. Surprisingly, he found himself in a similar situation once he thought about what waited on the other end. Hating to admit his fears of Crystal Woods, he desperately wanted to change the topic.

"You know," Linx said, looking into Jaut's eyes, "they really aren't that scary."

"Who?"

Rolling her eyes, she said, "Everyone in Crystal Woods."

"I . . . I have no idea what you are talking about."

Rolling her eyes, she explained, "Really, the main thing is finding out where they're housing Zalia. I'm not afraid of them. I refuse to be."

Approaching the end of the tunnel, they observed light peering in.

Linx said, "We're almost there! Just stay alert."

Jaut agreed by moving his head up and down before walking into the sunlight. Exiting the cave, Linx felt a rush of adrenaline as she realized how close they were to the kingdom. Nothing could stop her at this point. Anger coursed through her veins, and resentment kept building. "I think we should attempt to get into the castle and see if Zalia is in the dungeons."

"Sounds easy enough." Jaut rolled his eyes while running his hand through his hair.

"She has to be in there. I don't know where else they'd keep her. You can overtake anyone with your wit and agility. Not to mention, your camouflaging will definitely come in handy."

Scrunching his eyebrows almost up to his hairline, Jaut stopped in his tracks. "I'm in trouble here, aren't I?"

"Huh? What do you mean?"

Jaut smirked. "I didn't know if your nice words were meant to instill false optimism. Are we screwed?"

Shaking her head side to side, she laughed for a moment.

"Well, how do we go about getting into the dungeon?"

Pursing her lips humorously, Linx said, "I, um, have an idea."

"And what's that?"

Releasing a breath, Linx looked around to see if she could spot the castle yet and saw the hill she had rolled down, which felt like ages ago. After climbing for a short distance, they neared where the hill met flat land. Scanning the potential battleground, she saw a few men walking in the distance, a guard near each entrance, and a family of people resting under a tree full of bright green foliage. It was strange watching the guards now. When she would walk that courtyard with Carter, it never dawned on her how many Crystal Woods had. Now that she was the enemy, it seemed like their forces had tripled. Or maybe they did.

"Um, are you going to answer me?" Jaut demanded.

"I just needed to see what we are up against," Linx slyly said.

"Well, what are we up against?"

Opening her mouth, she heard the free birds mocking her once more. "I don't know."

"You don't know? What are you talking about? We need to figure something out! We traveled all the way up here for you to say that? You've got to be kidding me."

"Woah, woah. I didn't say I don't have a plan because I do," Linx said. "I was just hoping I could think of a different one before saying anything."

"I'm waiting to hear it."

Pulling a branch covered in soft leaves out of her way, she glanced once more before speaking. "So . . . I can teleport to the dungeon."

"Oh, oh! Well, that's great!" A giant smile grew on his face.

"Um, kind of."

"What could go wrong? We get in, out, and return to Pangotha."

"The issue is that I don't know what awaits my arrival. They could have something set up to disable my powers, or worse."

"Like?"

Shrugging, she explained, "Not too long ago, they wanted me dead. I'm sure not much has changed since."

Another smile lit up his face. "Well, I'll be there with you too! We got this!"

"Hmm. About that."

"What?" he asked as the smile faded.

"I . . . need a distraction."

Raising his eyebrows, Jaut stood dumbfounded. "Huh?"

Letting go of the branch, the rustling leaves paused the conversation for a moment. She stepped to the side and leaned against the tree for comfort. "I don't know what to expect when I go in there. Heck, I don't know if anything changed in terms of an exit back out of the castle. As much as I hope to go in there and return quickly, I still need to find a girl I've never met before. Time is not on our side, but we can buy ourselves a little time if you help me."

"Of course! That's why I'm here. What do you need me to do?" Jaut eagerly awaited a response.

Gathering courage, she quickly said, "I need you to distract the outside guards as I search for Zalia."

Pausing for a moment, Jaut licked his lips as he absorbed her request. "Okay."

"I know it's a big ask, but—" she said. "Wait, what?"

"I'll do it. There's no better guy than me." Jaut laughed to himself, stretching his arms out wide. "I'll keep their attention for as long as I can."

Linx embraced his loving hug as she prepared to enter a place she had desperately tried to leave. Warmth coated her heart as she looked into his eyes. "Thank you, my dear friend."

"No need to thank me. It's what I do. Now, promise me something."

Confused, she looked at him. "What?"

"Promise me you'll make it out of there alive. I can't go back to Pangotha without you. Kateerah would have my head." He rubbed the back of his neck.

"I'll give it everything I got."

Stealthily running toward the castle, Jaut blended into tall bushes before sprinting behind a tree. He evaded detection as he got closer. Quickly making his way to the nearest guard, Jaut camouflaged against the castle's stone walls. Impressed by his skill, Linx awaited an opportune time to head toward the dungeon. Watching his performance, Linx laughed as she saw Jaut slap a guard on the back of the head and disappear into the stone. Flabbergasted, the guard frantically spun around to identify who dared to assault him. Unable to see anything, the guard stood back at his post once more, potentially contemplating his sanity.

Without seeing Jaut reappear, Linx almost lost herself when the guard flew forward. Instantly, Jaut took off, briefly revealing himself to ensure he grabbed anyone's attention. Between huffs of air, the guard yelled for backup as he pathetically tried to track Jaut's route. Like worker ants, numerous guards funneled out of the mouth of the castle. This was her cue.

Taking a deep breath, she filled her mind, soul, and purpose with any energy she could grasp. Then she switched her thoughts to the dingy, depressing confines of the dungeon. Focusing on the specific details of the room, like the smell and location within the castle, Linx hoped this would work. Letting go of her physical presence, she shut her eyes and exhaled.

The smell of rotting flesh and metallic liquid overcame her. Terrified to open her eyes, Linx envisioned her mother's massacred body in front of her. Bits of her dress decorated the trees like a sick, festive holiday. A lump formed in her throat, and tears surged toward her eyelids. Labored breathing trickled into her ears—it wasn't hers. *Open your eyes,* she screamed in her mind.

Forcing her eyelids open, she was shocked and proud to find herself where she had intended to go. Linx faced the dungeon door. The same vision burned in her brain while waiting to hear her fate. As she studied the wall and door in front of her, Linx's heart ached for the ill-fated soul who faced such an unfortunate consequence. Deep red blood splattered across the wall and down the door. Even the doorknob dripped with fresh blood. *Zalia? No,* she silently wept. Covering her mouth, her eyes dropped to the floor where blood covered her shoes from the puddle she stood in. The corners of the room had heaps of bodies still in netted bags, many of whom Linx could only assume were from Pangotha. Tears dripped from her jawline, swirling into and thinning the blood below. A high-pitched noise overcame her senses, and she felt as though she may faint. The noise got louder within the confines of her skull until—labored breathing. She heard labored breathing! The sound temporarily distracted her from the viscous scene, and she spun around to see . . . Carter.

CHAPTER 24

Staring at his bruised face, it was apparent the Pangothian creatures were not the only ones who suffered in this dungeon room. Strapped to a chair, Carter's head hung down in a daze. His blue, black, and red eye sockets, along with a busted and swollen nose, made him almost unrecognizable. Linx could only imagine what caused his strained breathing, but she pitied the old friend she saw before her. He looked broken—both physically and mentally.

"Carter?" Linx whispered.

Catching his attention, he lamely tipped his head in her direction and looked up through inflamed eyelids. Maybe he thought he was hallucinating, but it took a moment for him to register her presence. A thick choker was secured around his throat, making Linx wonder if it prevented him from using magic.

"Carter? Can you hear me?"

A pained smile pushed through. "Linx? W-what are you doing here?"

"I should ask you the same thing," Linx said in shock.

His eyes looked beyond her. "I learned the consequence of not trusting my gut and, instead, listening to others. Watching you walk away was one of the worst moments of my life. As you slipped away from me, so did my purpose. You were there for me when no one was, and you pushed me, stood up for me, and followed me literally to the ends of this world. And I failed you once again. Linx, I am so sorry."

Linx stood in silence, unsure if she could accept his apology. This toxic cycle drained her of all energy and emotions. A wall remained on standby, ready to be built quicker than anyone ever thought was possible.

"I can't ask for your forgiveness. I deserve everything that has happened and will happen, but I have to ask something of you. A favor, please. And I know why you're here."

Intrigued, she asked, "You do?"

"I began asking advisors about calling off the hunt for you. Explaining that you were not responsible for my mother's death, I thought they would settle the issue. They would bring up one reason after another about why I shouldn't trust you. At the end of it all, they wanted me isolated and powerless."

"As the king?"

Carter shook his head. "King of what when no one fears or respects you? There might be power initially; however, nothing lasts forever."

"Why then? What was all of this for?" Linx shook her head as she held out her arms.

"Conquering the next land. Simple as that. And once they

found out that I wasn't onboard with draining lands and pillaging, well, that's why I'm here now."

"I really don't know what to say, but I have to g—"

"They brought in prisoners—children and others."

Ready to leave him to rot in his sorrow, she shouted, "Get to the point, Carter. What do you want from me?"

His heart sank as he absorbed her anger. "I, uh, was hoping you could unlatch this thing around my neck. It prevents me from using any power at all."

Unamused, Linx walked behind Carter's chair and unlatched the lock.

"Oh, man. Thank you. I can't possibly thank you enough."

Looking at how vulnerable he was, Linx grabbed the strap tied around the chair and Carter's wrists as well. After she untied it, she started walking toward the door.

"Thank you."

Spinning around, she said, "You scratched my back—kind of —so I scratched yours. Don't ask me for anything ever again."

As Carter coughed up blood, something caught her eye in the back corner of the room. Curiosity pulled her closer. Within the pile of netting rested what appeared to be a heap of fur drenched in blood and mud. Only one small chunk of fuchsia remained near the creature's dark eyes.

"Pygo!" Darting over to the corner, Linx frantically ripped open the netting and untangled Pygo's body. She could barely feel a pulse. Gently caressing his face, she held him close to her heart. "Oh, please wake up."

A faint whisper poured out of his mouth, "My . . . lady."

"Pygo!" Linx cried, dripping tears onto Pygo's body. "Please stay with me. I'll do what I can to help you."

"Linx," Carter explained, "you need to get out of here as

quickly as you can. I'm not sure how much time you have left to save her."

Fiery green eyes waited for him to continue. Rushing to face Carter, she asked, "What did you just say?"

"The girl. I know where she is, but you have to hurry. Do you remember the pond that was cloaked by a force field?"

"The Eternity Pond?"

"Yes."

"Yeah, I do."

Struggling to sit comfortably, Carter said, "They have her there."

"Who?"

"The valuable girl from Pangotha, of course."

"What are they doing with her? Is she guarded?" Linx gently rocked Pygo closer to her like a mother comforting her young.

"I'm not sure if she's guarded, but they're keeping her alive for now—unless they find a way to siphon her powers. I'm not sure how long that'll last until they get bored, kill her, and just drain Pangotha."

"I can't believe you knew about all of this."

The pain and anger radiating from her gaze saddened Carter's heart more. "Just go get her before it's too late."

"Goodbye, Carter."

While holding Pygo, Linx teleported near the pond, hoping not to attract any attention. Quickly darting to hide, she impatiently waited in the brush to see if any guards entered or exited the force field. There was complete stillness. A beautiful bug buzzed past her nose, almost spooking her backward. Hopefully, no one saw her appear. Linx waited a bit longer before tingles formed, making their way up to her knees. Time was not on her side as Jaut remained a distraction to the guards while Pygo was slowly dying in her arms.

Assessing what to do, she could only see one option. Without sight into the Eternal Pond, she had to blindly enter a cloaked feeding ground. She thought in her mind, *Oh! How do I do this? I'm going to get us all killed if someone's in there.* A small, secluded pile of grass grabbed Linx's attention. Bending over slightly, she carefully laid Pygo on the soft, makeshift bed and stroked his cheek. Closing her eyes, she thought deeply about the day when she looked inside the Eternity Pond—the smells, sounds, and beautiful colors of that moment. Tightly squeezing them shut and holding her breath, Linx teleported inside the cloaked dome. Rapidly opening her eyes, Linx lit a flame in her hand and slid a force field around her body. Her focus thoroughly swept across the grass clumps, the damp dirt, and the shimmering pond. Peering over her shoulder, she couldn't see anyone there. *That liar.*

Kicking herself for believing Carter, Linx tried thinking about where they would keep a child. Her heart broke as her eyes led to the bright, shimmering pond guarded by a weeping statue. Glancing in the pond, she saw nothing odd or misplaced, but the water shifted. The colors faded and swirled, displaying an unsolicited picture into Linx's future. An undeniable smile naturally curled over her future self as the bright, warm sun soaked into her skin. Carefree and content vibes flowed from the picture. As she tried to look away, something else piqued her interest. A girl, clearly younger than herself, played next to her. Giggling, the girl ran near her without a care, her hair bouncing in the waterfall of sunlight. Instead of happiness, this scene brought a wave of sadness that made it difficult to breathe. Her senses were awoken by the tears running down her cheeks. She didn't know what it meant or who the girl was, but Linx hoped she would see her dear sister again. Turning to her side, her focus centered on the pain within the statue. *Sometimes my heart feels hardened from life,* she thought. *But other times, it turns into mush. Oh, how I miss Lyla.*

Right before she turned away, a glimmer caught her eye. Quickly, she saw a bright, beautiful ring around the statue's little finger. It was peculiar, reminding her of—the ring from the Gemenii? *No way! Why would this be associated with the Gemenii?* Then it clicked. *Is this . . . no way. It couldn't be. Could it? Was this statue Zalia?* Looking at the child's face on the statue, she was taken aback by the thought of Zalia being made of stone. Linx didn't understand why the Gemenii was made of stone, but she found it interesting that Zalia was as well—if this was Zalia.

Reaching down to pick up the statue, Linx gripped the base and vigorously tried lifting it. The statue wouldn't budge. Ambitiously trying to tip it, Linx couldn't believe how heavy it was and now felt the strain on her back. She gasped for a bit of air while she stood up, conjuring a plan in her head. As she considered moving a heavy statue and a fragile creature, muffled voices traveled in her direction. Linx desperately raced over to Pygo, cradling his body in her arms.

"Are you sure we should send out another wave?" a nervous man asked.

Letting out a disgruntled sigh, a regal voice said, "A good chunk of our men are chasing some buffoon around the land, and now a certain *someone* is missing. I've had enough. We're going to drain Pangotha for every ounce of energy and magic they have, and then we'll obliterate them until we find that other jewel."

"All right. Whatever you say."

The man shouted, "You don't see the value in this? Fool. You're all simple-minded idiots. It will be immaculate. We'll be able to pull and push energy whenever we want. Think about it. We'll be unstoppable. Others want to start a war with us? Good luck."

Clutching Pygo, Linx closed her eyes and appeared next to the statue. As she muted her heavy breathing, the mumbling quickly approached her location. Attempting not to panic, she desperately hoped her plan would work. Wrapping her other hand around the statue, Linx squeezed her eyes shut and teleported to the edge of the woods where she had last seen Jaut prior to them going their separate ways. Opening her eyes, Linx's heart felt as though it had sunk to her feet. The only thing she could feel in her arms was Pygo's blood-soaked fur.

"No," she whispered. Witnessing two cloaked figures advance toward the direction of the statue, Linx didn't know what to do. Pygo's high-pitched whimper drowned out any thoughts as her body involuntarily trembled. Everything she promised the Gemenii, Jaut, Pygo, Kateerah, and Pangotha was slipping away with each step the men took toward Zalia.

Looking down at Pygo's helpless body and then back up, Linx's gut ripped in two as she weighed out her options. How could she abandon a child, if that's what the statue was? But how could she save a heavy statue anyway? In the meantime, her friend would surely die from blood loss. The sound of a stick snapping behind her made Linx jump. Quickly turning around, she was taken aback once her eyes locked on the figure behind a branch.

"Jaut?" Linx whispered.

The figure stood still briefly before pushing the branch out of the way. A strange warmth rushed through her body as excitement mixed with heavy anger. Dumbfounded, she froze. "How did you get here? Oh, wait. Forget it. I'm an accomplice now, I guess."

Through bruised lips, Carter said, "I've been looking for you all over. There are guards everywhere. Did you find the girl?"

"Yeah, I think so. There is a new statue next to the Eternal Pond. Something seemed off about it. Is that her?"

"Oh, I'm not sure. The last time I saw her, she was . . . alive. Then I heard them mention taking her there."

Confused, they both eagerly stared toward the men who were approaching the Eternal Pond. Linx delicately caressed Pygo's fur, rubbing her thumb quickly up and down the side of his body. "Do you know who they are?"

Squinting his eyes, Carter said, "Yeah, I think so. It's hard to see, but the guy on the right looks an awful lot like one of my advisors, Lowe."

"Are you serious?"

"Yep. He tried to convince me that invading Pangotha was an excellent move. It's funny because he wasn't too thrilled once he realized I wasn't interested. I just can't make out who the other guy is."

"What should we do? I tried teleporting the statue with me, but it was a complete failure," she said, glancing down at her friend in her arms. "I need to help Pygo before he dies. Do you know of any healers?"

"Hmm." Carter thought about every person he encountered within the castle. "I don't."

"I wonder," Linx said.

"What?"

Letting out a heavy breath, Linx rubbed the ring on her finger. "I was given this ring to assist with the journey."

Intrigued, his attention bounced from the ring to her eyes. "What does it do?"

Turning away from him, Linx was reluctant to say much. She didn't know if she could trust him. *What if this was a setup?* She fought against the critical voice in her head. "Carter, how can I trust to tell you anything else? I want to, I do, but I can't bring myself to trust you anymore."

"It's fine. I get it. I don't need to know anything else. Do what you must, and I'll focus on them."

Despite feeling guilty, Linx watched Carter step closer to see what the men were doing as she rested her hand over Pygo's face. She had no idea how to utilize the ring's power to transfer power from herself to Pygo. Closing her eyes, she envisioned his happiness before this. Although she never saw his true happiness before the invasion, she knew he was kind, compassionate, and a fighter. Linx felt a flow of energy exit her body with an otherworldly exhale.

Pulling her eyelids open, tears flooded down her cheeks as Pygo's eyelashes gently batted. Visibly gaining strength, he scanned his surroundings and forcefully hopped out of Linx's arms. Shaking his head, he said, "My lady."

"Pygo! It worked! I can't believe it worked!" she said quietly, notating the shift in her energy.

Looking over his shoulder, Carter was stunned to see Pygo bouncing on the ground with his dark eyes and wide, sharp grin. "Oh, wow. That's incredible."

"You don't have to be afraid, Carter." Linx laughed at him.

"My lady, who is this?" Pygo cautiously asked.

"Carter. Or should I say, King Carter?"

Locking his eyes on Carter's position, Pygo flashed his teeth. "Of Crystal Woods?"

Stepping back and shaking his head, Carter held his hands in the air. "Woah, woah. I don't think anyone here views me as a king anymore."

"And why is that?" Pygo asked.

"They were interested in conquering lands, and I wasn't supportive. The noblemen have quite a gift for spinning stories and twisting words to fit their narrative, just like how they got in the middle of my relationship with Linx. It didn't take too long before everyone in the kingdom hated me. And I was targeted."

"It's not such a great feeling, now is it?" Linx crossed her arms and dug a heel into the ground.

Glaring at Carter, Pygo turned to face Linx.

"I can never apologize enough. In my gut, I knew I was making a mistake."

"Is that why you sent a goblin to watch me?"

At a loss for words, Carter looked down. "The goblin had been following you since you left the castle dungeon. I was hoping it would . . ."

"Spy on me?"

"No! Not at all. I wanted the goblin to protect you in case anything tried attacking you."

As she placed her closed fists on her hips, Linx said, "Oh, so I can't protect myself? I need *you* to help me survive?"

"That's not what I meant. It was just an extra security blanket in case anything happened."

"Oh, okay. I understand. Just in case," she began.

"Yes!"

"Just in case I were to have been trapped . . ."

"Yeah, sure. Anything like that."

Shaking her head from side to side, she continued, "If I were trapped in a dungeon, and I had to fight for my life."

"I guess," he said, flustered.

"Okay, I just wanted to make sure!" Linx laughed. "How about if I were trapped in a castle dungeon, fighting for my life, because I was accused of murdering a queen? Would the goblin protect me then?"

"Well, I mean, yeah. Why wouldn't . . ." Carter slowly caught on. "Linx! I will prove how sorry I am."

Gazing out into the distance as his brain painfully melted from the tense drama, Pygo observed something peculiar. "What are those men doing?"

"Huh?" Carter looked through the branches toward the Eternal Pond.

"Oh my god!" Linx shouted. "Is that Zalia?"

The two men violently dragged a girl across the grass as she lamely struggled within a net. Linx recognized the net—one very similar to what they dragged Pygo away in. Studying the situation, they could see something sealed across her mouth as well.

Crouching down, Linx asked, "Carter, is that Zalia?"

"Hmm." Carter stared for a moment before saying, "I believe so!"

"Oh, no." Linx's heart raced as she fought the instinct to rush over and decimate them where they stood. Knowing anyone else could be watching, and it would risk Zalia's life, she impatiently waited for the men to drag Zalia closer. Just beyond complete visibility, they frantically stumbled with Zalia in the direction leading into the woods toward Pangotha.

"Now what?" Carter asked. "Should we go after them, or is there a different plan?"

"I'd like to free Zalia, but I don't know what we're up against. Do they normally have guards popping out from dark shadows here? I only know what I saw, but hopefully, you have some insight into that."

"No, ever since they began invading Pangotha, they reduced troops on foot here. It seems counterintuitive, but they felt it would be a waste of manpower since the land we were destroying could barely fight back, let alone find our kingdom. Don't get me wrong, the stories about the ecknids and the tenacity of creatures within Pangotha's borders are terrifying. It's just that it's understandable if anyone loses with those odds."

Dumbfounded, Linx twisted her face, rolling her eyes. "Are you done yet? Like . . . I just asked a yes or no question."

"I'm sorry. No. No, they haven't been stationing soldiers willy-nilly throughout the forest here."

"Carter, would we be okay killing them and securing Zalia?" Linx asked very clearly.

"I don't see why not. No one is around." As his shoulders fell with an exhale, he said, "Let's do it."

Linx looked over with kind eyes. "Pygo, we can try to hide you somewhere close by."

At that moment, his pitch-black gaze locked with hers. Getting lost in the darkness, her mind envisioned a portion of outer space, a place beyond what she could comprehend, speckled with the brightest, vibrant stars. For a second, her breath steadied as a wave of purpose and strength overcame her.

With a soft chuckle, Pygo said, "My lady, I won't be hiding anywhere. I'm here for a reason."

Pressing her lips together, she dipped her head forward, gently nodding in his direction. Guilt threatened to spoil any positive emotion that blossomed. Linx believed that Pygo had suffered enough, but who was she to stand in his way of fighting for his home?

"Linx!" a deep voice whispered behind a tree. "Psst!"

Taken aback, the voice disrupted her thoughts. She stepped forward to listen if anyone or anything called her name again. The silence made her question her sanity. Examining each tree surrounding her, Linx struggled to locate where the voice came from. Confused and not wanting to waste time, she looked back toward Carter and Pygo.

"Linx! Are we going to do this or what?" Carter called.

Sighing, she trudged back. "Yeah, I thought I heard something. Are you sure you'll be okay, Pygo?"

Bouncing over, Pygo's eyes gleamed with excitement. "I've got your back. We must rescue Zalia and bring her home."

With a slight nod, they carefully stalked the men, waiting for the right moment to ambush them. An unbearable anticipation lingered in the air as Linx repetitively tapped her middle finger and then her pointer finger off of her thumb. Her heartbeat loudly pulsed throughout her body. Maintaining a strict gaze, her eyes stung from a lack of lubrication. The light prickle quickly turned into a burning sensation as she refused to blink her eyes.

"Ready?" Carter asked.

Linx nodded.

"Linx?" a whisper said from behind a tree.

Turning her head, Linx couldn't recognize anyone around

her. Raising her eyebrows, she abruptly glanced into the sky, but she didn't see anything. As she observed the land one more time, a color subtly changed in her field of vision. Caught off guard, Linx stared for a moment to make out the obscure figure.

"Linx!" Carter grew impatient. "What are you doing? Are you ready?"

"I—ugh—yes. Yes, I'm ready."

"Linx?" a male voice whispered.

"Linx!" Carter repeated. "Who's saying that?"

Closing her eyes, she felt like she was quickly going mad. "Enough!" Linx whispered in a raspy tone.

Bewildered, Carter's attention bounced from Linx to Pygo and back to Linx again. "Did I do something wrong?"

"Shh! Just shh." Peeking beyond a thin tree, Linx scowled. Her focus slid from one tree to the next, trying to hone in on where the voice came from again. Unable to locate anyone, overwhelming tension built up in her upper back and jaw.

Gently grabbing her arm, Jaut cautiously stepped out in front of her.

"Holy hell!" Linx shouted, grabbing her chest.

With a giant grin plastered across his face, Jaut held Linx's hands and whispered, "Shh! I'm so sorry, Linx. I was trying to rush over to you, but I didn't want to be seen."

"Well, you about gave me a heart attack!"

"I'm sorry!"

Carter looked over with curious and judgmental eyes. "Who's this?"

"Carter?" Jaut humorously asked.

"How do you know who I am?"

Jaut rubbed his chest while rolling his eyes. "Oh, I've heard stories."

"Is that so?"

Ignoring Carter, Linx anxiously stepped forward toward Jaut. "Is everything okay?"

"Well, I got a workout in for the day, to say the least. Hopefully, you were able to find out something about Zalia's whereabouts."

Hopping over, Pygo asked, "I see how it is. So you're just going to ignore me now?"

Jaut's eyes lit up with excitement, almost snapping his neck in the process. "Puffball, is that you?"

"You were always a charmer."

"How'd you get here? I'm so happy to see you, my friend." Jaut smiled.

Turning to Linx, Pygo said, "It was our guardian. I would've been dead if it wasn't for her."

"So, you're saying the Gemenii was correct?" Jaut tossed his hands playfully in the air, knowing he'd risk pissing off Pygo.

"Always have." Pygo shook his head firmly.

"There's our girl!" Linx interrupted, pointing through the branches.

Eyes wide, Jaut mumbled, "You've got to be kidding me."

"Huh? What?" Linx asked, peering through the leaves before looking up at Jaut. "Do you know them or something?"

"Hardly. But I saw that one on the right turn a man into stone with his bare hands while I ran through the woods. Luckily, he didn't see me."

"Are you serious?" Carter asked. "Are you sure it was him who did it?"

"As sure as the air that coats my lungs. I would bet my life and easily yours on it." Jaut scowled in Carter's direction.

"I wouldn't doubt that part," Carter said. "It's just odd because I recognize that man the closer they get. It looks like Brent Fille, a guard for the castle."

"So you know him?" Linx questioned Carter.

"Well, yeah. When I was king, I had an odd encounter with him. The weird thing was that Lowe, the man on the left, verbally destroyed him in front of me—to the point of embarrassment. I would think if he had that kind of power, he would've retaliated."

"Carter, I wouldn't dismiss anything too quickly."

"I'm not denying it. I just don't understand why he would allow others to treat him like that."

Linx impatiently said, "Hopefully, we'll figure it out shortly."

CHAPTER 25

Pacing back and forth, Linx explained, "Jaut, we need you to ambush them from behind. They won't see you coming, and we'll be distracting them. Pygo, attack when you can. We'll take the brunt of their attacks—whatever that may be. I'll rush them since I have my force field. Carter, you know what to do. Are we ready?"

"I'm ready when you are," Jaut said.

Pygo smiled. "I'm here to serve."

Carter nodded.

At that moment, Linx abruptly fell to her knees as intrusive thoughts infiltrated her mind. Humming and a unison pounding of footsteps created a musical composition performed across the land. The whooshing of swords slicing the air welcomed the grim reaper, serenading him with the screams of punctured and gutted soldiers. The blood from the fallen streamed together, forming a river of life that energized the surrounding lands.

"Are you all right?" Carter gently lifted her to her feet.

With fingers combing through her hair, she quickly snapped herself out of it. "Yes, I'll be fine. Please watch your backs. I feel this battlefield will get more crowded than expected, and I don't want to lose any of you."

Looking at each other, they acknowledged her concern and agreed to protect one another to the best of their abilities.

"Let's go!" Linx whispered, waving her hand toward Lowe and Brent's direction.

Jaut swiftly sprinted toward the men, hiding within the vegetation. Instantly, Carter stared at Linx, almost fearful of what might happen. Her bright eyes looked through him, reaching into his soul and mind. Regardless of his deepened terror of harming Linx again, she intertwined herself into his thoughts.

Her soft voice telepathically whispered, *Focus.*

Nodding in acceptance, Carter stepped forward and tightly closed his eyes. The familiar eerie calls and laughs amplified within the confines of his skull. He slowly unchained the gates within his mind, releasing the vicious demons that both protected and destroyed him. The effortless scratching into the ground, the heinous yells, and feral mannerisms could be heard rapidly approaching.

The stampede of nearly uncontrollable goblins caught the attention of Lowe and Brent. They quickly signaled other guards who were on standby to cover them as they passed through the remaining portion of open land. A stream of armed soldiers poured out of the castle. Heartbroken and embarrassed, Carter looked over at Linx. He felt like he failed the team by blowing their cover before they were even close enough.

"Focus! You got this! We can't afford to drop the ball, Carter!" Linx shouted, encouraging him to ignore the additional bodies.

For the first time in quite a while, Carter lifted the corners of his mouth into a slight smirk. Closing his eyes again, he dove deep within himself to travel with the goblins—exposing his energy and intentions to them. In his mind, he neared Lowe and Brent as they maliciously dragged Zalia between them. Their size overshadowed her tiny body, which tumbled within the net whenever she didn't keep up. Pointing to each man, Carter instructed them to attack with all their might. Mentally sinking deeper, Carter turned toward Lowe and slashed his face. Hoping he could guide the goblins with his psychological gestures, he imagined others bounding for Brent. Opening his eyes, the view shocked Carter as he witnessed Lowe grabbing for his face as red, thick liquid bled over his fingertips. Carter could not comprehend in a million years that his impulsive fantasy would actually come true.

Once his attention redirected to Brent, Carter was dumbfounded as he witnessed Brent effortlessly reach his hand out and grab a goblin by their throat. As they hung in front of him, the goblin fiercely shredded the skin off of Brent's hand, desperately attempting to escape. A chuckle escaped Brent's mouth, squeezing his fingers deeper into the goblin's neck, nearly crushing their trachea.

"Let them go!" Linx shrieked while throwing an energy ball toward Brent's arm.

Flexing his bicep out of the energy's path, Brent pulled the goblin close to his face, gazing into their eyes. The goblin's body turned to stone, dropping to the ground with a thud.

"What did you do?" Carter shouted, scrambling toward the unexpected victim.

"Oh, it's you!" Brent snorted. "I see you just can't keep your nose out of anything. And this—see, this right here will be the reason for your demise. You care too much about the puny servants of the world, making you miss the bigger picture. They mean nothing while the entire kingdom and its ascension rests on your shoulders."

"What would you know about a kingdom resting on your shoulders?" Carter shook his head. "You were beaten and bruised while providing the ultimate rags to riches story for the kingdom's occupants to pass down from generation to generation. Nowhere did I see you maintaining the castle culture or attempting to take charge. Instead, you were bullied by this man." Carter pointed to Lowe's half-dead body, convulsing because of blood loss from the group of goblins mauling him. "How can you even opt to work with him and borderline defend this insanity after how he treated you?"

"Because he offered me more than you ever did." Brent reached out to grab another goblin.

In a matter of seconds, Linx slammed an energy ball off of Brent's chest. As his feet flew over his head, sending him tumbling backward, he fractured his ankle and broke two ribs. Once his body stopped rolling, he held his sides, moaning from the pain. Linx scrambled toward the net that entrapped Zalia. Afraid to touch the sizzling, anti-magic mesh squares, her hand trembled while hovering over the child's limp body. She reluctantly reached for the handle, peeking over her shoulder. The weight of the net was surprisingly heavier than what Linx anticipated. Scanning the handle, she noticed two toggle switches strategically placed where the thumb would rest.

While avoiding pressing down on the buttons, she lifted the handle as best she could.

Exhaustion set across her shoulder blades as she released the handle, shaking her head. "Carter! I need help. I can't get her off the ground. We need to figure this thing out!"

"Good luck," Brent said, mumbling just enough for Carter and Linx to hear.

"What could they have possibly offered you that would make you like this?" Carter asked, barely able to close his mouth.

Shaking his head, Brent whispered, "You'd never understand."

"You're right. I don't understand. Frankly, there's almost nothing they could offer for me to throw myself to the wolves."

"Exactly. *Almost* nothing," Brent shouted, spewing particles of saliva.

Tilting his head and squinting his eyelids, Carter had no idea what Brent was alluding to.

"My grandmother was framed. No one would ever believe her, and she was sentenced to death for a crime she didn't commit. Her screams and cries still haunt me to this day. When she found out she was to be hanged, she lost her mind. Something inside her broke as she looked at me, but no one cared. Why would anyone care? Life moves on for everyone else. Anyone I would confide in said I should be grateful we found our way together."

Disarmed, the goblins backed away while Carter asked, "What do you mean?"

"Before this place, we were sitting on the living room couch, waiting out a heavy storm. I didn't think much of it. High winds whipped through the neighborhood while thunder rattled our home. Figured it would be like any other thunderstorm. Then our oak tree came crashing through our roof, pinning us to the floor. As I slowly bled to death, I looked over to see she was already gone. And then, I had the privilege of watching her die a second time." His eyes shifted toward Linx while he held his chest. "They said there's a way to find her again."

In Carter's peripheral vision, Jaut rapidly impaled a distant guard with his sword. After sliding the sword out of the guard's neck, he rushed behind another and jabbed the blade between a weak spot on the side of the armor.

"Carter! Others are coming! I need help!" Linx shouted, yanking on the handle.

Heavily sighing, Carter quickly said to Brent, "You poor fool. They were just using you."

"Whatever. It was a chance I had to take."

Frustrated, Carter shook his head before running over and kneeling beside Linx to figure out the lock on the net. "There's no way this thing can be difficult. These guys are complete morons."

"We're trying to save her! Insulting anyone right now won't help!"

"I'm not worried, Linx. Look," he said, flipping both switches to the other side.

The net popped open, and the sizzling sound of the mesh immediately dissipated.

Linx stared at Carter for a moment. "Zalia? Zalia? Why is she just lying there like that? Carter, why isn't she moving?"

"I don't know."

Speechless, they remained still. Linx scanned her surroundings for Jaut and Pygo, unsure of what to do. In her mind, they would surely know what to do—she hoped. *Where could they be?*

She couldn't find them anywhere. Her heart thumped heavily, feeling like she failed the land of Pangotha and this little girl in front of her. Linx's hands grew tingly as the rush of anxiety circulated throughout her body. Steadying her breath, she inhaled slowly, expanding her lungs to their capacity. Before calmly releasing the air between her lips, her vision crawled across the ground, expecting to see at least one of her friends. *Nothing.*

Peeling the net back off of Zalia's body, Linx stroked her curled hair gently as she assessed her for bleeding and acknowledged her weak breathing. *The ring! The ring can transfer some power to Zalia!* Closing her eyes, Linx pictured a funnel of powerful energy swirling out and leaving her body. The energy sprinkled across Zalia's body and soaked into her skin like a dry sponge that was thirsty for water. Opening her eyes, Linx noticed a peculiar glow that overcame Zalia's presence, creating a magnificent aura around her. Fluttering her eyelids, Linx's heart dropped as Zalia's bright green gaze stared back at her.

"Zalia?" Linx whispered in disbelief.

"Is she okay?" Carter watched quietly while still paying attention to Lowe and Brent. He couldn't bring himself to kill Brent, but he felt Lowe deserved every ounce of pain he experienced.

Blinking several times to focus her eyes, Zalia cautiously nodded.

"The Gemenii sent me to find you and bring you home. I'm here with others, Pygo and Jaut, to take you back safely. Are you hurt?"

After a moment, Zalia shook her head from side to side. Keeping her lips sealed shut, she remained curled in a ball on the ground, with part of her body still sitting on the net. Linx extended her hand to help Zalia stand up, but Zalia sat there, reluctant to accept any assistance.

"It's okay," Linx said. "You can trust me."

Zalia's vibrant eyes, almost matching Linx's, refused to blink. Terrified of what was to come, she glanced around to see who else was there. Once she spotted Lowe and Brent, she quickly scrambled backward in Linx's direction.

"Take my hand!" Linx said. "I will do my best to protect you, but you have to trust me. We need to get out of here."

Placing her hand on top of Linx's, Zalia furrowed her brows as she hesitantly stood up.

"I'm just trying to see where Jaut and Pygo went."

"What about me?" Carter whined.

"Ugh. Oh, yes. This is Carter. He was a king—not a very good one, if you ask me." Linx rolled her eyes.

As he threw his hands up in the air, Carter squinted his eyes at Linx before spotting Jaut rushing back with Pygo bouncing alongside him. Once they spotted Zalia standing near Linx, their faces lit up, and they sprinted as quietly as they could.

"Zalia?" Jaut questioned when he was close enough.

She shyly nodded.

"She hasn't said a peep," Linx whispered to Jaut. "Do you think she'll be okay?"

"I hope so, but there is something else I need to tell you."

Intrigued, Linx asked, "What?"

"I saw a group of creatures approaching from afar. When I was farther down, I heard marching and shouting. There's even some smoke traveling up this way. I don't know who they are coming for, but we might need to get out of here quickly. We killed several guards over there as well, but more are on the way."

The weight of gravity pulled down on every inch of Linx's face. In shock, she said, "The trolls."

"Huh?"

"The trolls. I had visions of them marching, slaughtering men, and—" Linx paused as she looked over Carter.

Confused, Carter asked, "What?"

"Nothing. We have to get out of here as soon as possible. Hopefully, we won't encounter any on our way back to Pangotha."

A faint, repetitive thump echoed throughout the land. They quickly glanced at each other with deep uncertainty. Linx knew they had endured the lengthy adventure to Crystal Woods to get revenge for Poba. Unfortunately for the trolls, the cape no longer existed and was a mere snack inside the stone stomach of a deinos. That wouldn't be any valid excuse for the trolls, though.

"Fine. Let's go," Jaut said, looking at Brent slowly scooching toward a hiding spot. "What about him?"

"What about him?" Carter asked.

Raising his eyebrows, Jaut combed his fingers through his hair. "So . . . we just going to leave him alive?"

"I . . . I . . . didn't know what to do. Lowe is a vile piece of garbage, but I couldn't bring myself to kill Brent. I feel like he was taken advantage of. What he did wasn't right, but he was their puppet."

"What are you talking about, man? You're leaving loose ends. It's unnecessary and dangerous."

Scrunching his face, Carter said, "What do you know?"

Jaut exhaled with a huff, whipping his hair to the side. Pulling his sword out of its sheath, he turned toward Brent. "If you can't, I will."

A tornado of thoughts uncontrollably swirled in Carter's head. *Did Brent screw up? Yes. Was he an evil being who deserved to die? No. I could have been—I was in a similar headspace. And someone manipulated a hurt, sad guy into doing something he normally wouldn't have done. I can't let this tool kill him.* At that moment, Carter rushed in front of Jaut. "Don't do it!"

"We have to leave—NOW!" Linx shouted, rushing Zalia in the direction of Pangotha. "Jaut, you know the promise we made with the Gemenii! I have to take her back."

Jaut turned toward Linx. "Go on! I'll meet up with you and Pygo shortly. I'm not sure about this flake, though."

Shaking her head in exhaustion, Linx continued escorting Zalia to safety, with Pygo bouncing next to them.

Carter shoved Jaut back a step. "What was that about?"

"You want to save an enemy! Why? I don't have time for this."

"Just let him go. Look, Lowe's about dead." Carter pointed to the puddle of blood that Lowe's body rested in.

Annoyed by the conversation, Jaut said, "And what? You and I both know that Lowe is only a small fraction of the problem within that castle right now. Get out of my way. I won't warn you again."

"Oh, tough guy. Or what? What will you do about it?" Carter twisted his face while clenching his jaw.

Letting out a loud chuckle, Jaut flashed his snaggletooth. "Is this about something else?"

"What the hell are you talking about?"

"Hmph. Get out of the way, clown." Raising his sword above Brent's body, Jaut swiftly brought down his arm.

Without a second thought, Carter reached out his hand and pulled Jaut's arm back, preventing the sword from piercing

Brent's chest. Capitalizing on the moment, Brent reached out his fingertips and grabbed Jaut's leg, hardening it inch by inch until even his hair turned to stone.

Stumbling backward, Carter shouted, "What did you do? I tried to save you, and you killed him!"

"Calm down. He's not dead—just stuck," Brent said with a smile.

"How is this funny to you? It's not. You must fix him. Change him back now!" Carter frantically looked around for Linx, hoping she knew what to do.

"I don't have to do anything, and I certainly won't do that!" Brent laughed.

The grunting and stomping from the incoming trolls crept up Carter's back. He knew they were incredible fighters, and they had something else that made them even more dangerous—a purpose. They finally found out the truth, or a portion of it, leading them to Crystal Woods. And Carter wanted to be as far away from their wrath as possible, but how could he leave Jaut?

"Do it. Leave him," Brent whispered.

"Huh? Why do you care?" Carter snapped. Pulling the knife out of Brent's boot, Carter held it toward Brent's face.

As he lifted his hands in the air, Brent remained calm and collected. "Hey, I'm just trying to help. But I wouldn't do that if I were you. If you kill me, you kill him."

Looking through his eyes and into his soul, Carter didn't blink. "You're lying."

"Fine. Kill me then." Brent shrugged.

Not sure what to do, Carter scanned his face for flinching or twitches. Deep inside his gut, he knew that something was off about his stare. His heart made him second guess saving Brent, but he gave Carter a disingenuous look—one that screamed cocky confidence. Knowing the trolls would kill him anyway, Carter figured Jaut would have the same fate regardless of who killed Brent, if Brent was being honest. Ultimately, Carter hoped Jaut had a better chance now. The trolls would not think twice about pulverizing any unknown creature.

"Enough talking," Carter said, slicing Brent's throat.

CHAPTER 26

As the blood dripped from Carter's new blade, he stared into Brent's eyes until he gurgled his last breath. Upset with himself for being so naïve, he turned to look for Jaut, but he was nowhere to be seen.

"Jaut?" Flabbergasted, his heart sank. Brent told him the truth, and now he killed a truly innocent guy. His chest felt constricted. How was he going to explain this to Linx?

"You okay?" a cheeky voice asked from a distance.

"Jaut?"

No response.

Glancing from side to side, Carter furrowed his brows as his fight-or-flight response kicked in. He couldn't wait anymore. Knowing it was a death sentence to wait, he fled to where he last saw Linx. It appeared as though she was going to head in the same direction as when he saw her for the last time before she left into the caves of Pangotha. As he climbed down the mountain, he heard footsteps behind him. Checking over his shoulder, he didn't see anyone or anything. Nevertheless, Carter could hear the tings from swords hitting shields, screams echoing through the woods from victims counting their last moments, and the shouting of trolls telling their army to move into the castle. Part of Carter felt awful knowing that many innocent lives would be taken by the morning.

As the sun disappeared for the night, it became increasingly more challenging to see into the woods. The familiar shapes formed by the trees and bushes shifted to threatening forms, taunting Carter's mind. He didn't know who might be waiting for him within the shadows. Although Lowe and Brent were dead, something shifted just an arm's reach away. "Jaut? Is that you?"

Stepping out of the shadows, a muscular figure blocked Carter's way. Startled and unsure of what to do, Carter backed away slowly, hoping to buy some time. Not seeing the creature's face, Carter could only assume it was a troll. He didn't know what to say—if there was anything he could say to make the situation better. At that moment, he saw a dip in the woods. The fall wouldn't be pretty, but it could get him out of there quickly and without incident. Without Linx's insight, he didn't know what she wanted to do. Regardless, he couldn't imagine her wanting the trolls harmed after the relationship that trolls and fairies had in Crystal Woods.

As he slightly bent his knees, he heard a loud voice shouting to the figure near him.

"You find him yet?" the grumbling voice asked.

Before the creature could respond to the other voice, Carter forced himself over the hill's edge, tumbling faster than he expected. Wanting to avoid hitting a tree trunk, Carter reached out his hand to reduce the speed of his tumbling. When he finally rolled far enough down, he slung his arm around a thin tree, sliding his body forward until it stopped abruptly. Standing up, he immediately sprinted away from the creatures' vicinity as quickly as possible.

Shouting ensued as Carter gained more distance between him and the visitors. He was at a loss for where Linx may have led Zalia, but he just had to go straight for now. Weaving between dark trees, he prayed he wouldn't encounter anything else. After running into several thorny bushes and over seen ditches, which luckily didn't sprain his ankles, light shone down from the stars in the sky, illuminating up his path. By a stroke of luck, he stumbled upon what appeared to be a familiar location. This was it! The cave where Linx had traveled to Pangotha! Carter was so grateful he felt like he could cry. Astounding relief overcame him as he approached the entrance. Simultaneously, an intense surge of guilt washed over his body. Jaut was nowhere to be found, and it was all Carter's fault. Had he killed Brent from the beginning, or just not physically stood in the way of Jaut, he might've still been alive.

As he was dipping into a secluded part of the cave, he heard a bloodcurdling scream that immediately stood out to Carter. Perking his ears, Carter listened to where the incident occurred. Deep inside his stomach, he knew he had to check out the commotion. It could be anyone, but Carter had to rule out that it was Jaut or Linx. Taking an extensive breath, he raced up the hill toward the shouting. *I can't believe I'm doing this! I was so close to escaping this dismal prison of a kingdom. If that is someone I know, though, I could never forgive myself. I'm hoping I can get there in time.*

Fortunately and unfortunately, the creature was no longer

waiting for Carter's return. Instead, there was an empty chunk of land that appeared to be uninhabited by anyone. Carter heard the sword's song as it collided with a shield. Frenzied chatter roared as a group of trolls encircled a fight.

"To the death!" one yelled.

A second troll laughed and said, "Rip his head off!"

Another creature walked over to the group, amused by the fight. "What's this?"

"Huh?" one asked. "Belv found 'em hiding over there."

As Carter made his way close enough to the action, he peered through a gap in the vegetation to observe a troll . . . and Jaut! Several minutes passed as Jaut and the troll fought intensely. One would direct their sword to strike the other, but they were both so quick that any damage was minimal. Impressed, Carter watched Jaut for a moment as he swiftly tried to stab the troll in the side. The troll quickly blocked the hit and slashed toward Jaut's stomach. Carter flinched as he witnessed the battle but didn't know what to do. He wanted to help, but he figured he'd do more harm than good interrupting them now. Holding his own, Jaut spun around, aiming for the troll's neck, before getting kicked in the chest and knocked down.

The troll laughed as he said, "You were good, but you weren't good enough!"

Sighing, another troll aggressively shouted at his friend, "Belv, stop wasting time! Kill him already! We have to help the others find the cape."

Carter's heart sank as he saw Belv raise his sword in the air to behead Jaut.

"Stop!" Carter shouted, flailing his arms. "Let him go! Please, let him go."

One troll snarled, asking, "Who's that?"

"Eh. Wait. Is that?"

Scratching their head, another troll asked, "What are you talking about?"

"Is that Linx's friend?" a troll shouted.

Another stepped in Carter's direction. "You really have some nerve thinking we'd help you."

Groaning under their breaths, the trolls reveled in Carter's fear of losing Jaut.

"Please! Please! I can help you in whatever way you need. He's a good guy that doesn't deserve to die."

"Ha! Listen to this fool. Like we care about how he can help us. There's no way we can trust you, so you're better off dead to us." Walking toward Carter, the troll raised his sword with anger behind his eyes.

"No! We aren't your enemy."

The troll rushed Carter, raising his sword into the night sky. The moon reflected off the blade, warning Carter of what was to come. "Everyone is our enemy now! Especially you! Everyone who left with you died, and for what? For you to be king of the land that sucks the life out of every other land? Over my dead body!"

Carter really didn't want to, but he felt he had no choice. Closing his eyes, Carter called upon his demons, his protectors. Chills covered his arms and neck, and intense pressure sank in his heart as his eardrums thumped with each step his vicious army took. Their fire eyes nearly glowed in the woods as they charged out, aiming to shred the troll and any other trolls nearby to pieces. The first goblin launched in the air while another ran toward the troll's ankles.

As Carter waited for the impact, he saw the other guards

flooding out of the castle to protect whatever they had left. At this point, he didn't know which advisors were alive—nor did he care. They all would soon get what they deserve.

"Stop!"

The shrill scream broke his concentration before an overwhelming curtain separated the goblins from the trolls. Once Carter realized that all his goblins were stuck within the vibrant dome, his head turned to see Linx standing hand-in-hand with Zalia. An incredible aura formed around their bodies, uniting their presence as one. Speechless, Carter's eyes scanned everything around him. It was the most spectacular thing he ever experienced—and that included when the wanderer brought him some odd and interesting encounters as well. His body felt heavy and restricted as a white semicircle created a dome over Carter, the goblins, and Jaut.

When he finally gathered his senses, Carter whispered, "Linx?"

With her body tense and her tone firm, she said, "I cannot let you harm the trolls."

"They were about to *kill* me . . . and Jaut too!" Carter's chest rose and dropped with each breath he took. He could not believe Linx would choose them over her friends. At that moment, Carter analyzed what his definition of a friend was—and that he still was a rotten one.

Looking from creature to creature, Linx said, "We need to help each other. We can't kill each other. There are enemies here who will drain us for everything we have and discard our bodies. Please."

A troll slammed his sword against the force field with all his strength. "We lose member by member with each journey or task, while giving everything we got, and for what?"

As the troll spoke, others marched over to hear the conversation between him and Linx.

"Juma, it's true. You and others have given everything. It isn't fair how the trolls of Violet Woods have lost so much. Our pact was meant to benefit both the fairies and the trolls, while allowing them to live harmoniously. Sadly, trolls have suffered the greatest without any retribution between the time of Poba's death and this current day. I also have a concern, though. Who sent you? And what did they want?" Releasing the force field, Linx slowly and confidently walked toward Juma, holding her hand in the air to signal Zalia and Pygo to wait.

Breathing loudly, with a gurgle in his chest, Juma frowned. "No one sent us. We got a message from an elder."

"What was the message they sent?" Linx asked.

Juma shouted, "The elder informed us that they found Poba's cape in Crystal Woods! Poba's cape, which was ripped from *his* body, was hung in this castle for display—mocking us! They wanted to let us know who was responsible."

Raising her eyebrows, Linx cautiously said, "Juma, wait."

"Don't you dare give me orders! We've waited long enough for answers. We demand Poba's cape and the blood of all involved."

"Juma! You don't understand!"

"No, I understand perfectly, Linx! This kingdom and everyone in it are garbage—including you."

Shaking her head, she looked him in the eyes. "If only you knew . . ."

"We know all we need to. *You* wanted the cape, and *you* killed the elder who guided you to Crystal Woods and the other elder who tried retrieving Poba's cape!" Gripping the sword, Juma was nearing his limit.

Finding the right words, Linx said, "Juma, you need to know the truth."

"About what? You murdering the elders or you failing Raza, Teshi, and Udin?"

Despite attempting to remain calm, Linx was starting break. Raging flames filled her body as the traumas experienced throughout the journey to Crystal Woods revisited her mind again. "How dare you! You come here fighting for justice while not knowing the truth or what anyone else has done in an attempt to right the injustices. The elders that you cling to are those who were created to divide us. They don't care about you, and they certainly don't care about me. They *never* did. They only cared about themselves and how they could manipulate us all!"

"You best watch your tongue, Linx!" Juma warned, pointing his sword at her.

"Stand down!" Pygo shouted from behind Linx. "Let her speak."

Smirking, Juma said, "Oh, how cute! Is that your pet? Don't worry, I'll kill that ball of fur too—then wear it as a hat when I get cold."

Laughing uncontrollably, Jaut shook his head while shouting, "You idiot!"

Linx's jaw dropped at the thought of what Pygo could do to disrupt their day. "Don't, Juma!"

As Juma went to strike Linx with his sword, Pygo threw himself high into the air before slamming into the ground next to Juma and the other trolls. With limited time, Linx immediately generated a force field bubble around herself, Carter, Jaut, and Zalia. Upon impact, the trolls and guards shot backward, forcefully catapulting in multiple directions. Bits of dirt, chunks of various rocks, leaves, and sticks speckled the air. Screams ensued as a handful of guards slammed into trees, puncturing their skin with branches. The guards who were not injured retreated back toward the castle.

"You are useless!" Juma cried.

"If you said that to me a while ago, I would've believed you," Linx said. "I may have argued with you, but deep inside, I would've agreed with you. I was taken and forced into labor, lied to, and tormented. I believed the elders, just like you. What else do we do? What else do we believe other than what was told to us? We arrive in this world from many other worlds, and what information do we have to go off of? Do you remember how you died in your previous life? Because so much of my memory was wiped out—until recently. Then, I tried to do what I thought was best when Carter came to Violet Woods. I sacrificed myself, as did the others. We wanted to know more, we wanted to help, and we wanted unity. You callously called me a murderer when you know *nothing* that occurred throughout our journey. You waited patiently as we experienced hell and back. I witnessed each of them go through things you couldn't imagine. Yes, you may have gone through the Dark Woods to get here, but you travel in a massive army of men, where we had a mere handful that quickly got picked away. With each life lost, I felt like a failure until I realized that it was simply the roll of the dice. We try to come prepared, but there are so many things you can't prepare for."

Groaning, Juma asked, "Like what?"

"Death!" Linx shouted, looking at Carter as he sank his head. "And then coming back after death to find myself buried, soon framed for a heinous act I never committed, and harshly imprisoned. I have served my time, Juma, and I tried my best to find your justice. I found Poba's cape, the one that an elder was going to steal for their own gain. Yes, I killed them, and it was for good reason. I wanted to bring Poba's cape to Violet Woods, but I was hunted by Crystal Woods after escaping imprisonment, since I was sentenced to death."

Juma's eyes lit up. "Where's the cape, Linx?"

"Gone."

Another troll demanded, "Gone? How is it gone?"

Stepping forward, Carter said, "It was my fault. If anyone should be held responsible, it should be me. I knew she was innocent, but she had to run from my men. They wanted her dead. She was a distraction from a bigger ploy."

Gazing into Carter's eyes while talking to Juma, she said, "As I ran, I tripped down the mountain. The cape adhered to my back. I had no intention of using the cape. I wanted to return it to Violet Woods, but I couldn't return. How could I?"

Juma and the trolls listened intently while awkwardly pulling themselves up from the ground.

"After finding myself involved with other issues in Pangotha, the cape was ripped off of my back by a deinos. The beast ate it. I've never seen anything like it," Linx said, shaking her head. "And here we are now. There's other big issues at play here, Juma, but I don't know where you stand. I gave everything I could, but sadly, it wasn't good enough."

Stomping over to Linx, Juma didn't blink until he stood a foot away. Discreetly, Linx observed Jaut camouflage close by, but she looked in his direction and shook her head. If she needed to fight, she would. But she needed to give Juma a chance to make a move. He stood in silence for a moment, gripping his sword once again. Rubbing her fingers together, Linx prepared herself to send an energy ball directly at his face if he decided to attack. Internal butterflies fluttered from her heart up to her throat. Juma inhaled deeply . . . before kneeling at her feet. Tears immediately streamed down Linx's face as hope filled her heart.

CHAPTER 27

"I'm so sorry for what you and the others went through, Juma. We've all wanted answers for so long, and now any piece of closure is underwhelming." Linx hung her head, sighing from the frustration they constantly encountered with this subject.

Juma shook his head and said, "As you know, we're only told so much."

"I know, and we can only believe a small portion of what we're told." Linx scanned her surroundings to keep an eye on Jaut, Pygo, Zalia, and Carter. "I don't want to cut you short, but I have to get someone back to their homeland in time. So, I'll have to leave you for now. This means the world to me, though. I hope to see you again someday."

As Linx turned to walk away, Juma mentally noted the kingdom's layout and the location of the surrounding trolls. "What's your mission, Linx?"

Despite wanting to open up, Linx had difficulty with

exposing Zalia's significance to Pangotha or even the Gemenii for that matter. Everything now felt like potential risks that may or may not be worth it.

Pursing her lips, she wanted to find the perfect, discreet way to slide this brief conversation into a message for Jaut or Pygo. She responded, saying, "Give me one moment, Juma."

Walking near Jaut, she quickly wanted to ask for his thoughts on the situation. She whispered, "Juma inquired about our current mission. I haven't said anything yet. I didn't know what to say. It seems like he can be trusted, but I don't want to risk Zalia's or anyone else's safety."

Rubbing his eyes forcefully, Jaut looked over and watched as Juma scouted out each of the trolls. As they made eye contact with him, he gave them specific directions for eliminating the approaching guards quickly. Without hesitation, the trolls fearlessly charged the guards. They had their swords drawn with pain in their eyes. Their capes draped protectively over their bodies, shimmering in the limited light. Swift blades sliced through the enemies, leaving no guard alive.

Focusing back on Linx, Jaut said, "I think it's a good idea to have them come with us. They'll have a place to rest, and they can help us remove the remaining guards within Pangotha."

"Are you sure?" she asked.

"Without a doubt," Jaut said firmly.

Rushing back over to Juma, Linx released a breath of air. "I'm sorry about that. We have an immense issue, and I fear giving anyone details. But—"

"It's quite all right," he said while standing. "I understand."

"But," she continued, "we may need you and your men more than you'll ever know. We'll be going on a journey to Pangotha shortly, and we have no idea if more guards will be there waiting."

His demeanor perked up, knowing he could help. "It would be an honor to come with you."

Sighing a breath of relief, her chest rose and fell, allowing the weight of the world to spill from her shoulders. She knew they were in for another arduous journey, but the trolls were undeniably valuable on the battlefield. As Linx thought about their fighting capabilities, the trolls gutted, with ease, more than a dozen guards that charged them. "What is your mission, though? I'm not sure how to help, since the cape is gone."

"The cape was part of it, but we wanted to dismantle their corrupted monarchy, making sure they never do this again."

"How can you possibly ensure that?"

With a vengeful smirk, he simply said, "Some men can stay here while others come with us. They'll take care of the rest of the problem ones."

Stepping forward, Carter said, "I can help you identify them."

Linx raised her eyebrow, studying Carter's facial reaction. It appeared genuine, but why? She couldn't understand why he was offering this now. "Carter, while I'm sure they'd appreciate it, we must leave. I'm not sure how much longer Pangotha can take the abuse. Also, we don't know who else may be interested in trying to conquer Pangotha."

"That's why I have to stay. I know everyone around here. The last thing any of us wants is to pay the cost with more innocent lives. It's the perks of being a former ruler," Carter said without hesitation.

"If you're sure," Linx said as her smile faded. "We've come so far, but if you feel you are more useful here, I completely understand."

"Yes, I feel good about this. I want to contribute, and I think this is the way to do it. There are so many corrupt advisors who need to leave this kingdom or face consequences. I feel confident that it can be done now. Although you don't need it, good luck, Linx." Carter stood awkwardly as he watched Linx trying to hide her automatic pout. Although he felt guilty, he couldn't help but smile.

Scrunching her eyebrows together out of frustration, Linx looked up at him. "What? What's so funny?"

Carter shook his head from side to side while pursing his lips. "Nothing."

In her gut, Linx knew Carter was lying. Walking toward him, she stared into his eyes despite not knowing whether he would have his mind blocked. For a moment, she heard nothing and chalked it up to Carter perfecting how to keep thoughts hidden. That was until an unfiltered thought passed through his mind.

I wish I could tell her.

Stepping closer, she looked deeper into his eyes. He neither flinched nor pushed her away, and a magnetic pull seemed to draw them together. Curious, she bluntly asked, "You wish you could tell me what?"

Caught off guard, he wanted to kick himself for being careless with his thoughts. He rubbed his neck while stumbling over his words. Carter surprised himself by saying, "I . . . um . . . wanted to tell you how beautiful you look."

Blushing, Linx turned her head away for a second. "Well, I wasn't expecting that."

"I don't know, Linx. No one knows what will happen. I

mean, I have faith in us. The trolls can annihilate most creatures they encounter, but if I don't see you again, I have to say that you're a special girl. You're funny, witty, smart, and—gorgeous. I can never apologize enough for how I treated you. I'm so sorry."

"Carter, I—"

Towering over her, he looked down and held out his arms. Pausing for a moment, she cautiously walked into his arms, and a single tear droplet slipped out of the corner of her eye. "Please keep yourself safe."

"You do the same too. Hopefully, our paths will cross again soon," Carter said before spontaneously kissing her on the forehead.

While butterflies danced in her stomach, she gracefully lifted the corners of her lips. Before she bade him farewell, she said, "Thanks for helping me find Zalia. You have no idea how much it means to me and Pangotha."

"You're welcome."

Linx turned to face Zalia and Pygo while Jaut made his way beside them. Nearby, Juma recruited a massive army of trolls while leaving a trustworthy leader and a significant chunk of men to fight in Crystal Woods. Once they had successfully divided their army, they exchanged words of encouragement. Together, they started marching toward the cave entrance where Linx and Jaut had traveled not too long ago.

As they continued on their journey, Jaut walked next to Linx. "Are you okay? I'm not sure what that was about back there, but I can only imagine."

She released a deep breath. "I'll be okay."

"All right. You don't have to talk about it. I was just wondering and a bit concerned. We don't know the status of

Pangotha right now, so we need to keep our minds clean." He rubbed the back of his neck, hoping to bring his friend to a calm state of mind.

"I'm okay. Don't worry about me. It's just complicated," Linx continued. "And it will always be complicated."

"That sounds exhausting. I don't know how you put up with it." Jaut shrugged, rolling his eyes.

Kicking some rocks in front of her, Linx said, "I don't know if it's surprising to you then, but I don't wish him ill will at all. In fact, I hope he soon becomes the happiest he's ever been. Everyone deserves happiness and joy. I've spent too much time locked in the darkness, and I've learned that we can never have too much light in this world. Yes, I was very upset with him a while ago, but part of me feels bad for all he's gone through, too."

"And what about you?" Jaut questioned Linx.

Confused, she stared at him. "What?"

"What about all you went through?" He shrugged. "I mean, it's not that ridiculous to ask. You were treated like garbage."

Slowly nodding her head, Linx remained silent. What could she say? He wasn't wrong. Hoping to drop the conversation, she looked over at Juma. "Have you ever traveled to Pangotha, Juma?"

"Hmm? Oh, no, no. Most of us haven't even left Violet Woods until now!" Juma chuckled.

"Well, it's a beautiful land. When I first stumbled upon Pangotha, it took my breath away. Apparently, it was even more breathtaking before I arrived—before they were robbed of their energy."

Unable to understand what she was describing, Juma asked,

"Huh? I have no idea what you are talking about. What happened?"

"Watch your step," she said, pointing to some loose rocks as they traveled down the mountain. Her gaze quickly connected with Zalia's. "In addition to kidnapping Zalia, Crystal Woods would coordinate a daily magical drain of Pangotha and everyone's energy. Then, following the drain, guards would invade Pangotha and slaughter or kidnap anyone they could find. Unfortunately, I witnessed this several times—not nearly as much as Jaut, Pygo, and the others who lived there."

Zalia observed everything around her—from the trees to the critters running by the creatures. "They wanted to siphon the energy from *everything and everywhere* to build their defenses and—"

"And what?" Juma asked.

"They had this plan to travel to planets or realms. They thought they could find routes back to our previous lives."

Jaut stopped and turned to her for a moment. "From what you've seen them doing, do you think that's possible?"

"I have no idea." Zalia shrugged.

"Some creatures get obsessed with jumping timelines, but I don't think we're at a spot to make that happen yet. I've seen issues arise because people want to contact others from their previous lives," Linx said.

"One of the men told me he was outright lying to another guy about the capabilities of jumping realms. He thought he was hilarious—a genius of some sorts. I always ignored him if I could. I'm not sure what I believe."

Shaking her head, Linx peered around a tree. "We need to go a little farther, and the cave will be right down there—hopefully undisturbed."

As soon as the words left her mouth, she heard laughing nearby and felt an eerie tickle sprinkle across her neck.

"What was that?" Jaut asked.

Hopping over a fallen branch, Pygo paused for a moment. "I don't have a good feeling about this."

Quickly signaling his men, Juma whispered orders and sent about a dozen down to scout the land. "They're going to check things out first before we get closer. The last thing we want is for you to get ambushed."

"Thank you." Linx graciously bowed her head.

"Let's hope it's something the guys get through quickly. We'll get through them, regardless." Juma smiled at Linx.

The rest of the group waited impatiently as laughs and a scream bounced from tree to tree, whispering sadistic intentions. Anxiety increased as the intensity of the shrieks rose. Pulled by emotion, Linx's instinctual drive tugged at her heart, begging her to locate the origin of the screams.

"Don't do it, Linx," warned Jaut.

Glancing over, Linx frowned. "What? Don't do what?"

Jaut raised his eyebrows and tipped his head forward, acknowledging her intentions. There was no point in playing any games. It would simply be energy wasted, so she looked away in disappointment. He walked over to her nonchalantly.

"What? I'm not going anywhere!" Linx snapped quietly so no one else would hear.

Amused, he smirked. "I know. I just wanted to say that you have a good heart."

Staring at him, she rubbed her lips together and sighed heavily.

"But that can be a flaw, too," Jaut continued.

"Oh, is that so?"

"Definitely! You have a responsibility to the Gemenii, Pangotha, and, most importantly, yourself. How would you feel if you ran down there to check out the situation and Zalia was somehow taken again—or worse?"

"Awful! I would feel awful. I get it already. No need to harp on it."

Bumping her arm playfully, he asked, "Well then, what's the matter?"

"It was something about the scream. I don't know." Linx hunched over for a moment in despair. She rarely felt torn inside for who to help, but she knew Jaut was right. In her soul, she was aware she had a purpose—to help Zalia reunite with Pangotha and potentially the Gemenii. They were counting on her, and she needed to allow herself to lean on the trolls and trust in their capabilities, strength, and skill.

Attempting to calm her nerves, a vision softly crept into her mind. The premonition consisted of breathtaking amber sunshine that melted over her skin, sweet dew mist over the vegetation, and a strong sense of contentment. Although the image and feelings were comforting, the persistent nagging of guilt tugged on her heart. She desperately looked at Juma, hoping to gather a sense of time for how long they needed to wait there. He stood almost motionless and listened intently, practically counting the trolls' steps as they located the noise. Right on cue, deeper screams and shouting echoed throughout the forest. Concerned, Linx didn't understand what was happening.

"We need to go help them!" Linx shouted, pleading with Juma.

Standing there, his lips curled into the epitome of satisfaction. "They don't need help, but we can proceed now."

Rolling her eyes, Linx asked, "Are you sure they don't need help?"

"Oh, I'm positive."

"All right! Let's go!" Jaut shouted enthusiastically.

Pygo looked at Linx as they walked down a tricky, sloped area. "My lady, is everything okay?"

Giving a half smile, she said, "Pygo, I'm not sure, but I guess we'll see."

"Well, I just want you to remember that I follow you." He stared for a moment to make sure she understood.

"Thank you, Pygo."

The further they descended, the more the moonlight faded through the trees, barely grazing the ground. Shadows from the leaves, rustling on the trees, danced across the woodland floor. A blanket of silence simultaneously calmed and spiked Linx's nerves while she fixated on any sounds around her. Moving branches out of the way, tiny flickers of light shone in the distance ahead. As the group approached an illuminated portion of the woods, a low mumble slowly became audible. A large campfire flickered, sending sparks floating into the air.

"Just over there!" Pygo whispered.

Some figures could be seen moving around, while others remained still. Once only a few trees stood between them, Linx noticed a slender figure seated on a log with their head and shoulders hunched forward. Interestingly, no one else sat near the figure. The trolls bickered back and forth, talking about what to do. Crystal Woods guards and bits of armor peppered the temporary campsite.

"Amazing!" Jaut said, impressed by the swiftness.

Stepping over a mangled arm, Linx said, "The trolls are the best warriors Violet Woods could ever wish for."

Intrigued, Juma disregarded Jaut and stared at the figure on the log. Unlike Linx, he had no interest in stepping over anything. Without a second thought, he crushed his boot into a broken skull as he asked, "Hmm. Who do we have here?"

"After we slaughtered the puny and pathetic tin men, we found her tied up. It seems like they did a number on her, but luckily, we came when we did," a troll reported.

"Thanks for the update, Farge. Has she said anything yet?"

"No, nothing."

Another troll circled around her. "How do we know this isn't a trap? I say we kill her."

"No! Don't! Leave her alone!" Linx desperately ran over to the log.

A troll asked, "Huh? What's your deal?"

"She's a friend! She's with us!"

Confused, Jaut waited patiently before saying anything. He had no idea what had gotten hold of Linx. "Who is it?"

Looking back at Jaut, Linx whispered, "Kateerah."

CHAPTER 28

Confused, Jaut asked, "Wait, what?"

"Kateerah! Jaut, it's Kateerah!" Linx shouted.

As soon as her name registered in their heads, Jaut and Pygo rushed over to see if she was okay. The dark light made it difficult to see all of her injuries. Her body had been severely bruised, and she had several slashes across her arms, legs, and back. A jagged gash ripped her skin beneath the middle of her left eye down to her jawline. Looking up at the trio, Kateerah's demeanor shifted. Her eyes lit up as familiarity finally sank in. "Jaut? Linx?"

"Kateerah! Are you okay? What happened?" The corners of Linx's lips dropped in despair.

Shaking her head, Kateerah said, "They found our hiding spot. I was so afraid they would've spotted the group, but I was able to distract the guards while the others got away."

"Oh, no! I'm so glad you're alive! What did they do to you?"

Linx cautiously asked. She hovered her hand over the laceration on Kateerah's face. "You don't have to answer that if you don't want to."

"They dragged me out and tied me up. There were so many of them. Whenever they'd ask a question, I refused to answer it. So, their anger and impatience got the best of them, and they beat me when I didn't give them the information they wanted. Some guards said they wanted to kill me. I had no doubt they were telling the truth. I don't know what would've happened by morning." Kateerah softly closed her eyes at the thought.

Shocked by the story, Linx asked, "What did they want? Did they ask for anything, or anyone, in particular?"

"It was just questions about the Gemenii—or you," she said.

"What? Who would be asking questions about me?"

Shrugging and shaking her head, Kateerah whispered, "I'm not sure. They were pathetic animals, though. I would've been able to defend myself if they didn't attack in a group like that." She shook her head before standing with her shoulders pulled back.

"I'm so sorry, Kat," Jaut said.

"I don't want pity. I want justice for Pangotha and Za—" Kateerah paused as her eyes flooded with tears. She quickly hobbled over to Zalia. "Oh! You're alive! I can't believe you're alive!"

"Of course, I'm alive." Zalia smiled as she hugged Kateerah.

Pulling back and holding Zalia's shoulders, Kateerah laughed. "I guess I should've just said I've missed you!"

"Are you okay?" Concerned, Zalia couldn't stop staring at all the blood and bruising on Kateerah's body.

"I'll be fine. Don't you worry about me. We have to find the others, though. I'm not sure how many guards are still lurking. They arrived group after group. We have to find them and kill them before they kill us."

"All right. Let's go," Juma shouted to his men.

Kateerah quickly glanced up at him in suspicion, maintaining her distance.

"Oh, I'm sorry, Kateerah. I didn't introduce you to Juma. He's from Violet Woods, as are the other trolls."

"I see."

Juma walked over to her and looked her in the eyes. "We've been wronged by the same people who destroyed your home. They stole something important to us, but unfortunately, it's gone now."

"Are you going to help us get rid of these monsters?"

"I can give you my word that we'll try our damnedest."

Nodding her head, Kateerah turned toward the direction back to Pangotha while releasing a deep sigh. Linx's heart went out to Kateerah as she readied herself to battle once more. She admired that she sacrificed herself for her community without even batting an eyelash.

An image—a feeling—flashed across her mind. Linx felt the sun's warmth absorb into her skin as happiness resonated in her soul. A sweet floral smell tickled her nose before embedding its scent in her brain. Her heart fluttered when she peered over to see someone similar in stature to her sister, Lyla. Laughter and joy swirled around them as they ran together in a field filled with purple and gold flowers. They continued to giggle as they raced into bliss. The feeling of belonging coated her spirit, exploding to each finger, toe, and breath.

Crunch. Someone's shoe snapped a twig that was resting on

the ground—instantly crumbling Linx's vision. The merriment shattered from her being, disintegrating each shard that fell. What did it mean? Would she see Lyla again? Oh, how part of her heart longed for that to be true, before remembering the cost. It would mean that Lyla would've died. Despite Linx wanting to reunite with the one being she loved most, Lyla deserved to be happy. She deserved to live a long life filled with happy moments, maybe kids or even grandkids someday.

"Linx, you good?" Jaut asked.

With a faint smile, Linx discreetly wiped a warm tear from her cheek. "Yeah. I'm coming."

For a brief moment, her ambition took a dip as she had to come to terms with her present reality. Looking around at all the faces, Linx channeled her focus to find her purpose. As she fought against the lingering shadow in her mind, someone caught her attention. Standing confident and tall, Zalia glanced in Linx's direction. Witnessing such a powerful soul destined to rule a land under attack, Linx admired her tenacity for her age. Maybe she didn't know what she was in for, but who's to say anything after she was a prisoner in Crystal Woods?

Turning to see Kateerah walking near Pygo and Jaut, an overwhelming feeling of respect jolted her brain. Linx almost felt indebted to them all. From the beginning, Pygo saw something in Linx she hadn't—as a guardian. Although this message apparently came from the Gemenii, the way he looked at her made Linx feel appreciated. That was something not many people could do. Then Linx thought about Jaut and Kateerah. They sacrificed so much for their community and even for Linx, guiding Linx and protecting her whenever they could.

"What's the matter?" Jaut asked.

Releasing a heavy sigh, Linx shrugged and shook her head. "I . . . don't know."

Confused, he stopped for a moment to walk beside Linx. "What do you mean, you don't know?"

"I just had a vision."

"I see. What was it about? Or can you not tell me?"

Quietly whispering, she said, "Lyla. I think."

Pausing with curiosity, Jaut thought about how he wanted to approach this topic. "Oh, yeah? Was it a good or bad vision?"

With her bloodshot eyes holding back heavy tears, she said, "It was beautiful, peaceful, and everything else I could've ever imagined. I had her back again."

"Well, I'm risking sounding dumb, but does this mean anything?"

Remaining silent, she thought about what it could mean. Focusing on the ground as they walked, Linx got lost in the warm feeling, holding it for as long as she could.

"I'm sorry, Linx. I—" Jaut pulled her back to reality.

Linx rubbed her arm. "There's no need to be sorry. I really don't know what it means, honestly. So many visions come to light, but I don't know what to make of this one."

Pressing his lips together, Jaut nodded with understanding. "I hope you find peace again, Linx."

"Thank you so much. That means more than you'll ever know."

"Despite what you may think of me, I'm not a complete jerk. I don't like to see people suffer—at least not everyone." He laughed, flashing his infamous grin.

Cracking a smile, Linx rolled her eyes and gripped a tree as they walked down a slope. "I never said that."

"Eh, but you thought it."

Shaking her head from side to side, Linx adamantly refused to agree with him. "I just want to focus on our journey to get Zalia back. It's the only thing that we have influence over."

Patting her gently on the shoulder, Jaut turned to Juma and said, "We have to head over there. I don't know if anything is waiting inside, but that cave leads straight into Pangotha."

Waving his men toward the direction of the cave, Juma walked beside Pygo, talking about something that made each other laugh. Curious, Linx wanted to know what they were bonding over, but she didn't want to interrupt. Nevertheless, she was grateful for everyone else's upbeat attitude. Lighting a bright flame in her hand, she helped to guide others through the woods, especially those who had difficulty navigating in the darkness. Luckily for her, there weren't many that required assistance. Linx held onto a thin tree with her other hand as she descended the slanted ground. Mere feet away from the opening of the cave, her heart started pounding as excitement sped through her body. There was still a decent journey ahead of them, but she knew they were one step closer to bringing some tranquility back to Pangotha.

"Yeah, this doesn't look suspicious," a troll muttered as others shuffled inside while cautiously observing their environment.

"I know it's nothing to look at, but at least we're on the right track," Linx explained. "Once we go through this cave, we need to locate the Gemenii's cave in Pangotha quickly, before we're spotted."

"We're not afraid of anyone," Juma shouted.

"I understand! I'm not saying you should be—really. It's just that it would be a shame to waste energy on unnecessary battles."

A concerned look crossed Pygo's face as he remained quiet.

"What's the matter, Pygo?" Linx asked.

Licking his teeth, he looked into the sky before entering the cave. "I just . . . don't know how well the Gemenii would appreciate a party of guests parading through their sacred caverns."

"Do you have a problem with us coming?" Juma was not afraid to show that he was offended.

"It has nothing to do with you but everything to do with everyone else. You just need to explain to your men the importance of keeping the Gemenii's location confidential," Pygo explained.

Snorting, Juma said, "Trust me, you have nothing to—"

"I'm serious," Pygo interrupted.

"Huh?"

Adamant to get his point across, Pygo raised his voice. "This is why we're in this predicament now. Someone leaked the location of the Gemenii to untrustworthy individuals who came back to ravage our homeland and take everything—including the strength and power of all who reside in Pangotha."

"Look, if it makes you more comfortable, we don't have to go toward any sacred land or location. We can wait anywhere you need us."

Linx peered over at Jaut, unsure of what to say. He simply shrugged his shoulders and chuckled. Once Pygo noticed how the environment had shifted, he took a breath and gently closed his mouth.

Jaut kicked a few pebbles his way. "It's okay. We know you're *very* dedicated to *your* Gemenii."

Turning to face away from the crowd, Pygo mumbled to himself, "Fool."

As the trolls proceeded into the dark tunnel, they reluctantly glanced at each other before marching down the same path Linx had . . . not too long ago. Although the trolls saw well in the tunnel, Linx knew Pygo, Jaut, and Kateerah did not have the same advantage, so she moved up to the front of the group and brightened her flame. Looking into the darkness with the army behind her, she felt an excitement that raised her spirits. There was a chance, a very good one in fact, that she could help all of those suffering in Pangotha.

"There is a good spot a little bit further where we can rest for the night. I can form a protection force field around us to assist with holding back any enemies who attempt to attack us while we sleep," Linx said with a gentle smile.

Jaut nodded with enthusiasm.

"That sounds great," Juma agreed. "We have traveled very far and could use some sleep. We can sleep in shifts, too, to help stand guard."

"We brought some food if anyone needs some," a troll in the back added.

"Oh, yes, please! I haven't eaten in a while. I'm starving!" Jaut yelled.

Pygo's eyes lit up as well. "Oh, that would be lovely."

"Let's set up camp, and we can distribute what we have." Juma smiled at them.

After a few minutes, Linx ushered the group into a giant space where the trolls and others made themselves as comfortable as possible. Forming a force field around the group, Linx smiled as she was reminded of the hubbub in Violet Woods when everyone sat down to feast. Resting beside one another, they waited patiently as two trolls dug into large brown sacks that they had strapped over their shoulders. Jaut and Pygo were impressed by the berries, melons, breads, and dried meats they carried. As they stared at each other, Jaut winked at Pygo while rubbing his hands together. Shaking his head in disgust, Pygo knew Jaut would wipe out the entire ration for the night, given the chance. Jaut's appetite was a beast to be messed with, so Pygo rushed over to get some dried meat and bread. Once he maneuvered around one troll, he quickly hopped over toward the two trolls distributing food. When he thought he was in the clear, Pygo picked up a little speed before accidentally bouncing off Juma's stomach.

"Woah there, little fella!" Juma shouted. "No need to rush! There'll be enough for everyone. Just wait your turn."

Holding in his laughter, Jaut discreetly pressed his lips together. "Yeah, there's no need to be greedy, little fella."

Fluffing up his fur, Pygo grunted as he took a seat. Linx caught wind of Jaut's teasing, so she brought over her portion to Pygo.

"Oh, my lady, you don't need to do that. I just didn't want to get behind this horse."

"Horse?" Jaut held his hand up to his chest and whinnied.

"I should've said jack—"

"Ignore him, Pygo!" Linx interrupted as she shot Jaut a disapproving glare. "And don't worry about it! I know you must be famished after your time in the dungeon. I can wait for some more."

"You are truly a kind soul," Pygo said, smelling the inviting aroma from her plate.

Sliding an extra piece of meat on Pygo's plate, Jaut said, "Ah, you know I'm joking with ya, fluff ball. Here, take this."

"Give me your berries. Maybe I'll forgive you then."

"Hmm. I don't like you that much, my friend!" Jaut laughed, popping three purple berries in his mouth.

While happily devouring their food and sipping lukewarm water from canteens, their voices echoed down the tunnel, providing a sense of warmth among the group. They briefly chatted between bites about past fights and strange encounters from their travels through the Dark Woods. As they passed around the remaining portions of various breads and fruits, they looked at each other to figure out who'd be keeping an eye out while others slept.

Juma asked, "Wronet and Bueron, how about we take the first shift? And Pon, too. The four of us can easily watch over everyone."

"Sounds good to me," Wronet said, biting into a chunk of bread.

Reaching for some berries, Bueron shook his head in agreement. He impatiently peered over toward Pon and kicked him in the leg.

"Ah! What was that for?" Pon rubbed the side of his shin.

"Juma's waiting for you to answer!"

Reaching for another chunk of bread, he squinted his eyes. "Yeah, I said yeah."

"No, you didn't," Bueron said.

Puffing out his broad chest, Pon sank his uneven teeth into his food. "I did, too!"

"Enough!" Juma said, pounding his hand off the wall.

"Juma, can you wake me up so you guys can get some sleep too?" Linx asked. "I want to make sure that everyone gets time to rest."

"It shouldn't be you!" Juma shouted and joked. "These free-loaders shouldn't be getting more shut-eye than you!"

"Freeloaders?" a troll yelled, grumbling while chewing his food. "After all we do, and we get called freeloaders."

"Eh, calm yourself. You sleep and complain more than you battle." Juma tossed a berry at the troll's face, and others laughed as it bounced off.

Creasing her forehead, Linx shook her head. "No, no. Don't worry about it at all. We need to make sure everyone has as much energy as possible. I'm really not sure what to expect. We might make our way through and see no one. I truly hope that's the case, but we might encounter countless guards with whatever new weapon they've created. I'm just trying to be prepared for the worst."

"I understand, Linx. I'll wake ya."

Partly smiling, Linx nestled herself into a comfortable ball, folding her arm under her head. Although hope clung to Linx's heart, she wondered if there would ever be a night in the future when she could sleep without worrying.

After the others scarfed down several remaining handfuls of food, everyone except Juma, Wronet, Bueron, and Pon managed to prop against the wall or lie on the ground, attempting to get in a position comfortable enough to fall asleep. Within a short time, snoring projected from every angle, bouncing from wall to wall. The four remaining trolls stationed themselves near each other, quietly telling stories in the fading light of the cavern tunnel.

"There ain't no way you slayed six jaks on your own," Wronet said. "You're out of your mind."

"I did, too! You're just jealous that you can't," Pon argued, squinting at Wronet.

Trying to calm his laughter, Bueron rolled his eyes. "Now,

now, leave him alone. Clearly, they came out when you were taking a dump behind the tree."

"I swear. You're supposed to be the best warriors Violet Woods can offer, yet you still argue about the dumbest crap." Juma pulled a knife from his pocket and ran his finger across the blade. "We're screwed."

Silence fell over the group as they thought about the devastation that consumed their homeland.

"Why can't we just kill her?" Pon moaned.

With her back facing the group, Linx's eyelids popped open. She began to breathe quickly as she did not anticipate any hostility toward her. Rubbing her fingers together, sparks flew out from her fingertips. Her mind remained on high alert.

Pulling his eyebrows into a tight line, Juma held the tip of his blade to Pon's throat. "I've told you before, no rogue missions. We came to find Poba's cape, disassemble Crystal Woods, and to right what's been wronged. Linx did not wrong us."

"According to . . . her." Pon sighed before sitting back.

Knowing she had at least one ally watching her back, she eventually drifted off to sleep.

"Linny! Linny!" a singsong voice shouted.

Opening her eyes, Linx looked around to see herself sitting on her family's wooden living room floor. A marble rolled past Linx's toes as she tried to assess the validity of her current reality.

"Linny! Catch that!" Running over quickly, Lyla dove to the ground, skinning her knees as she cupped the marble.

Wiping her eyes, Linx blinked several times before noticing a novel on the bookshelf. As she attempted to read the title,

Linx noticed the letters on the spine shifted and slid around on the book cover.

"Do you want to go outside, Linny?" The shiny, dark curls on the back of Lyla's head bounced with life as she sprinted toward the door. "Come on! Let's go play!"

Held by intense gravity, Linx pulled her legs through what felt like invisible quicksand that refused to let go. As she approached the door, the distance surprisingly increased. She wondered if she would ever escape.

A lighthearted giggle behind her shouted, "Linny!"

Turning around, the walls of the home broke away and shifted into a field outside. The long weeds whipped Linx's skin, stinging momentarily before disappearing altogether. She could hear Lyla's chuckle, but whenever Linx spun her head around, Lyla was nowhere to be seen. Trudging through the weeds, she obsessively followed the laughter. As she pushed past the branches, Linx heard splashing in the nearby creek.

"Lyla? Where are you?" Linx took the route she knew best, but she was struggling to find her. "Lyla?"

"Come on, Linny! I'm over here!"

"I need to talk to you about something." Walking around another tree, Linx finally saw where Lyla was playing. She splashed in the creek, sending droplets everywhere.

Stepping into the water, Linx didn't notice any temperature difference as the water rushed up against her skin.

"I have something to tell you."

Looking into Linx's eyes, Lyla had an eerily robotic approach. "What do you need to tell me?"

"I won't be coming back to play anymore."

"I don't understand." Lyla looked intensely into her eyes.

Twisting her soft hair, Linx released a deep breath. "I can't do this. It's not real—you're not real. It's just prolonging the inevitable. I hope that someday I can see your angelic face again. I hope wherever you really are, you find peace, happiness, and love."

"But I love you, Linny! You can't leave me!" Lyla stomped into the water, sending droplets in all directions. Upon realizing that she had no influence over Linx, Lyla burst into tears, sobbing loudly to keep her attention.

"I will always love you, Lyla. But I need to move on. You will always be in my heart. I need to go now."

CHAPTER 29

Forcing herself to open her eyes, she scanned the makeshift room to mentally note who was asleep and who was still awake. Surprisingly, everyone was fast asleep except Juma. He waited patiently while Bueron and Wronet rested on each other, snoring louder than anyone else in their hiding spot. As for Pon, he appeared to have been asleep for quite a while. Aggressively knotting some ration bags, Juma didn't realize that Linx was staring at him. After a few minutes, he felt the tingling on his neck of lingering eyes upon him. Glancing over, Linx waved her hand calmly so as not to wake anyone before giving him a thumbs up to nap.

"Are you sure?" he asked. "I can wake one of my men."

"No, I'm good. I'll wake Jaut shortly. Thank you, though."

Nodding as a thank you, Juma scooched his body over to the side, making room for him to lie down. Linx witnessed him release buried stress as he exhaled and his body sank into the ground. *Why did it have to come to this?* Linx thought to herself.

Life felt doable and contained several moments of happiness within Violet Woods. Trolls protected the land while foraging for magnificent crystals and gems, and the fairies had agreed to maintain peace and prosperity over the land. Unfortunately, this was the reality now. Staring off into the hypnotizing ridges of cavern walls, she hoped soon the near future would bring a stronger sense of calm.

Keeping herself occupied, Linx opened her hand flat and formed a flame that barely grazed her skin, pulling the energy from within her to grow the fire. Entranced by the beauty, her gaze followed the swaying and sharp flickers of the light. It danced across the palm of her hand, gliding gracefully while increasing speed.

"You okay?" Jaut asked quietly.

His voice went through Linx's skin, causing her to jump and crush the flame in her hand. With her heart pumping rapidly, she looked over toward Jaut. Linx said harshly, "What?"

"Woah, calm down. I had no idea what was going on."

"Don't tell me to calm down. You scared the crap out of me."

Rubbing his face with both hands, Jaut lightly grunted. "Look, I didn't know if you were under a spell or something by the way you stared at the flame."

Scowling, she said, "Under a spell? Are you serious right now?"

"Just forget it."

"Jaut, I was meditating. I wasn't under a spell or anything like that—I mean, unless it was my own. I was only trying to pass the time and calm myself!" Linx laughed.

"Well, how am I supposed to know? You were doing that for a while, so I figured I needed to ensure you were okay. I know it's getting stressful again. We were so focused on getting Zalia, and now that we found her, I can't wait to bring her back to the Gemenii." Jaut looked over toward Zalia, who slept soundly with a piece of tattered fabric draped over her body.

Nodding her head, Linx rubbed her eyes. "Yeah, I feel the same. Each part of the journey back, I'm terrified something will happen. We both know we'll give it our all, but I don't want to let anyone down. Everyone has treated me so kindly since I arrived. Well . . . maybe after the first several moments." She playfully glared at him.

"What can I say? I have to protect what means most to me. You seemed suspicious." Jaut smirked.

"I'm sure," Linx said, rolling her eyes before pausing momentarily.

Jaut noticed the shift in her face as Linx stared beyond him. "What? What is it?" He turned his head to see what she might be looking at.

"I . . . don't know. I could've sworn I saw something pass by quickly."

"Huh? Really? What did it look like?" Jaut inconspicuously reached for his sword.

Linx shifted to her feet as she tried focusing on the peculiar shadows that lurked just beyond her line of sight. Slight movements twitched in the darkness, but nothing could be identified. Carefully walking toward the opening and fluttering her fingers around, Linx slowly lifted her leg and tapped Juma's thigh with her shoe. Without a second passing by, Juma's eyelids snapped open, and he immediately locked onto Linx's eyes. Holding out one finger to keep Juma and Jaut on standby, she crept closer to the force field. Jaut glanced over briefly at Juma to see his hand reaching for his blade as well. Quickly shaking Pygo awake, Jaut held his hand over his mouth so Pygo knew he shouldn't speak. Little by little, others woke each other up to prevent an ambush.

Standing with her toes almost touching the force field, Linx peered down and then up the tunnel. Strangely enough, she didn't see anything at all. She was slightly embarrassed and wondered if she was seeing things. They needed to be hypervigilant, but they also needed plenty of rest before entering the center of Pangotha—or even just to continue through the rest of the tunnel. As she turned around to walk back to her empty spot, a gray figure jumped at the force field, trying to attack Linx. Startled, she flew backward, stepping on a sleeping troll's hand. The troll hurled his arm against her, sending Linx's tiny body flying against the wall. Whacking her head against the wall, she dropped to the floor in a heap. Instantaneously, the force field disintegrated, fully exposing the area to danger.

Jaut shouted, "You fool! How dare you hit her like that?"

"Pon, what is the matter with you?" Juma yelled. "I swear, if she doesn't wake up, it's your life that will be on the line!"

"I was sleeping, and she stepped on me!"

"So you can hit her so hard she smashes her head off the wall? Give me a break. Don't be weak, and hold your temper." Juma had no patience for Pon's problem with Linx. He didn't know if they knew each other too well, but Pon had a growing, transparent dislike for Linx that Juma couldn't understand.

As Pon went to defend himself against Juma's words, an agile creature ran in. Light shined off of its smooth, oily, gray skin. Running on all four legs, it almost looked manlike but with a sharp snout jutting from its face. The creature charged toward Linx, opening its mouth to reveal a double row of teeth on the top and bottom. Stumbling over the trolls' bags, it emitted a deep, frustrated growl. Jaut slid his legs to the side to spring up, bounding toward the beast without hesitation. Oddly enough, the creature focused on Linx's whereabouts rather than its own surroundings and the potential threats near it. Taking advantage of the moment, Jaut lightly ran behind the beast to avoid drawing any attention to himself. As he leaped onto the creature, he gripped his sword, pulling it up and quickly dropping the blade into the creature's back. As soon as the tip of the sword slid into its skin, the creature violently bucked, knocking Jaut on top of a rock pile.

Scrambling forward, Jaut couldn't move after being blocked by other trolls who were swinging their weapons at the agile animal. Trying to push between them, he was unsuccessful at navigating through the trolls. Devastated, he saw the creature reach Linx and look down at her. Jaut's heart dropped as he envisioned his friend being shredded to death. He was disgusted with himself as his eyes couldn't look away.

The beast brought its nose close to Linx's face. It licked her cheek and rested its head on her shoulder, whining from the pain in its back. Dumbfounded and confused, Jaut stared in disbelief as this monstrous beast cuddled up with Linx. No one moved as they were blown away by the outcome.

Jaut asked Pygo. "Should I try to wake her up? I don't know if we can, though. She hit her head pretty bad." He gave Pon an icy stare.

"I don't know. Maybe we should wait this out until she wakes up."

"What if she doesn't wake up?"

"All right, all right. Maybe we can give her a couple more minutes. The last thing we want to do is startle that thing, causing it to kill her. Oh, wait! Look!" Pygo whispered.

"Huh? What?" Jaut looked toward Linx.

Pygo bounced lightly up and down. “She moved her head a little bit.”

“Hey! Move! I need to get over to her!” Jaut shouted into the chaos, just to be ignored. Despite shoving the trolls, they were overly distracted by the beast.

“I wish we could get over to her.” Jaut ran his fingers through his hair.

“If you insist, I can get you over there.” Releasing a giant, mysterious smile, Pygo awaited Jaut’s response.

“What do you mean?” It took a second for it to click in his brain, and then he said, “Oh! Yes, definitely. Let me grab onto something, so I don’t float away!”

“Kateerah and Zalia, hold on to something,” Pygo whispered.

Some trolls overheard Pygo talking with the others, but they didn’t understand what was going on. Zalia and Kateerah quickly grabbed onto whatever they could, hoping they would be okay. After Jaut linked his arm with a nearby large boulder, he gave Pygo a wink to move on.

Pulling together all the strength in his little yet mighty body, Pygo jumped a few feet into the air in preparation for moving the trolls out of Jaut’s way. As his body came in contact with the ground, every troll around him buckled forward and fell to the floor. They shouted and blamed each other for the issue until they realized it was Pygo.

“What the hell was that for?” a troll screamed at Pygo.

Another chimed in while pushing three trolls off of him and said, “Yeah, what’s your deal?”

“Jaut needs to get over to Linx! All of you clogged up the way. Now move!” Pygo demanded without any waver in his voice.

Grumbling among themselves, they stood back up and shuffled to the side, allowing Jaut to pass. As he looked in Linx's direction, he was relieved to see that she was waking up. Initially looking at her face, concern overcame him as he wondered if she had head trauma from the impact against the wall. Would she be able to react quick enough?

While opening her eyes, she sat frozen in place as the creature looked down at her. Disoriented, it took a moment to realize who was hovering above her. As her mind desperately tried to adjust to reality after being slammed against the hard surface—now twice, most recently thanks to Pygo—she finally recognized the beast standing above her.

"Linx! We're coming!" Jaut shouted as Pygo hopped behind him.

Not focusing on Jaut, Linx dismissed his yelling and instead stared into the creature's eyes while tearing up. "It's been so long," she whispered.

Bringing its nose near Linx's face again, the creature licked her cheek and ever so gently rubbed its face against hers. Jaut grabbed a knife and readied himself to throw it when close enough.

Linx then let out a giggle and quietly said, "Rexil!"

Immediately stopping in his tracks, Jaut yelled, "Rexil? Who's Rexil?"

Looking over, Linx didn't understand what the commotion was about. "He's Rexil," she said, pointing to the creature in front of her. "Why? What are you doing?"

He gazed down at the blade in his hand and quickly hid it in a side pocket. "Ugh . . . saving you."

"Saving me? Saving me from what? Happiness?"

Perplexed, he held his breath while rubbing his face. With

the room now quiet and all beings focused on him, he bluntly asked, "*What* is Rexil?"

"Oh," Linx said, laughing. "I'm so overwhelmed by this surprise! Rexil was my childhood pet! He is the sweetest, but he can get quite protective."

"Ah, I see! Well, I'm glad you told me before I sent Rexil to a new home." Jaut opened his eyes wide and rolled them.

Scowling, Linx pet Rexil's head while furrowing her brows. "I would end you."

Jaut chuckled. "What? How am I supposed to know this hideous beast was your beloved pet?"

"How dare you!"

"I'm joking! I'm joking! However, I may have scratched Rexil."

While assessing Rexil's health, Linx noticed a minor gash on his back. "Jaut! What is wrong with you?"

"How was I to know? That thing charged toward you. I thought it would hurt you."

Tending to his wounds, Linx massaged Rexil's face and attempted to minimize his bleeding.

Jaut scanned the room, and by no surprise, everyone had woken up from the chaos. "Since we're all up now, should we get moving?"

Pressing on his eyes, Juma said, "I wish I could've slept longer than that, but we might as well get ourselves moving."

"Sounds good to me! How about you guys?" He pointed at Pygo, Kateerah, and Zalia before looking over toward Linx. "As long as you're feeling okay."

Shaking their heads, they all agreed to gather their items to prepare for the next portion of the journey.

"I'll be fine, I think. My head is just killing me, though." Linx gently held her injury as she stood up.

"We can wait if you need some time to rest," Jaut suggested.

"No, let's go. I'll rest on the way if I need to," she said, motioning for Rexil to follow her.

As she walked slowly toward the tunnel, Rexil obediently followed behind her. When he passed Jaut, Rexil glared at him, warning him to be careful. Jaut was flabbergasted by the intensity of Rexil's stare. His bright purple eyes with large pupils went straight through Jaut's soul.

"That thing is creepy," he admitted.

Pygo laughed at Jaut's facial reaction. "You're picking a problem, and all for what? If you quit threatening him, then maybe he'll spare your life."

Ushering everyone into the tunnel to resume their journey, Juma waited to speak with Jaut. When everyone finally left the small area, Juma asked, "So, speaking for all of my men, we haven't ever traveled to Pangotha. Is there anything we need to be wary of? I don't want us just walking in blind."

"Anything to be wary of? If you're not trying to kidnap people from our community or cause destruction to our land, it normally wouldn't be an issue. I truly don't know what to say now. The land and the residents' energy have been drained to almost nothing."

"I see." Juma scratched his chin. "Well, we're not here to harm Pangotha. I just hope the others see that."

"I'm sure they will. Let's hope for minimal guards along our travels. It will only slow down our journey, but it will not break us."

Nodding his head, Juma knew they wouldn't have any issues, especially with the setup. As the tunnel grew narrow, some trolls fought over how close they were to one another—pushing and shoving others when one would get bumped.

"Did you do that on purpose?" Pon shouted at Wronet.

"Huh?"

"You stepped on my foot, you clumsy fool!"

Snorting, Wronet slammed his shoulder against Pon's before he crushed Pon's foot beneath his boot. "If I wanted to step on your foot, you would know it."

"Ahh!"

Juma glared at the rowdy bunch. "All right, all right."

As she compared walking alone to now being surrounded by so many, Linx smiled to herself. She peered over at Zalia, watching her confidently walk among the crowd. Zalia had a warm, powerful aura that flowed from her presence. It was no surprise that Kateerah walked beside her, happy to be reunited again.

After quite some time, the narrow tunnel opened up, allowing the group to breathe as they trekked through the darkness. What was once a rambunctious environment soon became uncomfortably quiet. Whether it was due to the unknown or simply boredom, an uneasy feeling overcame the travelers. A deep, bitter coldness weaved around them, coating every inch of their beings. Although it was unclear what had changed, every being felt a shift. While walking and pressed against one another, they proceeded almost as a single entity, charging through the darkness.

Linx led the mass gathering, lighting a solid semicircle in front of her. She knew they were almost near the explosion site; however, the potential of an ambush threatened her excitement. Stuffing her nerves back down, she led the group onward with undeniable confidence and an undetectable light sigh.

CHAPTER 30

"Not to be rude, but are we almost there yet, Linx?" Jaut complained. "Maybe it's me, but it feels like this trip is taking twice as long to get through the cave. How much longer can this take?"

Acknowledging his concern with compassion, Linx motioned her head forward. "Hang in there. We aren't far."

"You said that a while ago."

With patience, she chuckled and said, "I know, I know. But we are."

"How can you be so sure?" a troll yelled from behind them.

"Because I came through here before, and that was a memorable experience, to say the least," Linx said. "It will narrow ahead again, and we'll finally be able to leave the cavern. There is also a wonderful vantage point at the end of the cave. We might want to take advantage of that prior to walking through the woods."

"I'm just hoping there is a land to come back to and save after all of this." Jaut shook his head.

"Our family and friends are a lot stronger than you think!" Kateerah snapped.

Turning his focus to her, Jaut silently looked at Kateerah for a moment. "You're right."

"You should've seen them before I was taken. They are doing what they can to stay alive. I made sure to let them know that we'd come back for them. In the meantime, I told them to hide in the safest place I could think of."

"How did you know that we'd make it back?" Linx asked.

Kateerah raised the corners of her mouth. "There was no doubt in my mind you would be back again."

A much-needed warmth swept over Linx as they approached where the tunnel narrowed a second time. The feelings of isolation, darkness, and suffocation instantly became vivid again, reminding Linx of her first time walking through. Dismissing those moments as quickly as she could, her eyes widened as she saw the hole where she had decimated the cave.

"Ladies and gentlemen, we're here," Linx whispered. A wave of excitement rushed over her legs, up her torso, and clutched her heart. Curiosity felt as though it would eat her alive. Would they make it to the Gemenii unharmed? At this point, all they could do was focus on one step at a time.

With an unsure yet accepting sigh, Juma walked toward the hole in the cavern wall. "I wonder what happened here," he said, scanning the rubble piled on the ground.

"Long story, but it was me," Linx admitted.

Raising his eyebrows, Juma nodded in respect. Impressed by the destruction, he kicked some rocks to the side before carefully peering out of the exit. Concern emerged beneath his scowl as he absorbed the devastation that was now Pangotha's reality. Linx hadn't yet looked out to see its current state, but after witnessing Juma's reaction, she frantically stumbled over a pile of debris to glance over the land. Her heart sank as her mind almost refused to believe what she saw. Green faintly covered the land while brown predominately shaded the ground and woods. Despite the lack of morning light, it was still apparent that Pangotha's state had significantly declined since when she had seen it last.

"Jaut," Linx whispered in disbelief.

Confused, Jaut climbed over several rock piles to stand near Linx. "What's the matter?"

"I . . . don't know what's happening to Pangotha."

Sinking his head down, Jaut said, "Pangotha is dying. Crystal Woods drained and killed off almost everything we had here—magic, power, safety, peace."

"But they can never take our hope!" Pygo hopped over to view the wreckage himself.

Jaut unenthusiastically asked, "What hope do you have left, puff?"

"That we can defend our home! Don't give up now, you buffoon! We're so close!"

"Looking out there, all I see is death," Jaut said frankly as Kateerah and three trolls came over to observe the land themselves. "It's hard to remain hopeful when our home looks so defeated."

Pygo asked, "We've come so far, been through so much, and for what? For you to give up?"

"I never said I gave up. I'm just being honest. It's not looking good out there." Jaut laughed, rolling his eyes. His lack of energy to entertain Pygo's motivational questions only fueled Pygo's fire.

"Well, you might as well have. If you give up hope, you give up everything. You made it to Crystal Woods and back again with everyone you care about."

"Don't flatter yourself," Jaut teased.

Irritated with the banter, Pygo bounced toward Linx. "I'm not trying to. Collectively, you found Zalia, rescued me from an unfortunate and painful demise, helped Kateerah, made it back, and formed an alliance with a powerful army." Ignoring Jaut, Pygo looked deep into Linx's eyes. "My lady, I believe in you, and I know that we'll make it. Regardless of what that imbecile says, I hope you feel the same."

"Hey! No need to say that. I'm entitled to my opinion. Besides, I'm not saying we're all going to die, but I know they didn't bring Pangotha's energy down this far without maximizing their gain in the meantime. I bet there are many hiding and waiting for us to come down."

"They very well may be, but what choice do we have?"

"Pygo, I'm mostly joking—mainly about the hope," Jaut admitted. "I do have hope, but I also know there are plenty of leeches lurking in the woods. We need to remain calm but not overly confident."

"Agreed!" Pygo huffed, turning to look toward Zalia.

Waiting to make sure the two had reached a common ground, Linx said, "If it means anything, I'm going to do everything in my power to escort Zalia to the Gemenii and protect Pangotha in any way I can." She gently smiled as her focus shifted from one being to the next. "We're all in this together."

"We have your back," Juma stated. "But I want to finalize a plan before we head out. Which direction are we headed?"

The sunshine slowly rolled over the hills, illuminating the unwelcoming path through the woods. Overseeing the route, Linx pointed toward the area where she had accessed the Gemenii for the first time. "It's over there. We have to stick together long enough so we can get Zalia to the Gemenii."

Nodding in agreement, Juma waved his men to come forward. "All right, we're about to head out. We don't know what this place looks like on a good day, so we must have our guard up! Pay attention because we don't know who or what might be lingering during our journey. I'll need men in the front, back, and sides. Our mission is to escort this group to the Gemenii's cave. I'll be following Linx's directions there, so I recommend you do the same and follow me. Again, pay attention, guys. We don't know what's out there, and I want to see you all come home—even you, Pon."

Chuckles bounced around within the group while Pon rolled his eyes. He wasn't the least bit amused. However, they all knew Juma meant every word he said. As the trolls discussed where each would be positioned within the group, Kateerah stepped toward Linx as Zalia trailed behind her.

"Linx?"

Turning to face Kateerah, Linx noticed that her mind seemed distracted. "Hey, what's the matter?"

"I know you need as many warriors as you can get to escort Zalia, but I'm also concerned about the people of Pangotha. I'm not sure how many are still alive, and I want to make sure they're okay."

"I completely understand." Linx kindly smiled. "We have a solid group, Kateerah. If you can't join us, please don't worry about it. They need you as well."

"What I can do is walk with you about halfway and then

head off to find them around that tree line," she said, pointing into the woods.

Nodding her head, Linx said, "Whatever works for you. If you can stay with us for a little while, that'll be perfect. Do you need anyone to go with you?"

"I can't possibly ask anyone else to go. I should be fine, though."

"Oh, nonsense. I can come," Pygo said, hopping over with a smile.

"Are you sure? You don't have to."

Eagerly clapping, Linx said, "That would be great! I honestly would've loved to join you, so this works out that Pygo wants to come."

"Well, okay. As long as you feel all right with the amount of men you have."

Jaut patted Kateerah's shoulder as he asked, "Are we ready to do this?"

Pygo said, "I've been ready for a long time. Anyone in our way will bleed. I'll bite off any fool's head that dares to challenge me."

"That's the spirit."

Scratching his chin, Juma shouted, "Yeah. Let's do this."

Linx lovingly looked over at Zalia. "Are you ready? I know this must be overwhelming."

Shyly shaking her head up and down, Zalia stared at the ground before bringing her attention to the journey ahead. While fidgeting with her hands, her shimmering eyes intensely studied the movement of the wind and the dips in the path.

"I won't leave you," Linx explained. "Even if it gets questionable out there, I will be by your side."

Breaking her trance, Zalia's lips formed a slight smile. As she allowed her hands to finally rest by her side, Zalia released a cleansing exhale. Without a second thought, she gently began petting Rexil's face. She giggled, emitting an adorable high-pitched jingle as Jaut winced and squirmed in disgust. To test Jaut's reactions, she caressed the top of Rexil's head with the side of her face.

"Look, don't come crying to me when that thing eats you."

Almost in tears, Zalia's angelic laughter soaked into the ears of everyone around her, raising spirits in a time of need. Several trolls smiled, including Wronet and Bueron, and Pygo rolled with amusement.

Meticulously rubbing her fingers together, anxiety set in as Linx waited for the rowdiness to calm. Despite being appreciative of the happiness surrounding her at that moment, she knew, in a matter of time, blood would be shed, and she would do everything in her power to make sure it wasn't theirs. "Okay, is everyone ready? I think we should head out sooner rather than later."

"Yes, let's go," Kateerah quickly responded.

Stepping through the abstract exit, Linx was surprised by the bleakness within Pangotha. Surprisingly, it almost didn't feel like the same place. Bare, dark trees stood like menacing shadows, watching their every move. Oddly enough, no visible creature walked through the woods—at least from what Linx could see.

"This is so tragic," Jaut explained while he walked through the exit behind Linx. "It just looks like haunted woods with no sign of life beyond the decaying trees."

"Where are the ecknids?" Linx asked, caressing the side of her face as she looked for them.

Scanning for a sense of presence from the ecknids, Jaut shook his head. "I don't see anything or anyone."

"Right before I was taken, the creatures knew there was no chance of survival if you showed your face. When you guys left, it was heartbreaking; however, it got worse." Kateerah's face grew solemn.

The feeling of doom tickled Linx's stomach with its long, bony fingers—threatening to take over. Inhaling deep into her abdomen, she pushed out feelings of dread and thought of every reason why this beautiful land and its people needed them to succeed. She would be damned if she let any enemy cross her and survive. Anger, rage, and a sense of responsibility overcame her. "We'll find them, Kateerah."

Signaling his men to move forward, Juma tightened his shoulders and continued to assess their surroundings, peering up beyond his bushy brows. A bead of sweat dripped from his hairline, curling around his ear. Juma's muscles seemed to tense more with each step, while his thick veins pushed up against his skin.

Wriggling her fingers toward Rexil, Linx quickly smiled before resting her lips in a line. Without warning, Rexil released a chilling howl, echoing through the dying land. Jumping in her shoes, Linx immediately brought her finger to her lips. "Shh!"

"Silence that thing!" Jaut hissed, waving his hand.

With her eyes still wide from the shock, Linx said, "I've never heard him make that noise before!"

"Well, it'll be the last thing you hear if he does it again! We have no idea where anyone is."

"Jaut! I get it." She rolled her eyes.

Sniffing the ground, Rexil whined in small spurts, raising his tail alarmingly.

"What's the matter, honey?" Linx gently caressed the side of his face and behind his ear.

With his bright purple orbs set perfectly on his precious face, Rexil looked compassionately toward Linx and rushed off into the shadows.

"Rexil! Rexil!" Linx frantically whispered. Her heart sank, knowing she may never see him again. *Where did he go?*

"Linx," Jaut quietly said. "Let him go! He knows what he is doing."

"I don't want to hear it, Jaut. You don't care about him at all. He was such an amazing companion. I hope he'll be okay." The corners of her lips tipped down, and tears pooled in her eyes.

"Look, I was never allowed to have pets, so I never got too close to any creatures besides this fur ball." He chuckled, motioning toward Pygo.

"Hilarious." Pygo glared at him.

"It never gets old," Jaut said. "But my point is that Rexil will be fine. He seems like a smart guy. Have some faith."

With a warm feeling inching over her chest, Linx said, "I hope so. I try, but everything I love gets taken away so easily."

"You're not the only one. Remember that."

As they crossed over several lonely hills consisting only of dirt, brown leaves, and dead trees, they attempted to focus on the Gemenii's mountain. Although they were making good time, their destination felt like a lifetime away. Not one creature was visible throughout their travels. Every so often, a large burnt lump rested on the ground.

"This is so bizarre." Linx twirled her hair between her fingers. "How did we not see anyone at all? Like no creatures of Pangotha anywhere and no guards or any kind of enemy. Where is everyone?"

"I have no idea. I know they were heading south before I was taken. However, I'm not sure if they made it. I'm surprised as well that we haven't encountered any of the guards," Kateerah said. "They were everywhere, walking up and down the paths."

"Wait," Jaut said, bringing attention to thick, ashy plumes of smoke rising into the sky. "What is that?"

Looking underneath furrowed brows, Kateerah whispered, "A devastating problem."

Sulking his shoulders, he said, "That's what I thought."

"What do you mean?" Linx spun around and studied Kateerah's face.

Shaking her head, a tear dripped from Kateerah's eye. "An ecknid has been engulfed in flames."

"Are you sure?"

Wiping her tear away, Kateerah nodded.

"Yes, it's something that isn't seen by many since they were always strong and crafty creatures. They could clear out armies if needed before any chance of harm. But on those very rare occasions, when someone managed to bypass the other ecknids and creatures, ecknids were killed. They immediately light up when threatened by flames—with thick smoke dispersing across the sky." Jaut hung his head for a moment.

"Let's get 'em," Juma said matter-of-factly while rage filled his eyes.

"Do you think it's a trap, or should we split up? I don't think it's a good idea to digress from the plan of getting Zalia to the Gemenii." Linx's attention bounced from Jaut to Kateerah to Pygo.

"I'm not sure if it's a trap, but we can all venture to where the path splits into a fork over there. That way, we'll be close to

Zalia. In addition, Juma and whoever wants to go with him can investigate until we figure out the Gemenii's plan or advice."

Walking over a mound of boulders, something caught Linx's eye. Purple orbs with a sharp snout sat at attention, staring at her until their lines of sight connected. "Rexil!"

Rushing over to him, Linx dried several tears dripping from her eyes. She fell to her knees in front of him as she wrapped her arms around his smooth back.

"See, that wasn't too long, was it? Little devil dog looks to be doing just fine!" Jaut snorted, picking up a thick stick wrapped in a browned vine off the ground. Glancing at the decaying vegetation in his hand, he whipped it into a pile of broken sticks and twigs.

"Jaut, look!" Linx whispered, pointing beside Rexil.

A strange shape caught his attention. "Is that—"

Her face winced as her vision focused on the blood-soaked ground surrounding two mutilated guards. Rexil's bright eyes stared, seeking approval for his swift actions. When Linx didn't respond soon enough, he emitted a soft whine and stomped his right paw.

Shocked, Linx bent down to acknowledge him. "Sweetheart, thank you! You're such a good boy!" She affectionately rubbed the side of his face, looking around to see if she could identify any other intruders.

"Wow. Unbelievable!" Jaut walked over and patted Rexil's head without a second thought. "I have no idea how he found them so quickly. And to think we would've been walking through here, potentially unable to see them in time."

"So, does this mean you'll be a little nicer to my boy?" Linx asked, smirking with delight.

"I guess so."

As Linx and Jaut mumbled amongst each other, Juma's footsteps approached, crunching over leaves and twigs. His men waited patiently behind him as he determined which route they'd take. "Do you want us to follow you to the cliff over there? We can, especially with the unexpected lurkers hovering around."

"No, we'll be fine. Thank you, though. Once we enter the cave, it would be quite difficult for anyone to follow us without our knowledge. Rexil can stay with you guys as well. I'm not sure if he'd be able to make it through the Gemenii's security defenses anyway." Linx held her hand out to pet Rexil once more.

"Are you sure? I don't even know how to keep him with me," Juma admitted.

"Yes, I'm afraid he'll get hurt. From deep water to protective bugs, I don't know how welcome he'd be in there."

"Protective bugs?"

"Yeah, like bees and such."

Scrunching his face, Juma shuddered. "Ugh. Protective bees? That's not a place I envy."

"Yup. Me neither." Jaut rubbed his face and frowned.

"I'm hoping after we meet with the Gemenii, we can easily find each other again. I'm not sure what will happen, but in case we can't find you, what direction should we head toward?"

"Hmm. I'm betting we can find them, especially if we're looking from the cliff." Jaut nodded toward the massive ledge.

Twirling her hair around her pointer finger, Linx wasn't convinced. "Jaut, last time, we came out through a different way. What if we aren't up there? Or what if they are in a different cave or hiding spot with the others? It'll be impossible to find them."

"Maybe I can send your pooch to come and find you after a while. Then he can bring you to meet up with us."

"All right." Linx bent over to nuzzle Rexil's face and kiss his forehead. "I'll see you soon."

Turning to finish the walk to the Gemenii's cave with Jaut and Zalia, Linx could hear Rexil's high-pitched whine and his paw stomping into the ground. Her heart broke, knowing she had to leave him once again. Looking over her shoulder, she lovingly smiled at her boy.

CHAPTER 31

Walking toward the familiar path, Jaut bumped his shoulder into Zalia's to lighten the mood. "Are you feeling okay?"

Shyly nodding, Zalia's eyes immediately looked in Linx's direction. Jaut could tell she was more comfortable with Linx, despite not knowing her.

Unsure of how to make her want to talk, Jaut tried asking anything that popped into his mind. "How did you meet the Gemenii? Were you able to get through on your first try?"

Zalia stared at the ground while they continued to travel over the remaining portion of the path.

"I'm sure trekking through the maze as a kid is no walk in the park. Even going through as someone older, it was quite intimidating."

Linx rolled her eyes and sighed. "Jaut, I'm not sure she really wants to talk. I know I wouldn't."

"You? Not talk? Haha. There's no way that you'd ever remain quiet!" Jaut chuckled to himself.

"Well, I wouldn't want to talk to some random, strange man trying to pry into my personal life," Linx said with a massive grin on her face.

Zalia held her hand over her mouth as she attempted to muffle a giggle.

"Oh, I see how it is. You two are buddies and are leaving me out of the cool group!" Jaut joked. Hoping to make Zalia more comfortable, he held off on any more questions.

As Zalia sped up near Linx, she grabbed her hand for support, weaving her fingers through Linx's while gleaming from dimple to dimple. Almost floating, Zalia grew light on her feet. Her curls joyously bounced off of her pulled-back shoulders. A sense of calm and warmth emanated from her being in their final moments before climbing the cliff.

With a rush of emotions, Linx was captivated by the light within her eyes. A burning tickle swept over her face, causing tears to form as Linx squeezed her eyelids closed. The bittersweet feeling rushed around her body. What she would give for her hand to be interlocked with Lyla's, but she now needed to be a role model to another. At the least, she needed to guide Zalia through the deadly cavern maze in a manner that required her to be brave, supportive, and protective.

Approaching the cliff wall, Jaut rested the base of his head against his back, looking up at the daunting and wicked ledges. "Well, are we ready for round two?"

Quickly nodding, Linx gripped Zalia's hand tightly and reached out her other hand to hold Jaut's. Envisioning the trio on the ledge above, Linx closed her eyes, sharply inhaled, and steadily exhaled, alleviating the stress from her anxiety. Hyping herself up to the task, she chanted in her mind, *You can do this. You got this. Who am I kidding? I got this. There are no surprises, so I know what to expect. Let's do this.* Within seconds, Linx gracefully teleported everyone to the Gemenii's cavern entrance.

Stepping back near the edge, Jaut almost lost his balance. "Holy—"

"Are you okay? Watch your step!" Linx shouted, pulling him toward her.

"Yeah! I expected us to wind up in the spot from last time."

With a proud glance, Linx said, "I know. I felt I could do it, though. So I wanted to give it a shot."

"I guess there's no better time to test out transporting up a deadly cliff than now." He combed his hand through his hair vigorously with the skin on his face lightening to a paler shade.

Chuckling, Linx shrugged. "If I didn't think I could do it, I wouldn't have tried it."

"No, no. You're right. You did it!" Jaut wiped a layer of sweat off of his forehead.

"Ha! I'm sorry. I should've told you," Linx said, soon turning to Zalia. "Are you okay?"

Gratefully nodding, she smiled with unwavering confidence.

Looking over her shoulder and over the land, Linx tried to spot her Rexil through the thinning woods. "Good! Well, let's push onward then. I hope this time is a bit easier since we have some experience coming through."

Stepping into the dimly lit entrance, Linx and Jaut curiously connected glances before absorbing the strange path in front of them. Bright symbols glowed on each of their foreheads the deeper they walked. Almost forgetting the Gemenii's gift, they stared in shock for a split second prior to remembering its purpose. Throughout the path, the walls and ceiling were covered in illuminated hieroglyphics, similar in style to the symbol on their heads. Linx didn't know what to make of it as her fingertips traced some of the lines. Why has the cavern changed? And the tunnel of symbols almost made her head spin as their trippy presence evoked an ethereal feeling.

"What happened?" Linx whispered to Jaut.

"I'm not sure. We can continue, but we need to be wary. I don't know what the Gemenii is trying to tell us. I'll go first, just in case." Jaut started moving ahead, cautiously walking down the tunnel.

Following closely behind, Linx analyzed every inch of the pathway they passed through. Tightly holding Zalia's arm behind her, she mindfully led Zalia through the enchanted passage. Bright white lights shifted into a neon lavender color, fading and then intensifying.

"Do you know what's going on?" Linx asked Zalia, hoping she knew something—anything.

Eyes wide and nervous, Zalia shook her head slowly from side to side. Her attention bounced from one wall to the next as they progressed into what appeared to be a new world.

Confused, Linx continued to scan every inch she could see, hoping to decipher something into a helpful message. The path shifted from what Linx had remembered. Slabs of mostly flat rock formed stairs that gradually increased height ever so slightly. She trailed behind Jaut, noticing his figure had a glowing blue aura. Entranced and distracted by the lighting in the cave, Linx jumped and her heart heavily pounded when she heard Jaut gasp.

"Are you okay?" Linx whispered. "What happened?"

Distracted a moment, Jaut said quietly, "Yeah."

"Yeah, what? What does that even mean?" Linx demanded.

"Sorry," he said. "You have to come over here and see this."

As he walked forward, the path opened into an enormous domed room. Linx entered the area, and what she saw blew her away. Luminous gems and crystals speckled from every inch of the room, sending Linx spiraling into a euphoric sense of comfort. From toe to neck and up to her crown, Linx was submerged in warm vibrations that covered her skin, sinking into her bones. She felt her sense of self extend beyond her fingertips. With eyes glistening, she asked, "What happened in here?"

"I don't know," Jaut whispered, almost holding his breath because of the beauty surrounding them.

Overcome with happiness, Zalia gracefully spun around, holding her hands above her head. Her hair appeared to levitate as she danced with the magic inhabiting the room.

"Over here," Jaut said, waving his hand. "There's an entrance to another room!"

Linx and Zalia quietly followed Jaut once more as they walked through a pathway lit by speckles of gold and silver. Rubbing her hands over the rough walls, Zalia remained intrigued by the environment within the cave. The path led them up a slight incline, ending by coming face-to-face with a familiar friend.

"The Gemenii!" Linx whispered with relief.

Slowly walking toward the Gemenii, Linx held Zalia's hand as they stood in front of them. Without saying another word, the Gemenii opened their eyes, glowing green.

"I knew you could do it, my dear. You are the true guardian of our home. Thank you."

Speechless, Linx stood for a moment, staring at the elegant being before saying, "Oh, I am no guardian. The pleasure is all mine. I'm just so happy to help you and the people of Pangotha."

"You and your friend are protectors of this land, and I thank you for everything you did. Yet I have one more thing to ask of you."

"Of course! Anything you need," Linx eagerly responded.

"Feel free to decline because it's not a light task. Zalia alone can guide Pangotha to tranquility; however, she needs help defending those who live within and communicating with those who live beyond our land. You have experience in many areas she has yet to develop fully," the Gemenii said, smiling. "Plus, I think you might find something you've been searching for."

Intrigued, Linx asked, "What would that be?"

"A home."

Thinking about everything she had experienced since waking up in this world, from her life in Violet Woods through now, her mind quickly knew the right thing to do. "Yes, I accept your offer."

"Are you sure? You can take some more time if you need to. It is not an easy question."

"I don't need more time. As much as I loved Violet Woods, too much has happened. It doesn't feel like a home anymore. Here, I can start over and have a purpose. The people of Pangotha have been so welcoming—some taking longer to accept me than others," Linx said, quickly looking at Jaut with a smile. "But it feels like the right move. I want to see Zalia succeed and rule Pangotha."

"Wonderful! She needs you as you need her. There will be a

day when you both see that. I'm hoping you can guide her as a mentor while she guides those who live on this land."

"I wasn't that bad," Jaut interrupted.

Linx faintly smiled. "You threatened to kill me if I didn't leave."

"I believe you're taking it completely out of context!" Jaut scoffed.

Rolling her eyes, Linx ignored his antics. "What is the next step for me to officially help Zalia?"

"Well, my dear, with the fate of Pangotha in good hands, my heart can rest happy knowing that it will thrive. As for its current state of well-being, it's not doing well. The ecknids rely on the energy within the soil to survive, as do other plants that assist in providing food to those who live here. I'm afraid, in time, the land will continue to die off until it can no longer sustain a habitable environment."

"How can we fix that?" Linx asked, saddened by the thought of everyone losing their home.

"My energy and power will help to provide the boost it needs to get back to where it must be. You two will have to protect the land and its creatures from harm. With those tasks in motion, Pangotha shall be restored to good health."

"I promise to protect Pangotha, its creatures, and its people from any harm I'm able to stop." Linx sighed heavily, releasing the underlying stress that had haunted her for a long time.

She never felt like she truly belonged anywhere and hardly ever felt a sense of purpose. Contentment settled within her body as she glanced at Jaut. Grinning, he shook his head—maybe from excitement or possibly due to his amusement. Regardless of the motive, Linx shot an unamused look at him.

"That's such wonderful news!"

Smiling from ear to ear, Linx said, "Am I able to give energy to Pangotha as well? That has to be a lot by yourself. Hopefully, it can reduce the amount of stress on your body."

"You're correct. It isn't easy on anyone's body. But no—I have to do this alone. This is how it's meant to be. I'm but a temporary guardian myself. When the danger was coming, Pangotha knew and created me. The magic that burrows into the soil, waters, and plants summoned me into what you see in front of you. Essentially, I am a safe for Pangotha's magic. By creating me, all its treasures and power wouldn't be immediately ransacked when the guards began desecrating our homeland."

Dumbfounded, Linx stared in confusion as the Gemenii rattled off this incomprehensible information. "So you're saying that you will die to save Pangotha?"

"No, my dear. I am Pangotha. We are one and the same."

Shaking her head in disbelief, she turned to Jaut. "Is there anything we can do?"

Jaut shrugged. "I don't know why you're asking me."

"Linx, you don't have to worry about me. You're releasing me to free the land once more."

With tear-filled eyes, Zalia looked up toward the Gemenii. In a quiet and soothing voice, she uttered, "Thank you . . . for everything."

The Gemenii smiled while saying, "Of course! Zalia, I'm so glad you're home. All right. Now I need both rings. Once I have them, we won't have much time after that."

"Thank you for trusting me with this journey. I wish there was another way for this to play out," Linx said with a single tear threatening to roll down her cheek.

Clenching his teeth together, Jaut bowed his head in respect.

One hand gripped the other as he focused on the floor. Before he lost his moment, he quietly said, "It was a pleasure to serve."

"You all will do great things for this land. And don't worry, I'll be watching." Rotating a hand, the Gemenii awaited the return of the rings.

Linx held one ring as Zalia pinched the other. Quickly glancing at each other, Linx nodded toward the Gemenii. Together, they gently placed them in the Gemenii's palm. Stepping back, they firmly held hands, unable to suppress their tears. Within seconds, the Gemenii's eyes began to close. The bright green light faded from their eyes until it was no more. Once their light had fully disappeared, the Gemenii's body instantly broke into bits, crumbling to the ground.

For a split second, the group felt devastated and lost—unsure of what to do next. However, a burst of rejuvenating energy rippled from where the Gemenii had been seated, sending outward an intense movement similar to an earthquake. The aggressive shaking led the ceiling to begin caving in, sprinkling the floor with dust, gems, and chunks of rock. A large piece of rock dislodged and fell, nearly missing Zalia's head.

"We got to get out of here! Now!" Jaut shouted, standing over Linx and Zalia to shield them from the falling rubble.

Instinctually, Linx grabbed Jaut's and Zalia's hands. As her fear of failure lingered, her legs involuntarily trembled, causing chills to shoot up her back. Shaking off the bad energy, Linx connected her eyes with Zalia's and then Jaut's. She knew it was up to her to save her friends, yet she wondered if the Gemenii knew about the cave collapsing. Breathing heavily and swiftly closing her eyes, Linx visualized the trio on the cliff's edge, safely outside the cave's opening. As she released her energy into the air, a jolt ripped her eyes open as they teleported to the front of the cave's opening, right where she hoped to be. In a matter of moments, they heard the cave's ceiling collapse with an unsettling rumble.

"Dang, girl!" Jaut said. "You saved our sorry behinds. I'm so proud of you!"

"Oh, thank you, Jaut. I'm just glad it worked!" she said, shyly smiling.

"I would've easily been dead had you not done that."

With a big grin, she said, "I'm going to remember you said that."

As they looked around, bright green colors gradually spread across the land, highlighting the beautiful mountains and lush fields. Linx noticed that even the crystal clear water sparkled once again—with a luster inviting anyone to come and swim. Overwhelming happiness, warmth, and comfort cushioned their souls as they slowly descended the mountain while admiring the environment.

"This is incredible! Pangotha was so beautiful before, but it's stunning now!" Linx shouted in amazement. "I didn't think it was possible."

"Oh, you have no idea," Jaut said. "Just give it more time for everything to get back to normal, and you will be floored."

"Well, I can't wait to see Pangotha thrive," Linx said, peering over the cliff edge. "If you want, I can teleport us to the base of this."

Laughing, Jaut said, "I thought you'd never ask."

"Let's do it. We have some friends to find." Linx opened her hands, waiting for the others to place their lives in her care.

Without a second thought, Zalia and Jaut intertwined their fingers with hers. Jaut's firm yet effortless grip and Zalia's calm demeanor reassured Linx. A soft feeling overcame her, causing Linx to lightly smile before closing her eyes. After smoothly transitioning the group to the base of the cliff, they quickly opened their eyes, scanning their surroundings. Unsure of what could attack, they were instinctively on high alert, attempting to locate Kateerah and the others.

CHAPTER 32

Consumed by the breathtaking view, Linx looked over and saw Zalia's eyes merrily gazing into the distance. Chills caressed Linx's scalp as she witnessed Pangotha shift from a vulnerable land to something almost unimaginably beautiful. Vibrant green, purple, and indigo vegetation rapidly flourished before her eyes. A surge of energy crept up her body, soaking deep into her core. It was a sensation she had never felt before—a clean, rejuvenating feeling that elevated her soul.

As they continued to explore, they couldn't find any trace of the others. They traveled through rocky terrain where plenty of hiding spots could be, but there was no sign of them anywhere.

"I don't get it. Where are they?" Linx asked.

Shrugging his shoulders, Jaut shook his head from side to side. "You got me. I have a few other places in mind. If they aren't at any of those, I'm not sure where they'd be. They could be anywhere."

After a few more footsteps, a light voice softly said, "I have an idea where they'd be."

Jaut and Linx quickly looked at each other and down at Zalia before staring at one another again. Afraid to affect the progress, he nodded over to Linx to pry for more details.

Inconspicuously raising and lowering her head in agreement, Linx excitedly asked, "Oh, really? Where do you think?"

"A little further down, there is a hidden entrance to an underground pathway. It leads to a secret place my friends and I used to visit. Before I was taken, I told others about it—in case they needed a place to hide." Zalia pointed down near moving water.

Once they got closer to the water, Linx noticed some creatures had come out of hiding, but they still made sure to reduce their chance of detection. Many cowered in the shadows or camouflaged in the trees, hoping to survive another day. Her heart ached to make them feel safe and secure in their homeland.

"We have to follow this river around the bend."

"I never knew this led to a secret hideout!" Jaut admitted with intrigue.

Rolling her eyes, Linx rubbed her temple before caressing her scalp with her fingers. "Well, it wouldn't be much of a secret if they told you."

"Wow." Jaut glanced at Linx with a straight face.

Trying to hold back her laughter, she pretended to observe the water. Large trees beautifully decorated both sides of the surrounding areas, cooling the ground beneath them. Nearing a small, rushing waterfall, Zalia ran ahead toward the curtain of cascading waters. Linx and Jaut picked up their pace so as to not lose Zalia in the excitement. The power of the waterfall sprayed a light layer of mist over the group as they walked alongside the plunge pool.

"Zalia, where are we going?" Jaut asked.

Releasing a big smile, Zalia said, "Follow me."

Climbing over several damp boulders sprinkled with moss, Zalia disappeared behind the overhanging waterfall. Linx sprinted past Jaut as she attempted to catch up to her.

"Wait for me!" Jaut shouted, looking around to see if anyone, friend or foe, was approaching. Once he confirmed no one was near, Jaut climbed onto a ledge to make his way behind the waterfall as well.

"Careful with that one, Jaut," Linx said, pointing to a slippery rock that slanted just enough to warrant climbers to take heed.

Keeping her eye on Jaut and Zalia, Linx hopped down on the rock slab that sat comfortably hidden. Perplexed, she looked around to see where Zalia had disappeared to. Starting to panic, she spun around, looking behind herself. Without a trace of where Zalia went, Linx backed up against the rock and tried to stare beyond the waterfall. As she waited for Jaut, she couldn't believe Zalia had vanished.

After hopping next to Linx, he asked, "Where did she go?"

"I have no idea." Linx cupped her face in borderline defeat. "I hope not far."

While they discussed what to do, Zalia popped out from behind the wall. "Boo!"

"Hey!" Jaut shouted.

"Woah! Where did you come from?" Linx held her heart.

Giggling, she waved them over to a sharp bend in the rock wall that provided the perfect cover for the pathway. The position of the back wall and front created the perfect illusion, protecting the secret location. Once they passed the bend in the wall, the pathway split in two—one leading left and the other leading right.

Looking left and then right, Jaut whispered, "So now which way?"

"Over here," Zalia said, leading the group down the right side.

"How did you ever find this?" Linx asked.

"We always play around here because it's fun to jump in the water. One day, we were playing hide-and-seek, and I hid back here. As my friend came to look behind the waterfall, I stumbled across this passageway. We gathered our other friends and explored them together," Zalia explained in a soft, happy voice.

Rock slabs lined the pathway, almost structured with the passages in mind. Drips of water raced down the walls, puddling on the ground. Reaching the end of the tunnel, they heard some concerned whispers echo from one wall to another.

"Almost there!" Zalia said with a grin. "If you're unfamiliar with this spot, it can get confusing. Stay near me. They must be down there. I hear them!"

Somewhat disregarding her own advice, Zalia began to jog toward the voices, zigging and zagging through various openings.

"Zalia! Slow down!" Linx playfully requested. "Jaut won't be able to keep up!"

"Oh, I'm so sorry," she said, slowing her pace.

"Hey, speak for yourself," he mumbled, stopping himself from saying more once his eyes noticed the movement of others.

The narrow, confusing walkway opened up into one room that led to several other connected corridors filled with creatures hiding from the guards. Joy and laughter broke out when the group stepped into the room.

"You're here! I'm so glad to see that you guys are safe!" Kateerah shouted, running over to the group and hugging Zalia.

Within moments, Rexil ran out from the shadows and jumped on Linx, resting his front legs on her shoulders. Stroking his head, she nuzzled up to the side of his face.

"How come I never knew about this place? Why has no one told me?" Jaut asked, staring in disbelief.

Laughing, Kateerah turned to look at the creatures and people behind her. "This place was unknown to most of us. Luckily, some children told us about this haven just in time!"

"This place is incredible! Has anyone stumbled across it?"

Furrowing her brows, Kateerah said, "No, thank goodness! Are the guards out there? We felt a rush of energy, but we wanted to wait a bit before going out."

"Everything seemed fine on our walk after our visit to the Gemenii." Jaut quickly stared at Linx.

"Oh, yes! I wanted to ask. How did that go? What did the Gemenii say after you brought Zalia?" Kateerah looked at Linx and then shifted her attention back to Jaut.

"Um, well," Jaut said, "maybe Linx would want to talk more about it."

"Thanks, Jaut." Widening her eyes and releasing Rexil, Linx fumbled in her mind, trying to figure out what to say. "Well, we brought Zalia to meet with the Gemenii, as they requested, and it's still hard to process what happened."

Concerned, Kateerah stepped closer to Linx. "Huh? What are you talking about?"

Linx scanned each and every face as the room grew quiet.

"Once we brought Zalia inside, the Gemenii was thrilled. However, they went on to explain that they were created in the first place as a means to protect and save Pangotha from enemies seeking to harness its energy. Sadly, I guess they were never meant to exist forever."

The Pangothians desperately absorbed every word that left Linx's mouth.

"The Gemenii crumbled right in front of our faces."

Gasps broke out in the room, sending Linx into a state of panic. Not knowing what her fate with the people and creatures of Pangotha would be, pressure on her chest made it difficult for her to inhale and exhale. Low mumbles and whispers erupted between the Pangothians. Unsure of how to handle the situation, Linx glanced at Zalia before staring at Jaut.

Stepping toward the Pangothians, Zalia shouted, "It's true!"

The room fell silent again as everyone listened intently.

"When we walked into the cave, beautiful lights sparkled from every corner. It was magical," Zalia said with her eyes lighting up at the thought. "And then we entered the Gemenii's room. They were happy to see us, but they had to go. The Gemenii said Pangotha needed its energy back. They were only created to protect the power and energy from the enemies."

Jaut said, "But one thing they did mention was that Zalia's meant to rule Pangotha—to nurture and guide every soul that lives on this land. Also, the Gemenii was very clear about who the guardian of Pangotha is—Linx."

"No surprise there!" Pygo chimed in, hopping toward the group. "I told you, peabrain. She was meant to protect this land!"

Looking over with a smile, Jaut said, "I'm sorry I doubted you, Pygo. You were right. Linx is meant to guard Pangothians, defend Pangotha, and protect and guide Zalia through tough decisions that come her way. We know the news of the Gemenii leaving us is hard to swallow, but it's not the end. They stated they're always around us as they are part of the land once again."

Before saying anything, Linx's eyes locked with Juma's. Knowing this was not what he might have been expecting, she took a deep breath and said, "I'm sorry for what Pangotha and all of its people went through. However, I vow to protect Pangotha and every single Pangothian to the best of my abilities. I hope you give me a chance to prove myself to you. I promise to not let you down."

"You aren't returning to Violet Woods?" Juma asked, while seated next to his men.

Shaking her head, Linx said, "I feel like I belong here. It's hard to explain, but this feels like the right decision. I'm pulled to be here, but I can always visit Juma, especially with the shift within Violet Woods."

"You'll always be welcome there. I hope you know that."

"Thank you, Juma."

"And the same goes for you," Zalia said to Juma. "You and your men helped save me, Pangotha, and all of its people. Please come back and visit."

"Oh, thank you. We might take you up on that offer." Juma smiled kindly at Zalia.

Rubbing his chin, Jaut asked Kateerah, "What should we do now? Are you planning on staying here for the night?"

"Well, we didn't know if everything would be safe. We slaughtered some guards on our way here, but we didn't hear any others passing by. I know that anxiety is rising since we're getting closer to the evening," she answered.

"We haven't seen any enemies out there, and the land appears to be rejuvenating itself. I know my energy level is definitely feeling better." Jaut stepped back against the rock wall, quickly camouflaging without issue.

Holding her hands out, Linx lit a flame with one hand while forming a test protection bubble with her other. Other Pangothians were inclined to see how well their powers had improved. Sparks and vivid colors painted the air while thumps, clicks, and various noises filled Linx's ears. The Pangothians were quickly regaining their powers and energy, as well as their autonomy.

To Linx's surprise, the room's energy rapidly shifted to a very enthusiastic attitude about their future and her involvement. Several Pangothians approached her and asked questions about her travels and meeting the Gemenii. A coating of comfort covered her chest as excitement overwhelmed her.

"I'm sure everyone is getting tired, but we have daylight left. Come outside! It's safe once again," Zalia shouted.

Following her lead, the Pangothians and trolls calmly traveled along the narrow walkway. Once they reached the outside, an inviting aromatic breeze caressed their noses, leaving them suspended in a tranquil state. Hopping over the boulders, the group safely made their way beyond the waterfall to dark green grass and rich soil beneath sturdy trees in the woods. Taking a moment to absorb their present moment, the Pangothians and their visitors stood with bright eyes and beaming smiles, chitchatting while admiring the magnificent transformation Pangotha underwent.

"Every moment that goes by, it gets more beautiful. How is that possible?"

"Because of the Gemenii—and you," Jaut whispered. "Thank you."

Twisting her hair, she said, "You're welcome, but I did what anyone else would do."

Right as she was enjoying the warm company of others, an odd, eerie feeling overcame Linx—like someone was watching her. The light clicking of nails tapping on a tree trunk triggered a heinous internal reaction within her subconscious mind. A mild sweat formed over her brow while she attempted to calm her breathing before it developed into a panic attack. Turning around quickly, she was met with the bright yellow eyes that sporadically haunted her nightmares. The little goblin's grin grew, knowing its mischievous superpower of creeping out most creatures was in full swing.

Looking away and then drawn back to its spooky stare, Linx demanded, "What do you want? Why are you still following me? Carter is back in Crystal Woods, and I'm staying here. So I don't know what you want."

Lunging forward, the goblin opened its mouth, displaying every razor tooth inside. Linx shrieked in fear while igniting a flame in the palm of her hand, expecting to be shredded once again. Instead, the goblin brushed past her, clinging to a new tree while giggling with amusement. Their pitter-patter faded off in the distance as they quickly retreated.

Taken aback, Jaut sprinted over to make sure that Linx was okay. "What happened? Is everything okay?"

"Yeah," she whispered.

Placing his hand on her shoulder, he asked, "Are you sure?"

"I'm fine. No matter how much time passes, it still can be an unsettling feeling to see them." Linx pressed her fingers into her eyes, rubbing them in a circular motion over her eyebrows and forehead.

While rolling his eyes, Jaut shivered. "I get it completely. Those little furballs are creepy."

Furiously hopping over a fallen tree toward Jaut and Linx, Pygo yelled, "I despise when you call anyone a furball!"

"Don't worry," Jaut said, laughing, "you are my favorite one."

"And you are my favorite fool!" Pygo sneered at Jaut before turning to face Linx. "My dear, thank you for helping to restore Pangotha."

"It was my pleasure to be able to help. I hope we can get Pangotha back to its natural state," Linx said, gazing into the sky beyond the tree branches. Revitalizing smells swirled around the group as tints of pink and purple melted from the highest stars down to the horizon line.

"It will be soon. Now that it's starting to get late, we need to figure out where everyone will be sleeping." Pygo looked around at the mass of people.

Kateerah perked up her head. "We can head back to our hideout for the night. We'd make good time if we traveled down that way. Tomorrow will be a fresh day, and we can start anew—fix what we can and rebuild what has been destroyed. Not to mention, we'll need to construct a home for the newest Pangothian." With a calm yet proud face, she stared at Linx, hiding a gleam in her eye.

"After some rest, we'll be starting our journey back home in the morning," Juma told Kateerah and Linx.

"Oh, thank you again for everything, Juma. I'm beyond grateful for everything you and your men have done for myself and the Pangothians. We can't thank you enough. Would you like company on any of your journeys back?" Linx asked.

Juma shook his head firmly and said, "Nah, you've got loose ends to tie up just the same as we do. We'll be swinging by Crystal Woods to gather the rest of the men before heading back. I know it won't be anytime soon, but I do hope for a visit someday."

"Although I can't make any promises, I will definitely consider it," Linx said, hugging Juma.

Reaching into a pocket, Juma pulled out a handful of crystals. He motioned for her to open her hands. While pouring them into Linx's cupped palms, he said, "Well, in case I don't see ya, I want you to have these. They're my lucky ones. Never leave without them."

Admiring the beauty of the precious crystals in her hand, Linx whispered, "But . . . they're *yours.* Are you sure?"

"Yes, I'm sure. I hope it'll at least remind you of your other allies in this world."

Squeezing her fingers tightly against her hand, Linx smiled. "Thank you so much! I'll treasure these stunning crystals and keep them safe."

Kateerah stepped back to attract the Pangothians' and the trolls' attention. "All right, everyone! Unless you prefer to go on a separate route, follow me. In the morning, we can gather supplies to rebuild what was damaged in Pangotha."

Walking through the woods, Linx asked Jaut, "Have you seen any ecknids? I noticed that it's only been trees everywhere."

"Sadly, no. I haven't seen them," Jaut mumbled, scanning their surroundings.

The corners of her lips sank. "How awful! What a shame. I wonder if there are any left and if we'll see them again."

"I hope so, but only time will tell," Jaut said, gently holding her shoulder as they traveled with the others.

CHAPTER 33

A few months later, the vibrant amber sunshine peered over the mountains, drizzling warmth over Pangotha's luscious fields. The fresh, sweet smell of dew swirled through the lands as a light blanket of morning mist gently lifted from the ground—revealing a world hidden for so long. As Linx jolted herself awake, her eyes glanced down to see that she rested safely under a thick blanket in her room. Looking around, she realized it would take more time to embrace her new life of acceptance and love from those surrounding her. The magnificent castle-like cottage sparkled in the morning sunlight. Shades of lavender reflected off of the crystals that hung near her window.

Sliding her legs out of the bed while trying not to wake Rexil, who was lying beside her, she wrapped herself in a soft, elegant green robe and strolled over to change into clothes for the day. Having many options was something she had never imagined. Her hand lingered over a fitted, cute, pale pink top with lacing that crossed and tied in the back. Picking it up, a smile grew on her face, and she spotted a matching skirt that flowed effortlessly as she moved it. While pulling the pink top over her head, it felt like a fresh beginning for her new life in Pangotha.

Gently closing the door behind her, Linx briskly strolled over to Zalia's cottage next door. The blue flowers crawling up the door frame emitted a light, fruity scent which tickled Linx's nose. She energetically knocked on the door, anticipating a similar reaction. When the door opened, Zalia's response did not disappoint. Her beaming smile spanned from one side of her face to the other. "Linny!"

"Good morning, Zalia!" Linx opened her arms, hugging Zalia tightly.

"Morning! How did you sleep?"

Linx briefly closed her eyes. "Very good. I almost didn't want to get up, but it's such a beautiful day out. I figured you'd have some plans on your list for today. How about you? Did you sleep okay?"

Pulling the door closed, Zalia nodded enthusiastically. "Yes! And I do have some plans that I think you'll like. I just stumbled across delicious fruit trees near the meadow yesterday. Can we go there today? I know you'll love them!"

Laughing, Linx agreed. "Of course. I would love for you to show me! Should we see if Jaut would like to come?"

Nodding enthusiastically, Zalia smiled. "Of course!"

As they started to walk down a path, something caught her eye. Observing the trees for a moment, Linx noticed something odd about them. Caught up in curiosity, she walked toward the strange trees while the feeling of being watched was crawling up her neck. Once she finally got close enough, her eyes widened. "The ecknids!"

Holding her hands over her mouth for a moment, Zalia jumped up and down. "Oh! Really?"

"Yes!" Linx examined the astonishingly soft white flowers that heavily decorated the razor-sharp branches pointing into the sky. "They look beautiful! I wonder if Jaut, Kateerah, and Pygo have seen them yet. They're hard to miss, though."

"I can't believe it!"

The more she glanced around, the more she realized the ecknids had been there for a while. White, pink, and light blue perfectly accented the hills and mountains of Pangotha while hiding a strong defense underneath.

"To see them healing is way better than any gift I could think of."

After a moment, Linx remained still, staring at the ecknids. "Are you just going to stand there?"

Squishing her eyebrows together, Zalia said, "Huh? What are you talking about?"

"Not you. We have company."

A deeper voice said, "I didn't know you knew I was here."

"I expected you to visit for a while now," she responded, raising an eyebrow and turning to face her old friend. "What are you doing here, anyway? It seems like your little spy took a while relaying information."

Carter laughed—because it was true. "I was just hoping everything was okay. It's hard to know if you could use help when you're so far away."

"I understand, but I can't handle seeing them randomly pop up. Regardless, we have a wonderful group of soldiers who are quick to defend our land. Not to mention, who's watching yours?"

"Since I last saw you, things have changed a lot within the borders of Crystal Woods. People are showing me more respect, and advisors—the ones I have left—are taking on some responsibilities that help lessen the burden on me."

"Wow. That seems like it's working out for you."

"Eh, for now. I honestly don't know if I want it."

"It was your mom's legacy."

"Exactly, and it isn't for me. I was wondering about something. I didn't know if there was a possibility of me being able to forgo living in Crystal Woods . . . and maybe restart life . . . here."

"I-I mean, I think it's fine, but we just want to make sure that it won't cause any problems with the Pangothians."

Zalia laughed while shoving Linx and whispering, "I don't know if you want him here, but he's more than welcome."

Linx glanced at Zalia before staring at Carter. She shrugged and said, "You can do whatever you want as long as it isn't harming anyone here."

He shook his head and said, "I would NEVER harm anyone here."

"Well, then, good. You can come with us to check out some fruit trees—if you're not busy. We were about to find Jaut as well."

"That would be amazing," Carter said. "I've really been looking forward to another adventure."

Bouncing up and down, Zalia shouted, "Yay! Let's go then, Linny!"

Confused, Carter asked, "Huh? Linny? Since when have you been called Linny?"

"It's a long story," Linx said, exhaling slowly.

Maneuvering in front of Linx and turning to face her, Carter said, "Luckily, I've got time."

A sense of relief and tranquility passed through Linx's body as she walked down the path to the orchard. She wasn't naïve to believe pain and sorrow would cease to exist, but she did strongly sense as though life was feeling lighter. After what seemed like endless searching up until this point, Linx knew she was finally home.

ACKNOWLEDGMENTS

To my dream team:

You all have shown extraordinary support and poured so much into this series from day one. Thank you for everything!

To my amazing husband, Gregory Jones, thank you is not enough for what you have done to help me achieve this dream. You've shown true dedication to this journey, and I can never thank you enough for your assistance and support. Editing, setting up/breaking down at book signings, entertaining the kids when I needed time to work on my books, marketing, and guidance are naming just some of your contributions. You consistently believed in me, and I appreciate you more than you'll ever know. Love you, babe!

To my children, Scarlett and Elliott, thank you for being the best kids I could've ever asked for. Your patience, interest, support, and love helped motivate me to continue this journey. I love you both more than anything!

Julię Wasilewski, thank you for absolutely everything you did throughout this series! I appreciate your kindness, support, and amazing feedback. Also, you were the first person to officially finish reading this book! I was so nervous to send it off, but I knew it was in good hands. You're incredible!

Mid Cook, Angela Coyle, and Sara McKnight, thank you for your support and contributions from Dark Woods through Pangotha! From editing to continuously sharing on social media, you are wonderful people I am so grateful to have in my life! You have provided such beautiful words of encouragement, and I'll never forget that!

Belle Manuel, thank you for reviewing and editing Dark Woods and Pangotha! I appreciate the time and effort you put into this project!

To my readers, family, and friends, thank you for your constant support and love! I cannot express enough how much it means to me. I see the social media shares, appreciate your time, enjoy the visits at book signings, and love your words of encouragement. Every single one of you has helped to create an incredible community. Thank you!

Sammy Jones is a fantasy author and writer. She is the wife of a loving husband and a mother of two beautiful children. Sammy obtained her master of social work degree with a specialization in behavioral health from Marywood University. She also has a bachelor's degree in psychology from Keystone College, with a minor in criminal justice. Sammy is fascinated by the whimsical, strange, and unusual. With a love of music and film, her favorite movies include: Labyrinth, Nightmare Before Christmas, and Alice in Wonderland. Sammy has a never-ending love for animals and enjoys hobbies that include singing, crafting, and baking during her free time.

FOLLOW SAMMY JONES

Website:
www.authorsammyjones.com

Facebook: Author Sammy Jones

Instagram: authorsammyjones

Tiktok: authorsammyjones

X: authorsjones

www.ingramcontent.com/pod-product-compliance
Lightning Source LLC
Chambersburg PA
CBHW030539310726
48979CB00010B/1961/J

* 9 7 8 1 7 3 5 7 3 8 5 5 0 *